THE RIB KING

THE RIB KING

LADEE HUBBARD

THORNDIKE PRESS
A part of Gale, a Cengage Company

GALE
A Cengage Company

LIBRARY OF CONGRESS CIP DATA ON FILE.
CATALOGUING IN PUBLICATION FOR THIS BOOK
IS AVAILABLE FROM THE LIBRARY OF CONGRESS.

ISBN-13: 978-1-4328-8723-0 (hardcover alk. paper)

Published in 2021 by arrangement with Amistad, an imprint of HarperCollins Publishers

Printed in Mexico
Print Number: 01   Print Year: 2021

This book is dedicated to my grandmother, Minnie C. Williams, whom I thank for doing all she could to make sure I was raised right.

■ ■ ■ ■

Mr. Sitwell, the Groundskeeper

1914

■ ■ ■ ■

Nothing seemed more absurd than to see
a colored man making himself ridiculous
in order to portray himself.
— GEORGE W. WALKER

1
THE CURRENT ORPHANS

Mr. Sitwell had finished work and was passing through the garden on his way to Prescott Avenue when he happened to look up at the house and see something he shouldn't have. One of the Barclays' current orphans was standing in the main hall. Dressed in a gray shirt and dark blue knee pants, black stockings sagging above his brown shoes. The boy had his hands on his hips and head cocked to one side as he stared, transfixed by the antique starter pistol on the third shelf of Mrs. Barclay's *cabinet d'objets.*

Mr. Sitwell frowned. The child had arrived from the asylum with two others five months before and Miss Mamie, the cook who was in charge of their apprenticeship, told them the very first day that scullery boys were forbidden from loitering in the front of the house. Yet there the child was, just inside the window, for all the world to see. Mr. Sitwell watched him reach into the cabinet and pull the pistol out. He peeked inside the chamber, then spun around and pointed it three times: left toward the velvet drapes, right toward the side table, and straight above him toward the chandelier. Then he smiled and mimicked the gesture of sliding the gun into an imaginary holster. When his game was finished he put the pistol back and then turned and continued walking down the hall. But instead of heading toward the kitchen where he belonged he moved farther away from it, toward the conservatory.

Mr. Sitwell cocked his head and looked around the hall, trying to find the other two. The Barclays always brought orphans home in batches of three and, following the example of the industrial college, always between the ages of fourteen and fifteen, making them old enough to work but not so old that, in Mr. Barclay's view, "the clay had so far hardened that it could not be reformed." For the past twenty years they had been brought in at regular intervals to learn a trade under the supervision of the cook. Mostly they washed dishes but by doing so fulfilled Mrs. Barclay's sense of charitable obligation. The current orphans were extremely close and Mr. Sitwell knew that if he saw one the other two were sure to be nearby. They did everything together and in fact so favored one another that the first time he saw them, standing in a row on the kitchen porch with their hands clasped behind their backs for Miss Mamie's inspection, he'd had a hard time telling them apart.

He'd soon realized that the easiest way to distinguish between them was to look for their scars. Frederick was the one with the three nasty welts running in parallel lines down his left cheek, a memento of a frantic fork slashing from a south side butcher with whom he'd had an unfortunate run-in when he was seven. Mac was the one who'd lost part of his right ear to a stockyard dog when he was eight. The one loitering in the hall now was Bart; Mr. Sitwell knew it as soon as he started walking. Bart had a peculiar way of moving, a staggered hop-step caused by the fact that, due to circumstances he claimed he no longer remembered, he was missing the toes of his right foot.

Bart hopped down the hall for a few moments and then stopped when he reached the door to the conservatory. Something, it seemed, was amiss with his trousers, and he reached down to make some adjustment to his buttons. When he was satisfied he swung his arm behind him, grabbed a fistful of fabric from his rear, and lifted his right foot to shake out his pant leg. He set his foot down again and, after a couple more hops, disappeared through the conservatory door.

Bart seemed awfully foolish. Mr. Sitwell's first thought was relief that he was not responsible for him, that all three boys were, technically, Miss Mamie's problem. But of course, Mr. Sitwell was the one who'd seen Bart and, having seen him, realized he had to make a choice. Either he would continue walking toward his streetcar stop as planned or he would go back inside and drag Bart to the safety of the kitchen before any of the Barclays saw him too, in which case he would no doubt be sent packing.

Then the door to Mr. Barclay's study opened, unleashing a wide swath of light just inside the window where Mr. Sitwell stood. He ducked down as a woman's voice called out, "Fine, Herbert. But remember this is not the Monte Carlo. We have not been to the Monte Carlo in a very long time." Mrs. Barclay appeared in the window, skirt swishing and heels clicking as she moved down the hall toward the stairs and the upper chambers. Without thinking, Mr. Sitwell found himself jogging along the side of the house, headed for the kitchen.

It wasn't until he'd reached the back

porch that it occurred to him why he was doing it. He liked these boys, cared about them, wanted them to do well. In the twenty years he'd worked for the Barclays he'd seen dozens of orphans come and go and always thought it a shame that Miss Mamie's predecessor, Mr. Boudreaux, never did much to help them. He wasn't certain if it was something about these particular children or simply the fact that Miss Mamie handled her orphans so differently than Mr. Boudreaux had handled his that had made such an impression on him. He'd noticed how careful they were not to tramp on his flowers when they walked through the garden and he liked that they asked a lot of questions about herbs; he also liked that, when they did ask questions, instead of scolding them for slacking the way Mr. Boudreaux would have done, Miss Mamie seemed pleased they took an interest in something she considered useful. She was determined to actually teach them something and wanted them to leave the house knowing more than they had when they arrived. It was clear that she cared for them and, because of that, Mr. Sitwell found he couldn't help but care for them too.

He stepped inside the house. Also, of course, there was the fact that he had started out like them: waterfront orphan, beneficiary of the peculiar mingling of the Barclays' need for cheap labor and their relatively liberal views on children's reform. Mr. Sitwell was only fourteen when he was plucked from the yard of the asylum. He'd started in the kitchen and, while other orphans came and went, had managed to stay on, gaining more and more of the Barclays' confidence through a combination of talent, wit, and fealty.

He passed through the pantry, pushed into the dark kitchen, then stopped when he saw Jennie, the new chambermaid, standing by the window next to a large stack of napkins set out on the worktable, all tucked into three corner folds. She had her back to him and was looking out at the yard, a cigarette in her hand. When she heard him come in she turned around and smiled.

"Evening."

Mr. Sitwell nodded. He could feel the muscles in his face tighten and was glad the room was dark. He'd been practicing talking to Jennie in his mirror at the rooming house where he lived; he knew he had an unfortunate habit of frowning at pretty women and also that he looked ugly when he did. "You're here late."

"Had to finish these." She nodded to the stack.

Mr. Sitwell struggled to fit his face into a smile as calm and cool as hers. "Miss Mamie making you stay to do all that?"

"Honestly? She told me to do it this morning. I forgot," Jennie said, one arm wrapped in front of her waist, the other hand holding the cigarette. "Don't tell her."

Mr. Sitwell arched his eyebrows in an effort to keep his brow from furrowing over.

"How you getting home, Jennie?"

"What on earth do you mean?"

"I just mean it's late."

"Is it?" She glanced at the clock on the counter near the stove. "Nine? Well, I guess it depends who you ask."

She was still smiling. Mr. Sitwell had noticed that about her. She smiled a lot, had a way of talking to people as if what she really wanted to do was laugh at them. When she first started working there two months before it had hurt his feelings a couple of times before he realized she talked to everybody like that, even Miss Mamie. That it was just her way.

"I could walk you to the streetcar. If you'd like. Make sure you get there safe." He looked away from her, toward the sink, and was disappointed when he saw the stack of dirty pots still piled there.

"Well, aren't you sweet," Jennie said. "That's real nice, Sitwell. Honestly, I can't imagine a girl needs much protection in this neighborhood, never mind the hour. But I certainly would appreciate the company."

Mr. Sitwell nodded and looked back at the pots. If the Barclays didn't send those boys back to the asylum for wandering the halls at night, Miss Mamie just might, if they were stupid enough to leave a mess like that.

"Could you wait a few minutes? I've got to take care of something right quick."

"Alright, Sitwell. I don't mind waiting. Gives me a chance to put these napkins away." She flicked her cigarette out the window.

Mr. Sitwell reached down to straighten his tie, then pushed through the swinging door that led to the front of the house.

As he passed through the dining room his heart was beating fast, but he had to figure that hadn't gone so bad. He'd been trying to think of questions to ask Jennie since she'd started working there, but that was the first time they'd been alone. Jennie, he decided, was a nice person, and looking back on their conversation, not scary at all. A lot of people on staff didn't know what to make of her, in part because of the smiling, but also because they were still adjusting to the fact that Petunia, the woman she'd replaced, was indeed gone. Petunia's termination had been a shock, not because she'd been good at her job but because she'd been there doing her job badly for so long. When Mamie got promoted and took charge of the kitchen, it seemed like the first thing she did was send Petunia home.

He walked up a short flight of stairs and entered the main hall, the chandelier above him shining a harsh light on the objects in Mrs. Barclay's cabinet. He looked at the pistol that had so entranced Bart and noticed at once that the gilt was peeling on the handle; several other items on the shelves were chipped or otherwise damaged. Electric lighting, which seemed necessary only because everyone else on the block now had it, had not been kind to this house. There was a reason for the care Mrs. Lawson, the parlor maid, took to ensure each lamp was covered with a cloth of a particular weight when company came to dinner. Some of the rugs in the halls were worn down and frayed from overuse, there were water stains on the side tables in the parlor, and the velvet cushions of the couch in the conservatory were sun-bleached in places.

All these flaws had been there for years but were made disturbingly visible in the new glare.

He continued down the hall. He still remembered when he was a boy like the three he was looking for now, how fine that house had seemed to him, the glitz and glitter of the various curios in Mrs. Barclay's cabinet sparkling in the warm glow of the gaslights. There'd been a time when he'd been convinced this was not simply the finest house he'd ever seen but perhaps the finest there ever was. Then, one day when he was fifteen, he was standing in the front yard and happened to look beyond the Barclays' fence. For the first time it occurred to him that most of the houses on the Avenue were twice the size of the one where he worked, that the Barclays had neighbors who, if they wanted to, could have bought and sold both his employers and everything they owned several times over. He must have looked over that fence a thousand times before this actually occurred to him. Before that the house had always been just another part of the block, an extension of the world it belonged to, and therefore, extremely precious.

He moved past the stairs. Perhaps the Barclays weren't as rich and important as they once were, but it was still a good house. The boys had a good thing there, whether they realized it or not. What they'd been given wasn't exactly charity but it was better than the industrial college where scores of boys and girls shivered on cold factory room floors fourteen hours a day. Here they worked hard but they slept on warm cots at night and Miss Mamie made sure they were always well-fed. The Barclays were not crazy enough to be unmanageable and, miraculously for the times, still maintained an entirely colored staff. The Barclays had come to the city from Missouri thirty-five years before with their cook, Mr. Boudreaux; they did not believe in race mixing in the kitchen, rightly thought it caused too many problems. Because Mr. Boudreaux had been colored the rest of the staff, out of necessity, had to be colored too. When he finally left, Miss Mamie, his former assistant, had been the obvious choice to take his place. This meant that so long as she continued to cook and maintain order to the Barclays' satisfaction, the opportunity to be reformed in the kitchen would remain the exclusive preserve of three colored orphans between the ages of fourteen and fifteen.

When he reached the conservatory he

heard a loud, "Oooooohhhh!" followed by a series of childish giggles. He pushed the door open and found the three boys huddled together on the floor near the piano with Frederick at the center. From the halting sound of Frederick's voice, Mr. Sitwell could tell he was reading.

"Now that Cherokee knew that Wash Talbot, his former deputy, had been arrested, he had to make a choice: keep his vow to never again set foot in Seminole County, or let the last remaining member of his gang fall into the hands of an angry mob."

"What are you boys doing?"

They spun around in unison and blinked at him with enormous brown eyes. They were handsome children with bright round faces, thick eyebrows, full lips, and skin the dark red color of cedar wood. Their features were so similar that anybody would have mistaken them for actual brothers. In truth they were not blood relatives at all; their strong bond was formed in the interest of survival, on the waterfront.

"Nothing, sir." Mac smiled, eyes all innocent. "Just sitting here reading."

"In the front of the house?"

"Oh, nobody saw us. We made sure them folks was long gone before we came in

20

here," Frederick said. He lifted his arms and rocked back and forth, in imitation of someone else's waltz. "We waited until they finished dancing."

Mr. Sitwell frowned. "Somebody saw you. I did. Saw Bart playing in the hall when I was on my way out. Then come to find you haven't even finished cleaning the kitchen."

"Not true, sir. Kitchen's all done," Bart said. "Well, except for the pots. But remember last time, how Miss Mamie told us not to disturb Mr. Barclay's guests with a lot of banging while folks were eating dinner? Figured this time we'd just wait until the dinner was over, so as not to bother nobody."

The boy looked very proud of himself.

"It's alright, sir. We don't mind working late."

"The last guest left over an hour ago," Mr. Sitwell said.

"Really? Dang. It didn't feel like we'd been in here but five minutes. . . ."

The boys stared at one another, as if there were something wondrous about their shared trance.

"You mean to say we've been sitting here reading all that time?"

Mr. Sitwell held out his hand. "Give it to me."

21

Frederick gave him the book. On the cover was a picture of a tall, thin, white man with green eyes and a long red beard, clutching a pistol in each hand.

"What is this?"

"*The Life and Times of Cherokee Red, Wild Man of the Reconstruction,*" Frederick said. "You ever read it?"

"No."

"But you heard about him, right? Started out during the war, robbing from the rich and giving to the poor. Now his gang's all busted up. He and his ladylove moved out west to put the past behind them and he's been trying his hand at being a farmer. But, just when it seems like his gunslinging days are over, he finds out Wash Talbot, last surviving member of his gang, was caught stealing hogs and got himself locked up back in Florida —"

"What?"

"He stole a hog."

"Who did?"

"Wash Talbot."

Mr. Sitwell squinted at the cover. He'd never heard of Cherokee Red but he knew the name Wash Talbot. From when he was a boy back in Florida. Just like in the book.

He handed it to Frederick. "Where does it say that name? Show me. Wash Talbot."

22

Frederick opened the book and started flipping pages. After a while he set his finger down and read.

"Another infamous member of the gang was Wash Talbot, who never would renounce his lawless ways. For years after the gang disbanded he was still hiding out in the swamps of Seminole County, a terror to the neighboring towns —"

"That's enough," Mr. Sitwell said. "Pernicious lies."

"Sir?"

"I knew that man."

"Who? Cherokee Red?"

"Wash Talbot. He was a simple farmer."

The boys looked disappointed.

"Probably not the same man then," Mac said. "Was your Wash from Seminole too?"

Mr. Sitwell shook his head. "I don't recall."

He was lying, compelled by a childhood admonishment to say nothing about where he came from, even though he realized there was no cause for it any longer. It was the same reason he'd refused to give his real name when, lured by the promise of food, he'd voluntarily entered the doors of the asylum twenty years before. And then again, a few months after that, when he found himself standing on the Barclays' back

23

porch, hands clasped behind his back and wedged between those other two boys.

"Where did you get this?"

"One of Mr. Barclay's guests gave it to us after Tuesday's party."

Mr. Sitwell frowned.

"It's the truth, sir," Frederick said. "We didn't steal it, Mr. Sitwell."

"I'm going to have to ask Mr. Barclay about that."

"That's fine but . . . can we finish it first? We were just getting to the best part."

"What part is that?"

"It's the beginning of the end."

Mr. Sitwell sighed. Despite the lives they'd led and the work they did, they were still such children. Yet he knew if they did not learn certain lessons they would not last long in the Barclay house, to say nothing of the world outside it.

"You boys are going to have to be more careful. You've got to remember who you are, you've got to remember where. You shouldn't be in the front of the house. You shouldn't be talking to Mr. Barclay's guests, much less, as you say, accepting gifts from them."

"I didn't lie." Frederick pouted. "I tell you he said we could have it."

"That's not the point. What if you misunderstood the man's meaning? Or what if the man simply changed his mind? Don't you realize that an accusation of theft can be just as bad as a theft itself? Sometimes it's even worse."

"No, sir, I suppose we didn't think about those things." Frederick nodded. "I understand."

Mr. Sitwell frowned. He could tell from the boy's expression that Frederick thought he understood but also that, in truth, he did not.

"Best get back there and finish that kitchen before Miss Mamie sees it."

"Yes, sir."

They scrambled to their feet and sprinted down the hall. Mr. Sitwell stood for a moment with the book in his hands, trying to decide what to do with it.

He looked at the cover. Mr. Sitwell was only nine when he left Florida, and there were many things about those early days he no longer recalled — the name Wash Talbot, however, was not one of them. The man had been a neighbor-friend of his mother's and, as he'd told the boys, came from a family of subsistence farmers much like his own family had been. It certainly seemed more than mere coincidence that, as was true of the outlaw in the book, the Wash he remembered had come to his end over conflicting claims with a man from the neighboring town over livestock. Except — and this too Mr. Sitwell remembered with perfect clarity — the Wash he'd known hadn't been jailed over a hog. It was a mule. And he hadn't stolen it.

He'd shot it.

He watched the boys push through the swinging door to the dining room. You had to be careful in this world. Had to take precautions, always be prepared, even if you were telling the truth. That was the thing he remembered when he thought about Wash Talbot. One thing at least. If he didn't want the boys getting in trouble it was best to take care of this now, make sure there was no misunderstanding. He reached the door to the dining room then walked past it, headed toward Mr. Barclay's study.

The room, as expected, was still lit. Mr. Barclay did most of his work at night; the dinner parties that preceded these long evenings were just a part of how the man conducted his business. Through the half-opened door he saw his employer seated behind his desk, hunched over a stack of papers. A man in his sixties now, he'd gotten fat and lost most of his hair in the twenty years Mr. Sitwell had worked for him. He had bushy eyebrows and small, pale eyes that reminded Mr. Sitwell of glass beads.

"Is that you, Sitwell? What on earth are you doing in my house, lurking about in the dark, at this time of night?"

Mr. Sitwell nodded and tried to smile. He was already in the room before he recalled the foul mood his employer had been in lately. Mr. Barclay was a speculator by trade, which, so far as Mr. Sitwell could tell, meant he bought and sold properties he hadn't the least amount of knowledge about or interest in. Somehow he managed to make a good living this way, but it was a bit like musical chairs. As had happened a few times in the past, following the recent financial panic he'd found himself sitting atop ownership shares of several food manufacturing plants, charged with the sudden and somehow unexpected task of actually trying to make them profitable.

"Yes, sir. Hope I didn't startle you. I was just on my way out when I come across the kitchen boys with this."

He held up the book.

Mr. Barclay squinted. "What is it?"

"A book, sir. It looks like a book."

"What are you showing it to me for?"

"Kitchen boys had it. Told me one of your

guests gave it to them after Tuesday's party. Sounded unusual is all. I just wanted to make sure it was alright for them to have it."

"Last Tuesday?" Mr. Barclay blinked. "Who was that? The Southerners? That doesn't make sense. Southerners don't give books to colored children. Hand it over."

He took the book. Mr. Sitwell watched him strain his mind to recall the events of the Tuesday before, the effort making him seem very old. After a while he set it back down on his desk.

"Alright, yes, I do remember. One of those Florida jokers was passing these out like party favors. I forget why. Might have been claiming some relation to the protagonist."

"Yeah? From Florida?"

"The two I'm after, yes. Had a whole group of them in here, trying to make them feel at home. Got a concern I'm after down there. They'll be back on Friday. I'm still trying to unload some of this junk. . . ."

Mr. Sitwell nodded. He was aware of Mr. Barclay's current negotiations, at least so far as they affected the kitchen. After accepting that there was no way to divest himself from the food business without taking a substantial loss, Mr. Barclay had discovered an urgent need to shift production at one of his plants to the South where labor was cheaper. There was a functional plant on the market that Mr. Barclay was interested in purchasing but could not afford to do so until he sold one of his current ones. This meant he was negotiating two deals at once: one with a group of New Englanders he hoped to sell to and the other with a group of Southerners he hoped to buy from. Because of the particular way Mr. Barclay conducted his business, this also meant a lot of entertaining. Mr. Barclay was convinced that contracts were best negotiated on his home turf, preferably after a good meal, and Miss Mamie had been complaining all week about the difficulty of trying to come up with menus for two such divergent palates on the tight budget she'd been allotted for it.

Mr. Sitwell nodded to the book. "You say these Florida men claim some relation to this man on the cover?"

"I don't know, Sitwell. I don't listen to all the nonsense coming from the mouths of fools. I've got other things on my mind."

"But the ones you're dealing with . . . there's two of them?"

"That's right. Cousins."

"They tell you their names?"

"Well, of course, they . . ." Mr. Barclay

29

sighed. "Look here, Sitwell. What is this? Why are you bothering me with all these questions? Are you saying the boys are thieves? You come here to tell me you suspect they stole this book?"

"No, sir. Just the opposite," Mr. Sitwell said quickly. "I just wanted to make sure that they didn't get nothing confused somehow. Don't want them getting into trouble. Thought it best to bring it to you straightaways."

He watched Mr. Barclay's eyes glaze over.

"What do you think I do in here, Sitwell? At night, when you see a white man sitting behind a desk? And it's late and he's tired and should be in bed sleeping? I'm asking because I'd really like an answer. Do I look busy to you? Because it occurs to me that maybe if a man hasn't got a hoe or a shovel or a slop bucket in his hand, it doesn't appear to you that he's actually working."

Mr. Sitwell said nothing.

"How long have you been here anyhow?"

"A long time, sir. A very long time."

"Well, that's true now, isn't it?" Mr. Barclay said. "Never mind, Sitwell. You did right coming to me instead of Mamie. Matter of fact, speaking of the boys . . . Why don't you shut that door for a minute? I have a question for you."

Mr. Sitwell shut the door and sat down.

"How old are those children, anyway?"

"Mac and Frederick are fourteen. Bart just turned fifteen."

"And they are doing alright in that kitchen? You and Mamie are pleased with them so far?"

"Extremely pleased," Mr. Sitwell said. "They are good boys."

Mr. Barclay nodded. "Something I need to know. Can't ask Mamie, she's worse than you with the questions. So maybe you can help."

"Certainly, sir."

"I want you to tell me, if it came down to it, which one of those boys would you let go first?"

"Sir?"

"It's a simple question. I'm asking you to make a choice."

"But why?"

"I have to cut back on household expenses. Things have been hard since the downturn and, as much as I am dedicated to continuing my wife's charity work, I'll not endanger the stability of the house to it. And that means one of those boys has got to go."

Mr. Sitwell shifted in his seat. Had he been inclined to speak his mind he would have reminded his employer that it was only charity so long as one discounted the fact that a grown man asked to do the same work would have demanded more than the two dollars a week the three boys were content to split between themselves.

Instead he said, "Are you sure you need to do that? I mean, I can't imagine those boys account for a very large expense. If we need to cut back, perhaps there's something else we might do, something that would have more of an impact on the actual —"

"No. Now, look, I don't expect you to understand. But I've given this a great deal of thought and I simply cannot go on supporting all three of those children. We'll just have to hope that the time the child has already spent here will have some sort of enduring civilizing effect."

"Yes, sir. But . . . the boys are so close. They work so well together. How could I possibly pick one?"

"Well, you pick the one you deem the least valuable, of course. That's usually how such things are done. It's a simple question, Sitwell. Just answer it."

"I really can't say, sir," Mr. Sitwell said. "I'd need time to think about it."

"Well, you do that. You think about it. But do it in your own home, understand? Because it's late and I want you out of mine. You can give me your answer tomorrow."

"Yes, sir."

Mr. Barclay gave the book a push toward the edge of the desk with the tip of his finger. "Take this nonsense with you. Let them keep it, I really don't care."

Mr. Sitwell picked up the book and walked out of the man's study.

When he got back to the kitchen, the boys were hard at work washing pots. Had they simply followed instructions they would have been finished hours before, but by the way they laughed and jostled one another he could tell they'd been telling the truth: they didn't mind working late. They'd meant what they'd said, had only been trying to be helpful and not disturb Mr. Barclay's guests. They were good boys.

"Miss Jennie went to put the napkins away," Frederick said. "Said to tell you she'd be right back."

Mr. Sitwell nodded.

All at once, without thinking about it or even wanting to, Mr. Sitwell realized that he did know which one he would send away if it ever came down to that: Frederick. Not because he was the least valuable but, on the contrary, because he was the strongest. He'd seen the way Frederick looked out for the other two. The boy was a natural leader, the one of the three who stood the best chance of surviving if he ever were to find himself alone in the world. He was also the only one who could actually read, which would have meant the removal of a powerful distraction for Mac and Bart, and yet might also make him seem more desirable to a potential employer who had not had occasion to take such a consideration into account.

This thought and the ease with which it manifested itself in his mind disturbed Mr. Sitwell so greatly that he had to look away from them. He could feel his heart pounding in his chest and his left eye began to twitch. Before he knew it, he had worked himself into such a state that when Jennie walked up behind him and tapped him on the shoulder he was so startled he flinched.

"Goodness, I'm sorry," Jennie said. She'd put on her coat and had a small green hat fitted on her head. "I didn't mean to frighten you. Where'd you go anyhow?"

"Had to do something for the boys."

He started to tell her about seeing Bart through the window but realized that might somehow lead to having to talk about his conversation with Mr. Barclay.

"They're sweet, aren't they?"

"I worry about them," Mr. Sitwell said.

"Why? They look happy to me."

Mr. Sitwell could feel Jennie studying his expression. He nodded and tried to look normal.

"You started out like them, didn't you? Apprentice in the kitchen? How old were you when you came here from the asylum?"

"Fourteen, maybe."

"And you're not from around here are you?"

"No, ma'am. Florida."

"Oh, yeah? Had some Florida white folks over last week. Miss Mamie was complaining about how ignorant they were. . . . Not a lot of your people up here, I imagine. You get lonely?"

"I don't hardly remember it no how."

"No?"

She looked back at the boys.

"Well, you shouldn't worry about them. They've got each other. And they've got Miss Mamie looking after them, teaching them how to cook. Wants them to leave here knowing how to do something. It's a lot more than I had at their age, believe me. I suspect they'll be alright."

They walked out together, through the garden, down the driveway, past the front gate, and onto Prescott Avenue. The streets

35

were quiet at that time of night, the sidewalk lit up by the dim glow of the gas lamps. They moved past the great houses that lined the block then turned onto Olliana; when they got to the omnibus stop the only other people there were two white women with thick ankles, gray coats slung over their matching maids' uniforms as they talked to each other in a language that sounded like German.

Mr. Sitwell stood next to Jennie with his hands in his pockets. He looked at the trees running down the center of the Avenue and tried to think of something to say that wasn't dull. His mind was still rattled, not so much by Mr. Barclay's question as the ease with which he'd found an answer to it. And now Jennie was standing right beside him. She looked so pretty and he knew he was frowning, which somehow made everything he thought to say to her sound that much duller in his head. So he kept quiet.

The omnibus pulled to the stop and they followed the two maids inside. The four of them rode two stops together and the maids got off; a skinny drunk got on, rode the car one stop, and stumbled off again. The car was empty for a little while and then a large group of people got on; Jennie saw someone she recognized and threw her arm up to wave. All of a sudden Mr. Sitwell found himself a part of a crowd standing over him and smiling, all of them just as pretty as Jennie was. They were laughing and talking fast as they gripped the handrail and swayed from side to side.

Mr. Sitwell did not sway. Instead he stared down at his hands in his lap. He still had the book in the pocket of his jacket and, while Jennie talked to her friends, he pulled it out and looked at the cover, pretending to be distracted by the words on the front, although in truth Mr. Sitwell did not read. Still, just looking at the picture was enough to make him think about it. He remembered Barclay saying that the two men passing the book out had claimed relation to the man on the cover. He wondered if it was possible that there really was another Wash Talbot in Seminole County, an entirely different Wash from the one he'd known. And if this white Wash had happened to meet with a fate parallel to the colored Wash he still remembered.

He glanced at Jennie, remembered Mamie saying something about being glad she'd found a girl who'd been to school. If they were alone he might have asked her what the book said. But they weren't alone and he didn't want to spoil what seemed to be a happy mood.

"Come on out with us tonight, Jennie. You can bring your handsome man too."

"Oh, Aggie. He's not my man. He's a friend from work. Anyhow, I can't. You know I've got to get home."

"You mean that big old girl can't take care of herself yet?"

Someone snorted and a couple of people laughed while Jennie frowned. For a moment, the swaying seemed to stop.

"That was a joke, Jennie. I didn't mean it. We just miss you is all."

Jennie glanced at Mr. Sitwell then turned back to her friend. "Still?"

"Yes, girl. Still."

A hand reached out and squeezed Jennie's shoulder. "Always."

Jennie nodded. "I'll stop by Saturday if I get a chance."

"Any time. You know you're always welcome."

The car lurched to a stop near the theatre district and they all filed out at once. Jennie spun around in her seat, rapped her knuckle on the glass, waved good-bye, and laughed at something she saw out the window. Then the doors closed and the car started moving. She sank back in her seat and stared straight ahead.

When the car stopped again she stood up.

"Well, Sitwell. This is me. You take care and I'll see you tomorrow."

But Mr. Sitwell stood up too.

"No. Really, it's alright. You're sweet, but I don't need anybody to walk me home. Believe it or not, I've been doing it for years."

"That's not the point," Mr. Sitwell said. He tucked the book into his pocket and followed her out onto the street.

They walked along the crowded avenue.

"So you live around here too, do you?"

"Sure," Mr. Sitwell lied. "Anyhow, it's a nice evening and I like to walk. . . ."

Jennie didn't say anything. They made their way to the end of the block and turned a corner. She stopped in front of a two-story brick building.

"Well, now, Sitwell. This really is it. I would ask you inside for a cup of tea but —"

"I know. It's late," Mr. Sitwell said. "Perhaps some other time? I imagine you eat dinner."

"Once a day," Jennie said. "I mean, yes, that would be very nice. . . ."

She looked toward the house. Mr. Sitwell turned and saw the silhouette of a young woman waving back at them from a window on the second floor.

"That where you stay? That your room-mate?"

"Something like that." Jennie took a deep breath and shut her eyes. "That is my daughter, Mr. Sitwell."

Mr. Sitwell looked at the girl in the window for a moment then looked back at Jennie.

"Don't act so startled," Jennie said.

"No, I'm not. It's just . . ."

But he was startled. He couldn't help it, without wanting to he was adding numbers in his mind. The girl in the window was at least as old as the boys and Jennie couldn't possibly have been older than twenty-five. . . .

"What is it, Mr. Sitwell? Something wrong? Women do have children, you know. They have them all the time. And sometimes when they do it's a blessing, understand?"

"Yes. Of course, I know that. It's just . . . I didn't know you had a child."

Jennie frowned. "That's because I didn't think it was appropriate to talk about such things at my place of employment. It's nobody's business. I do my job and then I come home. Alone. Understand?"

"Yes. Of course."

Jennie narrowed her eyes.

"Why don't you run along now, Sitwell? You've done enough. Got me safely to my door. Think about whether you still want to have dinner sometime. And when you decide, let me know."

"No. I mean, yes. I mean, of course I do."

He shook his head. He didn't understand what was happening but could feel things going wrong. He knew he needed to change the subject. He still had his hand wrapped around the book in his pocket; he pulled it out and tried to smile.

"You really been to school?"

"Why? I said so, didn't I? Never said I graduated. Got through a whole semester at the nurses' college before I had to stop. Had responsibilities. But I'm not a liar if that's what you —"

"No, I didn't mean . . ."

It was hopeless. He could feel a foul mood creeping up on him, like a shadow.

"I should let you see to your daughter."

"Yes, you should," Jennie said. "Thanks again for walking me. Real nice of you. But maybe now you'll understand when I tell you it's not necessary. I've got no problem taking care of myself, Sitwell."

"Yes, ma'am. . . ." He tipped his hat. "I understand."

He turned around and started walking home.

It seemed as if he'd messed up everything, first with the boys and then with Jennie. He tried to remember what he'd thought would happen that night and found that vast parts of his mind were blank. It seemed nothing but foolish to have imagined she might have liked him. She belonged with the bright happy pretty people who rode the streetcar. People whose eyes danced when they talked. People who swayed.

The city was full of them and as he moved down the sidewalk they were all around him, everywhere he looked. Everybody rushing past him in a hurry to get somewhere. As long as he'd been in that city he'd never felt like he truly belonged. A part of him would always be country; his true home would always be a small village hidden in the swamps of Seminole County that, for the first nine years of his life, was the only world he had known. Founded by three runaway slaves back in days when much of the state was still unsettled land; they'd stolen a map from the man who'd owned them, run toward its nearest edge, and then kept running, wanting nothing more than to get off it. They'd made a home in the swamps, out of a landscape so wild and unmanageable that for a long time no one thought to claim it. Over time they had been joined by others — runaways like Sitwell's mother and his uncle Max, vanquished indigenous, deserters from various wars. For years they'd kept safe by sticking together and keeping to themselves. It wasn't until after the Civil War that people like Sitwell's mother and Wash Talbot started venturing outside, lured by the promise of paper money in exchange for work in what was by then one of several nearby towns.

He pulled the book out again and stared at the cover: a sneering white man whose eyes had been rendered a vivid green. And there in the quiet of his own thoughts, he started to remember things. He remembered how, as a child back in Seminole, he'd once met a man with eyes that color, and also that, when he'd asked who the man was and what he was doing there, his mother told him he'd come to attend funeral services for Wash. But aside from the color of his eyes, the man on the cover, with his straight hair, long beard, and top lip curled back in a savage grin, looked nothing like the one he was thinking of. That man had been small and compact, with a smooth, tan face and a high, bushy mop of brown hair. Mr. Sitwell couldn't recall the man's name, but he'd never forget the day he'd showed up on his mother's doorstep. It was the day before the shooting started and the last time he'd helped his mother bake a cake.

Mr. Sitwell kept walking. Before she ran away his mother had been a slave in a grand house in St. Augustine; it was there that she'd learned to cook. She was so good at it that even after Wash's hanging, when all the other villagers who worked in the town had been sent home and told not to come back, Mrs. Farley, the woman his mother cooked for, had kept his mother on because Mr. Farley's birthday was coming up and Mrs. Farley wanted a cake.

He rounded a corner and remembered how, when he and his mother got into the wagon to go to town that last morning, the green-eyed man had sat on their porch waving good-bye. And when they returned that afternoon he was still sitting there, a rifle laid across his lap.

"How did it go, Lotta?" he'd asked Sitwell's mother.

"About what you expected."

The man helped her unload the wagon then followed them back inside the small cabin they shared with Uncle Max. Sitwell's mother took off her jacket. She set her bag down on the kitchen table and said, "Mr.

Farley called you a ghost nigger."

"Did he now?" The man smiled. "Well, now, Lotta, I got to admit. That's actually kind of funny."

Mr. Sitwell stared at the book's cover. Was that man Cherokee Red? A colored version to go with the colored Wash? Mr. Sitwell could not recall ever seeing him before the day he showed up for Wash's funeral and didn't remember ever being told the man's actual name. But of course he must have been told; it was just that so many people had come back to attend Wash's service and he hadn't known which ones he should be paying attention to, hadn't known what was important to remember. It was entirely possible that other people had called the man Cherokee and Mr. Sitwell had simply forgotten.

Now, amid the noise and clatter of the city streets, the man's voice came back to him, followed by his mother's laughter. Sounds from his past, which, though soothing in some ways, were not actually comforting. Because he *missed* those sounds and hearing them again only reminded him of how alone he now was, how far from anything that resembled home. They reminded him of a time when he'd been part of a world he hadn't paid much attention to because he'd never imagined himself being outside of it. Reminded him that his real home would always be a small village in the swamps of Florida that twenty-five years before he'd been forced to stand and watch as it burned to the ground.

All these memories summoned by a book he hadn't even read. Things he hadn't thought about in years seemed to push against his current mood, filling him with a sense that there was something he was supposed to do. He looked at the cover. The man staring back at him sure looked white, but what if he'd only been drawn that way? There'd been people in his village who looked just as white as the Barclays, a couple of them with blond hair and blue eyes. But they'd been colored; he'd known they were colored simply by the fact that they were there. That's how things were in Seminole County; everybody seemed to just know who belonged where. If the man who drew the cover didn't understand that, he might have gotten confused.

He turned another corner, walked across the street, and finally saw the awning for his rooming house. He passed through the door and made his way to the front desk where Billy, the nephew of the woman who owned the house, was working behind the counter.

"You read don't you, Billy?"

"When I got to. Gives me a headache. Why? What you want, Sitwell?"

Mr. Sitwell put the book on the counter. "I want you to find the name Wash Talbot in there. I need to know whether he's colored or not."

Billy shook his head. "Afraid I'm gonna have to charge you for that. Not so much for the reading as the headache that comes with it."

Mr. Sitwell pulled a penny from his pocket.

Billy took the coin and picked up the book. He flipped through the pages, stopping every time he saw the name Wash Talbot written inside. The name appeared several times, usually in relation to some shoot-out or robbery. It was clear, from the brief passages Billy read aloud, that this Wash was not part of any community Mr. Sitwell remembered but rather a brutal savage who'd spent his youth as a lawless outlaw hiding in the swamps.

Furthermore, Billy assured him, the book's Wash was, like the man on the cover and all the other people inside, without question white.

He shut the book. "Satisfied?"

Mr. Sitwell shook his head. Whoever wrote

the book, if they hadn't even got that part right, surely didn't know what they were talking about. Perhaps the author had heard of the terrible events that had taken place in Seminole after Wash Talbot's murder and simply fabricated what he considered to be a suitable tale to precede it. The fire that had destroyed his village and sent Mr. Sitwell running all the way to the northern city where he now lived had, in truth, sent people running from all over the county. Perhaps someone told the book's author about the violence, or maybe he'd read about it in a newspaper. The rest he must have made up on his own.

He looked at the cover again and could feel his confusion give way to anger. What did this Cherokee and a white Wash have to do with his people, with him? And now there was someone sitting in the Barclays' parlor, claiming relation to the man on the cover, passing out this book full of lies?

He slapped the book back on the counter. "See if it's got a Lotta Smith in there."

"Why? Who's that?"

"My mama."

"Mama? I didn't know you had a mama."

Mr. Sitwell narrowed his eyes. "Everybody got a mama, fool."

"I know, I just . . ."

Someone walked to the counter wanting his mail. Billy sighed and shook his head.

"Give me a minute." He went to fetch their mail.

When he came back Mr. Sitwell asked him, "How much I have to pay you to just go ahead and read the whole thing?"

"What do you mean? You mean read it to you? This whole book?"

"I got some questions. Need you to read enough to answer my questions."

"In that case, the cost is gonna depend on what your questions are."

Mr. Sitwell told him what he wanted to know and they agreed on a price. He gave Billy his money and went upstairs to his room.

He unlocked the door and tossed his keys on his table. He changed out of his clothes and watered his plants. Then he clicked off the light and went to bed.

That night Mr. Sitwell had troublesome sleep, full of strange dreams he did not understand. In the one he remembered when he woke up the next morning, he was lying in the grass reading a book when he felt someone reach down and tap him on the shoulder. He looked up and saw a woman in a long white dress standing over him, one hand gripping the bar handle of a mask with a face drawn on it, which she held in front of her own.

"Put that away," she called from behind the mask.

Mr. Sitwell looked down at the book in his hands. "But this is the best part."

"Fair enough," the woman said. "But you're gonna have to finish it later."

She held out her free hand.

"Right now, we've got to go."

2
A MATTER OF TASTE

Mr. Sitwell woke up the next morning feeling no more rested than he had the night before. He lay on his back and stared at a long, thin crack that ran along his ceiling like a vein for a full twenty minutes before he even realized that he was actually awake. Then he turned his head, saw the potted plant on the windowsill beside his bed, the washbasin on the stand in the corner beneath the mirror, and the small wooden table and single chair in the middle of the floor. Somehow soothed by the blank familiarity of his own room, he realized he was no longer angry.

If anything, he had a hard time recalling how he'd managed to work himself into such a state the night before. It wasn't like him, and he felt a little silly thinking back to how he'd slapped that dollar on the counter and demanded Billy find answers to questions that, in the clear light of day, no longer seemed to matter much at all. He already knew the book was full of lies. And even if that wasn't the case, it was hard to see why it should have made such a difference. That was his past, a reminder of a world he barely remembered and far from the life he lived now.

Out in the hall one of the other men renting a room on the second floor cleared his throat as he shuffled past Mr. Sitwell's door on his way to the washroom. Mr. Sitwell had lived in the house since he was sixteen years old, when he'd had to clear out of the Barclays' cellar to make room for a new group of orphans; the two he'd arrived with had been caught stealing and sent away long before. Things were harder back then; it had been difficult to find a place to live that was both decent and affordable and also in a neighborhood that didn't prohibit colored people from moving in. He'd felt lucky to find a room in a gas-lit house on Union Street with an elderly widow willing to rent out one of her bedrooms to him. Then, a few years later, the widow, eager to profit from a sudden influx of colored people moving to the city, had paid to have renovations done to the downstairs, installed a proper front desk, and converted the parlor and library into four additional rentable rooms. The result had been a sharp decline in quality as suddenly Mr. Sitwell found himself no longer renting a room in a house but living in a proper rooming house.

"That's what I said. Isn't that what I just said?" a woman's voice came through the wall. Technically, women weren't allowed inside, but the widow was hard of hearing and if you slipped Billy enough money, pretty much anything was possible. The man living on the other side of the wall was a Pullman porter who only used the room for weekend trysts when he was in town. The other two rooms on Mr. Sitwell's floor were currently occupied by a waiter and a nervous man who was unemployed but claimed he was a hairdresser by trade. Mr. Sitwell didn't expect they'd be there long; people passing through the house now rented a room for a month or two while they were looking for something else — sometimes something better but more often, something even cheaper. Still, Mr. Sitwell saw no reason to leave. He was comfortable enough and so, at the age of thirty-four, was technically the building's most senior occupant, aside from the widow herself.

"You better tell that heifer to let you alone," the woman shouted through the wall. He listened as she and the porter laughed. Then he stood up, grabbed his towel from his night-stand, and washed his face in the basin. He put on his clothes, locked the door, and walked downstairs.

He pushed through the front door and stepped out into the gray dawn. Mr. Sitwell walked two blocks and made his way to the corner stop, where a row of women in sturdy shoes was already waiting for the omnibus. When it arrived they all climbed aboard and together rode past the two-story brick buildings that made up much of the south side.

Mr. Sitwell stared out the window until they reached Magazine Square, at which point he sank down into his seat and lowered his eyes. Although technically against city ordinance, it was common knowledge that blacks were not welcome to live or shop there; the neighborhood was notorious for the violence in their efforts to keep black people out. Because of this, most people avoided the area altogether and Mr. Sitwell, for his part, didn't even like to look at it through the window as they rode past. He'd been taught from a very young age by his uncle Max that some people required the same treatment as wild animals: do not feed or molest them. Keep your dealings with them to a minimum and under no circumstances look them directly in the eye, because they tend to regard this as a threatening gesture and become enraged. This advice seemed particularly prudent lately because a large group of them had been on strike for several months and staged protests almost daily. It was his understanding that part of their antagonism toward the colored race stemmed from the fact that, as opposed to addressing their demands, the Employers' Association had attempted to blunt the effects of the strike by hiring scabs, most of whom were black men.

He was back at the Olliana stop by seven thirty. He walked down the Avenue, then pushed through the Barclays' front gate and made his way up the long drive. As he rounded the back of the house he heard the kitchen door slam shut, looked up, and saw Mamie hurrying down the steps, headed toward the larder. Mrs. Lawson, the Barclays' parlor maid, rushed out after her.

"Don't try to hide from me, Mamie Price," Mrs. Lawson said. "I want you to look at what your girl did to Mr. Barclay's shirt."

Mamie made it all the way to the larder door and had her hand on the lock before she stopped and turned around. Just over five feet tall, she was a woman in her late thirties who always looked harried without somehow looking hard. She was wearing a long gray smock dress and work boots and, as Mrs. Lawson scowled, she kept her hand on the lock clenched so tightly that it seemed like her grip was all that was holding her upright.

"That's not her job."

"Since when? Where do you think we are? That's not how things work around here and you know it."

Mrs. Lawson, a tall, thin, hazel-eyed woman in her mid-fifties whose long nose and stony profile reminded Mr. Sitwell of a cigar store Indian, stopped talking as soon as she saw him walking past them on his way to the porch. He nodded and then, instead of going into the kitchen as planned, turned toward the vegetable garden. He had no intention of being drawn into their disagreement; he'd been working in that house for twenty years and knew that when the two of them started arguing the best he could do was stay out of it.

"Wasn't doing anything but sitting out here smoking," Mrs. Lawson said. "I told her if she had time for that, she could come back in the house and help me. And just look what she did." Mrs. Lawson waved one of Mr. Barclay's shirts over her head like a

56

white flag. "It doesn't even make sense, starching a collar the way she done."

"The girl just got started," Mamie said.

"Well, that's the point, isn't it, Mamie? We don't need anybody who 'just got started' here. Not now. As if I don't have enough to deal with now that Mr. Thomas is gone. . . . Petunia might have been slow, but at least when she finally got around to doing something she did it the right way."

"Petunia's gone."

"Yes, Mamie. I realize that. I'm asking you why. When you sent Petunia away from here I just assumed you were going to find someone with some experience."

"Experience costs too much," Mamie said. "You know Barclay can't afford that right now. Had to settle for smart enough to train."

"So how is that any better than what we had before?" Mrs. Lawson shook her head. "You ought to be ashamed of yourself, Mamie Price. Turning Petunia out like that. Maybe nobody else around here has the nerve to tell you to your face but don't think they're not talking about it. It's starting to seem like nobody's safe so long as you in charge."

"Yeah? Well, I am in charge."

"For now."

"That's right. For now. And so long as it's true, I suggest you take your bony behind back inside and get to work. I mean, if you want to keep your job."

There was a brief silence, then the sound of a door slamming shut.

Mr. Sitwell kept his head down. A full minute passed before he found the nerve to glance behind him, and when he did, Miss Mamie was still standing on the porch.

"You heard that didn't you, Sitwell? The nonsense I got to deal with? And every damn day? I know you heard it."

Mr. Sitwell nodded. He didn't want to talk about it, but the fact was Mrs. Lawson had been telling the truth — she wasn't the only one in the house still feeling prickly about Petunia being sent away.

"You think I wanted to send anyone away from here? Mr. Barclay made me do that. Said we needed to cut down on expenses, that someone had to go. Either it was Petunia or somebody else."

Mr. Sitwell said nothing. He'd figured as much. Just like he knew that Petunia's leaving wouldn't have been so contentious if they weren't already so understaffed. Shortly after Mr. Boudreaux left, Mr. Thomas, the butler, had suffered a heart attack. The man was over eighty so his passing was hardly sudden, but Mr. Barclay had been distraught. When Mamie took over for Mr. Boudreaux she'd naturally assumed that her first job would be to help find a suitable replacement for the butler. Instead Mr. Barclay had told her it would have to wait and reluctantly adjusted to being forced to dress himself, which he seemed to regard as a form of mourning. For the time being, not only would Mr. Thomas not be replaced, she would have to make further reductions to the staff.

"You know, Mr. Sitwell. I got to say. Every time I come out here it occurs to me just how smart you are. Stay out here in the sun all day, with the trees and the plants and the flowers. Flowers don't talk nasty to you, do they, Mr. Sitwell? Flowers don't try to call you out by your name, do they, Mr. Sitwell?"

Mr. Sitwell shrugged.

"Yeah, you're smart, alright," Mamie said. "You and your durned plants . . ."

The porch door slammed shut.

Mr. Sitwell frowned. He'd planned on warning her about what Mr. Barclay had in mind for the boys as soon as he saw her that morning, but now he was glad he'd kept the troublesome news to himself. It seemed odd, but the best thing he figured he could do for those children was not tell the one person in the house he knew cared even more than he did. But now was not the time. So much depended on Mr. Barclay's negotiations going well and, to the extent that those negotiations were at all affected by the meals that accompanied them, the best thing Mamie could do to help those boys was focus on doing her job.

Besides, sometime during his commute that morning Mr. Sitwell had managed to convince himself that things with the boys would never come to that. Mr. Barclay was in a state because of the stress of his current negotiations and Mr. Sitwell knew that there was no point trying to reason with him when he got like that. But it was also clear the man was not thinking straight. It was just a fact that the care and feeding of three boys was such a meager expense that it hardly made a bit of difference to the household finances one way or another. Once Barclay sorted out his deals with the New Englanders and the Southerners he was bound to be in a more reasonable mood. All Mr. Sitwell had to do was find an excuse to hold off on Barclay's request for another week or two; after that he was certain he could convince the man to pursue a more sensible course.

When the coast was clear, he stood up and went to the kitchen to have his morning coffee. Seated at the table, eating the biscuits Mamie left out for staff, was Mr. Whitmore, the Barclays' driver. As he walked to the stove, Mr. Sitwell glanced at Mr. Whitmore's rheumy eyes.

"Rough night?"

"Not so much rough as long," Mr. Whitmore said. He bared his teeth as he smiled, and Mr. Sitwell was reminded how little he seemed to belong there. Mr. Whitmore had worked as a meat cutter for twelve years before he came to work for the Barclays. The career change had meant a sharp cut in pay, but he seemed overly fond of the jacket, starched collar, and doffer's cap of a chauffeur.

"Woman kick you out again?"

"She thinks she did. Truth is I ran," Mr. Whitmore said. "Got half a mind to stay gone this time too."

Mr. Sitwell nodded. "What was it this time?"

"Same as always. Nothing. She got mad because I went out for drinks with my uncle."

"Uncle?"

Mr. Whitmore and Mr. Boudreaux were related through marriage. Mr. Whitmore's installation on staff had been one of the final changes Mr. Boudreaux had made to the house before he was told to leave it.

"That's right, Sitwell," Mr. Whitmore said. "Just because he's not working here doesn't mean the man has ceased to exist. I still see him from time to time, have a drink, catch up on old times. What's wrong with that?" He shook his head. "But it's all just carousing to her. Well, I'm sick of it, and Uncle says I got cause. Who wants to come home to a woman like that? No, sir. Not me."

He smiled. "Truth told I've been thinking about moving on to greener pastures for a while now."

"That right?"

Mr. Whitmore grunted. "Got my eye on that new girl, that Jennie. What do you think, Sitwell? She's looking mighty ripe to me."

"Don't talk like that in here," Mr. Sitwell said quickly. He nodded toward the boys. "It's not the place."

"No? Well, what is the place? We're in the kitchen aren't we? How should I talk in the kitchen?"

"Quite frankly, Louis, I'd prefer it if you didn't talk at all. If you must, try to talk like you understand what it is you are doing here. Like you understand this is a place of business."

"Place of business?" Mr. Whitmore laughed. "Your whole life is a place of business. Does that mean you always talk like that? Like you're being paid to work?" He squinted. "It's the tone I'm curious about. Like say you're laying up in bed with a woman, assuming such a thing would ever happen." He winked. "What do you sound like then, Mr. Sitwell?"

"Ask your mother," Mr. Sitwell said.

Mr. Whitmore reared his head. For an instant he appeared mad enough to strike Mr. Sitwell. But then he looked around and seemed to remember where he was.

He laughed.

"See? There it is. That's what I was looking for. I knew you were still in there somewhere. I'm just trying to draw it out."

Mr. Sitwell sipped his coffee. Mr. Whitmore was a troublesome fool. Mr. Sitwell knew that the only reason Mamie hadn't sent him away instead of Petunia was because, even if it wasn't his actual job, the man still handled a knife like nobody's business. It saved a lot of money to have a man on staff who, regardless of his official title, knew how to properly butcher a hog. Mamie had told Mr. Sitwell that, for all the meat that passed through that city, it was a sight more difficult to find someone with Mr. Whitmore's skills who was willing to work for what they could afford to pay than she would have imagined before she'd actually had cause to try.

He saluted the man with his cup. "Just be careful you don't draw something else out, Whitmore. Something you wouldn't like."

"Yessum, boss," Mr. Whitmore said in an exaggerated southern drawl. "Whatever you say." He smiled. "How's that? For your kitchen talk?"

Then the swinging door opened and Mamie came into the kitchen. "Why are you still sitting there, Whitmore? I asked you to bring in those boxes."

"I'm gonna get to it as soon as I have my coffee."

"Nobody paying you to drink coffee."

"No, ma'am. But then again nobody paying me to bring in boxes either," Mr. Whitmore said. "I'm just kidding."

Mamie nodded. "Sitwell? Would you mind taking a sniff of Mr. Whitmore's cup, make sure there's no whiskey in it? Understand drinking is hereditary. Might turn out unemployment is too."

"I was just joking around," Mr. Whitmore said.

"Well, don't. Just finish your coffee, get

up off your ass, and do what I told you to do."

She pushed back through the swinging door.

"Bitch," Mr. Whitmore said.

"Watch yourself."

"It's true isn't it? I mean you saw what she did to Petunia. To say nothing of my poor uncle. Man trained her and how does she repay him? By taking his job first chance she got."

"Your uncle was caught drinking in the larder. Mamie had nothing to do with that."

"You believe that? That somehow Mr. Barclay just happened to go into the larder during my uncle's midday nap? What the hell was Mr. Barclay doing in the larder? No. My uncle was set up. By that woman. Because she wanted his job."

Mr. Sitwell shrugged. "Maybe she did want his job. Doesn't change the fact that she wouldn't have gotten it if he hadn't been drinking."

"So what if he was? What difference did it make, so long as he got the job done? That woman can't run no kitchen. Why do you think every time I turn around she's asking me to do something back here? Wasn't like this on Uncle's watch because the man handled business. Plus you got to give it to

65

him. He can cook."

"She's better," Mr. Sitwell said.

"You think?"

"It's just a fact."

Mr. Whitmore, who clearly did not agree, walked out the kitchen door.

Mr. Sitwell finished his coffee. Then he took his cup and placed it in the sink. Truth was there were a lot of things going on in that house that would have to be dealt with sooner or later; it wasn't just Whitmore. Ever since she took over, Mamie had been doing many unconventional things to try to keep down costs, like having Mr. Sitwell stand in as footman on those occasions she considered too important for the boys to handle. Mr. Sitwell did not mind the added responsibility; he understood it was temporary and was more concerned about her increasing reliance on ingredients taken from the fields near the fairgrounds as essential components of her evening meals. Some of these Mr. Sitwell had stumbled upon growing wild and some were there because Mamie had asked him to plant them. Mr. Barclay would have fired them on the spot if he knew how many field roots and vegetables had found a place on his dinner table. But there was not enough room in the vegetable garden to grow everything

Mamie needed for some of the Barclays' favorite recipes and, quite frankly, some of these ingredients would have cost a fortune if Mamie tried to buy them at the market. It was an inconvenience, but so far the biggest problem was making sure that the tramps who slept there at night did not eat them themselves.

"Mr. Sitwell?"

He turned around and saw Frederick standing behind his chair.

"We're running out of bicarbonate. And I heard Mrs. Lawson say something about needing more bluing for the wash. And it occurred to me that perhaps you might like some fertilizer. You want me to ask Miss Mamie if she don't mind letting us go to the market to pick that up for you? I mean if you want it now. That way we can just go out and get it all at once."

Mr. Sitwell squinted at the peculiar phrasing of the offer.

"I take it all three of you must go?"

"Yes, sir. Take three to carry all that," Frederick said. "Also, it's Colored Day at the fair. Don't come but once a month and we already missed the last four. They keep changing the day, for some reason. Thought maybe we could stop by on our way to the market. I figured if I said you needed us to

67

go, Miss Mamie's bound to say it's okay."

Frederick smiled. The boy was just so clever. Mr. Sitwell couldn't help but feel sorry for him.

"Alright. But I want all of you to come outside with me for a minute first. We need to talk."

"We do something wrong?"

"No, I just want to talk."

He walked out to the yard. The three boys came out to the back porch and sat in a row along the bottom step.

"I'm curious to find out how much thought you boys have given to what you will do when you reach maturity."

"What do you mean 'maturity'?" Mac asked.

"Well, when it's time for you to leave here, of course. It must have occurred to you that Mr. Barclay couldn't possibly afford to keep all three of you on indefinitely. Have you thought about what you will do then?"

The boys shook their heads. "No."

"But it's important."

"We're just happy to be here now," Frederick said. "Try not to muck it up with thinking too much."

They all nodded as if it were agreed: they must not muck it up with thinking.

Mr. Sitwell frowned. "Well, you have to

think. Even if the Barclays did let you stay, eventually you'll get too big for the room downstairs. What if one of you was to meet a nice girl?"

To his chagrin, the boys began to blush.

Bart giggled. "Well, sir, I guess the other two would just have to scooch over and make room. . . ."

"I'm serious. You'll be adults one day, sooner than you think. What happens when you find yourself grown men, trying to make it out there on your own?"

The boys were still jostling and pinching one another, thinking about the imaginary woman coming to join them in the cellar. For a moment it actually made Mr. Sitwell angry. He could not, for the life of him, remember ever having been so young.

"Stop that now. I'm trying to help you. I'm telling you it will happen. And when it does, you'll wish you'd thought about it, you'll wish you'd been prepared. You can't spend the rest of your lives sleeping on a cot in some white man's cellar."

"We know that, sir. But we just want to stay together," Mac said. "Long as we stick together, figure we'll be alright. . . ."

All three of them nodded in agreement. He could tell they were serious and something occurred to him that hadn't before:

the likelihood that, if one of them were sent away, the other two might very well go with him, in solidarity.

This thought so upset him that his hands were shaking as he reached into his pocket and pulled out a few coins.

"Take this." He nodded. "We'll discuss this again later. Go ahead and tell Miss Mamie I need you to go. But don't dawdle. You can stop by the fair if you want, but you can't stay all day. I expect you back in three hours. Tonight's dinner is very important."

"Thank you, Mr. Sitwell. And don't worry. We won't be late."

They ran off toward the driveway.

"You gave those boys good counsel, Sitwell."

When he turned around, Jennie was sitting on a stump near the water pump, watching him.

"Imagine they do well to listen to you."

Mr. Sitwell nodded and said nothing. He was still confused by what had happened the night before. He'd done something wrong, offended her, when that was the last thing he'd wanted to do.

"I mean that. You're one of those decent men I've heard stories about, aren't you? Walking ladies to their door. Passing out money to orphan children . . . Just all around decent." She frowned. "I feel like I wasn't half as decent to you last night. Made me nervous, is all, having you at my door like that. I don't like things to get too mixed up."

"What's that mean?"

"It means I've got work and I've got my life at home. I try to keep the two separate. Because as strange as it might seem to you, I've never actually worked in a white man's house before. Just trying to be careful is all. Can't always tell when I'm about to offend somebody around here."

"What did you do before?"

"Honestly? I was a cakewalk delineator."

"What's that?"

"A performer, Sitwell." Jennie stretched her arms out in a sudden graceful movement and bowed her head. "Toured with Happy Hillman's Baby Blackbirds for seven years. Came here to do *The Creole Show.* You see that?"

"No."

"Well, that figures. Anyhow, when they left, I stayed." She sighed. "Miss Mamie took a chance hiring me, I do realize that. I'm just trying to fit in."

"Well, you seem to be making a lot of assumptions about what you're fitting into."

71

"That occurred to me last night as well."

Mr. Sitwell shook his head. "I never would have thought something bad about you for having a child, Jennie. Hope you know that. Just surprised me is all."

"I believe you. Truth is you have been nothing but nice to me since I got here. And that's why I wanted to apologize. While I still have the chance."

"What's that mean? You going somewhere?"

"Maybe." Jennie shrugged. "I don't know. Honestly, I wasn't planning on letting Mamie down quite so soon. But then she gives me this." She held up a piece of paper.

"What's that?"

"I do believe it's a shopping list."

"Can't you read it?"

"Yes, I can read it. I just don't understand half of what it says." She looked down at the paper. "What on earth is a mirliton, Mr. Sitwell? You ever heard of that?"

"Of course I have. Must be something she's got planned for when the Southerners come back for dinner on Friday," Mr. Sitwell said. "Didn't Mamie explain about the shopping to you?"

The shopping would have needed explaining. Mamie knew that. But maybe she was getting tired of trying to explain things.

"Would you like me to go with you to the market?"

"Would you do that? Could you do that?"

"I could."

"And you won't get in trouble for leaving?"

He smiled. "I'm the groundskeeper. Nobody knows what I do around here all day, unless something goes wrong. And it won't. So let's go."

They walked out to the Avenue.

"Really, Sitwell," Jennie said. "I am sorry I was rude to you last night. Felt bad about it as soon as you left. This is all new to me and I don't really know how you people think, I mean the kind of people who don't go to *The Creole Show. . . .* Just trying to be smart. Not so much for my sake, you understand. But my child."

"What's your daughter's name?"

"Cutie Pie. Cutie Pie Williams." Jennie smiled. She paused for a moment, as if expecting him to recognize the name, then seemed to remember whom she was talking to.

"We used to have an act together. The Dancing Darling Williams Sisters. But she's getting too big to play the Pick and I don't think I want her playing anything else."

"That why you quit the stage?"

She nodded. "Tired of touring. It's dangerous out there. Believe me, I had a hard enough time trying to keep myself out of trouble. Anyhow, I want her to go to a proper school."

"And the girl's father?"

"What do you mean?"

"Is he a performer too? Or somebody you knew before?"

"Ain't no before, Sitwell," Jennie said. "I don't mind talking about myself. I'm not ashamed of anything I've done. But as far as I'm concerned life started when I was fifteen and Cutie Pie was three, when the two of us hit the road and took to the stage. We'll just have to leave it at that."

They climbed aboard the omnibus and got off again near the Water Street Market, a noisy crowded space made up of over one hundred fifty stalls. Mr. Sitwell led Jennie to a large busy stall where, behind a low counter, a thin man's hands were moving fast as he stuffed a bag with beets.

"See this man? He's from Louisiana. Mamie ever give you a list like this again, especially if you know the Barclays are entertaining Southerners, just show it to him, he'll help you out. Matter of fact, anybody here would be willing to help you, Jennie. Just so long as you let them know you work for the Barclays. The Barclays throw an awful lot of parties and don't nobody out here want to lose their business. It's what will keep them from trying to cheat you too."

"I will remember that." She looked around then pointed to another stall. "Looks like you can get the same cheaper over there."

"Taste cheaper too." He sniffed. "Go ahead and pay the man."

After they'd purchased vegetables they went to the butcher for meat. When they were finished, they only had about two thirds of what Mamie had written down on her list, but there were only a few coins left.

"Now what?"

Mr. Sitwell nodded. This was the part that needed explaining.

"You want to get in good with Miss Mamie? I'm about to show you how."

He took her to the fields, a large green hill located on the back end of the fairgrounds. During construction for the Exposition, the land had been cleared and transportation tunnels dug beneath it to bring in building materials. Once the fairgrounds were complete the area had been reimagined as a public park. They put in grass, planted trees, and built a fence around it. But the area had not been maintained due to funding issues and had long since been taken over by tramps.

As he led Jennie through it, Mr. Sitwell explained, "I'd say a fourth of what she's got on this list you can find growing wild if you know where to look. Especially the herbs. You want to make a good impression on Miss Mamie? You've got to figure out what's worth paying for and what you can get for free."

He looked around.

"Over there is the asparagus. And that there is mustard greens. I'm not entirely sure Mr. Barclay realizes it, but he and his wife eat an awful lot of greens. Mamie just sautés it, covers it with seasoned manioc flour. Sometimes she uses it as a garnish for bean soup."

Jennie shook her head. "I don't understand. How do the Barclays expect her to make dinner if she doesn't have the money to buy what she needs?"

"It's stupid, isn't it? The Barclays don't understand what Mamie does in that kitchen. They just eat. They'll tell her to go ahead and make a substitution then complain when it doesn't taste right. But they're not the ones who are going to be sent packing if one of their dinner parties doesn't go well. And I'll tell you something else people like to pretend they don't understand. In that house, the color of the staff will always match the color of the cook. That means if Miss Mamie goes, most likely we all going with her. That's why she's got to always be thinking. For all our sakes. Understand?"

"I do," Jennie said.

To his great relief, he believed her.

"The last thing I want to do is let Mamie down. But I've got to be honest. I don't know much about herbs and vegetables."

"I don't mind teaching you, if you're willing to learn."

He pointed to a bush heavy with red berries. "In a couple days I'll come back for these. They make an excellent jelly, believe it or not. But you've got to be careful not to confuse them for their cousins — they're very poisonous, which is why folks sleeping out here know to leave them alone. I'll teach you how to tell the difference. Got to look to the leaf. See how they're different? When you see that, don't get near the berries on that bush. The leaves can be made into a powerful soporific, if you need one. But really the whole bush is just too dangerous to mess with if you don't know what you're doing."

"You speak from experience?"

"I've had cause to serve it once or twice."

"To Barclay's guests?"

"No. I got a before too, Jennie. Don't forget that. These leaves are a part of how I got here. I was in New Orleans at the time and needed a way up the Mississippi. Wound up feeding 'em to a ship captain who was not particularly amenable to providing me with passage on his boat."

Jennie squinted. "How old were you then?"

"Twelve."

"Well, you must have been a very clever child to have managed that on your own."

"I imagine you must have been pretty clever yourself." Mr. Sitwell smiled. "None of that matters now, does it, Jennie? It's past. A long time ago. And far, far from here."

It certainly seemed so as the two of them walked out of the fields and back onto the crowded avenue. They got on the streetcar and rode back up the city's south side. This time when Mr. Sitwell sat next to Jennie he found it easy to talk. She seemed interested in the things he said and that made him feel funny and clever. Everything went so smoothly between them that the turmoil and distance he'd felt the night before seemed to evaporate every time she smiled. In all respects it felt like a new day.

Mr. Sitwell was in a good mood when they pushed through the back door. When they entered the kitchen Mamie was sitting on a stool near the main worktable, Mrs. Lawson standing behind her, braiding her hair.

"What took you so long?"

"Got a little held up at the market," Jennie set the bags on the table. "Don't worry, it won't happen again. Mr. Sitwell was helping me out."

Mrs. Lawson sucked her teeth. "Girl, what's he got to help you out with? He's the groundskeeper, remember? You oughtta be telling him what to do."

Mr. Sitwell shrugged. "House is on the grounds."

"It's an entirely different sphere."

"Well, he seems to understand how things work around here well enough," Jennie said. "I appreciated it."

"That's not the point." Mrs. Lawson shook her head as she fitted a small kerchief over Mamie's braids. The bobby pin clenched between her lips bobbed up and down like a cigarette as she said, "There's still something called discipline and order, a chain of command. But see, you wouldn't know that because everything is all mixed up around here. We got the meatman driving the car, we got the yardman supervising

79

household staff. . . ." She looked Jennie up and down and sniffed. "Quite frankly I still don't know what the heck you're doing here."

"Why, she's the cakewalk delineator, of course." Mr. Sitwell winked.

"You think this is funny? You think it don't matter what your title is, what somebody calls you? Well, you're wrong about that, Sitwell. It does matter. It matters a great deal. Trust me, I've been working in this house for thirty years and if there is one thing I've learned it's that there is a reason there is an order, a way things are supposed to be done. Because without it everything is bound to fall apart eventually. It's only a matter of time."

Mamie said nothing. She submitted to Mrs. Lawson tugging at her braids with a scowl on her face. As soon as the kerchief was tied she hopped off her stool, signaled for Jennie to follow, and stormed across the room. The door to the supply closet slammed shut behind them.

Mr. Sitwell turned to Mrs. Lawson. "Why you got to keep going on like that? You know it's not helping anything."

"I'm not trying to help that woman. I'm trying to tell the truth. Everything has been a mess around here since Mr. Boudreaux left and you know it. Quite frankly, if anybody should be upset about all this foolishness going on, it's you. You're the one she's got working two jobs. What time you get out of here last night anyhow?"

"Nine."

"Well, now, see? That's just wrong."

"It's temporary," Mr. Sitwell said. "You know there's no money around here right now and we're understaffed."

"What the heck did she bring that girl in for? Why didn't she just hire a man when she had the chance?"

"A man costs more than a girl, Mrs. Lawson. You know that. Mr. Thomas will be replaced soon enough."

He squinted.

"Nobody is trying to replace you. You know that, don't you?"

"I didn't say anything about me."

Mr. Sitwell nodded. "Good. Because nobody could. Need you too much around here, even I know we wouldn't last a week without you. But I also know you are smart enough to realize what is going on. There's no money until Mr. Barclay works out his business deals. Quite frankly, if things keep going the way they have been, it's only a matter of time before that man realizes he's got no business having a staff this large. And then what? You really want to be out there right now, trying to find another job? Or haven't you noticed what's going on in the streets, all the protests and strikes? People out there starving, fighting just to survive. So even if you don't want to help Mamie, I would have thought you'd have sense enough to help yourself."

Mrs. Lawson was quiet.

"You hear what I said?"

"I hear you." She frowned. "I'll say one thing, Sitwell. Mr. Boudreaux sure did name you right. Because the title does suit you."

Mr. Sitwell said nothing. Because it was true: the only thing Mr. Sitwell could remember Mr. Boudreaux ever giving him was his name. Shortly after he arrived at the house, because he'd refused to divulge his real one, Mr. Barclay had asked Mr. Boudreaux to assign him a moniker that might best remind him of those characteristics he should build upon as he sought to make himself useful to the household and hopefully someday a productive member of the society that surrounded it.

Sit well.

It could have been worse. He might have just as easily wound up *Mr. Don'tbothermenow.*

Or *Mr. Keepyouropinionstoyourself.*

Or *Mr. Don'tcryinmykitchenorIwillgiveyou-areasontocry.*

"I know you and Boudreaux never got along," Mrs. Lawson said. "Just like I know the man had problems. But even you have to admit he would have never let things get this bad. Plus, you got to give it to him. The man could cook."

Mr. Sitwell shrugged. "She's better."

"You think?"

"It's just a fact."

Then the door to the supply closet swung open. Mamie came back out wearing a uniform identical to Mrs. Lawson's: a light blue, long dress and a thin muslin apron with straps that fluttered over her shoulders in short, puffed sleeves. She was still pulling at the straps as she charged through the kitchen, the kerchief on her head flopping up and down in counter rhythm to her heavy strides. Jennie trailed behind her, trying to tie her sash. When Mamie reached the swinging door she stopped, turned around, and slapped Jennie's hand away. Then, without a word, she pushed through to the front of the house.

Mrs. Lawson looked Sitwell up and down. "At least wash your hands."

He washed his hands in the sink and then

followed Mrs. Lawson out to the hall. They found Mamie standing near the front door with her back to them and her head down, softly muttering to herself as she prepared for the arrival of Mr. Barclay's guest.

"Mamie?"

Mamie raised her right hand as a signal for them to keep quiet. She took a series of deep breaths then raised and lowered her shoulders as she rolled her head from side to side.

Through the window beside the door, Mr. Sitwell could see the car pulling to a stop in front of the house.

"You ain't got time for all that now, woman," Mrs. Lawson said. Mr. Sitwell glared at her.

"What I mean to say is, I hope you didn't take offense at what I said before. All that kitchen talk," Mrs. Lawson said. "That's all it was. I know you doing the best you can."

"You think you could do better?" Mamie said, still facing the door. "Because trust me, you wouldn't last a day."

"Now, Mamie Price, I am trying to apologize to you."

"I don't need your apology. Everything is gonna get sorted out soon enough and, in the meantime, try not to get too confused. I know exactly what I'm doing."

She took a final deep breath, then turned around.

"Open the damn door, Mr. Sitwell."

He pulled it back just in time to see Mr. Barclay bounding up the stairs. Beside him was a man in a dark blue suit whom Mr. Sitwell had never seen before.

"This is my cook, Mamie. The one I was telling you about," Mr. Barclay said as they stepped inside the house.

Mamie bowed and did a small curtsey.

"And she is clear on the restrictions for tonight's dinner?" the man asked. He handed Mr. Sitwell his hat.

"Yes, of course. You haven't forgotten have you, girl?"

"No, sir." Mamie smiled. "No meat. No meat by-products."

"That means no lard," the man said.

"Yessum, sir." Mamie batted her eyes. "No lard. No ham hocks."

Mr. Sitwell stared straight ahead. This was the performance Mamie had been gearing up for, another element of the complexity of her role in the house. All the other servants were expected to make themselves as inconspicuous as possible, but the cook was often called upon to interact with the guests, to become part of the entertainment. Smiling and bowing in the front of the house was just another part of her job.

Mr. Barclay took a deep breath and said, "This man is Mr. Pound, Mamie. He's the progenitor of the cookless breakfast."

"Cookless breakfast? Why, what on earth is that?"

"Delicious wafers of whole meal flour, molasses, and dried fruit. All baked and pressed under a patented process, introduced right here in the city, at the World's Fair."

"And do you eat them with ham and eggs?" Mamie blinked.

Mr. Barclay laughed. "No, Mamie. You pour them into a saucer of milk and serve it cold. Now when a man stands up from the breakfast table, instead of feeling sluggish and weighed down, he is energized, full of the fuel he needs to start the day."

"Mo' fuel than ham and eggs?" Mamie's eyes opened wide. "Lawdy, y'all white folks is a true wonder. What will you think of next?"

Mr. Sitwell looked at Mr. Pound. It was difficult to tell how much the man appreciated Mr. Barclay and Mamie's performance. He nodded his head, looked around the hall, and smiled as if vaguely amused.

"Tell me, Barclay. Is your entire staff colored?"

"Yes, as a matter of fact," Mr. Barclay said. "I prefer to maintain a staff of a uniform hue. Cuts down on conflict, and I've found, perhaps counterintuitively, the problem of theft."

"Is that right?"

"Indeed. I realize there is a fad these days to go with the Irish. But, quite frankly, from what I have seen, I still believe that if one is able to manage it, one is better off sticking with the colored race, in part because of the unfortunate prejudice. By which I mean that a perfectly respectable colored will happily work as a servant while the white man content to do so will inevitably be of a lower caliber."

"This is unfortunate," Mr. Pound agreed. "Yet so often true."

"Well, of course," Mr. Barclay said. "It is why even if one is able to find a decent Irish man he will so often prove surly, and I simply cannot abide surly. Ultimately it comes down to a simple question of genetic aptitude. One can't argue with generations of breeding; one can't argue with science. Isn't that right, Mamie?"

"I'm still trying to wrap my mind around this here cookless breakfast," Mamie said. She cocked her head and gave Mr. Barclay a puzzled look. "But tell me, sir. Why is it

I've never heard of this marvelous invention before?"

Mr. Barclay sighed. "Alas, Mamie. Mr. Pound's fine product is not yet available in stores here in the city. But that is why our friend is here. He is thinking of purchasing one of my manufacturing facilities. This will cut his transportation costs in half so that soon his nutritious wafers can be made available not just in the city but throughout the entire country. Isn't that marvelous?"

Mr. Pound clucked his tongue. "That's enough now, Barclay. I'm well aware of what this deal would mean over time. Your Mamie couldn't possibly understand such matters and you and I shall have plenty of time to discuss them tonight, over dinner."

"Yes, of course," Mr. Barclay said.

"And in the meantime, don't you worry none, Mr. Cookless Breakfast Man. About yo' restrictions. Much as it pains me to not throw a ham hock in there somewhere, I got something planned that I think is gonna satisfy you this evening. Yes, sir. Whip you up something real nice, leave you feeling proper energized."

"Thank you, Mamie," Mr. Barclay said.

She bowed and, with a wide swing of her hips, walked back to the kitchen.

"You'll forgive my enthusiasm," Mr. Barclay said. He and Mr. Pound began walking down the hall. "It's just so rare that I have the opportunity to play a hand in the distribution of a product I so deeply believe in."

"It's quite alright. I must say I am curious to see how our diet finds interpretation at the hands of your Negro cook."

"I'm sure you will be pleasantly surprised." Mr. Barclay smiled. "It will be a treat for me as well, to see what is to be made of this diet of yours, as clearly it has served you well. You are looking quite fit, Pound. Not a day older than the last time I saw you."

"It has been a while, hasn't it? When did we last see each other?"

"I believe it was that night at the Monte Carlo."

"I believe you are correct."

"Well, perhaps this will prove another benefit of our transaction, the opportunity to see more of you in the city. Tell me, have you given much thought to who you intend to market your wafers to?"

"Yes," Mr. Pound said, just before they disappeared into the parlor. "All of them."

Mr. Sitwell waited until the door closed behind them. He hung Mr. Pound's coat in the hall closet, then turned around, walked through the dining room, and pushed through a swinging door.

When he got back to the kitchen Mamie was already hard at work at the stove. Despite the theatrics at the front door, Mamie was well aware who Mr. Pound was: an old friend turned health reformer from Mr. Barclay's college days. He ran a longevity spa in the Berkshires and was currently making a great deal of money selling his breakfast wafers and a series of books meant to promote the moral lifestyle that was to accompany their consumption. He was now interested in purchasing the plant with the ambition of making his wafers available on a national scale. Mr. Barclay had made a point of telling Mamie about Mr. Pound's peculiar dietary restrictions two weeks in advance, and ever since she had devoted a few hours each day to experimenting with different ingredients in order to come up with a meal that would be both sufficiently flavorful and would accommodate his particular needs. The elaborate seasoning she'd created was a combination of several ingredients, including dried onion, garlic, dill, horseradish, mustard, parsley, white pepper, turmeric, green and red bell peppers, rose hip, summer savory, mushroom, safflower, coriander, fenugreek, basil, marjoram, oregano, thyme, tarragon, cumin, ginger, cayenne pepper, cloves, spinach, rosemary, cinnamon, paprika, yeast, celery, and orange and lemon peel. In combination these had produced a seasoning that was not only remarkably economical but also unlike anything Mr. Sitwell had ever tasted before.

It was absolutely delicious.

He watched her shut the oven door.

"Twenty-eight minutes," Mamie said to Mac as she wiped her hands on a dish towel. "Not a second longer, understand?"

"Yes, ma'am." Mac set the timer.

She turned to Mr. Sitwell. "You stay in the house for now. I need you to help serve dinner tonight and that means I can't have that man seeing you out in the yard."

Mr. Sitwell nodded. He sat down on a stool near the side window, glad for the excuse to be in the kitchen. He loved watching Miss Mamie work, knew for a fact that, though Mr. Boudreaux got credit for having trained her, she was a better cook than he had ever been. In some ways, Mr. Sitwell thought, Mr. Boudreaux was like the house itself in that there had been a time when he had been very impressed. Then, one day when he was fifteen, he'd gone to the larder in order to do some errand for Mamie and found Mr. Boudreaux lying facedown on

91

the floor. It was the first of what would be many times he'd seen the man passed out drunk.

"Best to just leave him there," Mamie told him when he ran to fetch her. That day had marked an important advance in his maturity, for it was when he began to understand how things in that house really worked. Throughout the time Mamie had been Mr. Boudreaux's assistant she always acted on his authority. Every command that came from her lips was prefaced with the words "Mr. Boudreaux wants . . ." or "Mr. Boudreaux has asked . . ." when the truth was Mamie had been carrying him for at least a decade before she got her promotion. It was why, as the years went on and Mr. Boudreaux's drinking and absences from the kitchen became increasingly frequent, there was scarcely any change in the daily operations of the house. If anything, it was an improvement.

Quite frankly, everything was more pleasant when the man slept.

Bart brought out a pitcher of iced tea and set it on the table. He filled two glasses with ice and placed them on a silver tray. He handed the tray to Mamie, who passed it to Sitwell in turn.

"Go on, Mr. Sitwell."

"Yes, ma'am."

He pushed through the swinging door.

"Really, Barclay, you must visit, even if it is only for a few days," Mr. Pound said as Mr. Sitwell entered the parlor with the tea. "We now offer a wide variety of services for men such as yourself. Many find that even a short stay promotes substantial improvements in terms of vitality and cognitive functioning."

"Is that right?" Mr. Barclay said. Mr. Sitwell set the glasses on the table between them.

"Absolutely. Our mineral-infused colonic provides significant relief in just a few days. Depending on the level of blockage, of course."

"Enticing," Mr. Barclay said. "Perhaps someday soon."

"Well, not too soon I'm afraid. I'm told we are booked solid until the following spring."

"Oh? Business is that good?"

"Business could not be better," Mr. Pound said. "This venture has proven remarkably profitable. Has brought me success beyond my wildest dreams." He smiled. "Looking back, Barclay, I must say I understand perfectly why you chose not to invest. Quite frankly, when I came to you seeking funding even I had no idea how much money there was to be made in the field of rejuvenation. But I suppose everything happens for a reason. Because, of course, it all turned out for the best."

Mr. Sitwell handed Mr. Barclay his glass.

"That will be all," Mr. Barclay said.

Mr. Sitwell bowed and took his leave.

Back in the kitchen, he watched Mac set a bowl on the worktable, shake out three cups of flour from the five-pound sack, and add a teaspoon of baking soda to a sifter.

"Make sure you don't put too much soda in it," Mamie said. "Last time it was a little too much. . . ."

Mr. Sitwell smiled. He wondered why Mrs. Lawson could not see it, how much better things were now that Mr. Boudreaux was gone. For all the hardship they had endured since his departure and Mr. Thomas's passing, Mr. Sitwell did not miss either of them. This was how a kitchen was supposed to feel. Warm and nurturing, a place of comfort and learning. More like the kitchens he still remembered from his childhood.

He watched Mac crank the handle. He'd spent a lot of time in the Farleys' kitchen growing up and had learned a great many things from watching his mother work, much like Mac and Bart were learning from Mamie now. It was in the Farley kitchen that he'd learned the difference between a grate and a grind, a chop and a cut, a twist and a taste. Outside in the Farleys' garden was where he'd learned how to identify herbs and edible plants, to distinguish sweet berries from their poisonous cousins. But above all the kitchen was where he'd come to understand all the things the world outside the village had to offer. The Farleys' cabinets had been full of things you needed paper money to buy: heavy cream, powdered sugar, tea biscuits, almonds, and dates. Things that, once you'd had a taste of them, you couldn't help but want more.

Bart came in from the pantry carrying a plate of finger sandwiches. Mr. Sitwell watched him arrange them on a silver tray. When he was finished he held the tray up for Mamie to inspect. She arched her eyebrow, then nodded.

"Nice work," she said and handed the tray to Mr. Sitwell.

He pushed back through the swinging door.

"Of course, it's not really the Italians I am worried about," Mr. Pound said as he entered the parlor with his tray.

"Well, of course not. It's an adjustment,

to be sure. But I've been here for thirty-five years and I'm telling you, they are no longer the primary issue. If this is a matter that concerns you in the slightest, allow me to put you in touch with the Employers' Association. They are the ones who are handling it."

"Importing scabs, I understand." Mr. Pound reached for one of the sandwiches Mr. Sitwell held out to him.

"It is effective. If you want a docile workforce, sometimes you have to go out and find one."

"A docile workforce? They are also potential customers, are they not?"

"Are they?"

"They could be. I wonder, has it ever occurred to any of your associates that, instead of constantly reminding them how inconsequential they are, perhaps the better course would be to offer them some investment in the existing order? Perhaps then they would not be so determined to tear it down."

"So that's what you are selling now, is it? The opportunity for inclusion?"

"Shared habits, shared identity. Why not? Patriotism may be the banner of inclusion, but consumerism might very well be the anvil," Mr. Pound said.

Mr. Barclay bit into one of the sandwiches

96

then nodded toward Mr. Sitwell's tray.

"Leave it," he said.

Mr. Sitwell set the tray on the table then bowed and took his leave.

When he returned to the kitchen Mamie and the boys were still hard at work with dinner preparations. He watched Mamie pull a cake out of the oven and smiled.

It had been years since he'd helped his mother bake a cake but he still remembered — not simply the taste, but also the gestures of the making. The look of her strong brown arms reaching for the powdered sugar, her long thin fingers wrapped around the handle of a cup as she scooped it out and added it to the butter. She mixed them together and spread it across a flat pan. Then the two of them sat together at the worktable and created a sugar cookie daisy chain to line the sides of a birthday cake. . . .

The clatter of a pan being dropped snapped him out of his reverie.

"Careful, Mac! What did I tell you about that?"

He sat up on his stool, startled by the ease with which his thoughts had drifted back to Seminole County once more. When he recalled the strange delirium that had seized him the night before, he realized he needed to be vigilant about the melancholy such nostalgia seemed to provoke. It was why he was relieved when, a few minutes later, Mrs. Lawson came back into the kitchen and set an empty serving tray in the sink.

"Get on back out there."

"That quick?"

"Yes, that quick. It seems Mr. Pound has another engagement."

When Mr. Sitwell reached the front of the house the two men were already standing in the hall.

"You misunderstand me," Mr. Barclay said as Mr. Sitwell handed a jacket to Mr. Pound. "I was merely referring to taste."

"And I was referring to the fact that you are a snob." Mr. Pound slipped his jacket over his shoulders. "One day you will realize that this sometimes prevents you from seeing the opportunities right in front of your face."

"Yes, this may very well be true. Perhaps you are right. Perhaps if we could all just sit down together and enjoy your breakfast wafers, all the problems of our modern polyglot society would finally be solved."

Mr. Pound frowned. "You think it's funny? I assure you it is not. I see this product as a calling. I will not be satisfied until every man, woman, and child has had the opportunity to experience its benefits. Someday good health will no longer be the exclusive preserve of the wealthy; that will be my gift to them. I can see how that may seem absurd to someone like you. Perhaps you forget that unlike you I am a self-made man, I have had to work for everything I have become. If I believe so strongly in human potential it is because I know myself to be the proof of it."

"I am well aware of your circumstances, my friend," Mr. Barclay said. "As I said, I was merely referring to taste. Speaking of which . . ."

He turned to Mr. Sitwell then reached into his pocket and pulled out one of Mr. Pound's breakfast wafers.

"What are you doing?" Mr. Pound said.

"I think you will find this amusing, Pound. . . . Mr. Sitwell?" He held out the wafer. "I would like you to hold that to your nose then recite a complete list of ingredients to Mr. Pound in descending order according to volume."

Mr. Sitwell took the wafer.

"Seriously, Barclay. What is this?" Mr. Pound said.

"Just watch."

Mr. Sitwell held the wafer to his nose. "It's . . . . fairly simple, sir. Wheat flour, malted barley, salt, yeast, and a touch of molasses."

"Is that all?"

"Yes, sir."

"No nuts? No berries?"

"No, sir."

Mr. Barclay nodded. "Is he correct?"

Mr. Pound frowned. "How did he do that?"

"Well, in truth no one knows. But he did do it, didn't he? It's a trick of his, some sort of genetic adaptation, the origins of which I have not yet had time to investigate. Perhaps I would find that in the jungles of Africa such olfactory skill was useful for determining the proximity of predators, although it serves no actual purpose here, in the modern city. Yet it is amusing, is it not? And now it seems we have a complete rundown of the key ingredients for world peace."

He patted Mr. Pound on the back.

"Oh, Pound. Don't be so serious. You know what I said was meant only in jest. And really, what does it matter what I think? Marketing longevity products is your area of expertise, not mine. The plant will soon be yours and you will run it as you see fit. And while I may not understand everything you have said today, I do know that you are a man of a keen intellect and that your product is one possessed of a unique value.

I am fully confident that you shall make it a success."

Mr. Pound nodded. "Very well, Barclay. Until tonight, then."

"Yes. Looking forward to it." Mr. Barclay smiled.

Mr. Sitwell turned to take his leave but Mr. Barclay stopped him.

"I'd like a word with you."

Mr. Sitwell frowned. The only thing he could imagine Mr. Barclay wanting to talk to him about was his decision about the boys. He racked his mind trying to think of an excuse for why he had not come up with one yet.

He watched Mr. Barclay wave as his guest made his way to the awaiting car.

"Negotiations going well, sir?" Mr. Sitwell asked.

"As well as can be expected. The man is a pompous buffoon."

"But a rich buffoon, yes?" Mr. Sitwell said. "Perhaps from our vantage point there could be no better combination."

It was an attempt to change the subject but Mr. Barclay arched an eyebrow at the comment. As Mr. Whitmore started the car and drove toward the gate, Mr. Barclay looked Mr. Sitwell up and down and frowned.

"Getting a little ahead of yourself don't you think, Sitwell?"

"Yes, sir. Apologies. I meant no disrespect to your guest. Only that —"

"Not him. Never mind that idiot. I'm talking about the boys."

"The boys?"

Mr. Barclay frowned. "I saw them walking down the block as Mr. Pound and I were pulling into the drive. It certainly did not escape my attention that there are only two of them now."

"Two of them?"

Mr. Sitwell glanced toward the side of the house. In the distance, near the water pump, he saw Mac and Bart struggling to lift a heavy pail.

"Understand me. I do recognize the possibility of confusion stemming from our conversation last night. I asked you to take care of it, and perhaps you thought you were doing so. On a certain level, I appreciate that. But it is not your place to terminate anyone without my express permission. Not even a kitchen boy."

"No, sir. Of course not. I would never . . ."

His eyes searched the yard, looking for Frederick.

"It's alright," Mr. Barclay said. "Or in any event, what's done is done. I realize that I have at times allowed you to take certain liberties in this house, to conduct yourself with a degree of independence not at all appropriate to your station. But that freedom is predicated on your ability to demonstrate that you understand the limits of your actual position. There is still a chain of command. An order, a way that things must be done."

"Yes, sir," Mr. Sitwell said. "Of course. I realize that."

"Good." He patted Mr. Sitwell on the shoulder. "Just make sure it does not happen again."

Mr. Sitwell walked back to the kitchen. He checked the pantry, then the cellar, but saw no sign of Frederick. He went through the back door and walked toward the water pump, where Mac and Bart were still struggling with the pail.

"Where is Frederick?"

Mac and Bart stopped what they were doing at once. They looked at each other and then at Mr. Sitwell.

"He's not here, sir," Mac said. "He . . . got a little bit held up at the fair."

"Held up? What does 'held up' mean?"

"It means they're holding him," Bart said. "It means they won't let him leave."

"Won't let him leave?" Mr. Sitwell

squinted. "Are you saying he's been detained?"

"Yes, sir. A little bit," Mac said. Bart nudged him with his elbow. "I mean he's not in jail. They got him in that room underneath the boardwalk, where they used to put the drunks. Said they're gonna keep him until closing and then decide what to do with him."

"Why? How on earth did that happen? What were you all up to out there?"

"Nothing, sir. At least not today," Mac said. "The man selling passes for the Ferris wheel knew him from before. A long time ago, before he got to the asylum, before he was properly reformed." He shook his head. "Seems the man used to have a fruit cart, and it's possible Frederick might have taken an apple from it. It was so long ago that Frederick figured the man wouldn't remember him. But he did."

Mr. Sitwell looked at the clock. It was three in the afternoon.

"Why didn't you say something before now?"

"We wanted to," Mac said. "But Frederick told us to wait until after the party, said he didn't want us disturbing Miss Mamie making dinner. Said he knew it was important, but if he wasn't back by then we should tell you straightaways."

"Look here, sir," Bart said. "I can see you're upset but I promise you, it's alright. Frederick will get it straightened out. He always does, he's smart like that. Until then, Mac and me can cover for him, no problem."

They nodded in agreement.

"You won't even know he's gone."

Mr. Sitwell frowned. It was clear the boys did not grasp the seriousness of the situation. But Mr. Sitwell knew that in Mr. Barclay's mind there was no greater sign of moral turpitude on the part of a servant than theft. Mr. Sitwell had seen orphans sent away after being caught stealing a single silver spoon because Mr. Barclay insisted the pettiness of the object could never outweigh the implications of the act itself. If the Barclays found out what had happened, it wouldn't matter when the transgression had occurred or whether Frederick had stolen a single apple or a hundred. Mr. Sitwell already knew what Mr. Barclay's response would be: "The child has decided his own fate. Best leave him to it."

He reached for his hat.

"Don't say a word about this to anyone until I return. Not even Miss Mamie. Just focus on getting everything ready for tonight's dinner," Mr. Sitwell said. "I'll take care of it."

3
NEEDS WARNING

Mr. Sitwell hurried through the garden and out the gate, headed toward the omnibus stop. As he ran he thought about all the other orphans he'd known over the years, boys caught stealing and sent away, never to be heard from again. So many boys had come and gone since he'd started working in that house that he couldn't even recall most of their names. Their features blurred and blended in Sitwell's mind so that they all seemed sad semblances of the two who'd stood beside him on the back porch the day he arrived. Those boys had only lasted a few months before they were sent back to the asylum for stealing silverware and ever after, that theft was how Mr. Sitwell knew that deep down he was still one of them. Because the truth was, when those two others were banished from the house, Mr. Sitwell had been stealing too. Somehow he'd just managed not to get caught.

For the next twenty years he'd worked in that house and never once thought to intervene — yet here he was, running. What was it that made these boys different? What was it that made him run? All he could think was that it had something to do with Barclay asking him to choose between them, that somehow it had had the effect of making him feel responsible for them, accountable not only for the answer he had come up with but also for his own determination not to give it.

The bus pulled to the curb. He climbed aboard a crowded car and found himself wedged between two men in sanitation uniforms. He paid his fare, pushed past the men, and stood near a group of women in frock coats arguing in some Slavic language. The driver yelled, "Push back," and Mr. Sitwell took a few more steps toward the rear of the car. He stopped next to a heavyset man in a blue fedora. He reached for the handrail and looked down at the elderly woman in the seat in front of him, humming to herself with her eyes closed. The car lurched and rumbled down Olliana Avenue, then rounded a corner headed past the Magazine. He climbed down near the park and made his way through the remnants of the fairgrounds.

During the Exposition it was estimated that more than one million people had come to the city to see the fair, but there wasn't much to look at anymore. The entire Exposition had been conceptualized as an "object lesson for the modern worker," meant to demonstrate the many marvels of capitalism, a display of the collective fruits of industrial labor. Its actual construction had involved five years of brutal, backbreaking labor on the part of hundreds of men tasked with the arduous job of clearing an entire swamp. Several had died in the process and for most of the survivors the glories of the fair had not proved sufficient compensation. Much of it had been reduced to cinders not a year after the Exposition closed, a casualty of a workers' strike.

He walked past the brackish water of a man-made lagoon where, during the Exposition, people had ridden paddleboats carved in the shape of swans. The year of the Exposition was the same year Mr. Sitwell came to work for the Barclay house. He had gone to visit just once before it was burned: on Colored American Day. The other two orphans brought in with him had been sent away just a few weeks before when Mamie, then a chambermaid, found him crying beneath the kitchen table following some altercation with Mr. Boudreaux. She had managed to coax him out from under the table, dried his tears, and then, in an effort to cheer him up, insisted that he accompany her to hear Frederick Douglass speak.

They'd ridden to the fairgrounds, pushed past the aggressive crowds, and made their way to Festival Hall. He remembered Mamie holding his hand as they walked through the front rotunda, pointing out the display tables full of charts and indices of Negro improvements since Emancipation. He'd nodded at the sight of them although in truth he could barely read and so was able to make little sense of the progress they claimed to record. Then there was the thunder of applause and Mr. Sitwell turned around in time to see the old man take the stage on the arm of a small white woman whose mother, Mamie explained, had written the script for the very first *Tom Show*.

For the next two hours Frederick Douglass spoke in a deep, sonorous voice that reverberated throughout the hall, a memory supplemented by the rapid flutter of several hundred handheld fans in the audience. When Douglass was finished there was more applause; people rose to their feet and Mamie, deeply moved by the dignity of the man, had begun to cry. She and Mr. Sitwell went back outside and walked around the ethnic pavilion, where "exotic specimens" from various lands had been invited to perform their native songs and dances for the public.

Mamie bought him a box of Cracker Jack and then, for the very first time, told him about her life before she'd come to work for the Barclays. She told him how her mother had been born a slave to one of Mr. Barclay's cousins and that she'd spent her childhood working for the same people who once would have owned her. She told him that this fact had caused her mother a great deal of pain and that she'd realized the only way to change Mamie's fate was for her to leave home. So arrangements had been made for her to come work for the Barclays at the age of maturity, which, in her case, was apparently fourteen.

She told him she missed her mother terribly but insisted that wasn't why she was crying. Instead it had to do with the fact that it wasn't until she'd come to the city that she'd even realized Mr. Douglass was colored.

"I'd heard his name spoken a few times while I was helping my mother serve dinner, always in the most disparaging terms

111

and always, it seemed, in conjunction with a Mr. John Brown. Somehow I must have got it in my head that the two were related." She dabbed her eye with a handkerchief. "Can you imagine, Sitwell? Being so ignorant? It never occurred to me that such a Negro man could even exist. And then I think that perhaps I would have never known if my mother had not had the strength and courage to compel me to come here and leave everything I knew behind."

Mr. Sitwell sat and watched her cry. They were only separated by five years but what a difference that small span of time had made then. He hadn't the slightest idea how to comfort her.

"But he does exist," Mr. Sitwell said. "Doesn't that make you feel better?"

"Of course it does."

"So why are you sad?"

"I'm not sad." She took a deep breath as she attempted to regain control of her emotions. Then she smiled. "People don't always cry because they are sad, Sitwell. You should remember that."

Then they shared the box of Cracker Jack while they stood on the boardwalk and watched the Dahomey men dance for money.

That was twenty years ago. The Dahomey

men were long gone; in their place a penny arcade had been set up along the boardwalk. He walked until he found the stairs that led to the security compound underneath it, which, during the Exposition, had been used to hold drunks and petty thieves.

"Mr. Sitwell?" A voice called to him from one of the darkened cells. He turned toward a small barred window.

"Frederick? Is that you?"

"Yes, sir. It's me. . . ."

He could hear the rattle of chains scraping against concrete as the boy came and stood near the window.

"Thank goodness you've come. . . ."

Mr. Sitwell looked at Frederick's face and was horrified. The bright happy child he had given a coin to just a few hours before now appeared completely transformed. His hair was matted and covered in cobwebs, his left eye was swollen, and there were the salted stains of dried tears streaked down his cheek. Mr. Sitwell could feel his own eye start to twitch in empathetic response.

"Who did this to you?"

Frederick shook his head. "It's the man who sells the tickets for the Ferris wheel. He used to have a fruit cart down on Cornelius, and I'll tell you right now, he's not wrong. I did used to steal from him. But it was a long time ago, sir. Before I was reformed. And I was awful hungry them days."

"So this happened more than once?"

"That I was hungry? Yes, sir. . . . But it wasn't like I was the only one. And it was so long ago I didn't think he'd remember it. Turns out he's still mad." Frederick began to cry. "Please don't tell Miss Mamie about this, sir. I don't want to be sent away. I want to learn a trade, make something of myself. . . ."

Mr. Sitwell stared at the boy's swollen eye.

"Never mind that now. Hear me? Calm down. Let me get you out of here first."

"Thank you, sir."

Mr. Sitwell walked around to the front of the building and knocked on the door. A metal shutter peeled back to reveal a set of eyes.

"Nigger Day finished," a man said.

"I'm not here for Nigger Day," Mr. Sitwell said. "I'm here about the poor child you've got locked up in that dungeon."

"Ain't no poor children locked up in that cell. That cell is for degenerates, drunks, and thieves. If he got himself locked up, he must be one of those."

"He is fourteen years old."

"All the more to his shame."

114

Mr. Sitwell frowned. "Listen here. He works for me and I've come to take him home."

"Well, you can't. Not until he's made restitution."

"Restitution for what?"

"I couldn't tell you. I'm not the one that brought him in. Anyhow you're wasting time talking to me. I'm not the one that does the negotiating with niggers. Hold on a minute and I'll get the man that do."

The shutter slammed shut.

"See?" Frederick called through the window. His voice was cracking. "They not right around here."

Inside the compound Mr. Sitwell heard a sound like the rustle of heavy keys, then a drawer being slammed shut. The door swung open and a large man in a parks uniform walked out of it.

"You here about the monkey?" the man said. He was six feet tall, had dirty blond hair, and was clutching a set of keys.

"I've come to take him home."

"That right? Well, you can't. Not until he's made proper restitution."

"Restitution? For what? What exactly has he done?"

"It's not about what he's done. It's what he is. A thieving menace. Run me out of business. Used to steal my apples, back when I had my own cart. Back when Cornelius was still a decent place to live."

"It is my understanding that this theft of your apples occurred years ago, long before you were an employee of this park."

"It's not about the apples."

"Yes, well, my point is you have no right to hold this child based on a theft of an apple you claim happened years before."

"It's not about the apple."

"Furthermore, all this talk of Nigger Day? You think I don't know what that is? It's against the law, a violation of his right. I understand children call it that among themselves, but an actual park official in a park official uniform? If you do not release the child at once I shall be compelled to file a complaint. Because it is quite clear an injustice has occurred here. And I'm not referring to your apples. In fact —"

The fist came out of nowhere, a quick sharp jab to the gut that sent Mr. Sitwell reeling forward. It knocked the wind out of him, and he let out an audible gasp.

"How many times do I have to tell you it's not about the apples?" the man said.

Mr. Sitwell was hunched forward, clutching his stomach. He stared down at his hat, which had been knocked from his head and now lay on the ground between them. Lying beside it was a small plank of wood with several nails sticking out of it. It occurred to Mr. Sitwell that, from where he stood, it would have taken him less than a second to pick it up and swing it at the man's head.

But then he glanced at Frederick watching him through the bars, a terrified look on his face.

He shut his eyes.

"I understand," Mr. Sitwell said. He stood up. "Clearly I made a mistake in coming. I'll give your message to Mr. Barclay at once. Tell him you need to speak with him directly." He spoke calmly and smoothly although his eye was now convulsing violently.

"Who?"

"Mr. Barclay. Of Prescott Avenue. My employer. He is a member of the board of trustees here, so I suppose, in a manner of speaking, he's your employer too." Mr. Sitwell raised one hand to cover his afflicted eye and with the other hand, reached down to retrieve his hat.

"Mr. Barclay is the one who has taken charge of the child's reforms. Sent me to fetch him, in the hopes that this matter could be taken care of without having his dinner disturbed."

The man squinted. "I thought you said the boy worked for you."

"Yes. And I work for Mr. Barclay. Need the boy to serve dinner tonight. But no matter — I'll tell Mr. Barclay you have demanded to speak to him in person, let you explain to him directly about your need for restitution."

He nodded toward the dungeon.

"Until Mr. Barclay gets here, I would advise you to make sure the boy does not further injure himself. That particular monkey is his favorite, don't ask me why. But you can expect Mr. Barclay to be in a foul mood when he sees the conditions in which you've been holding him. Mr. Barclay doesn't like to see his pets damaged."

Then, without another word, he turned around and started walking back toward the boardwalk. As he did he could hear Frederick crying from his cell.

"Mr. Sitwell? Where are you going? Please don't leave me here!"

But he did not stop walking until the man called him back.

"Wait."

Mr. Sitwell turned around.

"How do I know what you say is true?"

"Well, of course you don't. We'll just have

to wait for Mr. Barclay to come and confirm it."

He could feel the man sizing him up, wheels turning in his mind as he tried to make sense of what was being said to him.

"Hold on," the man said. Then he turned around and went back inside.

A few moments later the door opened again, and the man came out, gripping Frederick by the collar.

"Take him." He gave the boy a shove toward Mr. Sitwell. "There is no need for this, no need to disturb the gentleman's dinner. But let this be a lesson to him, you hear me? I don't want to see him or his little friends in this park again. If any of them come back they will regret it. I don't care who you work for. . . ."

Mr. Sitwell stepped forward, seized the boy's hand, and led him toward the stairs.

The two of them began walking back along the boardwalk.

"I'm sorry, sir."

"You've already said so," Mr. Sitwell said. His eye was still twitching. He raised a hand to cover his convulsive eyelid and felt his lashes flutter against his palm in successive spasms.

"But I am sorry, Mr. Sitwell. Sorry you had to go through that." Frederick shook his head. "Honestly? I don't know what would have happened to me if you hadn't come."

"Don't you?" Mr. Sitwell said. He stopped walking, tilted his head back and stared up at the sky. "Wash Talbot," he said.

"What?"

"From your book. Cherokee did not get to him in time. He was dragged from his jail cell by an angry mob the same night he was arrested. By the time Cherokee got back to Seminole, Wash was already dead."

It was what he'd been thinking about since he first saw Frederick sitting in that cell. Somehow it was a relief to say it out loud; it seemed to ease some of the pressure on his eye.

"How do you know? You been reading ahead?"

"I told you I knew him. He was a farmer, like all my mother's people were. He did not steal a hog. He shot a mule. And he was colored," Mr. Sitwell said. "Some white man from the neighboring town made like he wanted to buy a mule off Wash, then elected to not pay him for it. Wash tried to get the sheriff to help him out, but he told Wash he couldn't do anything, had to take the white man at his word even if he knew that word was a lie. Wash must have figured if he wasn't going to get paid for that mule, he would claim it back another way."

"You're telling me that a mob did that to him because he shot his own mule?"

Mr. Sitwell sucked his teeth. "Didn't nobody care about the mule, boy. Nobody except Wash and the one who stole it off him. They did it because he was black and had the nerve to come to their town in the middle of the afternoon, carrying a loaded rifle."

That was all it had taken to end Wash's life. It was why his uncle Max had warned Sitwell's mother to stay away, that the only way to be safe was to keep to themselves. None of them should have gone to town in search of paper money and maybe it wasn't until what happened to Wash that they understood how surrounded they now were.

He looked at Frederick. "Never forget who you are in this world. Never forget where. Got to take precautions, even if you are telling the truth. Got to make sure there's no misunderstanding. Like it or not, you must always remember that you live in a world where your life doesn't mean much compared to some rich man's need to have his dinner served on time." He frowned. "I mean to some people. Most maybe. Not me . . ."

"What should I do, Mr. Sitwell?"

"Whatever you've got to, son. Be smart, survive. And if a white man ever tries to put you in a cage again, have sense enough to realize that you shouldn't count on ever getting back out of it."

They kept walking, back along the boardwalk, past the spot where, twenty years before, he'd stood and watched the Dahomey men dance for money.

By the time they got back to the house the dinner guests had already begun to arrive.

"Where were you?" Mamie said as they entered the kitchen. "Mr. Sitwell, I told you I needed you to work the floor this evening. Instead you just disappear . . ."

She caught sight of Frederick's face and stopped.

"What happened?"

The boy didn't answer.

"Mr. Sitwell? What is going on?"

"It's alright, Mamie," Jennie said. "You've got enough to worry about. I'll take care of Frederick." She put her arm over Frederick's shoulder. "You just focus on dinner."

She led Frederick down to the cellar.

Mamie glared at Mr. Sitwell.

"You and I will talk about this later. Right

122

now, Jennie's right. I need you on that floor."

Mr. Sitwell picked up a tray and pushed through the swinging door.

He found the guests assembled in the conservatory, where they were being entertained by a musical trio Mrs. Barclay had hired for the occasion. The ladies were seated in a cluster near the front where Mrs. Pound, a lively blonde woman no more than half the age of Mr. Pound, appeared to be holding court.

"It was a wedding present from my husband," she said as Mr. Sitwell walked past her. She ran her hand along the large strand of diamonds around her neck and smiled at Mrs. Barclay. "He asked me to wear it tonight, said that it reminded him of a necklace he saw you wear once, I believe at the Monte Carlo. He told me that you looked so elegant that evening that when he saw this one, he had to buy it for me. . . ."

The men were standing farther back, drinking bourbon.

"And how are the Berkshires these days?" he heard one of them ask Mr. Pound.

"Marvelous. We've recently purchased another two hundred acres and are expanding the organic farm. It is, in all respects, an utter idyll. . . ."

Also in the room, to Mr. Sitwell's great dismay, were Bart and Mac. Mac was holding a bottle of wine, refilling empty glasses while Bart stood beside him with a silver tray, passing out hors d'oeuvres.

Perhaps it was the stress of his recent ordeal combined with the memory of what had happened to Wash, but as soon as he saw them his eye began to twitch again and he could feel a strange hysteria bubbling up in him once more. He hurried across the floor, snatched the bottle out of Mac's hand, and took the tray from Bart.

"What did we talk about yesterday? Get back in the kitchen where you belong."

The boys looked around nervously.

"You weren't here so Miss Mamie said —"

"I don't care what Miss Mamie said. I'm here now, aren't I?"

The boys hurried out of the room.

It wasn't until they were safely beyond the door that Mr. Sitwell realized a few people seated nearby were watching him. He had spoken too loudly, behaved inappropriately, and now, apparently, the guests were disturbed.

The only thing to do in such circumstances was smile.

"Begging your pardon, ladies and gents."

He grinned as he tucked Mac's bottle in the crook of his right arm. "There seems to have been some confusion as to who has earned the privilege of serving you this evening."

With a flourish, he spun Bart's tray around and then set it on his right forearm. He reached for an empty glass on one of the side tables, picked it up with his free hand, then flipped it in the air so that they could watch it land right side up on his tray. He repeated the trick four times, which seemed to sufficiently soothe their alarm. A few of them began to applaud.

"Wait a minute, Barclay," Mr. Pound called out. "Is that the same one from earlier? The one that does that trick?"

He turned to his wife.

"This man is possessed of the most amusing talent. Barclay? You must show my wife."

"Of course," Barclay said. "Sitwell?"

Mr. Sitwell set the tray on the side table.

"Would one of the ladies be kind enough to lend me a handkerchief?" Mr. Barclay smiled.

"Give him mine," Mrs. Pound said. She handed her handkerchief to her husband, who in turn passed it to Mr. Barclay.

Mr. Barclay held it to his nose and smiled. "As I suspected, it retains the scent of your perfume." He handed it to Mr. Sitwell. "Now Mr. Sitwell. Will you kindly tell our assembled guests what that perfume is composed of."

Mr. Sitwell held it to his nose.

"An elegant composition consisting of essences of lemon, bergamot, neroli, rosemary, petitgrain, myrtle, and cedarwood."

Mr. Barclay nodded. "Is that all?"

Mr. Sitwell inhaled again. "A hint of sandalwood to round out the aroma."

"How marvelous," Mrs. Pound squealed. "I'll have you know that is one of the most expensive perfumes in all Paris."

"Well, I must say, dear," Mrs. Barclay said, "if that is all it is made of, it sounds to me as if perhaps you were overcharged." She seemed to enjoy the laughter this comment produced.

"An amusing talent," Mr. Barclay said. "Even if it serves no real purpose!"

The guests laughed and smiled then began to demand their own demonstrations in turn. Mr. Sitwell sniffed and recited the contents of the perfumes on four more handkerchiefs and the ingredients of a stick of chewing gum. Then he recited the different vintages of three glasses of wine. Finally he heard the tinkling of a little bell, turned around, and saw Mamie smiling in the door-way.

"Dinner is served," she announced.

The guests stood up and walked to the dining room. Mr. Sitwell stayed behind to collect their empty glasses. Jennie came out to help.

"I see I am not the only performer in this house," she said.

"Hardly."

Everyone danced for money in this world, Mr. Sitwell thought. The jailer danced for the rich man, the rich man danced for his investors. Mr. Sitwell, it sometimes seemed, danced for all of them at once.

In the dining room the guests took their seats. Mr. Sitwell made a show of fussing over the gentlemen, holding napkins out for the ladies while Mamie stood at the head of the table and began introducing the meal. The food was brought out and lowered before the assembled guests. Then he poured the wine. As he bent over the table to fill Mrs. Pound's glass she flinched, then quickly recovered and eased back into her seat.

"So much shade in your house, Barclay. I'm afraid we New Englanders are not quite accustomed to it."

"I imagine it is the intimacy of contact

that many in New England object to," Mr. Pound said. "But you, Barclay, are originally a Southerner, are you not?"

"Missouri."

"What I mean is, this is all perfectly normal for you, is it not?"

"The presence of black servants in the home? Why, it is the most normal thing in the world."

"I hope you enjoy it," Mamie said and took her leave.

The guests began to eat.

"Gracious, this is delicious," Mrs. Pound said. "Tell me, Barclay. Do you eat like this every night?"

"Not every night, no. This meal was prepared especially for you. An effort by my cook to accommodate your dietary restrictions."

"And the recipe?"

"Something Mamie came up with."

"Well, I must say, if they all cook like this, it's a wonder everyone doesn't have a darkie cook," Mrs. Pound said. "If they all cook like this, I want one too!"

Mr. Sitwell picked up his tray and pushed back into the kitchen.

"How is it out there?" Mamie asked him as he passed through the swinging door.

"Good, I imagine." Mr. Sitwell shrugged.

He set his tray in the sink. "Everybody wants a darkie cook now."

Mamie frowned. "Are you going to tell me what happened with Frederick?"

Mr. Sitwell shook his head. "A misunderstanding. He ran into someone he shouldn't have at the fairgrounds and —"

"Fairgrounds? What was he doing at the fairgrounds? They were supposed to go to the market then come straight back."

Mr. Sitwell was quiet for a moment. "I told them they could go."

"*You?* Without asking my permission? Why would you presume to do such a thing?"

"I did not foresee any danger in it. It was Colored Day, I thought they deserved a little fun."

"Colored Day? Fun?"

He could hear how foolish it sounded given what had happened. For the first time it occurred to him that he was partially responsible for it.

"Listen, Sitwell. I know that maybe no one else around here cares what happens to those children. But *I* care."

"I know that, Mamie. I care too."

"Then you should have the sense to realize there is a reason I try to keep them with me in the kitchen, where they are safe."

"It won't happen again."

"Better not," Mamie said. "Because I realize a lot of hincty things have been going on around here lately and would hate to think that one of those hincty things is you. There are about to be some big changes, Mr. Sitwell. You hear me? Everybody is about to get put right. Or else they're getting put out."

She walked back into the dining room.

He knew she was right: it was a mistake to tell the boys they could go to the fair, a lapse of judgment. And perhaps it was not the first time. Perhaps if he had not brought Mr. Barclay the book he would have never been asked to choose between them. The more he thought about it the more it seemed as if every time he tried to do those children a kindness he only wound up exposing them to more danger. And what if it were true? What if all his efforts to help those boys were only making things worse?

"Mr. Sitwell?"

When he turned around Frederick was standing behind him. Jennie had washed his face and a linseed bandage was now pressed against his forehead.

"I want you to know how much I appreciate what you did for me today and how sorry I am for it. Also I want you to know

130

that it won't ever happen again. From now on, every time I go out of this house I'm going to make sure to take precautions, like you said. Make sure I'm prepared."

"Is that all?"

"No, sir. It's not," Frederick said. "Also . . . about that book. I didn't steal it but the truth is, it wasn't a gift either. One of Mr. Barclay's guests was passing them out and I heard someone say he didn't want it, making fun of the one what give it to him. . . . He left it on a settee and I took it. Figured otherwise it would have just gone in the trash."

Mr. Sitwell nodded. "Well, thank you for telling me the truth. Let's not talk about it anymore. So long as you've learned your lesson and won't do it again, I'm satisfied."

"Thank you, sir," Frederick said. "I won't."

Mr. Sitwell watched him leave, still thinking about the part he had played in Frederick's ordeal, puzzling over the extent to which he was responsible for it. It weighed on his mind for the rest of the dinner and then as he rode the streetcar home. He was so distracted by these thoughts that when he finally pushed through the doors of the rooming house he didn't even notice Billy sitting behind the desk until the man called out to him.

"Should be ready for you by tomorrow."

Mr. Sitwell looked up. "What?"

"Your book, Sitwell. Thing you paid me a dollar to read? Actually, it's a pretty good story." Billy smiled. "Listen to a bit."

"Wash had been sitting in that jail cell for ten days when Dupont come into the Sheriff's office one morning in a frightful panic. Someone had seen Cherokee pass through the market the day before. When asked about his sudden reappearance, Cherokee had told them he was just there to visit his uncle Max, but everybody knew that was a lie. Cherokee coming back to Seminole County could only mean one thing: trouble."

Billy smiled. "About halfway through. Ain't come across no Lotta yet, just so you know."

Mr. Sitwell was quiet for a moment. "Did you say 'Uncle Max'?"

"That's right. Just a local drunkard living in some run-down shack. I wouldn't worry too much about Max. He's what you call a minor character. Not really important to the actual story."

Sitwell nodded. His eye was twitching again. "What about a Farley?"

"He's the sheriff."

"Sheriff?"

"That's right. He's the one who organized the posse to take Wash into custody."

"Posse? You mean lynch mob, don't you?"

"What? No, wasn't no mob." Billy shook his head. "They were just holding Wash, peaceful-like, until the marshals could transport him to the state prison. Then Cherokee shows up, guns blazing. And poor Farley can't help but feel responsible for that, seeing as how he was the one who brokered the peace."

"Peace? What peace?"

"With Cherokee's people. When Cherokee promised to leave the county once and for all."

He opened the book, flipped through the pages, and started reading again.

"It had been ten years since Sheriff Farley brokered the deal that sent Cherokee away. Sheriff didn't want any more trouble from the gang and Cherokee said he didn't want any more harm coming to his kin. He told Farley he was tired of fighting, tired of all the bloodshed. Said he would get his people to lay down their weapons, then promised to go away and never return so long as Farley gave him his word that that would be the end of it, that there would be no retaliation against his people once he was gone.

So the sheriff let him go. At the time it had seemed the surest way to keep the peace. Now Farley regretted it. Because if Cherokee was back, then all signs were pointing to an inevitable showdown. And the truth was, if it came down to that, Cherokee was the better shot."

Billy smiled. "I'm about halfway through."

Mr. Sitwell pursed his lips. "So Farley's the sheriff?"

"That's right."

"Any mention of Farley's servants?"

"Servants? Naw. Ain't no servants in here. It's not that kind of book. These are simple country folk. Farmers mostly. Everybody in this book is just trying to survive."

Mr. Sitwell nodded. "I need it back by Friday."

"No problem. I should be finished by then."

"That good?"

"Oh, it's a page-turner alright. Through and through."

Mr. Sitwell nodded and walked up the stairs.

First Wash Talbot, now Uncle Max and Mr. Farley. All of which made it impossible to dismiss as mere coincidence: the book was, without question, telling a story about his people, the world he had come from.

And yet everything it said was a lie. But it was such a strange lie because it seemed to constantly remind him of the truth.

He thought about that last day at the Farleys' house. At one point Mrs. Farley had come into the kitchen and asked about the green-eyed man. Her agitation over rumors of his return had in many respects paralleled the anxiety of the townspeople from the book in the passage Billy had read to him, upon hearing that Cherokee had been seen in the market.

It was from her that he'd learned there was a reason he'd never seen the green-eyed man before, but from what she said it had nothing to do with any peace brokered by a local sheriff. Instead it had something to do with a conflict with the National Guard over conscription labor in the immediate aftermath of the war. There'd been some violence over this, which had led to Cherokee's arrest. After serving his term he'd been required to vacate the state. According to Mrs. Farley, if his mother knew anything about him coming back, she was required by law to inform the authorities.

It was the first time he'd heard his mother lie. When Mrs. Farley demanded to know whether the man was in fact staying with Uncle Max, his mother had smiled, looked

135

the woman directly in the eye, and told her she had no idea what she was talking about. There were indeed many people who had come to mourn the passing of their fallen brother, but the green-eyed man was not among them.

This had confused him. He hadn't understood the reason for this lie, and prior to it, had not been aware that his mother was even capable of lying. Mrs. Farley was a friend, was she not? They had worked in that house six days a week for years. They were safe in that kitchen, were they not? So why on earth would his mother lie?

The effects of the lie were equally confusing. Because if his mother was trying to soothe Mrs. Farley's alarm, she had instead done the opposite. Mrs. Farley was so upset that she told his mother that when she left that afternoon she was not to come back. In fact, she said she did not want to see his mother again; instead of having his mother serve the cake, she asked that Mr. Sitwell do it, the woman who normally served having already been fired.

The townspeople had attacked the village that very night, completely unprovoked. That, ultimately, was why the book's lies upset him so much. The story it told was not simply a fiction but an erasure of the truth, thereby paralleling the erasure of his village through a cowardly act of violence from which it was only by some miracle he had managed to survive.

He reached his door and stepped inside his room. He watered his plants, took off his clothes, and lay down on his bed. He listened to a woman in the room next door laugh, a man move slowly up the stairs and down the hall, the sound of a closing door.

He shut off the light.

In his dreams that night he was alone and running down a dirt road when a wagon traveling in the opposite direction pulled up beside him. In the front a man sat holding on to the reins.

"You're going the wrong way, son," the man said. "You go back there now, there's a good chance you won't ever come out again. Best turn around now while you still can."

"I'm trying to get home."

"Ain't no home in that direction." The man shook his head. "Not anymore."

He looked and saw it was true: there was nothing but the road he was standing on and, in the distance beyond it, a plume of smoke billowing up to the sky.

The man nodded toward the rear of the wagon. "Get in. I can take you as far as the state line. Just put those blankets over your head, stay down, and keep quiet."

In the back of the wagon, the woman in the white dress was sitting on top of a flour sack, holding the mask with the hand-drawn face with one hand and a blanket for him to hide under with the other.

"Be quick about it —"

Mr. Sitwell shook his head and took a step backward. "No. I have to go back. I've got to get home, my mama will be looking for me."

The man who held the reins frowned. "Son? I don't know your mama. But I do know don't nobody want their child walking that way, in that direction. So you're going to have to be a big boy now. Going to have to do what I tell you. Get up in this wagon and act like you got some sense."

He held out his hand. "Hurry now. Ride with me. While you still got a chance."

4
HOW HE GOT THERE

When Mr. Sitwell arrived at the Barclay house the next morning, he found Bart sitting on the back porch with his shoes off, stuffing rocks into the toe of his sock.

"Morning," Bart said.

Mr. Sitwell nodded. Without wanting to, he glanced down at Bart's mangled foot.

"What's that you're doing?"

Bart shrugged. "Old trick of mine. Keeps my shoes from popping off when I'm running upstairs."

He held out the sock weighted down with rocks, wedged his damaged foot inside it, then shook the stump at Mr. Sitwell.

"Doesn't that hurt?"

"No, sir. Not at all. Not for a long time. Itches sometimes, but that's about all."

Mr. Sitwell said nothing. He'd meant the rocks but the boy apparently thought he meant the foot itself. He started to ask why he didn't massage the foot in linseed oil to keep the skin from cracking and then wrap it in something softer, like a cotton bandage. But instead he kept quiet. The boy was not his responsibility, he thought. Let someone else help him, someone who actually worked in the house.

Bart stood up and hopped a few times. "See that?" Bart said proudly. "Takes a lot more than a couple of missing toes to keep young Bart down." He held open the kitchen door. "Coming inside?"

"Not today."

Instead Mr. Sitwell turned and walked toward the yard. He'd spent the whole night thinking about what had happened the day before and decided the best he could do for those boys was stay away from them. He'd let himself get too caught up in the drama inside the house and was now convinced that nothing he did was actually helping. For once he was determined to stay out of it and focus on his actual job.

He walked through the flower garden and looked at the grounds beyond it, taking stock of all the work he had sacrificed to Miss Mamie's constant need of him inside the house. Given how much time he'd spent neglecting his own duties he was not surprised to discover that an invader had taken root near the north fence: choke weed.

He went to the shed, put his weeding tools inside the wheelbarrow and pushed it to the northern fence. Then he got down on his knees and began the arduous task of trying to uproot everything that did not belong.

Vigilance: that was what was required to keep the weeds out, what he had started to lose sight of by spending so much time in the house. And this was true not just with respect to his responsibilities to the yard. For, in going over the events of the day before, it occurred to him that in telling Frederick the truth about Wash Talbot, he'd revealed more about his past than he'd ever told anyone since he arrived in the city, even Mamie. He'd told Frederick that story because he felt the boy needed telling, but he wondered why he'd not chosen another way to convey the message he was trying to express. He'd always been taught that one kept safe by keeping hidden; because of that, he was not sure if his telling what had really happened to Wash was not, in fact, a symptom of his finally beginning to forget who he actually was.

At some time around eleven, when the sun was high in the sky, a voice called out to him.

"There you are."

He turned around and saw Mamie standing behind him.

"You didn't come get your coffee this morning. Where you been, Sitwell?"

"Right here. Working." Mr. Sitwell shrugged. "I'm the groundskeeper, remember?"

"Yeah, well about that . . ."

She was quiet for a moment, distracted by something going on near the front of the house. Mr. Whitmore had brought the car around and was holding the door open as Mrs. Barclay and Mrs. Lawson climbed inside.

"You heard the news? Mr. Pound made Barclay an offer last night. Coming by this afternoon to finalize the contract."

"Glad to hear it."

"Nothing is settled yet, of course. Barclay still has to deal with the Southerners. But it's a step. A big step."

"Good for you." Mr. Sitwell nodded.

"Good for me, good for everybody . . ."

The car wheeled past them, out the front drive.

Mamie chuckled.

"You see that? Mrs. Barclay is going shopping. Deal is not even finalized and they're already celebrating. Isn't that just typical?" She shook her head. "Know why Mrs. Lawson is going with her? She's buying fabric

142

for a new uniform. I finally got the go-ahead from Barclay to hire new staff."

Mr. Sitwell nodded. "So, you're finally getting a real butler?"

"No, I'm finally getting a real grounds-keeper." Mamie smiled. "Don't look at me like that. I'm not putting you out, Sitwell. I'm bringing you inside."

"What?"

"Already talked to Barclay about it. And honestly, he didn't take much convincing. Man is getting tired of trying to dress himself for one thing. And I imagine you impressed him with all that clowning you did last night. He said he understood you might need some training, but he thought it was a fine idea. You know how he is; man-aged to convince him it was better than bringing another stranger into the house."

"What are you saying? You want to make me the butler?"

"Don't act so surprised. It's something I've wanted to do for a long time. Now maybe folks won't act so confused about your proper 'sphere.' You'll be the butler, and that means you'll take charge of the staff. It's called delegation of authority. I'm tired of listening to people complain."

Mr. Sitwell stared. "I don't know what to say, Mamie."

"Say thank you."

"I mean I'm flattered, of course. But you know very well I'm not properly trained."

"I shall train you. You are smart and you shall learn. Anyhow it's more money. And it's where you belong."

She sat down on a stump and looked around the yard.

"How old were you when Boudreaux sent you out here? Fifteen? I remember because it was right around the time he finally agreed to make me his apprentice. That man sure had a way of making it hard to like him. I spent an entire year pleading with him to let me come into the kitchen and when he finally consents, what does he do? Forces you out the very same day. He knew you were like a brother to me."

"Perhaps he had cause."

"No, he just didn't like you. Imagine he figured out pretty quick you were smarter than him, imagine it intimidated him. You don't intimidate me, Sitwell."

"Yes, well, regardless of the circumstances . . . ." He looked back at the house. "Perhaps it's better this way. Truth is I'm happy here."

"That right?" She gave him a pitying look. "Well, too bad. Because your exile is now over. You're coming back inside, like I said.

And that is final."

She stood up. "Enjoy your flowers while you still can. I intend to have a proper groundskeeper hired by the end of next week."

He watched her stomp back to the house.

She was angry, had no doubt been expecting gratitude and instead he'd told her the truth. He was relieved to hear that things were finally getting back to normal, if only because it meant that he could finally get the matter of the boys sorted out with Mr. Barclay. But he'd already decided he didn't want to be in the house. He didn't trust himself inside of it, found it too confusing for reasons he could not fully explain.

He was still thinking of ways he might prevent it from happening when a woman's voice called out to him once more.

"Hello, Sitwell."

This time when he turned around Jennie was standing behind him.

"Miss Mamie sent me to fetch you. Said to tell you Mr. Barclay wants to talk to you. Congratulations, by the way. Understand you are going to be the man in charge from now on. Which is funny because I was under the impression that you already were that. Guess they're just making it official."

"Nothing's official," Mr. Sitwell said. "Mr.

Barclay got two deals to work out, remember? It's why we're having another dinner on Friday. Nothing around here has really changed and there is not really anything to celebrate. Not yet anyhow." He shook his head. "Seems like everybody else around here has forgotten that except me."

"Well, now you just proving my point, aren't you?" Jennie said. "Frederick told me what happened yesterday, by the way. He was crying in that cellar while I was trying to wash his face. He told me he figures you saved his life."

Mr. Sitwell frowned. "Probably best not to repeat that."

"Yes, I realize that too. I wouldn't tell anybody who didn't already know. Just wanted to make sure you know the boy understands what you did for him. Just wanted to make sure you knew that I understand it too."

She smiled. "You do realize that, if it is true that you are coming into the house, it means the two of us will be forced to spend more time together."

"I suppose it would."

"Well, we shall just have to find some way to endure it."

She shook her head, let out a dramatic sigh, then, in the most graceful movement he'd ever seen, spun around before him and bowed.

"What are you doing?"

"Cakewalk."

Mr. Sitwell watched her glide back and forth through the yard.

"Must be hard for you, working in this house."

"There are harder things."

"I mean I imagine you must miss the theatre."

"Oh, I loved my life. And it was a good thing too, seeing as how when I started out I didn't have much choice in the matter. Perhaps Cutie Pie will choose to go back to it someday. But if she does decide to go back, that is what I would like it to be. A choice. I owe her that much. She did save my life."

He watched Jennie dance. "One day I would like to thank her for that."

"Perhaps one day you will get the chance. Perhaps over dinner sometime?"

"Dinner?"

"You do eat dinner, don't you?"

"Once a day." He smiled. "I would like that, Jennie."

"How about Saturday? After Mr. Barclay's deals are sorted out. What do you say?"

"That sounds grand."

147

She spun around one last time and curt-seyed. Then she bowed and took her leave.

Mr. Sitwell watched her walk back through the yard. As he did it occurred to him that he'd been so busy worrying about his past that he hadn't even realized what Mamie was actually offering him by giving him that promotion: a future. If he wanted to court Jennie, he'd be a butler asking her out to dinner, as opposed to a groundskeeper. A butler, walking down the street, holding Jennie's hand . . . It made a difference, he knew that it did and deep down realized that Jennie knew it too. Knew she thought about such things because she had to think, if not for her sake then for the sake of her child, Cutie Pie.

When he walked back to the kitchen Mamie was sitting at the table dicing onions. Mr. Sitwell stood behind her chair.

"Mamie?"

"What is it?"

"Thank you."

Mamie sighed. "Never mind, Sitwell. It's alright. Just go on out there, do like I told you, and stop acting like a fool."

"Yes, ma'am."

Mr. Sitwell pushed through a swinging door. He walked down the hall and knocked on the door to Mr. Barclay's study.

"Come in," Mr. Barclay said, then smiled when Mr. Sitwell entered the room.

"There you are, Sitwell."

"How can I help you, sir?"

"Yes, well, this time I believe it is I who can help you. Have a seat, my boy."

He eased into the chair in front of the desk while Mr. Barclay gave him an appraising look.

"I have news. You may not be aware, but I am currently in the process of negotiating a substantial business deal. Once negotiations have concluded, the house will once again be on secure footing, and when that happens, I've decided to give you a promotion."

"A promotion, sir?"

"That's right, Sitwell. We are in urgent need of a new butler and I have decided to give the position to you."

"Me, sir? Well, this is indeed an honor." Mr. Sitwell smiled. "And most unexpected."

"Of course, initially it shall be on a trial basis. You should consider it an opportunity to prove yourself. An opportunity I believe is well within your reach."

"Thank you, sir. For the opportunity."

"Not at all. I have already informed Mamie of my decision and found her highly amenable to it. She told me how much help you have been to her these past few months, a fact that did not surprise me in the least. Truth is I have long believed you belong in the house, never fully understood why Mr. Boudreaux seemed so convinced you would work better in the yard. It has always seemed to me that your instincts were better suited to an entirely different form of service. It's not a groundskeeper whose advice I count on. Not a groundskeeper who would think to take the initiative, to step in and handle the situation with those boys."

"Thank you, sir. And . . . about that," Mr. Sitwell said. "I can't tell you how bad I feel about our misunderstanding."

Mr. Barclay waved his hand. "Never mind. It's past."

"Still, I feel bad. And seeing as how things have changed and the house is back on firm footing . . . perhaps there is some way we could correct my mistake."

"What do you mean?"

"Bring the boy back. The other two are still in contact with him. Perhaps it is not too late to have him reinstated. After all, we do need three to handle the workload in the kitchen."

"Yes, that has always been the official number. . . ."

Mr. Barclay pursed his lips as he thought

about it.

"Perhaps, Sitwell . . . Why don't we give it a few days, let things get sorted out here first? Wait until the contracts have been signed. We don't want to get too ahead of ourselves. . . ."

Mr. Sitwell smiled. "No, sir. Of course not. But thank you."

Mr. Barclay turned toward the window and sighed.

"You know, it's funny. Those children do look so much alike. Yesterday I would have sworn it was the other one you'd sent away. The one with those dreadful scars." He ran his finger along his left cheek. "But now I see quite clearly it was the one with the deformity. It didn't affect his hearing, did it? The missing ear? Is that why you chose to get rid of him?"

Mr. Sitwell turned toward the window and saw Bart and Frederick working together in the yard.

"Never mind," Mr. Barclay said. "Leave it for now. We can discuss it later, once my negotiations have concluded."

"Yes, sir. And thank you again, sir." Mr. Sitwell stood up. "I won't let you down."

Mr. Barclay smiled. "I know you won't, Sitwell. You never have."

Mr. Sitwell bowed and took his leave.

He walked outside to where Frederick and Bart were crouched in front of the water pump.

"Where is Mac?"

Bart shrugged. "He had to run a quick errand. Should be back straightaways."

"Errand?"

"Don't worry, sir. It's nothing like yesterday," Frederick said. "Just went to pick up something right quick. From the field."

"What?"

"Berries, sir," Bart said. "The nonpoisonous kind."

"The nonpoisonous kind? What are you talking about? Did Miss Mamie send him out there?"

"No. It was for Miss Jennie," Frederick said. He took a deep breath and then tried to explain. "When we came upstairs this morning she was at the stove boiling berries. She said you'd taken her out to the field and told her they'd make a fine jelly someday. She wanted to make some for you, as a surprise. Thing was, soon as we looked at what she was doing we could tell she'd picked the wrong ones. Got some of the bad berries mixed in with the good. And we remembered how you told us we had to be careful with them on account of the poison."

They went back inside and led him down

to the cellar, where they'd taken the berries and hidden them so that no one would eat them by mistake. He took one whiff of the concoction and could tell it was true: Jennie's jellies were poisonous.

"She was very upset, of course, when we explained it to her," Bart said. "Started crying and everything."

Frederick shook his head. "I told Mac to let it alone. But, you know . . . she's so nice and sometimes Mrs. Lawson gives her such a hard time. Mac said he'd go back to the field, get some good berries so she could make her jelly and wouldn't have to feel bad about nothing. Said he figured it wouldn't take more than an hour. If it wasn't for that, I would have told him not to go. Something must have happened to hold him up."

"I heard Mrs. Lawson say there was some kind of protest going on downtown," Bart said. "Might be they blocking the streetcar. Might be he had to walk."

"How long ago did he leave?"

"Must have been around seven."

Mr. Sitwell looked at the clock above the stove. It was eleven thirty.

"Look here, sir. I can tell you're upset, but I mean it when I say you got no cause to worry. Mac will be alright and Bart and me can cover for him until he gets back."

Frederick smiled.

Bart nodded in agreement. "You won't even notice he's gone."

Mr. Sitwell sighed. "Honestly, what foolishness. Just keep those jars where no one will find them. Then go and help Mamie in the kitchen. Mr. Pound is coming back this afternoon. I'll deal with cleaning the jars properly when I get back."

"Yes, sir." Frederick gave him a serious look. "I'm sure Mac is fine. Matter of fact, you'll probably pass him coming in on your way out."

But Mr. Sitwell did not pass him on his way. He looked for him too, as he hurried toward the streetcar stop, then all along the Avenue as the omnibus shook over the pavement. When the car trundled past the Magazine he could see Bart was right about the protests; there was a great throng of people crowding the sidewalks, much larger than on previous days. From the signs they carried he gathered it was some sort of tailors' strike. They were shouting chants and waving their fists and the car was forced to stop several times in order to avoid hitting those who, lost in a trance of their own outrage, would every now and then wander directly in front of it. When the driver dared to honk his horn their anger only seemed to intensify. Before long, rocks were being thrown.

Mr. Sitwell kept his head down as both rocks and fists battered the windows of the car. After a long series of starts and abrupt stops, the car finally made its way past the turmoil. Mr. Sitwell kept riding until they reached the park then climbed off and hurried toward the fields.

He entered through the gate and began walking up the hill. He walked the entire length but saw no sign of Mac. He turned around and walked back the way he'd come; he'd almost reached the gate when, in desperation, he began shouting the boy's name. To his surprise a voice called out in response.

"Mr. Sitwell?"

He stopped walking. The voice seemed to be coming from some place nearby, but when he looked around he saw no sign of Mac.

"Mac?"

"Yes, it's me!"

"Where are you?"

"I'm right here," Mac's voice cried out. "I'm in a hole."

The voice seemed to be coming from behind a large patch of reeds near the fence.

"Careful, sir. Watch your step. . . ."

He pushed through the reeds and found, hidden behind them, a large hole, so deep and dark that he could barely see Mac trapped inside it.

"Thank goodness you've come," Mac said.

"What happened to you?"

"A terrible thing," Mac called from the hole. "Just came out here to run a quick errand. Figured I could do that and get back before anyone even knew I was gone. And I was right about that, only took me a few minutes to get the berries. Then I was on my way back to the omnibus stop. And that was when I saw him."

"Who?"

"The boardwalk man. The one who locked up Frederick. He was standing on the corner, arguing with a group of men about the protests. He said the strikers were foreign anarchists and that he hoped they were all shot. Then he saw me and stopped talking to give me the most hateful look. So I did the only thing I could do. I ran. Ran all the way back here trying to find some place to hide. I looked back one time to see if he was following me and it seemed like the ground just gave way beneath me. Next thing I knew I was stuck in this hole."

Mr. Sitwell looked at the broken planks of wood on either side of the hole. He realized that Mac must have managed to fall into one of the many transportation tunnels that had been dug underneath the fields as a means of getting supplies to the fairgrounds during the construction of the Exposition. The tunnels had been boarded up, but the wood must have rotted in the neglect of the years that followed its demise.

"Are you alright down there?"

"Not really, sir. I hurt my leg. It's why I can't get out."

"Don't cry, Mac. It will be alright."

"You talk like somebody who's never been stuck in a hole before."

"You should feel around down there. Perhaps there's something you could use to pull yourself up."

"There isn't."

"Perhaps there is. Something you can't see."

"No, I can see everything just fine. I see in the dark, sir. Did you not know this about me?"

"I did not."

"Well, perhaps it simply never came up." Mac cried, "Woe is me that it ever should have. . . ."

Mr. Sitwell listened to the boy sob. "You know, Mac. I have already walked by this spot twice trying to find you. If you couldn't get yourself out, why didn't you call for help?"

"I didn't know it was you."

"Yes, but how did you expect anyone to help you if you would do nothing to make yourself known?"

"I don't know," the child said between hiccupping sobs. "I guess I was scared. First I was scared of that boardwalk man and then I started thinking of all the other people I done met in my life who I'd not want to ever find me in a circumstance like this. I figured Frederick and Bart were bound to come out here to look for me, eventually. So I thought it best to just stay quiet until I heard someone actually calling my name."

Mr. Sitwell looked out across the field. Yes, he could see the wisdom in that. It was a warning he himself had been given once, a long time ago.

From the green-eyed man: "Stay hidden and keep quiet. No matter what you hear going on outside, promise me you will not cry out until someone actually calls you by your name."

"I understand," Mr. Sitwell said. "No, you did right, Mac. Just . . . please don't cry. I'm going to find a way to get you out."

"Thank you, sir."

But when he looked around him, he realized he didn't have the slightest idea how to do that. It was a very deep hole, so deep he was surprised that the boy had only injured his leg.

"I'm going to have to get some help."

"No! Please, Mr. Sitwell. Don't leave me alone. I'm scared!"

The boy was hyperventilating.

"Mac, stop crying. Try to relax."

For some reason, Mr. Sitwell found himself patting his pockets. His instinct was to give the boy something to hold on to, in order to vouchsafe his return. But his pockets were empty.

"I promise I'll be back."

As he hurried out of the fields and back onto the street, he puzzled at the strangeness of his own gesture, wondered what it was he'd expected to find in his pocket. It wasn't until he reached the omnibus stop that he remembered: that it was not true that he'd never been trapped in a dark place underground. He had once spent an entire night alone in the darkness, not in a hole but a cellar. It was where the green-eyed man had thought to hide him the night the townspeople raided their village. He'd hidden Mr. Sitwell then told him he had to go back to help the others; but before he'd left, he'd reached into his pocket, pulled out a

159

locket, and tucked it into Mr. Sitwell's hand.

"Keep that for me. That's how you know I'm coming back. Because that there is precious to me. It's kept me safe and it will keep you safe too. Best believe I'd never leave it behind. . . ."

When the omnibus let him off near the Avenue, Mr. Sitwell began to run.

Back at the house he found Mr. Whitmore standing in the kitchen, chopping meat for Mamie.

"Stop what you are doing at once and come with me."

"Excuse me?"

"I need your help."

He ran out to the shed and searched for a length of rope. When he came back out, Mr. Whitmore was standing in the yard, watching him.

"What is this, Sitwell?"

"There has been an accident. . . . Just come along, I'll explain on the way."

"No." Mr. Whitmore shook his head. "I am not going anywhere with you. Whatever it is, I can't help you. Bad enough I've got Mamie after me all day, asking me to do things in the kitchen that aren't my job. I'm not gonna get started in all that with you too. I was hired to drive the car, remember? You're the yardman. Something wrong in

160

the yard, you can fix it yourself."

Mr. Sitwell frowned. "I take it you haven't heard the news?"

"What news?"

"I've been promoted. I'm the butler now."

"Butler? Says who?"

"At present, I do." Mr. Sitwell held out the rope. "That means you work for me."

Mr. Whitmore stared for a moment, trying to decide if Mr. Sitwell was serious or not.

He took the rope.

The two of them walked back out to the Avenue.

"So you say you're the butler now? Interesting. I mean it's a bit unusual, don't you think? Kind of makes me wonder if my uncle wasn't right after all."

"What does that mean?"

"Nothing. It's just that he figured it was what you wanted. Said he figured it was what you've been angling for all this time."

"Your uncle doesn't know a thing about me or what I want."

"Yeah, well . . ." Mr. Whitmore shrugged. "He said you'd say that too."

They climbed aboard the omnibus. When they reached the Magazine stop, the sidewalks were deserted; at first Mr. Sitwell was confused by this, but then they ran into the

161

mob two blocks later. He realized the strike had not ended abruptly; it was on the move.

Once again the car was forced to stop in order to avoid those who were passing in the street. Mr. Whitmore watched the windows nervously as people began banging on the side of the car.

"It's a tailors' strike," Mr. Sitwell said.

"No." Mr. Whitmore nodded toward the crowd. "Some of those men might be tailors. But I recognize some of the others. They are part of the gang sent out with the specific intent to assault men of color. The Good Time Gang. They're the same ones who ran me off the job."

"The Good Time Gang?" Mr. Sitwell squinted. "So that's what happened? Why you came to work for the Barclays?"

"Man came to recruit me back when I was still in Alabama. Said he wanted to make sure I was aware of opportunities that awaited in the North. Wasn't until I got up here that I realized I'd been hired to be a scab. In some ways, the man was right, of course. They gave us less than those white boys were making but more than I ever would have made in Alabama. Still, I can't say it sat well with me, nor many of the others who come up here. We tried to tell them that. Tried to form our own delegation, see if there wasn't some way to work something out between us. Man who volunteered to speak with them got a brick to the head for his trouble."

He stopped talking, distracted by something going on near the front of the car. A black man had risen from his seat and was standing nervously by the door, trying to decide if it was worth it to get off.

"Don't do it," Mr. Whitmore said.

"I've got to get to work."

"Sit back down. Can't work if you not living. Stay on the car until we get past it, then find some way to circle back around. Sometimes you got to be strategic. You try to get off here, those men will tear you to pieces and not think nothing of it. Trust me, I know."

The man nodded his thanks and waited until the car rumbled past the strike. When the coast was clear he carefully stepped out onto the street.

Mr. Whitmore looked at Mr. Sitwell. "What did you think I was doing in that house?"

"Honestly, Whitmore? We thought you liked the uniform."

"I could have bought myself a uniform with the money I was making before. But I get it. Y'all think I'm a fool. Well, you're wrong about that. I am not a fool. What I am is a cattle butcher."

"Push back!" the driver yelled.

Mr. Sitwell and Mr. Whitmore moved to the very rear of the car.

At last they reached their stop and Mr. Sitwell led Mr. Whitmore to the fields. Three paddy wagons were parked just outside the gate and several police officers were busy setting up a barricade on the opposite side of the street in anticipation of the protesters' arrival. Mr. Sitwell hurried into the fields and led Mr. Whitmore to the spot behind the tall reeds.

As soon as Whitmore saw the boy sitting inside the hole, he frowned.

"What is this?"

"I believe it's one of the tunnels they used to bring supplies into the fairgrounds. They run all across the fields. It must have collapsed."

"No, I meant how did he wind up in it?"

"I'm not sure," Mr. Sitwell said. "Never mind that. How is not important. We've got to get him out."

"You are wrong about that, Sitwell," Mr. Whitmore said. "It's very important. In fact, it's the most important thing there is."

He shook his head.

"How old is that boy? Fourteen? That's

far too old to just be falling into holes. Unless he was pushed. Did someone push him?"

"Nobody pushed him, so far as I know."

"Then perhaps he is simple. Is he simple, Sitwell? Because it's the only other possible explanation, so far as I can tell. And yet you know as well as I do this world is not made for the simple and the slow."

"He's not simple. You know very well he is not. It's Mac."

"Well, if no one pushed him and if he is not simple I can see no discernable reason a boy as big as that one should wind up in such a predicament."

There was a sound of breaking glass on the other side of the fence, some kind of commotion going on in the street outside the fields. Mr. Whitmore continued to stare at the hole.

"We shouldn't have come," Mr. Whitmore said.

"What?"

"I said we shouldn't have come. It's bad enough the boy managed to get himself into such a humiliating circumstance. The least we can do is let him get himself out."

Someone screamed on the street behind them.

"What are you talking about, Whitmore?"

165

"The larger picture, Mr. Sitwell. You might think you're doing him a favor pulling him out but trust me, you're not. Because it seems to me that if that big old boy can't figure out how to get himself out of a hole when there is no accounting for how he got into it, then he might as well stay there. Because we both know he's not got much chance of surviving outside of it."

Mac, who could hear Mr. Whitmore talking, began to whimper in the dark.

"It's the truth," Mr. Whitmore said. "You know it's the truth. You might like to act like you don't know what I'm talking about, but you do. Deep down, I know you do."

Mr. Sitwell could feel his heart pounding in his chest as he listened to the protesters chanting, just beyond the gate. Mr. Whitmore stared down at the hole, almost as if he were in a trance.

"It's the mob, isn't it?" Mr. Sitwell said. "Those strikers have rattled your nerves. I don't know what you went through before you arrived at the Barclay house but believe me, you are not the only one who has lived through an encounter with the mob. The point is, I don't care. I don't care what you've been through, I don't care how Mac got in that hole and I don't care what it means. I want him out of it and that's all that matters. Because you work for me now, and so long as that's true you are going to do what I tell you and you are going to do it when I tell you to. Or else you can go right back out there and join the rest of those men who don't have jobs."

Mr. Whitmore looked up.

"I'm not Mamie, Whitmore. I'll cut the meat myself before I allow you to disrespect me. I do everything else in that damn house. No reason I can't do that too."

Mr. Whitmore nodded toward a nearby tree.

"Might be we could tie the rope to that and make a pulley," he said.

"Then do it."

Together, they tied one end of the rope to the tree then dropped the other end into the hole and instructed the boy to tie it around his waist. They stood on the edge of the hole, a length of rope in each of their hands. Behind them they could hear the chanting getting louder as the protesters got closer to the fields.

"Now pull," Mr. Whitmore said.

Mr. Sitwell pulled on the rope. And as he struggled to summon strength from his muscles, he heard the mob drawing closer and could not help but be reminded of the night the townspeople had raided his village. The sound of the guns, the screams of his neighbors as the green-eyed man led him to his hiding place in the cellar. He'd told Mr. Sitwell he would be safe there and promised someone would come for him; until then Mr. Sitwell had to stay hidden. Then he'd reached into his pocket and held out a small locket on a chain with a picture of a woman inside.

"Your uncle Max give this to me, a long time ago," the green-eyed man had said. "See, when I was your age I didn't live in a nice place like this. I was born a slave in Saint Augustine; figured I would die there too until I met a woman who told me she could get me free. I went with her and I was not the only one. She had a whole group of us traveling with her, which is why when I got sick with the fever she had to leave me here on account of all the other people depending on her too. It's how I wound up living with your mother and uncle Max. By the time I got better, she was long gone, which of course produced a powerful sadness in me. So your uncle Max drew this picture for me, so I'd have something to remember her by."

"Pull," Mr. Whitmore shouted.

"Hold on to that," Mr. Sitwell remembered the green-eyed man telling him.

"Keep it safe and it will keep you safe too. Promise me that no matter what you hear going on outside you will stay here. Don't come out until you hear somebody call you by your name. Because I promise, someone will come for you."

Then the green-eyed man had gone back out into the chaos and left him alone in the dark. And even though Mr. Sitwell never saw him again the man had kept his word. Because someone had come for him. Just before dawn someone had called his name and led him out of the burning village and back onto the main road; there he'd met a man in a wagon who'd taken him all the way to the state line. He'd explained the need to be careful, that everyone knew his family had been harboring the green-eyed man, that if he were caught he'd be held responsible for his mother's lie.

"Pull!" Mr. Whitmore said.

It wasn't until the following day that he'd opened the locket and understood what it was he'd been given. Inside it was a picture of a woman's face, hand-drawn by his uncle Max. It was the face of the woman who had tried to lead the green-eyed man to freedom. It was the face on the mask held by the woman from his dreams, who'd been coming to him almost every night since.

The sound of a gunshot startled him from his revelry. He looked up and saw a woman in a torn blue dress running frantically past him through the fields. Mr. Sitwell pulled on the rope as hard as he could, then fell backward as the tension gave way and Mac appeared on the ground in front of them. He still had the berries he'd picked tied up in a handkerchief he'd strapped to his waist.

"Thank you, sir," Mac said.

Mr. Sitwell clutched the boy to his chest. Behind Mac he could see an enormous crowd of people now running through the fields, a row of men on horseback charging after them swinging billy clubs left and right and all of them heading toward the reeds where the three of them stood. He held on to Mac and shut his eyes, as for a moment it seemed as though the three of them might be trampled.

Then something happened. The earth began to shake beneath him, followed by a loud crack as the wooden boards sealing the transportation tunnel gave way a few yards from where he, Mac, and Mr. Whitmore stood. A section of the crowd was sucked into the ground, replaced by a cloud of dust that came billowing out of it. Mr. Sitwell raised his hand to shield his eyes then squinted at the chaos and hysteria that surrounded him. Through the fog of dust he saw a line of men with linked hands moving slowly and deliberately through the crowd, their footsteps tracing strange patterns in the ground as they wove their way through the fields. Mr. Sitwell recognized some of them as the tramps who lived there; he took Mac's hand and motioned for Mr. Whitmore to follow them all the way through the fields to a small hole in the fence on the opposite side.

The three of them slipped through it and carefully made their way back to the Avenue.

When they got back to the kitchen Frederick and Bart clenched Mac in a tight hug. Mr. Sitwell looked at Mamie standing near the stove.

"Am I late?"

Mamie smiled. "Quite the contrary. You are right on time."

She handed him a serving tray.

He found Mr. Barclay and Mr. Pound sitting together in the parlor.

"So it is settled then?"

"I should think so. Just a few minor details to work out. I have one more meeting tomorrow; I just want to feel confident that I fully understand what I am getting into. I shall be more than prepared to make you an official offer by Friday."

"But if you are getting into it, if that much is firm . . . I don't see what this meeting has to do with our negotiations."

"Rest assured, Barclay, the deal will go through. You have my word on that. Really, I find myself distracted by an altogether different matter."

"Oh?"

"I take it you are aware of the current chaos downtown?"

"The strike? Yes, but it's hardly chaos. More of a controlled burn. Sometimes it is best to let them rage a bit, get it out of their systems. I can assure you it is being closely monitored by the authorities."

"Well, whatever you choose to call it . . . It appears it does have consequence. I told you about the luncheon my wife is intent on hosting tomorrow? Now the caterer she hired has pulled out at the last moment and she is convinced that it is due to the turmoil that she has not been able to locate a suitable replacement."

"Whatever might be going on downtown, I assure you the two have nothing to do with each other."

"Perhaps not. But I am concerned that it speaks to larger themes."

"Nonsense, it speaks to no theme at all.

As a matter of fact . . . It occurs to me . . . Why not have her lunch here?"

Mr. Sitwell looked up.

"You're certain you don't mind?"

"Of course not. No trouble at all. My wife will be delighted."

"That would be marvelous. And of course, I could pay you for the catering if that is an issue at all."

Mr. Barclay laughed. "Nonsense! The opportunity for more of your company is payment enough." He turned to Mr. Sitwell.

"Run and fetch Mamie so that Mr. Pound may explain what he requires."

Mr. Sitwell frowned. "Yes, sir."

In the kitchen he told Mamie she was wanted in the parlor. Before she pushed through the door he reached for her hand.

"It will be alright," he told her.

He waited a few minutes then returned to the hall. He retrieved Mr. Pound's coat from the closet, then stood listening to the muffled voices on the other side of the parlor door. After a while the door opened and the two men walked out.

"Tomorrow then."

"Yes, looking forward to it. Hopefully we shall be doing business together for a long time."

Mr. Sitwell handed Mr. Pound his coat.

Mr. Whitmore drove the car around to the front of the house and Mr. Pound was already seated inside it when Mamie finally emerged from the parlor, the expression on her face a mix of anger and profound fatigue.

"So we are clear then?" Mr. Barclay asked her. "Everything must be ready by noon."

"What would you have me serve them?" Mamie said.

"What do you mean? You know very well what to serve."

"I know what I was asked to serve. And I also know we do not have the provisions to prepare it in the house. I barely have enough provisions to get through the week, including Friday's dinner."

"Is that not what the market is for? Go buy more. What is the matter with you?"

"Those who sell in the market expect to be paid," Mamie said. "We owe money to every grocer in the city."

"What did you just say to me?"

"I'm not telling you anything you don't already know."

Mr. Barclay frowned. "Yes. We have indeed passed through a difficult period in this house. And yet somehow despite this, you have always been paid and paid on time. Is that not correct?"

Mamie said nothing.

"I do not expect you to understand everything I do, all the sacrifices I have made to ensure the stability of this house. Why should you understand? You are the cook. Cooking is all I have ever asked of you. I must say, however, that when Mr. Boudreaux left, I did have my reservations about giving the responsibilities of head cook to a woman. But you assured me you could handle the job, did you not?"

"I did," Mamie said. "I do."

"Then figure it out."

He turned and walked down the hall. A few seconds later, the door to his study slammed shut.

Mr. Sitwell followed Mamie back to the kitchen where the three boys were busy washing dishes. They noticed her expression and frowned.

"Miss Mamie? Are you alright?"

Mamie stared straight ahead.

The swinging door pushed open again and Mrs. Lawson rushed in, followed by Jennie.

"What is this I'm hearing about a luncheon tomorrow?"

Mamie did not respond.

For a moment the room was quiet. Everyone stared at Mamie. They looked frightened, as if they'd all suddenly realized how

175

much they had depended on her these last few months. Depended on her confidence, on her assurances that things would get better. Without that, it was clear they hadn't the slightest idea what to do.

Fortunately, Mr. Sitwell did.

He reached for Mamie's hand. "What did I tell you before? It's going to be alright."

He went to the refrigerator and brought out what was left of the sauce she had prepared for the dinner the night before. He raised it to his nose, inhaled deeply then smiled. He went to the pantry and brought out a can of stewed tomatoes, brown sugar, and vinegar and set them out on the table. He chopped garlic and onions then set the saucepan on the stove while Mamie watched.

"What are you doing?"

"Wait and see."

He mixed Mamie's sauce with the new ingredients.

Then he began to cook.

When he was finished he tasted it, then held a spoon to her lips. Her eyes lit up as if smelling salts had been placed under her nose.

"What is this?"

"A meat sauce."

"It's delicious. I did not know you could

cook, Sitwell."

"My mother taught me a few things when I was a child."

"Your mother?"

"She was a cook, like you. A fine cook and a fine woman . . ."

"I don't doubt it. But I can't recall you ever speaking of your mother before."

"Her name was Lotta," Mr. Sitwell said.

Mamie tasted the sauce again.

"Did Mr. Boudreaux know you could cook like this? And yet instead of making you his apprentice, he chose to send you to work in the yard? Why, Sitwell?"

"What does it matter? I'm not outside anymore. I'm right here. With you."

When he returned to his rooming house that night Billy was sitting behind the front desk, reading.

"How is that coming along?"

"Oh, there are dark days ahead, that much is clear. Cherokee's assault is now inevitable and the town is bracing itself for what promises to be an attack of extreme violence."

"Is that right?"

"And yet there is some beauty amid the terror. According to the author, the threat of attack is what brings the townspeople

177

together. They've put aside all petty griev-
ances and are determined to meet the threat
as a unified force. As a result, perhaps the
first time in its existence, the town is able to
see itself for what it truly is."

"And what is that?"

"A beacon in the darkness. A lonely
outpost of civilization carved out of a
wilderness that had them surrounded on all
sides."

"Is that right? And what of the village not
a mile down the road?"

Billy shook his head. "There is no village
down the road."

"No, perhaps not. Perhaps not anymore.
But there was. It was a beautiful place. Full
of beautiful, strong, proud people. Until
those townspeople whose story you seem so
moved by decided to burn it down."

"What are you talking about? There is no
village. There never was. And these are good
people in this book. They would never do
something like that."

"And yet they did. I know because I was
there. I used to live there. This story you
are reading is my story and that is how I
know it is full of lies. And all these people
you've mentioned from the book? Wash,
Cherokee, Uncle Max, Farley, Lotta . . . I
knew them, I knew what they were really

178

like. The village existed and it still exists. Because I'm still here and I remember."

Billy frowned. "I've already told you, Sitwell. There is no one in this book named Lotta."

Mr. Sitwell nodded and walked up to his room.

That night, when the woman appeared to Mr. Sitwell in his dreams, he was waiting for her. For the very first time, when she stretched out her hand he did not hesitate.

He took it.

5
WHAT PEOPLE CALL YOU

It wasn't until the next morning that he learned what had happened in the fields. It was all anyone was talking about on the omnibus. From what they said, the strikers had planned a march to the financial district in order to compel those who owned the factories to look at them. The police had allowed the strikers to get as far as the fields, at which point a barricade had been set up, supported by a phalanx of armed men on horseback. Another phalanx of men, supplanted by members of the Good Time Gang, had been moving up the block behind them. Not only had this blocked the strikers' progress, it had boxed them in so that the only means of escape was through the narrow entrance to the fields.

The exact purpose of the authorities in doing all this was not entirely clear; what was clear was that no one had anticipated the ground collapsing beneath all of them.

It turned out that the illusion that the field was situated on solid ground was dependent upon the relatively small number of tramps who could be found congregating there at any one time. The transportation tunnels ran beneath the entire length of the field, and it had never had the strength to support the weight of several hundred stamping feet followed by the gallop of a phalanx of police on horseback. Dozens of people had been sucked into the ground, and on the morning commute there were varying opinions as to who was actually responsible for this.

"The police forced those people into that place knowing full well what would happen. Even if they'll never admit it," one passenger stated. "They killed those people just as surely as if they'd executed them."

"If it's true it's no less than they deserve," said another. "Violent rabble rousers, marching through downtown! It was anarchy plain and simple."

"Nonsense, it was a peaceful march. They have legitimate complaints and a right to protest. Do you have any idea what it is like to work in the Magazine?"

"No, and I don't want to know. It's why I've worked so hard, so that I never will. No one owes those people anything. Americans persevere through hard work and dedication, but you see most of those people don't understand that because they are foreigners."

"We'd be better off without them is what I say. This is America, and they should respect it enough to obey our laws or they should go back where they came from."

This diversity of strong opinions swirled about him throughout his entire ride to the Avenue. At several points, the conversations became so heated that Mr. Sitwell found himself concerned that his fellow passengers might come to actual blows.

He was relieved when at last he arrived at his stop, where it seemed the turmoil had not quite ended. When he turned onto the Avenue, two men were waiting on the corner. When he tried to walk past them they put out their hands to stop him.

"Where do you think you're going?" one of them said. But then the other one shook his head.

"No, this one's okay. He works for the Southerner, Barclay."

The first man backed away. It turned out they were both off-duty policemen, hired by the neighborhood association to ensure the security of homes along the Avenue in case of a possible anarchist attack.

"No one is to be allowed in or out without express permission until further notice. Make sure these men know who you are."

"Yes, sir. I will do that."

Once he'd gotten past the security detail he found the rest of the Avenue completely unchanged. Everything was as tranquil and lovely as it always was and as he walked down the block, Mr. Sitwell felt fortunate that somehow, twenty years before, he had found such a good place to hide.

For the first time since arriving in the city, he found himself wondering if perhaps there was no need to hide any longer. Mr. Barclay's negotiations were almost completed and he no longer had to worry about the boys. The house was stable again and now that he was back inside it he would be in a position to help ensure it stayed that way. He wasn't entirely sure why, but remembering who the woman in his dreams actually was had changed something inside him; for the first time since he'd been in the city, Mr. Sitwell felt safe.

What's more, he had dinner with Jennie to look forward to.

He pushed through the gate, then smiled when he saw his three boys standing in the mud near the water pump.

"Why is it every time I turn around you

three are playing with that pump?"

"We're not playing with it. We're trying to fix it," Mac said.

"Fix it?"

"No water comes out," Frederick said. "Hasn't been for the past week. We know how busy you are, so we've been trying to fix it ourselves."

Mr. Sitwell smiled. They were such good boys.

"Well, that's very thoughtful of you. But mind what you're doing. You don't want to make it worse."

He crouched down and rolled up his sleeves. He was just about to reach inside the pipe when the sound of Mamie's voice stopped him.

"Mr. Sitwell? What do you think you're doing?"

"The pump is broken. It needs to be fixed."

"Perhaps, but not by you. I told you the yard is no longer your responsibility."

"What if there was a fire?"

"There shall be no fire, Mr. Sitwell. Hear me? Not until the new man is hired. I forbid it. Now come away from there. I've got a surprise for you in the kitchen."

Mr. Sitwell stood up. He looked back at the boys.

184

"You heard the woman. Let it alone for now. Apparently it's not for us to worry about. We'll let the new man take care of it as soon as he is hired."

In the kitchen Mamie was standing near the stove, smiling as she held something behind her back.

"What is it?"

She brought her hands out in front of her and held up the new uniform Mrs. Lawson had made for him.

"Do you like it?" She held the jacket to his chest. "Go ahead. Try it on."

She smiled as she watched him drape it over his shoulders then fit his arms into the sleeves.

"How fine you look. How that jacket suits you. I would like to see you wear it all the time from now on. Because you are part of the household staff now, Mr. Sitwell." She gave him a serious look. "You understand that, don't you? The yard is no longer your responsibility. Perhaps this morning it's just the water pump but I know you. If you don't stop now people will continue to ask you to do something in the yard, and the next thing I know, Mr. Barclay will be telling me there is no need for a new grounds-keeper when Mr. Sitwell is content to perform the duties of two men. And then I shall have to watch him throw a grounds-keeper's salary away at some gambling hall. Do you understand?"

"I do."

Mamie nodded. "Good. Now, if you please." She pointed toward the kitchen table. "Have a seat."

He sat down at the table. Mamie reached into the oven and set a covered dish before him.

"What is this?"

"One of the perks of management."

When he removed the cover, he found two poached eggs, a side of ham, and a biscuit covered in gravy.

"Mr. Thomas, the man you are replacing, demanded this of me every morning." Mamie smiled. "For you I shall do it with pleasure."

"Thank you. But I'm not Mr. Thomas. It's not necessary."

"I feel it is. For you, part of the challenge of being a butler is going to be learning to behave like one."

Mr. Sitwell nodded and picked up his fork.

Mamie took a seat across from him. She looked around the kitchen and smiled.

"Isn't this something? After all we've been through together? Who would have imagined it when we first started? Me, a shy

186

chambermaid being bullied by Mr. Thomas. You, a frightened little boy hiding from Mr. Boudreaux under the kitchen table. Now look at us. Mr. Thomas is gone. Mr. Boudreaux is gone. I am the cook of a respectable house and you are the butler of the same."

"Yes, Mamie. It's wonderful."

She sighed. "So the next time this happens, perhaps I won't have to worry."

"Next time?"

"Next time the Barclays find themselves in a state of near destitution. Because you and I will both have options."

Mr. Sitwell stopped eating. "I thought the house was fine now."

"It is. For now. But I think we've both worked here long enough to realize there is a reason the Barclays wound up in their situation. After all, it's hardly the first time. Remember seven years ago? When Mrs. Barclay's inheritance finally ran out? The panic and confusion? All the hysteria over Mrs. Barclay having to sell some of her precious jewelry? And yet it seems they learned nothing from it. Today's lunch, Mrs. Barclay's shopping . . . Always spending money they do not yet have. That's why this house will never truly be stable. Quite frankly, I no longer believe, as I once did, that there is much stability in being a household servant at all. No, Sitwell. What we must do, if we want to avoid such situations in the future, is find work in a hotel. Some place like the Fowler."

"The Fowler?" The Fowler was the finest hotel in the city.

Mr. Sitwell looked at her. It occurred to him that of all the remaining servants Mamie was the only one who could leave there with the expectation of finding a position that was better than what she had now as opposed to one that was worse. She had spent years cultivating both her skills in the kitchen and her reputation among Mr. Barclay's many dinner guests. Her value was no longer specific to the house. It was simply undeniable.

"You've thought of leaving, haven't you?"

"Haven't you? I couldn't before, you know that as well as I do. As a cook's assistant? And a black woman to boot? Where would I have gone? No, it would have been simply trading bad for worse. But I have a title now. A title that I have more than earned. And soon enough so shall you."

Mr. Sitwell set down his fork. "So that is what this is really about then? You want me to come into the house not so much to be the butler but so that I will be able to say I am a butler should I need to seek other employment?"

"You need the title. Mrs. Lawson was right about that. Out there, in the real world, it matters what people call you. It matters a great deal. And like it or not, there is a difference between a former butler of a good house trying to find employment and a groundskeeper trying to do the same."

"I hadn't realized my prospects gave you such cause for concern."

"It's not you that gives me cause for concern. It's the world out there." She shook her head. "Have you not heard what happened in the fields yesterday? What has become of the poor people who slept there? No, I could never in good conscience have left you to fend for yourself as you were, a groundskeeper as a result of Mr. Boudreaux's caprice."

She reached for his hand.

"Why are we talking about this? There is no need and perhaps there will never be. It's not true that getting you a title is the only reason I want you in the house. I need you here. I need someone I can count on, someone I can trust. I could not have gotten through these past months without you. And I may have no confidence in the Barclays, but I have always had a great deal of confidence in you."

Mr. Sitwell nodded and, touched by her words, finished his breakfast. Then he put his empty plate in the sink, buttoned his jacket, and pushed through to the front of the house.

Now that he had accepted his new role he understood that being the butler was far different from pretending to be one. He was now in charge of supervising the entire household staff, and it was up to him to make sure the day's event went well, a responsibility complicated by the fact that, as was true of most things that went on in the Barclay household, he would be required to compensate for a serious lack.

Mr. Pound had made his requests with respect to the menu and Mamie had endeavored to accommodate him, making all manner of substitutions based on what food was actually available in the house. Even with the substitutions there was, according to Mamie, enough food on hand to satisfy the appetites of ten women; Mr. Pound had told them to expect twice that number. The only way to make up for this would be to find a way to sufficiently satiate their hunger before they actually sat down to eat.

Hence the significance of the sauce. Mamie had instructed Mr. Whitmore to deploy his butchering skill to salvage every edible portion of meat left in the larder, save that which was needed for the following night's dinner. These scraps were ground down then mixed with egg, onion, and flour, constructed into an appealing shape, and then deep-fried on skewers. The skewers were to be accompanied by copious amounts of Mr. Sitwell's sauce and offered to the ladies as soon as they entered the front door.

It was the best they could come up with and therefore it would have to do. Mrs. Lawson, however, seemed personally offended by the unorthodoxy of it.

"There's giblets on those skewers," she complained. "Giblets."

"No one will know unless you tell them."

"*I* will know. And because Mamie has seen fit to replace Petunia with a girl who lacks the slightest competency on the floor, she insists that I must serve them as well. What should I say if someone asks me what this barbarous concoction I am offering them to eat actually is?"

"You should lie, Mrs. Lawson," Mr. Sitwell said. "You should lie as if your job depended on it. Because quite frankly, it very well might."

Yet, in part inspired by the anxiety caused

by Mrs. Lawson's conviction that the women would be able to detect the poor quality of the meat, a further innovation was seized upon. Mr. Sitwell had planned on greeting the ladies at the door with tall flutes of orange juice and soda water. It was decided that a small portion of vodka should be added as well, in the hopes that the alcohol would further promote the sense of satisfaction with the day's event that they were all hoping to achieve.

At noon the ladies began to arrive. They were an imposing group, the wives of some of the most prominent men in the city. Mrs. Pound and Mrs. Barclay both greeted them at the door while Mr. Sitwell, Mrs. Lawson, and Jennie formed a row of hands along the front hall, ready to take their hats and coats and shawls. Mrs. Pound was a charming host and Mrs. Barclay, her mood no doubt buoyed by the purchase of a new dress, was far more sociable than she had been during dinner. They gathered together in the sitting room and chatted happily with one another as Mrs. Lawson and the three boys walked around them, distributing copious amounts of both the skewers and flutes. For an hour or so, everything seemed to be going as Mr. Sitwell and Mamie had hoped.

Then something changed. It was subtle at

first — a few odd outbursts of laughter, the occasional slurring of words. By the time he realized the cause, some of the women had become maudlin. He grabbed Bart and told him to stop distributing the flutes.

"What's wrong?"

"They are drunk from the vodka."

"Oh, dear!" Mamie said. "This is terrible."

At that point, almost every one of them was holding a flute.

"What should I do, sir? I can't just take the glasses from their hands."

"They need a distraction," Mamie said. "From the alcohol."

"No," Jennie said. She looked around the room. "They need a distraction from themselves."

She smiled at Mr. Sitwell, gave him a small wink.

"I've got this." Then, without a moment of hesitation, she walked to the front of the room and began to sing.

Everyone stopped what they were doing at once, riveted by the sound of her voice. She stood at the front of the room and without accompaniment let her voice glide and jump through a series of notes with such startling dexterity that all he could do was stare, amazed. And as he listened he felt as though she were speaking directly to him, calling out a song of comfort and grace and joy. He felt both calmed by her voice and somehow recognized — as if all the restlessness and confusion he'd tried to keep hidden inside him for so long had been found out, pulled to the surface, and then soothed. It was a beautiful voice and for the rest of his days, long after he'd forgotten both the words and the tune he would still remember what he'd felt at that moment, standing at the back of the Barclay's parlor, listening to Jennie sing.

It provided enough of a distraction to allow Bart to remove all the flutes that contained alcohol and replace them with glasses of juice and soda water. Mr. Sitwell stood by the door listening to it, then at one o'clock, just before the ladies were to be seated for lunch, he walked out of the room to see if Mamie needed his assistance in the kitchen.

He shut the door behind him, thinking to himself that one day he would have to find the words to tell her how beautiful she was, how her song had made him feel. Then he looked down the hall and, through the window, saw Mrs. Lawson walking through the garden carrying a pitcher of milk.

Puzzled by this he walked outside, still carrying a tray of appetizers, surprised to find a group of a dozen men gathered together near the gazebo. Based on their manner of dress, they did not appear to be the type of men who usually came to socialize at the Barclay house. Ill-fitting suits of inferior quality, flat caps, rubber-soled bluchers. One of them was actually wearing work boots. In fact, there were only two who wore the type of clothing that Mr. Sitwell had come to associate with visitors to the house: Mr. Barclay and Mr. Pound.

"There you are, Sitwell. I was just about to send for you," Mr. Barclay said as Mr. Sitwell entered the gazebo with his tray. As soon as he did several of the men rushed toward him and began hungrily stuffing skewers into their mouths.

"It seems Mr. Pound had something else in mind for today, in addition to his wife's luncheon."

"It only occurred to me yesterday." Mr. Pound smiled. "I had my assistant put an ad in the paper, soliciting volunteers to sample my wafers so as to better ascertain their appeal."

"Appeal?"

"It seems we are hosting a tasting party," Mr. Barclay said. He leaned close to Mr. Sitwell's ear. "Would you believe that he actually wanted this gathering to take place in my parlor? I had a time trying to convince him that these men would be more comfortable out here, where they would not disturb the ladies."

Mrs. Lawson walked around the table with her pitcher of milk, a look of extreme discomfort on her face. She poured half a cup into each of the bowls. When she was finished she stood up stiffly.

"Will you be needing anything else?"

"No, that's fine," Mr. Sitwell said. "Perhaps it would be better for you to go back inside and see to the ladies."

"As you wish," she said between clenched teeth.

Mr. Sitwell looked at Mr. Pound. Having sampled the man's wafers himself, he could not imagine much good would come from a tasting party.

He leaned close to Mr. Barclay's ear. "Perhaps you should try to dissuade him."

Mr. Barclay tittered. "Do you not think I haven't already? These men will not eat his wafers. I have told him that many times. Their palates, saturated in garish spices and heavy seasonings, lack the capacity to appreciate the simplicity of his wafer. And even if they did appreciate it they still would not purchase it. What money they do have will never be expended on something so bland and banal as breakfast wafers. No, they will spend their money as they always have, on sport and cheap liquors."

"Yes, well . . . my point is you are so close to concluding your negotiations. Surely we would not want anything to happen that might dampen the man's enthusiasm."

"Oh, have no fear, Mr. Sitwell. This man will not dampen. Whatever the outcome, I am quite certain it will only reinforce his resolve. He is that determined to prove me wrong."

"Wrong, sir?"

Mr. Barclay looked at him and frowned. "Do you not understand what is going on here? The man is trying to humiliate me. Has been trying to do so ever since he arrived. That's all this really is, the true purpose of inviting this rabble into my home." He sighed. "My only compensation shall be the wager."

"Wager, sir?"

"It was his idea. As I said, he is quite determined to prove me wrong."

Mr. Sitwell nodded. A wager was a dangerous proposition so far as Mr. Barclay was concerned. The man had already lost so much over the years as a result of his gambling. All he could do was hope his employer realized that for once it behooved him to lose.

He was just about to remind Mr. Barclay of this when a voice called out to him.

"Don't you look well in uniform."

Mr. Sitwell turned around and, near the rear of the small crowd, saw a tall, angular copper-colored man in his sixties biting down on one of the skewers he had brought out on his tray. It was Mr. Boudreaux.

"What are you doing here?"

"I have come in response to an ad in the paper, in order to sample this man's breakfast wafers. When I saw the location where the event would be held, of course I had to volunteer. I am to serve as representative of the Negro palate." He smiled. "As you can imagine, many men were vying for the rare opportunity to dine at the Barclay house. But when I informed Mr. Pound of my connection to the house, my selection was all but assured."

"Does Mr. Barclay know you are here?"

"Of course he does. He seemed to find it amusing. You, on the other hand, appear perturbed."

"You should leave," Mr. Sitwell said.

"I will not." Mr. Boudreaux reached into the pocket of his jacket, pulled out a small flask, and took a sip. "I am to be compensated one dollar for the simple task of

198

providing my honest opinion. And believe me I intend to earn it."

"I'll pay you two dollars to leave."

Mr. Boudreaux reared his head in a look of feigned horror. "And deny myself the rare opportunity to eat at the Barclay table? You ask too much." He shook his head. "Thirty-seven years I cooked for these people. And do you know that not once was I invited to sit down? But I suppose that is how it always is with these people. Always a place on the table. Never a place at it. Don't let proximity fool you, in that respect, Mr. Sitwell."

Then he heard a small pinging sound. When he turned around Mr. Pound was standing at the head of the table, tapping the side of his glass with a spoon. Mr. Boudreaux took his seat at the table with the other men.

"Good afternoon, gentlemen," Mr. Pound began. "I have asked you all here in order to provide you with a sample of an extraordinary new product, one which represents the latest in scientific research on health and rejuvenation. This research was conducted for the benefit of the most elite segment of society, those who have the time and resources to devote themselves to the cultivation of total fitness of body and mind. It has produced remarkable results and has

199

therefore proven remarkably popular among them and my intention now is to expand its distribution to the masses, in the hopes that it may one day serve as an important bridge over the otherwise ever-widening chasm between the haves and the have-nots.

"You see, the fact is, despite all appearances to the contrary, many of the conflicts of our society today are not, in truth, about economics at all. They are about dietary deficiencies. Research has shown that the average worker consumes a diet that is dangerously low of everything save sugar, starch, and sodium. As a result, men such as yourselves are subject to a wide variety of diseases that are all but nonexistent among the class of men who employ you. Jaundice, pellagra, melancholia, scurvy . . . What if I were to tell you that all that is required to remove the threat of these diseases is a healthy diet? Yet I assure you it is the truth. Not to mention greatly reducing incidents of work-related injury, many of which are the results of poor circulation and the resultant fatigue. Now when a man prepares to put in a hard day of work at the factory —"

"I do not work in a factory," one man called out. "I am a bookkeeper."

"Yes, well . . . the point is that my wafers

will keep you strong and healthy, your faculties sharp. In this manner, you will find yourselves equipped to realize your full potential as workers, nay, as citizens of this, our great democratic capitalist society."

He glanced at Mr. Barclay and frowned.

"Now, some have suggested that it is only the elite who are capable of appreciating the value of good nutrition and that therefore only they are capable of reaping its benefits. But I say, who is more in need of these benefits than the working man? Who is more deserving? Is he not the one ultimately responsible for actually producing the vast cornucopia of products on which our economy rests? I truly believe that it is only through internal rejuvenation that one is truly able to realize one's full potential. And I know of which I speak. Believe it or not, there was a time when people who live in houses such as this would have hesitated before welcoming me to their dinner table. . . ."

"Here it comes." Mr. Barclay sighed.

"I came from a decent family but it was not until I went to college that I was made to understand that I did not come from a good one. Not good enough to work in some of my peers' family businesses. Not good enough to marry some men's daughters. Yet through diet and exercise, discipline and hard work, I stand before you now an extremely wealthy man. So wealthy in fact that, lo and behold, the same men who once would have denied me an invitation to sit at their tables now find themselves compelled to solicit my favor when in need of financial assistance."

Mr. Barclay narrowed his eyes but said nothing.

"But, of course, in order to fully understand my meaning, you must eat. So go ahead — replenish." Mr. Pound saluted the men with his own bowl of wafers. "To good health."

The men looked down at the bowls set before them. After a brief hesitation, they picked up their spoons and began to eat. For a few moments the only sound was that of teeth crunching down on hard wafers while Mr. Pound looked on expectantly.

"Well? What do you say?"

"Good exercise for the jaw," one man offered.

"Hearty," said another. "That is a word that comes to mind. . . . One of several."

Mr. Pound nodded. "And the taste? What do you make of the taste?"

Silence.

"I'll be frank with you," Mr. Pound said.

"Some have suggested that this meal will not appeal to you. That your palates are not sufficiently —"

"May I be frank with you?" Mr. Boudreaux called out. He set down his bowl and dropped his spoon into it with a loud clank. "It tastes a bit like dirt."

Mr. Pound stared. "I beg your pardon?"

"Not just any dirt, of course," Mr. Boudreaux said. "High-quality dirt. Mineral rich soil."

Mr. Sitwell narrowed his eyes. It was an appalling comment, but when he glanced at Mr. Barclay he saw something more appalling still: the man was smiling.

"It is terrible," Mr. Boudreaux said. "Without question the worst thing I have ever put in my mouth."

The bookkeeper, noticing Mr. Pound's crestfallen expression, offered a suggestion in sympathy: "Perhaps if you were to add copious amounts of sugar to it. Might help blunt the effect."

A few of the others nodded in agreement.

"Or even better," Mr. Boudreaux suggested. "What if instead of serving it in milk you served it with this sauce, which I must say is, in marked contrast, delicious." Mr. Boudreaux dipped a wafer in the sauce, popped it in his mouth, then smiled in exaggerated satisfaction. The gesture was quickly copied by several of the other men.

"Do you know, I think he's on to something," the bookkeeper said. He dipped a wafer in sauce. "Much better."

Soon enough all the men were dipping their wafers into the sauce and contentedly chewing.

"There it is. . . . Delicious."

Mr. Pound watched the men eat.

"So there we have it," said the bookkeeper, wiping his mouth with a napkin. "Kudos to you for taking an interest in the health of the working man. I appreciate scientific research, as I'm sure many of us do. I would like to eat better, that is certain. If what you say is true and the point is to get these so-called vitamins and minerals into the system, then what matter is the manner of delivery? Instead of serving it with milk, serve it in the sauce, better to hide the actual taste."

Mr. Pound said nothing. He looked down at the half-empty bowl of sauce, picked up one of his wafers, and scraped it along the side of the interior. He bit down on it and began to chew.

Mr. Barclay smiled. "Never mind, Pound. I tell you this proves nothing. I tried to tell you before and you seemed to find my comments elitist, despite the fact that I have told you repeatedly that I was only referring to taste. Your product will do very well with those who have the underlying palate to appreciate . . . let us call it the subtleties of its flavor. Which is not to say I do not enjoy the taste personally. Quite the contrary. I intend to eat it every day, just as soon as it is available."

Mr. Sitwell watched Mr. Pound chew on his wafer. Mr. Barclay's behavior was not helping and, with so much at stake, he felt compelled to speak.

"Sir? If I may say something? I would like to point out that this is but a small sample of potential customers, randomly selected. Quite frankly, it is not at all clear to me that these men represent any population larger than themselves. You should not put too much trust in their opinions."

He pointed to Mr. Boudreaux. "Certainly not his."

Mr. Pound looked up. "You mean my Negro palate?"

"Yes, sir. Your Negro palate. He is the former cook here, no doubt embittered against your wafers due to resentment over the circumstances of his termination."

"Termination?" Mr. Pound stared. "He told me he left this house on good terms."

"Well, he has lied to you then. It is something he does with great frequency and only underscores my point. The man was terminated for drinking on the job."

Mr. Pound turned to Mr. Barclay. "Is this true, Barclay?"

Mr. Barclay shrugged.

"And you did not think to inform me? Let me conduct my test without warning? Why, Barclay? So that you might win a wager? Are you really that desperate for money?"

Mr. Barclay stopped smiling. "Well, of course, the wager is but a small matter. I shall forfeit it at once."

Mr. Pound looked at the bowl of sauce. "What is this?"

"My dear sir. It is a meat sauce," Mr. Boudreaux shouted out.

"Is there more?"

"The rest was served to the ladies inside," Mr. Sitwell said. "Had I known there would be additional guests, I would have prepared more, but —"

"*You* would have prepared?" Mr. Pound squinted. "You prepared this?"

Mr. Sitwell was quiet. His actual role in the house had been so confused lately; perhaps he had begun to confuse himself.

"No. I meant Mamie. She is the cook."

Mr. Boudreaux snorted. "You seem a bit

206

unsure, Sitwell." He took another sip from his flask.

"Please do not make too much of this," Mr. Barclay said.

"Of what? The fact that you sought to cheat me once again?"

"Cheat you? I have never sought to cheat you of anything."

"Just like the Monte Carlo," Mr. Pound said. "Or did you think I'd forgotten about your behavior then? How you sought to humiliate me?"

"Me? Humiliate you? This was all your idea. You are the one who invited these men into my home without a word of notice, who sought to compel my servants to wait on them. And do you think I don't realize your true aim in doing so? What is this, Pound? Are you trying to renege on our deal? Because of some absurd test? We had a gentlemen's agreement, but perhaps that means little to you."

"No, Barclay. I am indeed a gentleman. And unlike you, a man of my word. I fully intend to honor our agreement. However, in view of what has happened here today, there will be some alterations with respect to terms."

"Alterations? What does that mean?"

"We will discuss it tomorrow."

He reached into his pocket and pulled out an envelope.

"What is that?" Mr. Barclay said.

"Can't you smell it? It's money," Mr. Pound sneered. "Like truffle pigs, the lot of you . . ."

"I beg your pardon?"

Mr. Pound turned to Mr. Sitwell.

"Go on now, distribute it to the men," Mr. Pound commanded. "Then send them on their way. The tasting is over."

Mr. Sitwell said nothing. It was as if Mr. Pound had forgotten who it was he actually worked for.

He turned to his employer.

"Do as the man says," Mr. Barclay said and gave a dismissive wave of his hand.

Mr. Sitwell took the envelope stuffed with dollar bills. He distributed the money to the men, thanked them for their opinions, and told them their services were no longer needed. Mr. Boudreaux accepted his dollar with a laugh.

"Happy?" Mr. Sitwell frowned. "Of course you are."

Mr. Boudreaux snorted. "How could I be happy when I still have the taste of that man's revolting wafers in my mouth?" He slipped the dollar into the pocket of his jacket.

Mr. Sitwell shook his head. "You truly will not be satisfied until you have destroyed this house, will you?"

"Nonsense. If anyone shall be the destruction of this house, it is you. I think we both know that."

"Everything I've done has been to protect the people who work here. I think we both know that as well."

"Is that how you justify betraying me? Or do you think I did not realize who sent Mr. Barclay out to the larder that day?" He pulled a flask from his pocket and took a drink. "Go on and admit it. I know it was you. At first I assumed it was Mamie. But she is not that cunning and, besides, would never betray a fellow servant that way. But you know no such loyalty, do you? You knew about Mr. Barclay's gambling debts, didn't you? You knew someone was bound to be sent away in order to cut down household expenses. There were two cooks in the kitchen. And so you made sure it was me Barclay got rid of and not Mamie."

"I did what was best for the house."

"So you do admit it was you."

Mr. Sitwell frowned. "As I said. I did what was best for the house. If Mr. Barclay had the slightest inkling of how things actually worked in the kitchen, he would have known

209

it was for the best too. But, of course, he has no idea what goes on back there. You and Barclay have always gotten along better; he finds you amusing while he finds Mamie abrasive. But the truth is everything would have fallen apart if he had fired her instead of you. All of us would have been out on the street. Deep down, even you must realize that."

"What I realize is that I should have sent you away years ago, when I had the chance. Instead I took pity on you, that was my mistake. I banished you to the yard."

"You did not banish me out of pity. You did it as a punishment."

Mr. Sitwell watched him take another sip from his flask.

"I want you to leave," Mr. Sitwell said. "I want you to leave now."

Then he went back to passing out dollar bills. By the time he was finished, Mr. Boudreaux was gone.

When he returned to the kitchen Mamie and Mrs. Lawson were arguing.

"What is the problem?"

"The fact that you have to ask merely proves my point," Mrs. Lawson said. "This place is a disgrace. You and Mamie have rendered what was once a fine house into little more than a lunatic asylum."

210

"It is temporary."

"Is that right? With you as the butler? You are entirely unqualified for such a position. But all of you behave as if managing a household was some sort of game. When it is not a game. It is a profession. One that I take seriously."

"Mrs. Lawson, I know you are upset about being asked to wait on men of the same class as yourself. But I assure you, Mr. Barclay had no idea they were coming here. In fact, he was just as disturbed by it as you, just better at hiding it. Still, he should have known better than to ask you to set the table. I suppose it did not occur to him that this was something both he and his parlor maid have in common. You are both snobs."

Mrs. Lawson stared at him. At first she looked hurt, then she looked angry.

"Snob? Is that what you call it? Because I take myself seriously, and do not want to see my profession reduced to a joke? I understand that this is just a game to you, but it is not to me. It is my life."

She removed her apron.

"What are you doing?"

"I will not be taking orders from you."

"Mrs. Lawson. Please —"

"No. I've had enough. I'm tired, Mr. Sitwell. Tired of coming in here every day,

211

waiting to be sent home, either as a result of Mamie's caprice or simply because Mr. Barclay can no longer afford to pay me. I have worked in this house for thirty-five years, have given good service, have always tried to conduct myself with the utmost professionalism. I have also put up with more than you could possibly imagine. Well, I won't do it anymore. I can't, my nerves won't tolerate it. I deserve better and you know it."

"Yes. We all do," Mr. Sitwell said. "Mrs. Lawson, I'm sorry. I did not mean to hurt your feelings. I did not realize my comments would offend you."

"Of course you didn't. That's precisely my point. How could you have? Because you are not the butler, Mr. Sitwell. You are the groundskeeper."

She handed him her apron.

"Good-bye, Mr. Sitwell. And good luck."

And just like that, she was gone.

It was not until two hours later, after the ladies had left and the remaining servants had cleaned the gazebo and dining room, that Mr. Sitwell realized Mr. Boudreaux had not, in fact, left the premises. Mac found him on the floor of the larder, nestled in his old hiding place and snoring loudly. The man was pitifully drunk. When Mr. Sitwell tried to revive him he realized he would require assistance getting him out of there. But there were very few left to help him. Mr. Whitmore, after driving the Pounds back to their hotel and returning the car, had left for the day, completely unaware that his uncle was still there. Mamie was in the kitchen but was so angry about Mrs. Lawson's departure, which she saw as a betrayal, that it seemed extremely unwise to ask her to assist in carting her once-again-intoxicated former supervisor out of the larder. Mac was still hobbling about on his injured leg and Frederick, still rattled by his experience in the cell, had not been able to bring himself to leave the premises since Mr. Sitwell retrieved him from the fairgrounds three days before. That left only Bart or Jennie.

He chose Bart.

"Bart? I need you to help me with something."

"Right away, sir. What's going on?"

"Mr. Boudreaux is in the larder. I need to get him out of there and off the premises."

"Alright, sir. You can count on me. Just let me get my coat."

Mr. Sitwell went back to the larder. He managed to hoist Boudreaux onto his feet, then slung him onto his back and dragged him into the garden. When Bart came out of the house they each took one of Mr. Boudreaux's arms and carried him all the way to the omnibus stop. When they let him go he slumped to the ground, face forward. The man was so intoxicated he did not even have the ability to put his hands out to break his own fall. They sat him upright on the sidewalk by leaning him against a lamppost.

"What should we do?" Bart asked.

Mr. Sitwell shook his head. It was tempting to leave him there. But when he looked down the block, the new security detail was already watching them. It seemed imperative to get the man on the omnibus and far enough away that he could not cause a scene by wandering the Avenue, trying to make his way back to the Barclay house.

"We'll have to take him home."

When the omnibus arrived they hoisted him up once more, got him into the car, and sat him down in an empty seat. Mr. Sitwell sat beside him, leaned his head against the window, and shut his eyes.

"Shame, isn't it?" Mr. Boudreaux said.

"Many things fit that description. What are you referring to?"

"Myself, of course," Mr. Boudreaux said. "I mean look at me. For thirty-seven years I worked for that man. Only to be tossed out into the street like a dog. What does that tell you about the Barclays?"

"Very little," Mr. Sitwell said. "Mr. Barclay is our employer. We work for him because it is a mutually beneficial arrangement. Nothing more, nothing less."

"Is that right? Then what does it say about us? That you would betray me to a man like Mr. Barclay, after all I'd done for you."

"You never did anything for me."

"I gave you a name!" Mr. Boudreaux shouted. A few people across the aisle looked up at the sound of his voice.

"Stop making so much noise," Mr. Sitwell said. "Stop causing so much trouble."

"What is he going on about?" Bart asked.

"Ignore him," Mr. Sitwell said. "The man is intoxicated." He glared at Mr. Boudreaux. "Stop this. Can't you see you are confusing Bart?"

"That is not my intention. I am trying to do the opposite. I'm trying to unconfuse him." Mr. Boudreaux's head wobbled as he leaned forward and stared at Bart with red, rheumy eyes. "Do you not find it interesting that Mr. Sitwell is now the butler in that house, considering that he once tried to kill the previous one?"

"Shut up!"

"What are you talking about?" Bart asked.

"Exactly what I said. He once tried to poison Mr. Thomas. It happened a long time ago, when Mr. Sitwell was still a child, just a little older than you. One of Mr. Barclay's guests got a little too forward with Mamie at a party, back when she was still a chambermaid. It was hardly the first time such a thing had happened; quite frankly, any competent maid might have understood it as part of the job. From what I understand, Mr. Thomas told her as much. She must have complained to Sitwell who in turn complained to me. I told him I had nothing to do with it. He asked me to speak to Barclay about allowing her to come work in the kitchen and I told him that I did not want that dumb girl in my kitchen, did not need another apprentice because, so far as I knew, I already had one. Sitwell himself. Instead of being grateful this put him in a rage. Later that night, I found him in the kitchen mixing some strange concoction of poison he had planned to put in Mr. Thomas's soup. Apparently, his idea was that if I would not help him he would solve the problem himself, by getting rid of Mr. Thomas. He told me what he was doing, he told me why, told me it was his mother who had taught him how. I had to give him a good whipping to snap him out of it. When at last he calmed down he was inconsolable about the idea of Mamie finding out his murderous plan. It struck me that perhaps, instead of sending him away, the greater punishment would be to banish him to the yard so he could look upon the house every day and know perfectly well why he was no longer welcome inside."

Bart leaned forward. "Is that true, Mr. Sitwell?"

"No." Mr. Sitwell shook his head. "It is not."

"Of course it's true," Mr. Boudreaux said. "That is the true story of why Mr. Sitwell was banished to the yard."

Bart frowned. "I meant the other part. The part about someone being forward with Miss Mamie."

The car lurched to a stop. A half-dozen men got on, and when the driver yelled, "Push back," Mr. Sitwell and Bart stood up, grabbed ahold of Mr. Boudreaux's sleeves, and began making their way toward the rear of the car. There was an empty seat just in front of the rear door, but when he tried to deposit Mr. Boudreaux into it, Bart shook his head and continued to pull on Mr. Boudreaux's arm.

"What are you doing?"

"We've got to get off. Now." He nodded toward the front of the car. "It's the board-walk man."

Mr. Sitwell turned his head and saw several men standing by the driver, waiting to pay their fare. One of them might have been the man from the boardwalk but he wasn't sure.

"Don't look, sir," Bart said. "Just get off."

Bart was already walking down the rear steps. Because they were both holding on to Mr. Boudreaux, Mr. Sitwell found himself being dragged out the door with him.

"Quickly," Bart said as the three of them stumbled off the car. The doors closed behind them and the car lurched back into motion. They set Mr. Boudreaux down on the curb and watched the omnibus leave without them.

"Are you sure that was him?"

"Entirely sure."

"Well, I was not sure. And even if it was . . . There was no need to panic like that. We have every right to be on the train. . . ."

A woman walked by carrying a parcel of groceries. She stared at Mr. Boudreaux on the sidewalk. Mr. Boudreaux smiled and, by way of greeting, leaned forward and vomited on the pavement.

"Filthy wretch," the woman sneered. Then spit on the ground. Mr. Sitwell watched her hurry down the block then looked around and realized where they were.

It was the Magazine stop.

He looked at Bart. He started to scold him but could tell by the boy's face that he already realized his mistake. He looked petrified.

"Never mind. It will be alright." He looked up at the darkening sky. "Hear me, Bart? Another bus should be along any minute. Keep your head down and just wait for the next car."

An old man walked by, a startled expression on his face.

"You shouldn't be here," the man whispered. Then hurried down the block.

Mr. Sitwell glanced back at the sidewalk behind them. A small crowd of people were gathering near the front of a saloon on the corner, watching them.

"Perhaps he's right," Mr. Sitwell said. "Perhaps it's best to keep moving."

He hoisted Mr. Boudreaux back onto his feet.

"Come on, Bart."

But Bart shook his head. "No, sir."

"What do you mean 'no'?" A few of the men in front of the saloon had started walking toward them. "Grab his arm and come along quickly. We've got to go."

Again Bart shook his head. "No. I'll not run from these people."

"You most certainly will," Mr. Sitwell said. A rock whizzed past his shoulder. "You damn well will run, if I tell you to —"

"You misunderstand me. I don't run. Remember?"

And only then did Mr. Sitwell remember the boy's damaged foot.

Another rock struck Mr. Sitwell squarely on his back.

Bart watched the crowd in front of the saloon. "Look to me like those men mean trouble. But don't worry, sir. You just take Mr. Boudreaux, go on ahead without me. I'll hold them off."

"Hold them off? What are you talking about?"

"I took precautions." Bart winked. He opened his coat. Sticking out of the inside pocket was the antique starter pistol from Mrs. Barclay's cabinet.

"What the hell are you doing with that?"

"Precautions. Like what you told Frederick."

"Are you insane? Do you want to get killed? Don't you realize where we are?"

"Know exactly where we are. That's why I

220

brought it. Just in case."

Mr. Sitwell looked up and, to his great relief, saw the headlights of a car moving toward them.

"Give me that pistol. Give it to me at once."

"No, sir. Won't do it." He pulled the gun out of his pocket. "Y'all two just get on that car."

Another rock sailed past them. "Stop it, Bart. This is not a penny novel. You are not Cherokee Red."

The omnibus pulled up to the curb just as the crowd surged forward. Mr. Sitwell let go of Mr. Boudreaux. The man fell to the pavement as Mr. Sitwell snatched the gun out of Bart's hand. Mr. Sitwell shoved Bart inside the car. He slipped the pistol into his own pocket and dragged Mr. Boudreaux inside.

The driver looked at them and then at the crowd gathered on the sidewalk behind them. He shut the doors quickly.

Mr. Sitwell reached into his pocket. His hands were shaking as he took out a coin to pay their fare.

"What are you three doing in the Magazine?" the driver said. "Trying to start a riot?"

"We got off on the wrong stop," Mr. Sitwell said, still breathless. "Thank you. For closing the door."

The driver frowned.

"Don't bother thanking me, nigger. I'm just doing my job. Now push back." He nodded toward the rear of the car. "And I mean all the way back."

6
WHITE MAN IN THE KITCHEN

He and Bart wound up escorting Mr. Boudreaux all the way home. Then Mr. Sitwell felt obliged to ride the train back with Bart in order to ensure the pistol was properly returned to the cabinet. He did not get back to his rooming house until eleven thirty that evening.

When he returned to the house the following morning, he found Bart sitting calmly on the back porch, staring up at the sky and whistling to himself. A strange, trilling birdcall that stopped as soon as he noticed Mr. Sitwell watching him.

"Morning." Bart smiled.

Mr. Sitwell nodded. "I want you to stay inside the yard for the next few days. Hear me? No running errands for Mamie today. No going beyond the gate."

"Yes, sir."

"I mean it now. That was very foolish what you did last night, bringing that pistol. You understand that, don't you?"

"If you say so."

"If I say so?" Mr. Sitwell shook his head. "You act as if you don't even realize what you did."

"And you act as if you don't remember why I did it. I wasn't trying to start nothing with those people. It's not my fault I can't run. It's just a fact. Imagine it's why they cut my toes off in the first place. Because they didn't want me running."

"They? I thought you said you didn't remember what happened to your foot."

"I remember. Just don't like talking about it. The toes are gone and talking about them is not going to bring them back." He frowned. "It's not the only mark on me, you know. Just the one you've seen. But I got plenty of marks. You want me to show them to you, all the other places I been cut up, tell you about them too?"

"No. Of course not," Mr. Sitwell said. "Just promise me you will stay in the house until I tell you it's safe to go out."

"Whatever you say, sir," Bart said. "Also, there's a white man in the kitchen."

"Excuse me?"

"A white man. That's why Mamie got me out here, waiting on you. Told me to tell you as soon as you showed up for work this

224

morning."

He walked into the kitchen and saw it was true. A large white man in a gray suit was seated at the kitchen table while Mamie stood by the stove. He glanced up as Mr. Sitwell walked past him, but instead of acknowledging Mr. Sitwell's presence, looked back at the floor and muttered to himself, words that, although Mr. Sitwell could not actually hear them, were quite clearly angry curses.

He went and stood next to Mamie.

"Who is that?"

"Another cook," Mamie said between clenched teeth. "Mr. Pound brought him here. Apparently the plan is for me to reproduce the sauce we prepared yesterday. This man will watch me work and transcribe the recipe for Mr. Pound."

"The recipe?"

"It seems Mr. Pound is under the impression that I am unable to read and therefore incapable of transcribing a recipe myself. Can you imagine? How does he think I could possibly function as a cook in a house such as this without the ability to read a recipe book?"

"I don't understand. . . . Why?"

"Well, Sitwell, from what I gather — not from anything said to me, mind you, but

225

from what I have learned secondhand from Jennie — Mr. Pound has decided he is going to manufacture our sauce. To sell it, without a word to either you or me about it. Can you imagine?"

Mr. Sitwell frowned. "No, I cannot."

"Jennie says he and Mr. Barclay are in the parlor right now discussing it. Apparently, he now claims his deal with Barclay hinges upon it. Again, all without a word to you or me."

Mr. Sitwell glanced at the white cook. "Did you give it to him?"

"Of course not. And neither shall you."

"Why not? Give them what they want and send them on their way."

"Because I am not a fool," Mamie said, a little too loudly. The white cook looked up and shifted uncomfortably in his seat.

"I may play a fool on occasion for the front of the house, so perhaps Mr. Pound has an excuse for thinking me so. But Mr. Barclay knows better. And so do you. If Mr. Pound wants that recipe he should talk to one of us, not Barclay. And he should pay for it."

"Pay for it?" Mr. Sitwell sighed. "Mamie . . . I think you have misunderstood the man's intention. He does not actually mean to manufacture the sauce. This is about a wager. I'm sorry if the man insulted you, but none of this actually concerns us. He's upset with Barclay, wants to rub his nose in it. It's something between the two of them."

"Then let it stay between the two of them and keep the sauces out of it. I have made more than enough sacrifices for this house. I'm not going to allow these people to start stealing recipes from me as well."

"Why must you think of it as stealing? All he is asking is that you prepare the sauce once more. Same as yesterday. What harm is in it?"

"I'm not going to give them the recipe for free and neither shall you. Do you hear me? I forbid it."

Mr. Sitwell frowned. "Must you speak to me like a child?"

"Must you behave like one?" Mamie glared at him. "All I'm really asking is that you act like you've got the sense we both know your mother gave you. And say nothing."

The door swung open and Jennie rushed in. "Mr. Barclay would like to speak to you, Sitwell. Wants you to come to the study."

He pushed through the swinging door.

"At last, he arrives," Mr. Pound said as Mr. Sitwell entered the study. He was standing behind Mr. Barclay's desk while Mr.

Barclay sat in a chair that had been pushed to the side of the room and was angled to face the window. On top of the desk was a bowl in which a small portion of the previous day's sauce had been placed.

"Now, finally, let us take care of the matter once and for all."

"Sir?" Mr. Sitwell looked at his employer. "I don't understand."

Mr. Barclay sighed. "Mr. Pound seems quite intent in involving you in our negotiations."

"I want that recipe from yesterday. The one for the sauce," Mr. Pound said. "If you want me to take this plant off your hands, Barclay, then you will give it to me. It is as simple as that. Yet somehow, so far, I cannot get a straight answer as to who prepared it. For all I know none of you did. Perhaps it was purchased from a can."

"No, it was not purchased from a can," Mr. Sitwell said. "The truth is, and I apologize for any confusion about this yesterday, Mamie and I prepared it together. And, unfortunately . . . she is not amenable to sharing the recipe at the moment."

"Is that right?" Mr. Pound said. "Well, we don't need her to be amenable, do we?"

He held out the bowl of sauce. "Smell it."

"Sir?"

"Your parlor trick. As you did with the wafers and the wine. Perhaps she can't tell me what you put in it, but you can certainly tell me what she did."

Mr. Sitwell looked at Mr. Barclay, who said nothing. The man looked hideously rattled, as if his interactions with this man over the past few days had aged him several decades.

"Well? What are you waiting for?"

Mr. Sitwell looked down at the bowl.

"I . . . need a minute. The sauce is a bit more complicated than the wafers, you understand. Mamie is quite the artist in the kitchen as you are surely aware, having tasted her cooking. Her contribution to the sauce, the special seasoning she created to accommodate your dietary restrictions, was far more elaborate than mine, if less substantial in terms of actual volume."

Mr. Pound nodded. "You do understand that I intend to compensate you, don't you? Separate from my negotiations with Barclay."

Mr. Pound began rummaging through Mr. Barclay's desk. He pulled out a piece of paper from a side drawer and wrote a number on it. He handed it to Mr. Sitwell, who stared down at it, noting the three zeros.

"That is what I am prepared to pay you. Again, that is entirely separate from my negotiations with Mr. Barclay. You see I do mean to manufacture your sauce. Furthermore, once you sign proprietary ownership to me, I would like to put your image on the label of the can. It was always our intention to put someone on the label — why not you? That way, everyone will know to associate the product with you. It will mean that your role as the creator of the sauce will be recognizable even by those colored citizens who, like yourself, cannot actually read the copy. For everyone else you will be identified as what you even now seem determined to prove yourself to be: the epitome of the loyal servant."

Mr. Sitwell looked at Mr. Barclay, who clucked his tongue but said nothing.

"Perhaps we should send for Mamie," Mr. Sitwell said. "Include her in these discussions . . . Particularly as the most valuable portion of this recipe is, in my opinion, attributable to her. The precision and care that she puts into pretty much everything she prepares make her recipes hard to emulate. A talent like that . . . should be respected."

"Yes, well, speaking of talent . . . Once we have finished with this I would like to offer you a job. And I do not mean as a butler. I would like you to become my taste tester."

"Taste tester?"

"I am intrigued by your parlor trick, believe it could prove quite useful to me. You see, there are many products on the market today that make false claims as to their contents. It occurs to me that, for a man in my business, the ability to accurately account for the composition of my competitors' products would be invaluable. In other words, I believe you could make me a great deal of money."

He nodded toward Mr. Barclay. "The man you currently work for, unfortunately for him, does not always recognize talent when he sees it. Does not recognize human potential because he does not believe in it. This severely limits his ability to profit from it. But I do not share his limitations." Mr. Pound smiled.

Mr. Sitwell turned toward Mr. Barclay. "What would you have me do, sir?"

Mr. Barclay stared out the window.

"Sir? Are you alright?"

"Just as I feared," Mr. Barclay said. He nodded toward the yard outside. Three men were standing by the northern gate, peering into the yard.

"They've come back," Mr. Barclay said.

"Some of the men from yesterday's tasting, no doubt."

Mr. Sitwell squinted at the men. He knew at once that they were not from the tasting but, rather, from the Magazine.

"You see that, Pound? This is all your experiment has wrought. Now they know where I live and have no doubt returned seeking handouts."

"Yes, well, they've come to the wrong house then, haven't they?" Mr. Pound said.

Mr. Sitwell frowned. "Perhaps I should go speak to them. Tell them to leave."

"You will do nothing of the sort," Mr. Pound commanded. "Our business has not yet concluded. Your services are needed here."

Once again, he was behaving as if he had forgotten who it was Mr. Sitwell actually worked for. Mr. Sitwell turned his back on him and looked at Mr. Barclay.

"Sir? Are those men disturbing you? If they are disturbing you, I shall send them away at once."

"Yes, they are disturbing me."

Mr. Sitwell nodded. He left the room and walked down the hall.

He walked back to the kitchen. Mamie was standing by the counter, frosting a cake while the angry white cook watched her.

"What did you say?" Mamie asked him.

"Give me a moment." He pushed through the back door and found Jennie hanging laundry.

"Have you seen Mr. Whitmore?"

"He is gone." Jennie frowned. "For good, I'm afraid. Have you not heard? His uncle was assaulted this morning. Some sort of altercation with a group of men from some gang in the Magazine, apparently an attempted robbery. He had to be taken to Charity Hospital. Mr. Barclay told Whitmore not to go, that he was needed to drive the car and so if he did leave, he'd best not come back. He blames Mr. Boudreaux for what happened yesterday at Mr. Pound's tasting, seems to forget that the man is still Whitmore's uncle. I didn't know Mr. Boudreaux but it sounds terrible and I am sorry for it. Also I am sorry that it means you will have to perform double duty once more. It seems there is no one else to drive Mr. Pound back to his hotel."

Mr. Sitwell nodded. He took a deep breath, straightened his back, and walked toward the northern fence alone.

"What is it you want?" he said to the three men standing on the other side of it.

"Bring the boy out."

"Why? What do you want with him?"

"What do you think we want? Restitution."

Mr. Sitwell squinted. "How did you know to find me here?"

"My cousin works on the boardwalk. Seems he saw the three of you getting off the train in the Magazine as he was getting on. He said he also saw you in the fields just as strange tragedy struck, again in the company of a young boy. Given your propensity to show up in the wrong place at the wrong time, and always with a dangerous child, it seemed perhaps you might be the one we were looking for. Apparently, you once bragged to him about working in a big house on Prescott Avenue. Just a hunch. And lo and behold. Here you are."

"The child didn't do anything."

"He came to the Magazine carrying a gun."

"He was terrified. There were grown men throwing rocks at him for doing nothing more than standing on a corner, waiting for the omnibus."

"Bring him out anyway. Bring him out, we wish to speak with him. Bring him out, or we shall come in to get him."

"You'll do nothing of the sort," Mr. Sitwell said. "Where do you think you are? This isn't the Magazine. There are armed guards all around you, every one of them an off-duty policeman. You take one step on this property without Mr. Barclay's consent and you will be shot before you make it to the front door. You know it as well as I do."

The man smiled. "So that's it, is it? You actually think you can hide the boy behind this fence. Think no one can touch you because you work in a big house, have a master who sits inside it all day eating tea cakes and crumpets while children in the Magazine starve. And yet the truth is that's not your house. You just work there, and that means you've got to come out eventually. And when you do . . . so help me, if you don't bring that boy out to me, every black face I see walking off this property is going to pay for what happened last night."

Mr. Sitwell glanced behind him toward the house. He frowned when he saw Mamie standing on the back porch watching them. He shook his head. "It was a mistake. Don't you understand that? The child was frightened, that's all. What could you possibly gain from hurting him? How is that going to help the children starving in the Magazine while men like my master, as you choose to call him, eat tea cakes and crumpets?"

Mr. Sitwell frowned. "What if I could get

you money?"

"Money? What money?"

Mr. Sitwell pulled the slip of paper Mr. Pound had given him out of his pocket and handed it to the man. "That much. To compensate you. For whatever pain and suffering you experienced as a result of a terrified child you have already pelted with stones having a gun for his protection. Wouldn't that bring more satisfaction? And of course, my assurances that none of us will ever set foot in your neighborhood again."

"You've got that much, have you?"

"I don't have it now but I can get it. Come back this evening, once I've finished work. I can give it to you then."

The man nodded.

"Does that mean we have a deal?"

"Just bring the money. And this better not be a trick. You can't hide in that house forever."

Mr. Sitwell waited for them to back away from the gate, then returned to the kitchen.

"What was that about?" Mamie asked him. "Who were those men?"

Mr. Sitwell shook his head. "I'll take care of it."

He pushed through a swinging door.

"I'll do it," he said when he returned to

Mr. Barclay's study.

"Good," Mr. Pound said. "Then it's settled. Run and fetch my transcriber from the kitchen. Afterward you will accompany me back to my hotel and I will arrange to have sketches of your likeness made for the label."

"Very well, sir," Mr. Sitwell said.

He walked back to the kitchen.

"Your services are needed in the parlor," he told the white cook, who let out an exasperated groan and stomped toward the front of the house.

Mamie looked at him, stunned.

"You don't understand," he said.

"I think I do," Mamie said. "You have made a choice, haven't you? Without consulting me. Which means it looks like I have to make a choice too."

"What does that mean?"

"It means the Fowler. I have just decided to accept their offer of employment."

Very calmly she removed her apron and left.

Mr. Sitwell signed the agreement with Mr. Pound then told the white cook the recipe for the sauce. After that, in Mr. Whitmore's absence, he drove Mr. Pound back to his hotel. When they arrived Mr. Pound contacted an artist and had Mr. Sitwell pose for a series of sketches so that, at some later date, they could be used to create a label for the sauce.

When Mr. Sitwell returned to the house that evening, Mamie was still gone. In fact, the only one in the kitchen was the cook brought in to transcribe. He was now standing by the stove boiling pots of water.

"Where's Mamie?"

The man turned and looked at Mr. Sitwell. He started to say something then shook his head and looked back down at his pots.

Mr. Sitwell walked outside. He found the three boys sitting in the yard on a stump near the broken water pump.

"What is he still doing here?"

"Boiling water." Bart shrugged. "Been doing it since you left. Mr. Barclay asked him to stay and help with dinner on account of Mamie left like that."

"She's coming back, right?" Mac asked. He looked worried.

"Of course she is," Mr. Sitwell said. He knew she was upset, but that was because he had not yet had a chance to explain the situation. Once he had, she would realize he'd had no other choice. For while it was true that perhaps none of it would have happened had he not disobeyed her instruction to keep the boys in the house, that too had been a matter of necessity. One thing had led to another; a series of unfortunate events had transpired. But that was over now and things could finally get back to normal.

"Why are you three just sitting here? Dinner starts in less than an hour. Why aren't you helping Jennie get things ready for tonight?"

Frederick nodded toward the kitchen. "Man told us we are not allowed in there while he's sterilizing the pots. Told us to just sit here and wait until we were called."

Mr. Sitwell went back inside the house. As he walked past the new cook he said, "You realize that that's entirely unnecessary? Those pots are perfectly clean."

The cook shook his head and said nothing.

Mr. Sitwell pushed through the swinging door.

He found Mr. Barclay still in his study, still seated in the chair turned to face the window and looking much the same as when Mr. Sitwell had left four hours before.

"Mr. Barclay? Sir? May I speak with you for a moment?"

"What do you want, Sitwell?"

"The man Mr. Pound brought in . . . Why

is he still here? Mamie has already prepared the night's dinner and I am more than capable of serving it. We have no need of him."

"It is not for you to say what we have need of, Sitwell," Mr. Barclay said. "In any event, I was not aware that you still worked here. I thought you were leaving me to go work for Mr. Pound."

"Me? No, sir. Certainly not. I am quite satisfied with my position here."

"And you have told him this?"

"Yes, I have. While he was having my likeness sketched for his label. If it seemed as though I were going along with it, it was merely because I was trying to assist you in your negotiations. You understand that, don't you? I thought it was what you wanted. To end this business once and for all."

He sighed. "In all honesty, that's the reason Mamie left as she did. It had nothing to do with you. She is very upset with me, did not understand why no one spoke to her about Mr. Pound's plans for that sauce. She is, after all, the cook. She saw it as a betrayal on my part."

Mr. Barclay laughed. "Betrayal? Of Mamie? That is funny. When clearly the one who has been betrayed is me."

Mr. Sitwell was confused. "I don't understand."

Mr. Barclay turned away from the window and looked at Mr. Sitwell. It was only then that Mr. Sitwell could see how red and swollen the man's face was.

"You are *my* servant," Mr. Barclay said, so angry he seemed to spit his words at him. "You work in *my* house. That sauce was produced in my kitchen on my stove using ingredients that I paid for. All of which means that, in truth, the sauce was mine."

"Yours, sir?"

"Mr. Pound had no right to involve you in our negotiations, no right to offer you separate payment for anything. But you chose to ignore that fact, to accept his offer and thereby assist in my humiliation."

"Your humiliation?" He looked at the swollen veins on the man's neck, his eyes bulging in absolute fury. The stress of his negotiations with Mr. Pound had clearly taken a serious toll on the man's health.

"You are upset, sir. I understand. . . . Because of the stress of your negotiations. Perhaps we should talk about this later, once you've had a chance to recover."

"Perhaps," Mr. Barclay said between clenched teeth. "The Southerners will be here soon and, if you do indeed still work in this house, then I imagine I need you to serve the dinner. But the new cook stays."

"As you wish, sir."

Mr. Sitwell bowed and took his leave.

He shut the door behind him. He was confused. How could Mr. Barclay think he would want to humiliate him? After all he'd done, all the years he'd spent working in that house. He had been the man's gardener, his footman, his butler, his cook, and, as of that afternoon, his chauffeur as well. On many occasions he had been several of these things at the same time. Whatever the house needed, whenever the house needed it, there was Mr. Sitwell doing the best he could to provide. How then could Mr. Barclay possibly question Mr. Sitwell's loyalty? Was that not the definition of loyalty?

He looked out the window and saw a car pull up to the front of the house. He reached down to straighten his tie and began walking toward the front door.

It didn't make any sense. If nothing else, surely he was that: loyal. For twenty years he'd been nothing but loyal. Loyal servant to Mr. Barclay, loyal ally to Mamie. How could either of them question his intentions? Think that, after all they'd been through, he would ever intentionally betray or humiliate either of them?

He opened the front door and two grim-faced men stepped inside and handed him their coats. He took their coats and hung them in the closet.

Of course, the situation with Mamie was a bit different. He could see how, from her perspective, it might have appeared that he was betraying her, but that was only because he had not yet had time to explain why he had done it. He was quite certain that once she knew the circumstances, she would understand that he hadn't had a choice. And yet he also felt that, all things considered, she might have given him the benefit of the doubt. She might have thought to ask herself, before she removed her apron and left the house, *Wait a minute. This is Mr. Sitwell. Before I come to any unfounded conclusions let me at least hear him out.* He felt he deserved that much consideration, had earned that show of trust.

Mr. Sitwell went back to the kitchen and began preparing a pitcher of drinks for the guests.

Also it seemed ridiculous, given how long they'd known each other and all they'd been through together, that he and Mamie should have their most serious argument over a sauce. And not even a very good one. Mr. Pound had paid him for the recipe and it was enough money to satisfy the men at the gate, yet Mr. Sitwell still did not believe the man had any intention of actually trying to manufacture it. It was quite clear that the whole point was to humiliate Mr. Barclay; the amount of money Mr. Pound had paid for the recipe only underscored how much of it he could afford to waste in the face of Mr. Barclay's current insolvency. Having succeeded in making this point, Mr. Sitwell had no doubt that Mr. Pound would now put the ridiculous idea behind him and go back to his plans to mass-produce his breakfast wafers. Mr. Pound had gotten what he wanted and, once he'd recovered from the stress of actually dealing with Mr. Pound, Mr. Barclay would realize that he had gotten what he needed. Now all Mr. Sitwell had to do was resolve the situation with the men who'd shown up at the gate.

He put the drinks on a tray and pushed through a swinging door.

"Did you have occasion to read it?" one of Mr. Barclay's guests said as he entered the room. "I'm curious as to what you made of it."

"Made of it?" Mr. Barclay asked.

"The book I gave you when we were here last Tuesday."

"Oh. Well, yes, a rousing tale to be sure."

"It's based on a true story, did you know that?"

"No, I hadn't realized."

"More or less. Author did take some liberties with the facts. Still, there is enough truth in it that I thought you might find it useful."

"Useful?"

"Well, it occurred to my cousin and I that you were not actually familiar with the area. The labor situation is quite different from what you have up here. Thought the book might help you gain a sense of what you will be getting in to."

"I'm afraid I don't understand."

"What if I told you that, in truth, Cherokee was a Negro."

Mr. Sitwell looked up.

"A Negro?"

"That's right. So were all the other members of his gang," the man said. "Matter of fact, the town where the story takes place? It was pretty much surrounded by Negroes. It's located near a large swamp and slaves used to run into it all the time, trying to hide from the patrollers. They'd run off a plantation and hightail it straight in there, which was smart because it was dangerous in that swamp, full of alligators and disease. Didn't nobody actually want to go in after

245

them. From the outside it looked like the swamp just gobbled them up. But the truth was there was a pitiful group of Indians hiding in there who were willing to take these runaways in. Not just runaways, but sometimes deserters from the army too. And all of them hiding in there, more and more as time went on. Slept in the trees and ate roots and berries and whatever else they could find. Every last one of them filthy as rats. Wasn't an easy way to live, so, as you can imagine, the ones who survived were just about the nastiest, wildest creatures you could possibly imagine. The only reason that town exists is because a group of brave men and women recognized the importance of establishing a trade route through the area. The very route you plan on taking advantage of now."

"I'm confused," Mr. Barclay said. "I thought you said you were related to the protagonist. And now you're telling me he was a Negro?"

The two men looked at each other.

"You didn't read it, did you?" one of the men said. "Cherokee Red is not the protagonist. He's the villain. They just put him on the cover, probably thought it would sell more books. The real protagonist is a character by the name of John Farley. And this character is based on a genuine personage who happens to be our uncle."

"Uncle? You don't say."

"He was the town sheriff, right after the war. Not a job for the faint of heart, let me tell you. Some of those swamp niggers had been brought in to work in town. I think some people there had the idea to bring them in, clean them up, offer them a little money, and deal with them that way. But of course that didn't last. One of those nasty swamp dwellers got it into his head that somebody owed him money. Couldn't even count but he come into town one day, dirty and stinking and ranting and raving about being cheated, pointed a gun right at the man he'd been working for. That man would have been dead if he hadn't thought to hide behind a mule. The crazy fool shot the mule before one of the man's neighbors came up behind him with a shovel and put him down."

"How dreadful," Mr. Barclay said.

"Turned out this man was Cherokee's cousin or some such thing. He was so angry, he attacked the town the very next day. That was how it started. People realized they weren't going to take it anymore, that it was long past time they did what they had to do, what they should have done a long time before. Either they were going to let themselves be overrun or they were going to stand up and fight. So they went in and cleared that swamp. Braved the alligators and the filth and the disease and ran them all out, every last one of those swamp niggers; made sure they knew better than to come back. Nobody wanted to do it, but it had to be done. Someone had to step up."

He leaned forward and gave Mr. Barclay a serious look.

"Are you prepared to step up? To do what needs to be done? Before you make this purchase, I think it's important that you think about that. I know you are moving because you are thinking about the cost of labor and I'm trying to tell you honestly, that it's not quite as straightforward a proposition as you might think. You need to ask yourself if you can handle them and if you don't know the answer, if there is any hesitation in your mind, then I'm going to suggest that you consider keeping my nephew on, to run the day-to-day operations of the plant. He's been doing it for fifteen years, took over from my brother. And, trust me, he knows how to handle them."

"Interesting," Mr. Barclay said. "I will certainly take that into consideration. Thank you for sharing your insights."

"Not at all. We are selling you the plant but, as I said, we have strong ties to the area. We'd like your endeavor to be a success. Because that benefits everybody."

Mr. Sitwell set down his tray.

"That will be all," Mr. Barclay said.

Mr. Sitwell bowed and took his leave.

He returned to the kitchen. He sat on a stool by the window and thought about what he'd just heard. It was a lie of course, every word of it. Yet somehow, like the lies of the book, it had had the effect of reminding him of the truth. He might not have been familiar with the history the man had spoken of, but he knew for a fact that Cherokee was not the one responsible for starting the violence, realized that in truth he had always known.

Because Mr. Sitwell was the one responsible.

He looked around the empty kitchen. He thought back to that last day at the Farleys' house, the first and only time he'd heard his mother lie. This lie had so upset Mrs. Farley that after the cake was finished, she'd asked him to bring it out to the dining room. When he got there Mr. Farley was already seated at the table. He looked angry as Mr. Sitwell lowered the cake onto the table. Then, to his utter surprise, Mr. Farley had pulled back the chair beside his and told the boy to sit down.

Mr. Sitwell remembered doing as he was told. Then Mrs. Farley had cut the cake, set a piece before him, and told him to eat. He remembered looking at the cake and then at her holding out a fork. He remembered being very hungry but also hesitating before he took the fork, a little frightened that she actually meant to stab him with it. Then he had done as he was told.

It was the most delicious cake he had ever tasted.

"What did I tell you, Hank?" Mrs. Farley said. "The cake is fine. Lotta made it. You know Lotta. She would have never put poison —"

Mr. Farley had reached across the table and pulled the plate out of reach of the boy's fork.

"Like that, do you? You want more? All you have to do is tell the truth and it's yours. A man has come to stay with you, hasn't he?"

Mr. Sitwell nodded.

"And what color are his eyes?"

Mr. Sitwell hesitated. Even at the age of nine he was smart enough to suspect his mother must have had a reason to lie, but he had no idea what that reason was. Then he looked at the cake. A part of him must have realized he was being asked to make a choice between blind loyalty to his mother and the opportunity to sit at a table and eat a cake made by her very hand. It was an odd choice to be presented with, just as odd as the contrast between Mr. Farley's generosity and obvious anger. He racked his mind trying to think of any harm that might come of telling the truth, any harm that might outweigh his need for just one more bite.

"Green," Mr. Sitwell had said. Then took another bite of his mother's cake.

That was the real reason they had attacked the village that night. The real reason he would never see his mother or Uncle Max again. He had betrayed their trust, without fully understanding he was doing that, without understanding the consequences until it was too late.

All for a piece of cake.

He looked around the kitchen, saw the cakes Mamie had prepared for dessert sitting on the counter. How many people had died because he wanted to sit at a dining-room table and eat his mother's cake?

He stood up and walked to the cellar door.

"Mac? Are you boys down there?"

"What is it, sir?"

"Do you still have Jennie's jars of berries?"

"Yes. You told us not to touch them. Said for us to wait for you to clean them out properly."

"Bring them to me. Turns out they may be useful for something after all."

An hour later he walked outside and met a man by the northern fence. He gave him the money he had received from Mr. Pound, as promised. But he also gave him a cake box.

"What is this?"

"You said something earlier about my master eating tea cakes, while the children in the Magazine starved. And it occurred to me that you were right. You are just as deserving of this as any of the gentlemen in that house."

Inside was a large cake covered with copious amounts of jelly.

When he returned to the kitchen Jennie was sitting at the table, eating the soup he had prepared for the remaining servants in Mamie's absence and set out on the worktable. She smiled when she saw him.

"You've come back," she said. "Thank goodness."

She shook her head. "What a difficult day.

I don't even understand what happened. What exactly did Mr. Pound want that upset Mamie so?"

"Nothing important," he told her. "She'll realize that. I think it was more the stress of these past few weeks. I'm sure everything will be clearer tomorrow. You should go home."

"But the guests are here, are they not? The boys are downstairs; they ate their dinner and then fell asleep. I imagine it was the stress of thinking about Mamie leaving like that. But I thought you might need me to help serve dinner."

"No. I don't need any help. I'll take care of it."

"Are you sure?"

"Yes. Get some rest. Everything will be different tomorrow."

She smiled.

"In time for dinner, I hope. You're still coming tomorrow, aren't you?"

Before he could answer, the white cook stomped back into the kitchen. He looked Mr. Sitwell up and down then turned to Jennie. "What do you think you're doing?"

"She's eating dinner. And then she is going home," Mr. Sitwell said.

"Not until she's cleaned the upper chambers." He shook his head. "Go on now, girl.

Stop that eating and do as I say. This man is not in charge any longer. He just thinks he is."

Jennie put her plate in the sink and left the room.

The white cook glared at Mr. Sitwell. "When exactly do you intend to vacate this house? My understanding is that as of this afternoon, your services were no longer wanted."

"Perhaps. But I suspect come morning neither will yours be," Mr. Sitwell said.

The cook nodded. He nodded to the two cakes covered in berry sauce that sat on either side of the stove.

"What are these?"

"They're cakes," Mr. Sitwell said. "Mr. Barclay asked me to prepare them for him. Turns out his guests are from the same region of the world as I am. The sauce is composed of a particular type of berry they are sure to find familiar."

While the cook watched him, he picked up a knife and cut two pieces from the cake on the left side of the stove and set them on a silver tray. Then he cut two slices from the cake on the right.

The cook squinted. "Why are you doing it that way?"

"They are identical save for the berries I

have used for the compote. They are quite common where I come from but extremely difficult to come by in the city. I believe Mr. Barclay intends it to be a catalyst for conversation. Unfortunately there was not enough for both cakes. The cake on the left is for the exclusive consumption of our guests, in case it should turn out that one slice is not enough to satisfy their needs. You are welcome to try the one on the right if you like. What's left over was intended as the servants' portion."

The cook nodded. "So you are in the habit of feeding the Barclays from the servants' portion?"

"When necessary. I am indeed." Mr. Sitwell shook his head. "Listen, you might think you are equipped to work in this house but trust me, you are not. Because being a household chef is not just about being able to cook an adequate dinner. Every household is its own complex organism. To maintain it requires certain talents, which I'm sorry to say but I can tell by looking at you, you do not possess. Even if Mr. Barclay did give you Mamie's job. You would not last long here."

Again the cook nodded. He squinted down at Mr. Sitwell's tray. "Your slices are not even proportionate."

"Yes. That way I will be able to tell them apart as I serve."

The cook removed the slices Mr. Sitwell had prepared for the Barclays from his tray and dumped them back into the servants' portion. He got two new plates and cut two new slices from the cake on the left.

"Now there is no need," the cook said. "Understand me. Whether or not you do stay here, this is no longer a nigger kitchen. I am in charge now and so long as that is true, the Barclays do not eat from the nigger portion. Serve the dinner as you are supposed to and then clear out."

Mr. Sitwell looked down at his tray and then back at the cook. He began walking toward the dining hall, then stopped just before he reached the door.

"The cake on the left is for the guests. I made it for them. If you would like to try one, I would suggest you take it from the servants' portion, on the right. For that in truth is what it is. Not for Negroes, but for servants. And that is what you are. Same as the rest of us. A servant."

He pushed through a swinging door.

At nine o'clock that evening Mr. Sitwell returned to his rooming house for what would be the last time. He found Billy sit-

256

ting behind the front desk.

"Your book has taken a curious turn. One of Cherokee's many young cousins in the swamp was apprehended on the edge of town. The man who brought him in claimed he'd been trying to steal turnips. Such acts are apparently frequent but, in this instance, given the circumstances . . . no one is certain it was not a deliberate provocation. Farley's first instinct was to simply send him home, but then he thought better of it. Because what if the provocation was not the theft but the capture? What if Cherokee is testing them, trying to ascertain how they behave under stress, whether or not Farley will be able to maintain order? You see, some of the townspeople have their own opinions about how Cherokee's kin should be dealt with, but Farley has let it be known there would be no vigilante justice in his town. He put him in the holding cell with Wash. Then he gives a rather long, boring speech, which, I admit, I skimmed most of. But the point was he sought to remind them that it was precisely at moments such as these that a man revealed his true nature. Cherokee's assault will not change who they are. Just because they are dealing with savages does not mean they have to become one themselves."

Mr. Sitwell, who had just reached the foot of the stairs, stopped walking.

"That is not what happened at all."

Billy looked confused. "It is what happened. I just read it."

"I don't care what you read. Those townspeople were not civilized. They attacked Cherokee's village unprovoked, with the deliberate intention of driving out every man, woman, and child. And when Farley and his men were finished, the erasure was so complete that ever after I have had to live with not only the miracle of my continued existence, but the utter singularity of it. Because, you see, I am quite convinced I am the only one who got out alive. And because of that, I have always known I owe my people something. For a long time, I thought what I owed them was to simply survive. To make sure we are not entirely erased from this world. I had to live so that they could live on through me. But it occurs to me that perhaps this life, this world demands more of me. Perhaps the only way to ensure that the truth is what prevails is to make sure there is no one around to tell these lies."

Billy frowned. "Sitwell? As usual I'm not sure I understand your meaning, but . . . I wonder. Has it ever occurred to you that maybe this book isn't about you? I know you come from a small town, and I understand that a terrible thing happened there. But it occurs to me that this is probably true of many such towns in the South. And you keep saying you recognize the names in the book, but are you certain you did not get those names from the book itself? For example, this Cherokee. I notice you've taken to calling some man you once knew by that name but, as I recall, on the night you first gave me this book you said that you never actually knew a man by that name. And, on the other hand, there is the matter of Lotta — that's your mother, right? Well, I'm pretty far along, and as I have told you many times, I haven't come across anybody named Lotta. Not once. Furthermore, as I have also told you many times, everyone in this story is white."

"What is your point?"

"Well . . . when you asked me to read this you said that you wanted answers to some questions. But perhaps the reason you have not gotten any answers that seem to satisfy you is because they simply aren't there. I'm only saying this because it seems to upset you so, when the book doesn't conform to your own recollections. Perhaps the book is not trying to conform. Perhaps it's just a story. And a pretty good one at that. Perhaps, if you just took it on its own merit, it wouldn't upset you so much."

Mr. Sitwell turned away from Billy and walked back to his room.

He watered his plants.

He listened to the man next door snore.

He sat down on his chair. He had no dreams that night because he did not sleep.

In any event, it was not time for sleep.

It was time to wake up.

260

■ ■ ■ ■

Jennie Williams, the Maid

1924

■ ■ ■ ■

Some of our so-called society people regard the Stage as a place to be ashamed of. Whenever it is my good fortune to meet such persons, I sympathize with them for I know they are ignorant as to what is really being done in their own behalf by members of their race on the Stage.

— AIDA OVERTON WALKER

7
RETURN OF THE KING

Jennie Williams was hurrying down Central Avenue one morning, on her way to an appointment, when she happened to look up and see Mr. Sitwell's likeness hanging from a telephone pole. He was wearing a chef's cap, grinning beneath the caption, *"You've tasted the sauce, now meet the man!"* and a small drawing of a jewel-encrusted crown like the one on the cans of Rib King sauce they sold down at Schweggmann's Market. She hadn't seen the man in ten years, not since the night he poisoned the Barclays' dessert then set fire to the house, killing everyone inside it, save by some miracle Jennie herself. And this wasn't the wanted poster it by all rights should have been, but rather an advertisement for a series of cooking demonstrations he was giving that weekend at the Fowler Hotel.

It rattled her nerves. The thought of that lunatic not just coming back, but having the audacity to actually advertise it in the middle of downtown. She knew someone else had been blamed for his crimes, but a part of her always had a hard time accepting how someone could do something that crazy to that many people and not get caught. Made the world seem not just capricious and cruel but cunning. If people with the power and influence of the Barclays couldn't survive it, then what chance did someone like Jennie have? Because she hadn't even seen it coming. She'd worked with Sitwell for months in that house and not once had it occurred to her that he might be capable of such a thing. In fact, if things had gone a different way — if she hadn't been there that night, hadn't seen him prepare those cakes, and then if he had been arrested and she'd found herself called to testify — that's exactly what she would have said: "Mr. Sitwell could have never killed those people. He's honest, loyal, and just about the most decent man I've ever known." She would have been telling the truth and she would have been wrong.

But of course she never was called to testify because somehow Mr. Sitwell managed to do all that without ever being considered a suspect. The police had decided that the Barclay murders were a "white man's crime," a determination reached not so much because of the fire as the fact that it had been preceded by the use of two separate poisons, a nonfatal soporific added to the servants' soup and a lethal dosage of an entirely different substance added to the Barclays' dessert. This implied the type of intelligence, forethought, and horticultural knowledge that investigators attributed to an Anglo-Saxon mind. Angry black men, it seemed, were more likely to just come at you with a razor. The theory had been bolstered by the fact that the man named the responsible party — the white chef who'd been hired to replace Mamie that same day — could offer no argument against it. They'd found him laid out on the kitchen floor, still clutching a fork tainted with poisoned compote.

It was a conclusion that was both utterly false and one that Jennie, to her great shame, never tried to correct. She'd broken her ankle trying to escape the Barclay house and by the time she got out of the hospital the world seemed so satisfied with the lie she didn't trust what it would do with the truth. She could see how the revelation of intimate knowledge about how the murders had been committed might get confused for a confession; instead of seeing her as a victim they could turn around and accuse her of having had something to do with it. She had a daughter to think about, couldn't take that chance, and so instead tried to focus on cobbling together a new life from the wreckage Mr. Sitwell had left in his wake.

Mr. Sitwell, for his part, was simply gone. She was still in the hospital when she found out from Mamie that he was touring the country now, giving cooking demonstrations as the Rib King. A month later the cans of it were already stacked up at Schweggmann's. And they were just flying off the shelves.

"Excuse *me*," she heard a voice say, and she felt a quick push against her back. A teenaged boy in an unbuttoned porter's uniform sprinted past her and darted down a nearby alley. She realized she was blocking the sidewalk, forcing other people to jostle and push one another as they made their way down the Avenue. A man and a woman walked by arguing with each other, and two girls in plaid skirts wheeled their way around a man shaking a dirty coffee cup, which a woman in a maid's uniform dropped a penny into without breaking her stride. Three boys ran around an old woman in a brown shawl clutching her purse, and a high-stepping man in a threadbare jacket swiveled to the side to make way for two men passing in wool coats. One man groaned beneath the weight of the milk crate he had strapped to his back while another walked by singing as he gripped a racing form. One woman frowned as she clutched the wrist of a chubby toddler and another woman walked by humming to herself, the scent of her cologne trailing after her like a bridal train. It seemed as if the whole world were out there with Jennie on that city block, the haughty and the humble, the pitiful and the proud. People frantic with worry or nervous with joy, the ones who couldn't stop and the ones who had no choice but to try to keep going. People laughing and singing or sulking and frowning and all of them in a hurry to get somewhere. But who were they really? Who knew what any of them were actually capable of?

The only thing you could ever really know was yourself.

She looked back at the poster. The man grinning in it had tried to kill her, but he hadn't. Unlike the Barclays, Jennie had survived. Dragged herself out of a burning building, pulled herself up from the ashes, and emerged a completely different woman.

After the fire, she'd gotten a job working in a beauty parlor, and when the woman who owned it retired, Jennie figured she'd learned enough about the business to run it herself. Now she was no longer Jennie the maid; she was Jennie Williams, independent entrepreneur. She owned her own home, ran her own business, and had two employees whose paychecks she signed every month. On top of that she had a fine daughter she'd gotten all the way through high school who was now dating an equally fine young man. So maybe it wasn't a bad thing to look at the Rib King every now and then, if only to remind herself of all she'd accomplished despite him.

Then she remembered that there was a reason she was out there, hurrying down the Avenue. Inspired by the Rib King's success or, more accurately, her resentment of that success, Jennie had spent seven years trying to create a marketable product of her own, then another three trying to find a corporate sponsor willing to finance its manufacture. She'd finally succeeded and was on her way to a meeting with Mr. Holder, head of product development at Starlight Industries. After all that trying she was at long last dealing with someone who seemed to have both the vision to recognize the potential of her product and the money to see to it that it actually made it to market. So it behooved her not to let anything break her stride.

8
SOMETHING FOR THE BEAUTY AISLE

Jennie walked past the fairgrounds then kept walking until she reached Sutton Street, the heart of the financial district. The stock exchange, board of trade building, and the city's largest banks all had their offices on Sutton, which meant that all the real money in the city passed through it. This gave the area its own charged atmosphere and as soon as she turned the corner she could feel it, a certain shift in the energy that made her aware she was now in an exclusive part of town. The sidewalks were still crowded but less chaotic, as if everybody was determined to walk in straight lines. The men wore dark suits, there were very few women, and the only other brown people she saw were holding open doors.

In the middle of the block was a narrow brick building wedged between two skyscrapers, and a small orange sign out front that read, *"Monsieur Leclerc, le tailleur est ici.*" The building didn't look like much compared to all the bright concrete and gleaming steel that surrounded it but that, Jennie knew, was in truth an expression of power. Monsieur Leclerc's tailor shop had been there for almost one hundred years, built by the original Mr. Leclerc, who had come from France and established himself as the finest tailor in the city. During his lifetime his handmade suits had been the ultimate status symbol, instantly recognizable for their quality and unique buttons. Now it sat in the middle of the financial district that had been built around it, a symbol of power and influence hiding in plain sight like a rich man's handshake. The Leclercs did not advertise; their clientele was acquired entirely through word of mouth, and they continued to make custom-made suits for the most prominent men in the city, one of whom was Mr. Holder.

He'd agreed to see her while he was getting fitted for a suit. As she walked to the door she could see him through the front window, a tall, heavyset white man staring at his reflection in a three-way mirror, while her friend Aggie, who worked there as a shop assistant, was crouched down in front of him, making some adjustments to the hem of his pants. It hadn't been easy to

271

make contact with a man like Mr. Holder. Jennie might never have if it weren't for Aggie. Aggie was an excellent tailor in his own right and had his own business he ran out of his living room on weekends and in the evenings. But during the week, during daylight hours, he was here, taking measurements and doing minor repairs for the Leclercs. He'd seen Jennie struggling to make contact with someone who might be able to do something with her cream and finally suggested she let him try some of the customers at the shop. She'd gotten her proposal into the hands of three company representatives in this manner, but Mr. Holder was the first one to say he actually wanted to meet.

A bell rang as she stepped inside.

"Excuse me, Mr. Holder?" Aggie smiled as he nodded toward the door. "It appears your appointment has arrived."

Mr. Holder spun around as Aggie made the introductions: "Mr. Holder? Jennie Williams. Jennie Williams? This is Mr. Holder."

"Pleased to meet you, sir," Jennie said and put out her hand. "Thank you for taking the time."

Mr. Holder looked down at her hand and nodded. "Yes, well of course this is a bit odd. Not the usual way we conduct busi-

272

ness. Your proposal was brought to my attention through unusual circumstances, although, I must say, I'm glad it was. I'm curious as to how you managed to come up with it."

So she told him how, while working on a certain combination of ingredients in preparation for a meat sauce, she'd had occasion to utilize some of them as a poultice. She was immediately struck by the dramatic results when applied to the skin. She'd done some research, made some changes to the formula, and kept working on it until she'd come up with something she was sure would have mass appeal. Thus, what had begun as a sauce had been utterly transformed into a multipurpose beauty salve that she'd named after the woman who'd inspired it: Mamie's Brand Gold.

All this was more or less true. The only things she left out were why she'd been working on a sauce in the first place and how it was she'd wound up applying it to her face. The sauce was Mamie's idea: when she saw how successful the Rib King brand was becoming she'd suggested they work together to create something that could compete with it. This had seemed a reasonable goal given that between Mr. Sitwell and Mamie, Mamie was without question the better cook. Rib King sauce had started out as something cheap and easy, cobbled together from Mamie's leftovers, mixed with tomatoes and sugar and then whipped up one night precisely because it was cheap and easy. A few years later, it was one of the most popular store brands in the country. If that was all it took to have a successful store brand, they didn't see any reason why they couldn't have one too.

It turned out Mamie didn't know how to compete with cheap and easy. During the three years they'd worked together she'd come up with a whole series of recipes that were delicious but which, for one reason or another, were clearly unsuitable for mass distribution. Still they kept trying. Over time they'd come to enjoy each other's company so much that they might have still been trying if Mamie hadn't decided to pack up and move to San Francisco. The Barclay fire had caused such damage to her reputation that it had started to seem as if she might never find work in a decent kitchen again. One day she was considering offers from the Fowler and the next thing she knew, the best she could get was a job frying hot wings at an after-hours club. After a while she realized if she wanted to do the work she'd spent most of her life training to do, she'd have to do it someplace else. Jennie understood it but still had been devastated when she found out her friend was leaving. As opposed to having been carefully applied as a poultice to treat a wound, it was in the process of wiping tears from her eyes one night that Jennie had wound up smearing some of Mamie's leftover sauce all over her face. She fell asleep without bothering to wash it off, and when she woke up, her skin was positively glowing.

She figured Mr. Holder didn't need to hear all that. Instead she told him that Mamie was remarkably hydrating. It clarified the complexion and reduced scarring and the appearance of stretch marks. When applied to the scalp it soothed seborrhea and thereby promoted hair growth. But the quality that made Mamie truly unique was that it was also a cure for thrush.

"Thrush?" Mr. Holder said. "But that is a medical condition, is it not? And yet you claim your beauty cream cures it?"

"Don't just claim. It does cure it. That's why I prefer to call it a healing salve."

"And how do you account for that?"

Jennie looked at Aggie. She didn't want anybody stealing her ideas, but Aggie had convinced her that she needed to tell a potential backer enough about what the product was that they would understand why it was worth the investment.

"Vitamins, sir."

"Vitamins?"

"That's right. You advertise them in some of your breakfast cereals, so I know you are familiar with the term. From what I've read their discovery came about when doctors realized there was a connection between diet and certain diseases. Poor folks getting sick due to a lack of something rich people were getting in the food they ate. That something is called vitamins and it turns out they also have remarkable healing effects when applied to the skin."

"Is that right?"

"Absolutely. In truth this is something women have known for a long time without knowing why. But you ask any poor mother who can't afford to go to a doctor what they do when a loved one gets a rash or an infection or a condition like thrush and they'll tell you about all kinds of recipes for poultices that have been passed down over the years. They're called kitchen sink cures. A lot of them don't work, but some of them do."

"And you think it is vitamins that account for this? Based on what?"

"Research. Trial and error. Experimentation."

"Experimentation? What does that mean?
Were you working with a chemist?"

"No, sir. A cook."

"A cook?"

"Yes, sir. A very good one. A woman who
knew a great deal about food. Knew about
the effects of different foods on the body,
both inside and out. And like many women,
she knew what worked without always
knowing why. I didn't understand myself
until I started reading about vitamins."

Jennie reached into her purse, pulled out
a small vial that contained a sample of
Mamie's Brand, and set it on the side table
next to the chair. She pointed to it.

"Fish oil. Most potent source of vitamin
A and D readily available. Also essence of
seabuck berry, most potent source of vitamin C. Figuring out how to combine these
ingredients was not easy, and I'm not going
to tell you how I did it unless we have a
deal. I will tell you that it involves the use
of a very precise ratio of a certain stabilizer
that itself is very good at brightening the
complexion. After that, the hardest part was
dealing with the smell. As you can imagine,
fish oil and seabuck berry juice do not smell
like anything you would want to put on your

face, to say nothing of other parts of your body. It wasn't easy, but I found a way to manage that too. I realized it was impossible to get rid of the smell, and trying to mask it didn't work either. I had to find a way to change it. That's what most of the other ingredients are for. Don't so much disguise a bad smell as change it into something else."

"Impressive."

"Yes, sir. I imagine that's why it's done so well. I've got my own beauty parlor on Thirty-Seventh and I've been selling it there for almost a year now. It's gotten to the point where I can't keep up with demand. And that's where you come in. You get Mamie on those store shelves and I guarantee she will sell."

"What did I tell you?" Aggie said. "Jennie's smart, just about the smartest woman I ever met. She knows what she's doing and she's telling the truth. You should hear how people talk about her healing salve. Every time she makes a new batch, it's sold out within an hour."

The entire time they were talking Mr. Holder was assuming various poses as Aggie took measurements for the suit.

"It's true, isn't it, Aggie? Women spend a great deal of money trying to improve their appearance." He nodded, arms held out on either side, so Aggie could measure his wingspan.

"They do indeed," Aggie said.

"And yet . . ." He did a three-quarter turn then stopped and looked at Aggie. "What is the name of the specific condition it treats?"

"Candida, sir," Aggie said. "Affects the mouth and genitalia. Women get it, babies too. Can be quite serious if left untreated."

"And this is an issue for women?"

"It is indeed," Aggie said.

"It's not something ladies usually discuss in public, but there are a whole lot of homemade remedies that women use to treat it," Jennie said. "But, of course, they don't always work. My formula, in contrast, could provide consistent relief for anyone who might need it."

"You want testimonials?" Aggie said. "I know several women who have already tried it. I can get you testimonials if —"

"No, please, that won't be necessary," Mr. Holder said. He put his arms down and, measurements at last complete, took a seat in the velvet chair. "Testimonials would only be useful for extolling the product's effectiveness as a beauty treatment. And I think we are in agreement that that is what this product is. Something for the beauty aisle."

Jennie smiled. That was exactly where Mamie belonged: in the beauty aisle.

"After all, that's where the money is," Mr. Holder said. "Women will put anything on their faces it seems. And there are already more than enough brands of snake oil hidden behind the pharmacist's counter."

"Mamie is not snake oil," Jennie corrected.

"No, it is not. I have already had the sample Aggie gave me analyzed by a chemist. You see, I too have done my research."

He smiled. "Good work, Miss Williams. And more to the point, exceedingly clever."

Then he told her what he really thought.

He said he believed the desire for smooth skin and a discreet source of relief from the affliction of candida were concerns no doubt shared by all women regardless of differences in terms of race, class, or regional origin. This meant, if marketed correctly, Mamie's Brand had the potential to appeal to half the population. He said he was excited about being a part of the distribution of a product capable of contributing to the well-being of so many while simultaneously bypassing the more onerous aspects of the Comstock Law. According to him the Comstock Law had resulted in a profound unwillingness on the part of mainstream manufacturers to get behind any products which directly addressed even the most minor issue of feminine health — a fact which, in truth, represented an enormous opportunity, because it meant the market was wide open. Not only that but, thanks to Jennie's conceptualization of the product as a beauty supplement as opposed to a medicinal, it could be sold and displayed prominently in the front of the store instead of tucked away behind the pharmacist's counter.

This, according to Mr. Holder, was the true genius of Jennie's proposal: she had identified a real, pre-existing need and found a way to package it as an affordable luxury. That, he told her, was the key to a successful long-term campaign: finding a way to convince people that something they need is actually something they want. According to him, it was only the short sellers that insisted the opposite was true. The peddlers of fad products and flashes in the pan — those were the ones who operated on the principle of selling a lie as the truth. Mamie's Brand, in contrast, operated on the principle of selling the truth as a lie. He was convinced that, if properly marketed, Mamie had the potential to establish itself as a legitimate staple, simultaneously expanding the notion of what a staple was.

In other words, it seemed clear at the time that he honestly understood and appreciated Mamie's unique value.

"Well done, Miss Williams," Mr. Holder said and held out his hand. "Why don't you come by my office next week? I'll have my secretary contact you to set up the appointment. I should have something drawn up by then. Standard terms, half of which you will receive upon signing."

Jennie shook his hand while, behind him, Aggie grinned from ear to ear.

"Thank you, Mr. Holder," Jennie said.

"No, thank you. If everything goes as I believe it should, we shall make a great deal of money together."

Then he left.

As soon as the door closed behind him Aggie ran across the room and gripped Jennie in a tight bear hug. "You did it! It's actually happening! He wants to make a deal!"

Jennie nodded. "Thank you, Aggie. For all your help. I couldn't have done it without you."

"Me? Oh, you don't have to thank me. All I did was talk. You're the one who did all the work. I'm so happy for you. And believe me, there's going to be a whole lot of ladies looking to thank you too, once Mamie is in those stores."

Then the bell chimed and another man in a business suit walked into the shop. Aggie had to get back to work. Jennie told him good-bye and walked back outside.

Out on the sidewalk she was still having a hard time making sense of what had just happened. Was it possible that after all those years of trying she had finally found a distributor for Mamie's Brand? Because if it was, that meant everything was different. She was not the same woman she'd been when she walked into that shop an hour before. That woman had spent a decade of her life trying to create something of quantifiable value, never knowing if she would succeed. Now she was a woman who had ideas that people like Mr. Holder wanted to promote and get behind, who considered it "an honor" to play a part in their distribution. Jennie was a different person and somehow, because of that, everything around her seemed different too. The sun felt brighter, the sky bluer, the sidewalks cleaner. The people walking past her on the street seemed better-looking than they had before. And all this joy because at long last it was happening. Someday soon she would finally see Mamie where she belonged and where she deserved to be: lining the shelves of the beauty aisle.

Truth was that deal wasn't happening a moment too soon. As proud as she was to call her shop hers, being a business owner had not been easy and she'd been struggling to stay afloat pretty much since she bought it. It wasn't just the constant demands of work that made it hard; there was also the pressure of trying to pretend she could afford to keep her daughter in school at the same time. Cutie Pie wanted to be a nurse and Jennie was so proud of the ambition that it never occurred to her to give up on it, although it meant that even when business was good she had never known a time when money wasn't tight.

Borrowing from Peter to pay Paul had become not just a habit but an art form; still there'd been several occasions over the past few years when things had gotten so precarious that she'd actually considered letting one of her two assistants go. The only thing that had stopped her was the difficulty of determining which one of them she could actually afford to do without. They each had such different attributes that it was hard to say who was less valuable than the other.

Lala talked too much but she was also popular, pretty, and above all else, took pride in keeping up with the latest trends. Irene was the more dependable worker but had a narrow repertoire; she was older, set in her ways, and had a noticeable tendency to style women to look like herself. Then there was the matter of the scar, a long thin welt that ran down the left side of Irene's face and was the result of an unfortunate altercation with her third ex-husband. A lot of people thought it strange for someone with a scar like that to be working in a beauty parlor, but the truth was it was a look that appealed to a certain type of woman. But she also knew Irene would have trouble finding a job in another salon with another employer who might not think to take such a possibility into account.

A couple of months before, after she sat down with pen and paper and put together just how much a year of nursing school was going to cost, she'd finally determined to let one of them go. The next day, almost as if she knew what Jennie was planning, Lala announced that she was pregnant and that the man responsible had run off. This had frustrated Jennie to no end. She'd pretty much decided that Lala was the one who had to go and now, instead of finding herself with the prospect of one less paycheck to sign, she was instead forced to feel responsible for both the woman and whatever might happen to that baby should Jennie ever find herself compelled to turn Lala out.

Now maybe she wouldn't have to. By the time the streetcar reached Olliana Avenue, her initial euphoria about the possibility of seeing Mamie on those store shelves had hardened into thoughts of something far more practical: money. Was it possible that for once in her life she would actually have some? If the deal was real it meant that not only would she not have to fire Lala, she could pay both Cutie Pie's tuition and her mortgage. Maybe there would even be enough to expand the shop.

The car rolled past 27th and she looked out the window and saw some members of Harper's Army shouting on the corner. They were followers of Winston Harper, a man who preached that black people were the center of history. The implications of this were complicated but resolved themselves in the idea that most of what people considered to be the real world was in truth an insidious delusion propagated with the specific intent of keeping black people from realizing their true beauty and power. Winston Harper had spent the past decade touring the country and spreading his gospel before being indicted for tax fraud by the US government. Before that he'd attracted a large following in the city and now some of them were up on a small podium, dressed in matching suits and taking turns shouting passages from Harper's Doctrine through a bullhorn beneath a banner taped to the wall behind them that read, *"This World Is Not Your Delusion."*

Even though she couldn't hear what they were saying, seeing them had the effect of reminding her of yet another thing she could finally take care of now that she'd made her deal: her husband. Jennie had spent the past seven years legally married to a follower of Winston Harper, although in truth it was not a marriage so much as a business arrangement. When she'd come up with the idea of buying the shop, she hadn't had enough money to pay for it outright, and it turned out she needed a male relative to cosign for a business loan. So she'd come to an agreement with a man willing to provide his signature in exchange for a monthly fee. Her husband, Tony Marcus, hadn't had a problem doing this because in his mind a marriage wasn't valid unless it was to another Harperite and sanctioned by the organization's leadership. This had caused a great deal of turmoil in many households but worked out just fine for Jennie's loan application.

"Push back!" the driver yelled as a large crowd of people pushed their way into the car. Jennie walked a few steps toward the rear and considered the fact that that was seven years ago. For seven years she'd been paying Tony Marcus a monthly fee and only every now and then would it occur to her that their marriage meant that the shop and everything she owned was technically his. If she really was going to sign a contract, she couldn't actually do it until she got her divorce.

She got off at Union Street and hurried down 37th, past a row of street vendors and a small smattering of potential customers eyeing the various sundries laid out on their tables while the rest of the people hurried past them on the busy sidewalk. Technically 37th was part of a residential district, but it ran adjacent to the main shopping center on Union and a wide swath of commerce had grown up on the streets that surrounded it as people started converting their living rooms into places where you could find goods and services not available on the main strip. On her way to the beauty parlor she walked past a wig shop, a hardware store, a shoe repair place, and a West Indian restaurant. On the corner of Cornelius and 37th was Bosswell's Pool Hall, home base of one of the most successful of these independent entrepreneurs. In addition to the pool hall, Bosswell Banks ran the local policy game, a cash advance business, and a private security firm. The pool hall had live music on weekends, and at night it was always busy, but she was surprised to see people gathered outside at this time of day. It wasn't until she passed directly in front of the bar that she realized the door was missing. There were two police officers talking to a woman crying at the side of the building while a dozen people stood on the sidewalk, watching.

"What happened?" she asked a man standing next to her.

He shook his head. "They busted right through the front door."

"They?"

"They had masks on so nobody could see their faces. Shot the bouncer, then went in and shot the whole place up trying to get to Bosswell. A lot of people were in there listening to music. Some of them got hurt pretty bad just trying to get out the back door."

She looked back at the pool hall. Several

windows were broken and the front wall was riddled with bullet holes. A nervous-looking woman was crouched just outside the door sweeping up broken glass. Standing behind her was a row of five men in dark suits, one of whom was Mr. Whitmore.

When he saw her, he tipped his hat.

"Miss Jennie," Mr. Whitmore said.

Jennie nodded. After the Barclay fire Mr. Whitmore had given up on legal employment altogether and started running errands for Bosswell. Over time he'd risen through the ranks and was now the head of Bosswell's security business. Jennie didn't know the details of how that happened and didn't want to. They always said hello when they passed each other on the street, but besides that Jennie tried to stay out of his business. He'd earned quite a reputation for violence over the years and she knew enough to understand it was probably better to keep her distance.

People called him the Butcher.

"Afternoon, Whitmore. You alright over there? What's going on?"

"Nothing you need to concern yourself with, Jennie. Had a little trouble with some confused individuals last night. But it's over now. The situation has been handled. They're not confused anymore."

He looked out at the crowd. "You all hear that? No more confusion. It's over now so you can just go on about your business. Hear me? Just keep walking."

Understanding that this was less a suggestion than a command, the crowd, including Jennie, dispersed.

A minute later she reached the beauty parlor, the bottom floor of a converted duplex with a bright blue awning hanging over the door and a sign painted across the front window that spelled out the shop's name in yellow letters: *"Best Face Forward."* She'd inherited the sign and much of the interior decor from the previous owner, a woman from Mississippi who'd moved to the city with her husband twenty-five years before. The neighborhood was different then. Most of the people who lived there had been white and the entire block was made up of single-family homes. There weren't many black people in the city at the time and the woman started doing hair in her living room as a way to make a little extra money and also, Jennie suspected, as an excuse to socialize with her friends.

Then things changed. One by one her white neighbors moved out as more black people moved in, the homes carved up into smaller units to accommodate them. The woman became a widow and converted the front half of the ground floor of her house into a proper shop. But the transition to full-time enterprise had not been smooth, in large part due to confusion among her regulars as to whether they were customers or friends. They were in the habit of strolling in at all hours of the day, drinking enormous quantities of the complimentary sweet tea the widow always set out for them, and then just sitting there, talking either to her while she worked or among themselves.

Jennie figured it was why she'd been hired. She hadn't had any experience, but the widow agreed to teach her what she knew about hair and skin care so long as Jennie took charge of explaining to these ladies that they were trying to run a business. The first thing to go was the complimentary sweet tea. Jennie started charging one cent per cup and when people didn't like that, did away with the custom altogether. Then she'd introduced an appointment system, let it be known that anyone coming to the shop had to make arrangements at least twenty-four hours in advance, specifying day, time, and desired service. People were no longer welcome to stroll in whenever they felt like it, and as a result, many of them wound up taking their business elsewhere. This had upset the widow a great deal, but by the time she retired, Jennie had figured out how to replace them with women who understood the difference between a customer and a friend.

Actresses and prostitutes. She'd met plenty of both during the years she'd spent as a performer touring with Happy Hillman and knew that many were in the habit of visiting a beauty parlor several times a week. These women put a premium on hair and makeup because their livelihoods depended on it, so they were the ones she'd focused on when trying to drum up business for the shop. In the end they were the ones who'd kept the widow from going bankrupt. Yet all they got in return from the widow was a puckered frown.

It was Jennie's shop now. She pushed through the door and saw her two assistants, Irene and Lala, already inside. Irene was standing by the mirror curling her hair while Lala was busy setting up her station. Jennie could tell by the tight-lipped expression on Irene's face that the two of them were arguing.

"That's not true, Lala," Irene said between clenched teeth. "There's black people all over that place. Black people in there all the time."

293

"They got black people working in there."

"Well, that's all he's doing. Working. He's just a headliner is all. It's the same thing."

"What are you two going on about?" She hung her coat up by the door and walked to the cabinet beside the register, looking for her divorce papers. She'd had them drawn up soon after she got married and then tucked them away for the day she could finally sign.

"Lala went to hear Dr. Livingston give a speech at the library last night. Now she won't shut up about it."

"A speech about what?"

"All the progress we've been making," Lala said. "All our advancements in art and science and music. How our people are out there making great strides, but you wouldn't know it from reading a magazine or going to the theatre or the grocery store. Because everywhere you look all you see is some fool hawking pancake mix or dish-washing powder or meat sauce. That's why we've got to protest."

"Protest?"

"Haven't you heard?" Irene said. "The Rib King is coming to town."

Jennie looked up from her drawer. "I saw an ad."

"So you already know then," Lala said.

"Not bad enough having to look at those ads for that sauce all the time, now he's decided to come here and put on his coon show at the Fowler. A place that doesn't even let black people sit in the dining hall."

Jennie frowned and said nothing. She knew that even if people didn't know about his crimes a lot of them still didn't like the Rib King on account of his advertisement campaign. They said it promoted a bad image, which of course it did, although Jennie imagined it wouldn't have been such a big deal if the sauce weren't so popular. For a couple of years, it had seemed like the Rib King was everywhere. Face popping up on billboards across the city, ads in all the newspapers and magazines. Someone turned his slogan into a song they used to play on the radio and someone else made up a dance to go along with it, which, for about six months, was very popular. The character got to be so well-known that a decade later you could still use the phrase "doing the Rib King" to signify anybody acting a fool without seeming to realize that was what they were doing and pretty much anyone anywhere in the country would have known what you meant.

"It's not a coon show," Irene said. "It's a cooking demonstration."

"It's a coon cooking show. Cooking with a coon."

"So what if it is? The man is just doing what he's got to, to survive. Just like everyone else out here. Once he's got that money he can do whatever he wants with it. It's called being strategic. So white folks think he's a fool, so what? What difference does it make so long as he knows he's not one?"

"That's where you're wrong," Lala said. "Makes a difference what people call you, a big difference. It's why you should go to a lecture sometimes, get yourself educated. You'd find out that things are related, that it's not just about the Fowler, not just about one door. Doors are closing to us all over the city, and we can't just stand around doing nothing. They tell us we can't go here, they tell us we can't go there, and it don't matter how much money you've got. Why you think they got us all packed in here on the south side like a bunch of sardines? We got people moving in every day, and where are they supposed to go? And every time somebody acts a fool trying to slip in through a back door it makes it that much harder for all of us trying to get in through the front."

"And somehow you think that's the Rib King's fault? Why? Because of a cooking demonstration?" Irene shook her head. "Girl, where do you think we are? This is the United States of America. Things don't work like that around here and you know it. Or you should, anyhow."

Jennie kept her head down, still looking through the drawer. All this talk about the Rib King was making her nervous.

"I don't understand why you are wasting time talking about it. Got nothing to do with us, we're not going to the Fowler. What do you care what he does?"

"Because that's not all he's doing," Lala said. "Turns out that's not the real reason he's here. Apparently he used to live here. Got some kind of connection to the community. Now he got his name on a list of sponsors for the art show. People saying it's going to be the social event of the season, everybody else on that list represents our finest citizens. We don't want to look at his name, think about all the damage he's done, while we're reflecting on black genius."

"Black genius? Man out there trying to do something nice with his money and you still complaining. It's stupid anyway, standing around waiting for some white man to open a door for you. Instead of criticizing the man you ought to be doing like he do. Figure out how you can get inside so you can double back around and let somebody else in."

They looked at Jennie still riffling through her drawer.

"What do you think?"

"Me?" Jennie looked up. She hadn't talked about what the Rib King had done the night of the Barclay fire in ten years and she had no intention of starting now. "I'm not a clown. I think if that's all white folks see, then maybe it's all they want to see. Also I think that if someone really wanted to do something for the community, that money could have gone to something useful, like putting food in people's mouths. Got people out there starving and you all standing around arguing about some art show. Anyhow that's not why you here, remember? That's not what I'm paying you to do."

She looked back down at her drawer, pretended to be distracted by her continuing search for her annulment papers. She knew they were in there somewhere, but all she saw were bills.

"I just don't see how you can put all that weight on one man, Lala. I'm not saying I like all that he does, but he didn't make this world. And he's not like Dr. Livingston. He's not rich. Don't you know that? All you got to do is read the label. They got his whole story, right there on the back of the can. How he started out working for some cracker colonel down in Kentucky, how Rib King sauce was that old man's favorite recipe. Wasn't until the colonel died that the Rib King made his way north and started working for a man named Mr. Pound —"

"That's a lie," Jennie said. The other two women stared. "I knew that man," Jennie explained.

"Who? The colonel?"

"The Rib King. He used to work with me, at that house I was at when I first got here."

"What house? You mean the one that burned up in that fire?" Irene squinted. "How come you never mentioned that before?"

"I didn't think it was important," Jennie lied. "Anyhow he wasn't the Rib King when I knew him. But he's not from Kentucky. He's from Florida. And he wasn't the cook. He was the groundskeeper."

Irene nodded. "Well, see? Now you're just proving my point. Talk about somebody making something out of nothing." She looked at Jennie. "How did your meeting go, by the way? With Mr. Holder?"

"It went fine. He wants to make a deal."

"What? You serious? I mean, not that I

doubted you. It's just been a long time coming, don't you think? And then, when you didn't say anything . . . I figured it was probably best not to ask."

Jennie finally found her envelope wedged against the bottom of the drawer. She pulled it out and slammed the drawer shut.

"I got to go run an errand."

She pushed through the door and found two women waiting outside it.

"You all open yet?" the older one said.

"Not for another half hour. You got an appointment?"

"No, ma'am. Not specifically. It's why we come so early."

The older woman put her arm around the younger and gave her a little shove toward Jennie.

"This is my sister's child, she just come up from Alabama. I already explained it to Irene. Girl has no money and her mother can't help her, so that's what I'm trying to do. She's a singer and she can dance. She's been going to auditions but hasn't gotten any work. I keep telling her she got potential; it's just no one can see it yet. Still walking around looking country when of course she's in the city now." The woman smiled. "Hoping maybe Irene could help with that."

Jennie nodded. "Irene said it's alright?"

"She did."

"Come on in then. If Irene said she'd help you, then I imagine she can."

"You hear that? Go on inside," the woman said. "They're going to take care of you, fix you up. I'll come back to pick you up in an hour." She turned around and started walking down the street.

Jennie led the girl inside. "How long you been living here?"

"Six months."

"That woman really your aunt?"

"I guess."

"Enough of one to put you to work, is that it?" Jennie shook her head. Actresses and prostitutes. A lot of people acted as if they couldn't tell the difference. But Jennie could.

"Irene? Go on in the back and get this child a bottle of lactic acid."

"I was going to get to that. Later."

"Well, go on and get to it now," Jennie said.

Then she went to see her husband.

9
AN UNORTHODOXY

Mamie was the one who'd introduced them. Before she left for San Francisco, Jennie told her how she wanted to buy the shop but didn't have enough money to pay for it and couldn't get a loan because she was a woman. Mamie told her not to give up, said she knew somebody she thought might be willing to help if Jennie was willing to offer him a little money in return. She said this man was someone Jennie could trust, someone she was almost 100 percent certain would never try to cheat her. She said that the only reason she wasn't 100 percent was on account of she'd been so wrong about the Rib King.

She'd arranged a meeting at a local diner and Jennie was introduced to a tall, handsome man who owned his own store. He hadn't talked much, answered most of Mamie's questions with a simple yes or no and spent most of that first meeting staring down at a cup of coffee on the table between them. Jenny knew she was taking a chance by trusting him, but the only other option was trying to get money from Dewey Jenkins, the man who ran Bosswell's cash and loan business. That was where most people went when they needed money and needed it fast. Jennie was not yet convinced she was that desperate and so, largely on the strength of Mamie's having vouched for each of them as good, honorable people, neither of whom had any interest in taking unfair advantage of the other, she and Tony had gone down to the courthouse and gotten married. Jennie had vowed to make all her loan payments on time as well as pay Tony a small monthly fee for the duration of their marriage. Tony had vowed to be satisfied with this fee and otherwise stay out of her business.

In that sense, it had been a happy marriage. Their arrangement worked well, but she didn't know much about Tony's life outside of it. Harperism and the Doctrine Tony lived by were part of a philosophy and a movement she barely understood. It made sense in the broad strokes of slogans Harper's followers were fond of shouting on crowded corners: *Buy Black. Love Your Community. Stay Awake.* But anytime she asked

Tony to explain what those slogans actually meant, she wound up feeling more confused as opposed to less.

When she got to Tony's shop an elderly man in a gray coat was standing in front of the store, gluing a sign to the window. He stopped what he was doing when he saw her walk past him on her way to Tony's apartment.

"You going up to see Tony? Mind giving him this?" He held out a small cardboard box. Inside it was a roll of tape and stack of index cards with the word *"UNORTHO-DOXY"* written on one side of each. It was the same word spelled out on the sign he was gluing to the window.

"What are these?"

"Buyer bewares. Need to be affixed to all products not officially sanctioned for sale by leadership decree."

She looked down at the cards. It was a large stack.

"Tony knows which ones to put these on?"

"He should. All of them."

"All of them?"

A man in a delivery uniform walked by. " 'He who claims to know confusion best be careful lest confusion claim him,' " he said.

"You got that right," the old man called

304

back and smiled.

He looked at Jennie. "The beware is not so much for the product being sold as the man doing the selling. You see, Tony has been talking a little crazy lately. Someone asks him a question about something he's selling in that store, all kinds of crazy talk liable to come out of his mouth. Can't actually shut him down until the end of the month, when the elders meet. Until then I'm hoping this will be enough."

"Shut him down?"

A woman in a green frock coat walked by, brow furrowed and muttering to herself as she headed into the store. The old man tipped his hat.

"Afternoon."

"You ought to be ashamed of yourself," the woman said. "Doing that poor boy like this. 'The root of confusion is fear.' " She stomped inside the store.

The man sighed and looked back at Jennie. "Memetic device."

"What?"

"The cards. Just as much for Tony as for any potential customers. I'm hoping that when he looks at them he will think about what he's doing, reflect on his so-called choices."

Jennie shook her head. "I don't under-stand."

"That's why Tony needs to post the cards."

"You're saying he did something crazy, something unorthodox, and now you want him to close the shop?"

"Not what I want. Not what I want at all. But this is not about me. Not about Tony either. It's about what is."

"What?"

The man frowned. "You should come to a meeting sometime, girl. If you did, you'd know that the Doctrine teaches us what is. It is only through study and reflection upon what is that we come to understand what should be. Tony is out there confusing people, talking about some other mess al-together, something he calls 'what could be.' Which by definition is a heresy predicated on delusion."

"I still don't understand."

"How could you? You don't even know your own name."

"It's Jennie. Jennie Williams."

"Exactly." The man shook his head. "That's alright, girl. Nobody is coming to you for understanding anyhow. That's what the Doctrine is for. Tony just needs to affix the cards."

The woman in the frock coat walked back

out of the store. She took a deep breath and in a loud voice said, " 'He who knows what is will be held accountable for it.' "

To which the man responded, "And 'he who knows what's not is going to be held accountable for that too.' "

The woman put a hand on her hip. " 'I am the bulwark against darkness,' fool. 'That is the beauty of the I.' "

" 'Whereas you is the way of indifference,' " the man responded. " 'Not only are you fighting the wrong war, you not even on the right battlefield.' "

Jennie listened to them go back and forth like that for a moment, shouting passages from the Doctrine at each other, getting increasingly angry as they did. Confused, she took the cards and walked up the staircase that led to Tony's apartment.

She knocked on the door, still confused when a woman pulled it open, looked Jennie up and down, and said, "The answer is no."

"What?"

"You heard me. You are not welcome here. We're going to vote when the elders meet and until then, nobody wants to hear it. So just turn around and take your stupid cards with you."

Jennie looked down at the cards in her

hand. "Oh, no, these are not mine. You don't understand —"

"I do though. When the elders meet you will get your chance to speak. And I'll get mine. Until then you've got no business bothering the man in his home."

Jennie frowned. The woman was half a foot taller than Jennie and just the way she stood there, blocking the doorway with her arms folded across her chest, made Jennie bristle.

"I'm not here to see you. Here to see Tony."

"Well, you can't."

"Who says?"

"I do."

"And who are you?"

"Someone who actually believes in the future of the movement. Someone not so stuck in the past they can't see when it's time to make a change. That's who I am. Who are you?"

"I'm Tony's wife."

"Wife?"

That shut her up. She shrank away from the door.

"Oh. I'm sorry. . . . I didn't realize Tony was married."

"Well, now you do," Jennie said and pushed past her into the house.

She walked through the front room, one wall of which was covered with a large portrait of Winston Harper. The other sides of the room were lined with books: great stacks of them sitting on homemade shelves made of planks of wood separated by cinder blocks that stretched from the floor to the ceiling. There were still more books lining the hallway that led to the kitchen, where she found Tony sitting slumped at a small wooden table while a large man in a blue suit stood over him with his hands clasped behind his back.

Tony sat up straight as soon as he saw her pass through the door.

"What are you doing here?"

"Hello, Tony. Nice to see you too."

Tony shook his head. "Not a good time, Jennie. I'm in a meeting. Didn't Mary Jane tell you now was not a good time?"

"Mary Jane? Is that her name?"

"Who is this, Tony?" the man asked.

"That's his wife," Mary Jane said. She was standing in the doorway to the kitchen, watching them, lips pursed together as she frowned.

"Wife?" The man smiled. "Why, Tony. You didn't tell me you were married."

"That's because I'm not. What are you doing here, Jennie? Can't you see I'm busy

309

right now?"

"Oh, it's alright, Tony. I don't mind the interruption," the man said. "Seemed like our conversation was starting to get a little off track anyhow."

He put out his hand. "I'm Roderick Peters. Pleasure to meet you." He squinted. "Wait a minute. I know you. You work in that beauty shop on Thirty-Seventh, don't you? Just a couple blocks from Bosswell's Pool Hall? I took my sister there a couple of times."

"I don't work there," Jennie said. "I own it. That's my shop."

"You don't say?"

"Your shop, yeah, if you want to call it that," Tony said. "Really it's just a storefront. Seem like all somebody got to do these days is put a couple chairs in their parlor room and people will call it a shop."

Jennie blinked.

"Now, Tony, that's no way to talk about your wife's business," Roderick said.

"I told you, she's not my wife," Tony said. "We got a little arrangement going on, but we're not really married. The truth is, I barely know the woman." He looked at Jennie. "What do you want anyhow?"

"A divorce," Jennie said. She dropped the envelope on the table in front of him.

Tony looked at the envelope, then back at Jennie. His hands were shaking as he reached inside and pulled the annulment papers out.

"Mary Jane? Bring me a pen."

Mary Jane disappeared down the hall and came back with a pen. Tony signed the paper then handed it to Jennie.

"There you are, Jennie. Happy?"

"I guess." Jennie frowned. Somehow she'd been expecting something more from him, although when she thought about it, she wasn't sure what.

"Alright then. So it's settled. We're not married, just like I said. Why don't you go home, will you? I was right in the middle of discussing an urgent matter with this gentleman."

Jennie looked at Roderick. "Nice to meet you anyhow. Tell your sister to come back anytime."

She turned to Mary Jane. "You too, if you decide you want to do something about that acne. I got something for women like you, just so you know. You don't have to walk around looking like that if you don't want to."

"Bye-bye, Jennie," Tony said.

Jennie snatched her envelope from the table and stomped out. As she moved down the hall, she could hear them still talking about her.

"Well now, Tony, you're just full of surprises, aren't you? Why didn't you tell me you were married?"

"Because I'm not. Not really. Just trying to help a woman in need is all. Probably can't tell by looking at her, but that woman has had a hard life. Born on some dirt farm in Alabama. Mama married her off to some old man when she was eleven. Had a baby by him by the time she was twelve. Had to join the damn circus just to get away from that man and she's been hustling and struggling to take care of herself and that child ever since. Now here she comes wanting to open her little storefront, have some stability for once in her life. And all it took to make that possible was a man signing his name on a piece of paper. So that's what I did."

Jennie's jaw dropped. She couldn't believe what she was hearing, that that was how Tony saw her, how he talked about her when she wasn't around. And the worst part about it was it was all true. Jennie's mama had married her off to a man who'd had nothing to recommend him but a house with indoor plumbing. She'd lived in that house for four years, until Cutie Pie was finally old enough to run away with her. They'd joined a circus, then hooked up with Happy Hillman and spent the next eight years singing and dancing as the Dancing Darling Williams Sisters. But how did Tony know that? She'd never told him. Her past was something she didn't like to think about, much less discuss with other people.

She felt dizzy all of a sudden, a queasiness rolling up from the pit of her stomach, but somehow found the strength to keep walking. When she reached the door she realized she was still holding the box of cards and set it on the floor before she stumbled down the stairs and back onto the sidewalk where the man and the woman in the frock coat were still shouting passages from the Doctrine at each other.

" 'I am always with you, the bulwark against fear. I am the reason you never walk alone. . . .' "

It wasn't until she was back at the shop, one of her customers already sitting in her chair, that she remembered there was someone she had told: Mamie. When Mamie first came to visit her in the hospital, she hadn't been doing well. Still in shock from Mr. Sitwell's violence, laid up in bed with a broken ankle, staring at the walls, and crying all the time. All kinds of crazy nonsense had probably come out of her mouth while Mamie just sat there, listening to it. But she'd been so out of it at the time she couldn't really remember what she'd said.

Apparently, Mamie remembered. Jennie figured Mamie must have told Tony at least some of it when she was trying to convince him to marry her.

"Something wrong?" the woman in her chair said. She was watching Jennie scowl in the mirror in front of them.

Jennie nodded and tried to smile. "No, you're alright. Just keep your head down."

She looked around her shop. On one side of the room a teenaged beauty queen sat admiring her reflection while Lala crouched behind her and whispered compliments in her ear. On the other side, Irene was holding a curling iron over the head of a woman with a book balanced on her lap. While the woman read her book, Irene pivoted around her chair and stopped periodically to squint at both her handiwork and her own reflection in the mirror. That was how Irene worked: slowly and methodically, observing her client's hair from all possible angles, somehow managing to assume a series of dramatic poses as she did.

Tony had had no cause to disrespect her shop. As mad as she was about the things he'd said about her, she was more offended by his trying to downgrade her place of business. She was proud of her salon, proud of the work they did there, knew for a fact that the three of them together were up to the standard of any salon in the city. They each had different styles that complemented one another; they appealed to different types of customers and were capable of serving a wide variety of needs. Lala got a lot of requests from women who wanted to be pampered and petted, while Irene tended to attract serious, professional women, women who knew they were judged by their appearances but were no longer impressed by that fact. They were immune to Lala's flattery, didn't want their time and money wasted, and so preferred the cold, tight professionalism with which Irene carried herself, a performance they understood and respected all the more, Jennie suspected, because of the scar.

Jennie took care of what was left. Her beauty treatments were expensive, and so the women who requested her tended to be either the ones who could most afford it or the ones so harried and harassed by their daily lives that they hadn't been able to do anything about a problem until it got so bad they didn't have a choice but to see an expert.

"Everything alright?" The woman in her chair was staring in the mirror again, trying to intuit meaning from the expression on Jennie's face.

Jennie smiled. "Will be." She looked down at the woman's scalp. The woman had two jobs, five children, and a husband who was never home. She'd been using lye to smooth out her hair for years, not realizing how much damage she was doing until it started falling out in patches.

"Just relax."

Jennie dipped her finger into a small vial of Mamie's Brand. She massaged it into the woman's scalp and tried to think of the best way to tell her that sometimes things seemed to get worse before they got better.

After they closed for the night Jennie went upstairs to the apartment she shared with Cutie Pie. Despite her best efforts, she was still thinking about the things Tony had said. It seemed like the good feeling she'd had before giving him those annulment papers was long gone and she was having a hard time getting it back.

She went to the kitchen. She knew what her past might have looked like to other people. That's why she didn't like to talk about it. It was also why she would always be grateful to Mamie. When she'd gone to Mamie all those years ago needing a job, she'd never even worked in a house before. She'd spent eight years on the road doing whatever seemed necessary to survive. Instead of judging her for it, Mamie had considered her background and assessed it for what it actually meant: smart enough to train.

She opened the icebox, where a pound of ground beef had spent the day sitting in a marinade of one of Mamie's unmarketable sauces. As she set it in a pan she remembered the way Mamie had fussed at her while she was teaching her to make it. She hadn't minded because she'd recognized that Mamie's impatience had less to do with anger than a determination that Jennie get it right, a belief that she was more than capable of that. This determination and faith in her basic abilities had touched Jennie because no one else had ever taken the time to teach her much of anything.

She lit the oven. No, that wasn't entirely true. Her first husband, Cutie Pie's father, was the one who had taught her to read. He had owned a small store that sold livestock feed and had it in his mind that one day she would work there with him, not seeming to realize that she spent most of their marriage thinking up ways to kill him.

She placed the pan in the oven and set the timer for thirty minutes. That was how Jennie spent her childhood. Before she started performing with Cutie Pie she'd spent four years trapped in a small house trying to think up ways to kill her husband. And maybe that sounded pitiful but it was how she'd survived being married to him. How she'd learned not to complain, not to fuss, not to fight and above all, how to survive. It might have looked like acceptance, but in truth it was the opposite. She'd done her chores, studied her lessons, let him climb into bed with her at night. All the while convinced that one of them was about to die, that either she would kill him or he would kill her for daring to try. Either way, it would all be over soon.

Then she found out she was having a baby.

"Mama? Are you alright?"

She looked up from the stove and saw Cutie Pie coming in through the front door.

"Did something happen at the shop?"

"No, Cutie, everything is fine," Jennie said and wiped her eyes. "Just got a little upset on account of something with Tony."

"Tony?"

"I had to go see him today. He was talk-ing about my past, acting like he knows me when of course he's wrong. Bunch of old-timey stuff I don't even remember anyhow."

"Well, if you don't remember, how do you know he was wrong?" Cutie said as she hung up her coat.

"Because I know me," Jennie said. "I know who I am."

She smiled as Cutie came and took a seat at the table. Every time Jennie looked at her daughter she couldn't help but realize that whatever she'd been through in this life, it was all worth it if that's what it took to get Cutie Pie born.

"What are you doing home so early any-how? I thought you were having dinner with your beau, Theodore, tonight."

Cutie Pie had been dating the son of a doctor for the past three years, one of her fellow students at the private high school Jennie had insisted she attend. They'd gone without dinner sometimes just to cover the girl's tuition, in part because Jennie wanted to make sure that if her daughter was going to take up with a boy it would be one of the affluent students she was now surrounded by. If there was one thing her childhood had taught her it was that she would never allow her daughter to sell herself cheap. When

319

Cutie Pie got married it would be to someone who had a lot more going for him than
a house with indoor plumbing.

"Not tonight. Honestly, Mama? We had a
little argument."

"You did?" Jennie was surprised. She
couldn't imagine what the two of them
could possibly have to argue about. Cutie
Pie was beautiful and brilliant, Theodore
was rich and easygoing. They were a perfect
match.

"What were you arguing about?"

"Oh, it was stupid, really. Believe it or not
it started with a James Johnson song."

"What?"

"Remember the other night, when he took
me to that reception for his friend Reggie's
engagement? Remember? I told you about
that."

"That's right. I remember."

"Well, somehow we started arguing about
a poem by James Weldon Johnson. Theodore's friends didn't even know it was a
song. I told them I knew for a fact it was a
song because I used to sing it."

"That's right. You did. You sang it beauti-
fully too." Jennie squinted. "Did one of
those stuck-up people say something about
you being on the stage?"

"No, Mama. They just didn't know. Reggie

asked to hear it, so they'd know the tune. I sang it. Well, Theodore got mad about that. He said he didn't like me singing for other people, that he preferred to think my singing was just for him."

"Oh. Well, I can see how that's kind of annoying." She couldn't, really, but she nodded anyway. "But also kind of sweet. Don't you think? Just one of those sweet, annoying things boys do when they fancy you."

"But I don't sing for him, Mama. I sing for myself. It's not our thing. It's *my* thing. He's got nothing to do with it," Cutie Pie said. She shook her head. "It bothers me, Mama. I know we've been together for a long time. But it seems like he has a way of doing things that I know is supposed to be nice, but it doesn't actually feel nice at all. Honestly? They just make him seem simpleminded."

"Simpleminded?"

Jennie had to think about that. She was having a hard time understanding why Cutie Pie was so upset. But she tried.

"Well, maybe he is simpleminded. But I'll tell you something, Cutie. That's not necessarily a bad thing. You don't want no complicated man anyhow."

"No?"

"No. Too much work. Trust me on that.

The simpler the better when it comes to men."

The timer went off. Jennie walked to the oven.

Cutie Pie looked down at the envelope on the table.

"What's this?"

"Tony signed the divorce papers."

"Oh. Well, that's good news, right?"

"Yes. It's good news," Jennie said. "Means I'm finally free. Means I don't have to worry about some man waking up one day and deciding he wants to cheat me. And that's not all." She smiled. "Someone wants to buy my healing salve. Somebody who works for a big company wants to start selling Mamie in all the stores."

"For real?"

"That's right. Starlight. They sell products all over the country."

Cutie Pie squinted. "Really?"

"Really," Jennie said.

She set a pan of meatloaf on the table.

10
A CAKEWALK

The next day Jennie got word from Aggie that Mr. Holder's secretary wanted to know if she was available to come in for a meeting at Starlight's corporate headquarters the following afternoon. She said yes even though she had three appointments booked that day. She didn't care — either Irene would cover for her or she would cancel them; that was how important the meeting was.

Then there was the matter of figuring out what to wear. Aggie had made some comments about the dress she'd worn during her initial meeting with Mr. Holder. She told him it was her Sunday best and he told her that was exactly what it looked like. He said she needed to invest in some proper business attire, that when she went to that office it was important that she looked like she understood where she was and what she was doing there. He'd agreed to go with her down to South Parkway so he could help her pick out a new dress from one of the shops there.

When she went downstairs, Tony was sitting on her bottom step, waiting for her.

"I came to apologize for yesterday. Hope you know I didn't mean what I said. This is a fine shop, Jennie. I'm proud of what you've done, proud I had something to do with it."

"Oh, you didn't do that much. Just signed your name on a piece of paper is all, remember? And I paid you to do that." She shook her head. "That's something, isn't it? Here I am, just some poor, pitiful unwed mother. Yet I'm the one who has been paying you for the past seven years."

"Oh. You heard that, did you?" Tony frowned. "I didn't mean it, Jennie. I was nervous is all. Roderick seemed to be taking a little too much interest in your shop and I was trying to change the subject. It came out wrong."

"Who was that man?"

"Just someone I've got some business with. It's got nothing to do with you. I'd like to keep it that way, if you don't mind."

"Why would I mind? We're not married anymore. Never really were, like you said. I don't need to know anything about your

324

business. I don't even need to know who that woman was who answered your door."

"Who? Mary Jane? She's an ally."

"Ally? What does that mean? Never mind. It doesn't matter. The point is it's not my concern. Soon as they process that paperwork we won't have any claim on each other anymore. I don't really know you at all. And I don't need to."

"That's true. Because if you did know me, you'd know that I'd never look down on anyone for doing whatever they had to, to take care of their child. That's why Mamie told me those things about you, by the way. She wasn't trying to make me feel sorry for you so much as remind me that even if a courthouse marriage wasn't real for me it was very real for you. She was trying to make me think about my mother."

"Your mother?"

"That's right. A very resourceful woman, much like yourself. When my father died she took over his business, turned it into something even better than it had been before. Then she made the mistake of marrying the wrong man. That man took everything from us. Used to beat on her whenever she tried to complain. So that's what I grew up looking at. And I know a lot of people probably got the strength to rise above

325

something like that, but honestly, Jennie? I wasn't one of them."

He looked out at the street at all the people hustling up and down the block as they made their way to work, then looked back at Jennie.

He smiled. "Everybody's got a past, Jennie Williams. If you knew anything about mine, what I was like before I found Harper, you'd understand that I would never judge you for yours."

He tipped his hat.

Jennie watched him walk down the block. By the time he turned the corner she could feel herself getting upset again. She understood the confession as part of his apology but she didn't know what to make of the fact that he was confessing it now. It was the first time he'd ever said anything about his life before he joined Harper's Army and, if true, it was the most personal thing he'd ever told her about himself the entire time they had been married. Because of that, it didn't actually soothe her anger. Instead it made her feel something that was the last thing she ever wanted to feel: confused.

She frowned as she pushed through the door to the shop and found Lala already inside.

"You alright?"

"Why wouldn't I be?"

"I don't know, Jennie. You looked a little upset. I thought maybe it had something to do with the shooting."

"What shooting?"

"Didn't you hear? There was a shooting last night," Lala said. "Down by the waterfront, at one of Bosswell's warehouses."

"That's nowhere near here, Lala."

"Maybe not. But it means the trouble's not over. Who knows where it might pop off next. Anything can happen when you got the Good Time Gang involved."

"Good Time Gang?"

"They handle all the bootleg in the Magazine," Lala said. "Turns out they're the ones who shot up the pool hall."

"I thought those people were wearing masks."

"They were wearing masks, but someone saw their necks," Lala said. "That's how we know they were white. Come to find out Bosswell has been messing with the Good Time Gang, trying to muscle in on their territory." She shook her head as she thought about it. "What I don't understand is why he'd do that. I mean, you'd think Bosswell would know better. Everybody knows the leader of the Good Time Gang is cousins with the chief of police. From what

I hear, half the force got some kind of connection to that gang; a lot of them were in it themselves. That's why don't nobody mess with them. Mess with them, you're going to have the whole city government coming after you. Wait and see. It's about to get real ugly around here."

"Why? Because someone saw their necks?" Jennie frowned. "That's so stupid, Lala. Jumping to conclusions like that. Getting all worked up over nothing. Why are you always talking about things you don't know anything about? You don't know what's going on, don't know that man's business. You're not no gangster. And none of that has anything to do with you or me."

Then the door to the back room swung open. Irene walked out, laughing and smiling with a woman Jennie had never seen before. The woman was carrying a large parcel, and she and Irene were talking in low voices and leaning close to each other as they passed through the front of the shop. They walked right by Jennie, and then Irene stood by the door and waved as the woman walked back out onto the street.

"Who the hell was that?"

"Customer."

"But we're not open yet, Irene."

"Yeah, I know. Came to buy some of your

products. Said she wanted to avoid the rush."

"The rush? What rush?" Jennie squinted. "Why you got people coming in and out of here when we're not even open, Irene?"

"I don't know, Jennie. I mean it's kind of hard sometimes. We are running two different businesses and that means we got two different clienteles. I'm just trying to cope with it," Irene said.

"Cope with it?"

Irene shook her head. "She's just some church lady who wanted to buy some lactic acid for her diaphragm. It's part of the reason I think we should start selling door-to-door."

"Door-to-door?"

"That's right. I know you're all excited about the deal you got going but honestly? I don't know why. It seems to me that if some white man wants to buy Mamie from you then it just confirms something you should have already known. That she is worth something. And that being the case, I don't see why you want to get a bunch of men involved anyhow. Not when we can just hire more actual black women, start sending them out door-to-door. It's more work, but then you'd keep the profits, not have to worry about some man trying to cheat you."

"How is hiring more black women going to get Mamie in the stores?"

"There you go again, always talking about getting Mamie in the stores. What do you need to be in the stores for anyhow? Poro is not in the stores. Madam Walker is not in the stores. That's not the only way to sell something and you know it."

"I want Mamie in those stores, up on those shelves, where everybody can see her," Jennie said. "What the heck do you think I've been trying to do all this time?"

"Oh, I know what you've been trying to do, Jennie. But it's not the same as what you actually did do, now is it?" She shook her head. "Anyhow, as it stands now we got ladies coming in buying real personal items and maybe they don't want people seeing them doing that. Also maybe some of them got some funny ideas about the people who come here and don't want to be seen fraternizing."

"Fraternizing? What are you talking about?" Jennie said. "Are you talking about my customers?"

"Not all your customers. Just some of them. The ones who got reputations. Maisy Day and a couple of the others. Don't take it personal."

Jennie bit her lip. "Next time, you tell that

woman that if she wants to buy one of my products she can come get it during normal business hours."

"I'm not going to do that, Jennie," Irene said. "No. It's stupid. If I'm here and somebody wants to buy something, be stupid not to sell it to them. You are taking it personal when you shouldn't. It's just money."

"No, Irene. It's just *my* money. This is my shop, remember? I make the rules around here. If you think they're stupid you can go work somewhere else."

"I didn't say your rules were stupid," Irene said. "I told you not to take it personal."

"I'm the one in charge around here. Why is that so hard for you all to understand?"

She looked at Lala, still staring nervously at the streets outside.

"Come away from that window, girl. Stop worrying about stuff that's got nothing to do with you. I'm not paying you to gossip. Ought to be glad I'm paying you at all."

"What does that mean?"

"It means you're supposed to be working."

"I am working. I do work. You got a problem with how I do my job now?"

"No. I got a problem with the fact that you are five months pregnant. What do you think would happen to you if I turned you out of here, Lala? How would you support that child? You don't have a man, you don't have any money. Nobody else would hire you in that condition. Most people would have kicked you off the floor as soon as you started to show. Because it doesn't look right. We both know it doesn't look right."

She turned back to Irene. "Isn't that what you said, Irene? You got people coming in who don't want to be seen in my shop because something doesn't look right? Well, maybe it's not my customers who are the problem. Maybe it's the two of you."

Lala was quiet. Her lip started quivering and Jennie could see the tears welling up in her eyes.

"From now on, anybody coming through that door is coming in during normal business hours. You hear me?"

"Yes, Jennie," Irene said. "I hear you. Everybody hears you."

"Good. Now I've got to go out and buy a dress so I have something decent to wear for my meeting with Starlight. Can you handle things until I get back?"

"Yes, Jennie. Whatever you say. You're the boss."

Jennie pushed through the door and went to meet Aggie at the streetcar stop. As she stomped down the crowded street, she knew she shouldn't have been yelling like that. There was a reason for it, and everything she'd said was perfectly true, but seeing as how there wasn't much she could do about it, she knew yelling only made things worse. And yet deep down she knew the thing that was making her want to yell didn't have to do with them at all. It was Tony. Bringing up her past like that, acting like he knew her. The way he'd looked at her when he told her about his mother. Trying to confuse her mind.

When she got to the stop she told Aggie what she'd overheard Tony say about her to Roderick.

Aggie's jaw dropped.

"Is he crazy? Who is he to be acting like he feels sorry for you? Why? Because he owns a stupid store that doesn't sell anything but Harperite junk? You are an inventor and entrepreneur."

The streetcar pulled up and they fell into a long line of people waiting to get inside.

"I'll be honest with you," Aggie said as they climbed aboard. "I never trusted those people. I see how you went ahead and married one and I understand why you did it. But still. Those Harperites, always shouting on the corner, telling everybody what they are doing wrong. All that stuff about this world not being my delusion. It's not just stupid, it's dangerous. I mean, what does that even mean? Real or not, I've got to live in it, don't I? They do too, whether they like it or not."

He shook his head as he paid his fare. "A lot of crazy people running around the south side these days," Aggie said as they made their way to the rear of the car. "And I don't just mean Harper's Army. Bosswell's people too, shooting each other like that. It's madness and it's about to get worse. You know that, right? Shooting up Bosswell's Pool Hall? It means somebody wants him to know they aren't afraid of him anymore, wants everybody to know they're coming for him and aren't going to stop until they get him. And once they do? That's when it's really going to get bad. Going to be nothing but gangsters running around, trying to prove who's in charge. I've seen it before, when Bosswell first took over. He's the one who's been keeping people in line all these years."

He looked out the window. "All such a waste of time. You can't wish this world away and you can't shoot your way out either. You just have to find the strength to rise above it. By being excellent. That's how you cope with this world, Jennie. That's how I got my position in Mr. Leclerc's shop. And every day I make sure that everything I do is so fine that can't nobody tell me I don't belong there. Because I'll know they're lying. And deep down, they will know it too. That's how I fight. And in the end, that's all that counts. Trust me, Jennie. Quality is what endures. Excellence is what's real."

They rode the streetcar until they reached 57th, then got off and walked through the park, headed toward the section of South Parkway that had been taken over by a group of investors representing the city's black elite. Despite the housing covenants that restricted the sale of property to black people they'd somehow managed to buy some property and carve out a few blocks of stately homes and a small commercial district where, in addition to housing several black-owned boutiques and restaurants, the most successful black professionals in the city now had offices to cater to their needs.

The two of them stepped out onto a wide boulevard and tried to blend in with the people who lived there. Every time Jennie came here she thought of the cakewalk, a dance she had once specialized in when she was still performing with Cutie Pie. It was a performance that required strength and control, but when you looked at it, all you saw was effortless grace. Similarly, Jennie knew this world was not for the tired and the slow. As calm and cool as the people around her looked, their community was bordered on three sides by hostile neighbors, many of whom resented their encroachment outside the tightly packed southeast corner of the city where most of the black people lived. Businesses were routinely vandalized and several homes were firebombed in an effort to keep them from trying to expand the border of the black belt, making this the well-manicured frontline of a turf war.

Aggie stopped walking when they came to a large two-story building with a *"For Sale"* sign out front.

"What do you think, Jennie? You like it? It's where I want to put my shop."

"You're finally doing it? Opening your own place? Congratulations." She looked at the building. "You got enough saved up for all this?"

"No. I'd have to find a partner. Thought maybe you might be interested."

"Me?"

Aggie nodded. "I've been thinking about it for a while, but now that you are making this deal with Starlight, seems like a good

336

time to bring it up. I know you realize it's better for you. You probably know more about skin care than anyone in this city, learned all that trying to make Mamie. How much knowledge you think you have that you never get to use because your current clientele can't afford to pay for it? But see, you not going to have that problem with the ladies who shop here."

Jennie looked around her on the street. Proud, dignified women with long dresses and parasols, men in finely tailored suits and straw hats. It took grit to live there, making them not just a people of style and of grace, but a people of fierce determination.

They were also people with money, which made every single one of them a potential customer.

"I don't know if I'm ready for all that, Aggie. I mean, even with Starlight it would mean taking out another loan. And I just got my divorce from Tony."

"Forget about Tony. This time let me help you with that."

"You?" She was surprised to hear him say it. She knew how cautious Aggie was with his money.

"Why not? I mean I know how good your creams are. Got no doubt in my mind it'd

337

be a good investment."

"Investment?"

"I just mean I trust you, Jennie."

Jennie nodded and wondered if she trusted him.

"Just think about it, Jennie. There'd be more than enough room for both our shops in that building. And really, it's where you belong."

Then a cheery voice called out, "Why, Aggie Dawson. Is that you?"

Aggie stopped walking and without missing a beat, his serious expression changed to a bright, sunny smile. He whirled around and grinned at a woman in a large hat walking toward them with her arms outstretched.

"Why, Mrs. Nelson! What a delightful surprise running into you!"

"I thought that was you," Mrs. Nelson said. She leaned toward him, pausing between words to kiss the air beside his cheeks. "I've been . . . meaning to . . . thank you for that gorgeous suit you made for my husband. He looks so handsome in it."

"It was my pleasure. And I must say my work is always that much easier when I am dressing such a distinguished man."

"Oh, Aggie." She laughed. "Such a charmer. What brings you out today? Another delivery?"

"No. Today I'm enjoying a pleasant afternoon of shopping with a friend." Aggie put his arm around Jennie. "This is Jennie Williams. Have you two met?"

"No. I don't believe we have."

"Our daughters went to the same school," Jennie said.

Aggie smiled. "Jennie here is an inventor and entrepreneur. She owns her own beauty parlor on 37th and is also the creator of Mamie's Brand Gold."

"Mamie's Brand Gold?"

"It's a healing salve," Jennie said. "Draws on all the latest scientific research on skin care."

"Is that right? And how is it I have never heard of this product before?"

"You will soon enough. Jennie has just negotiated a distribution deal with Starlight Industries. Soon enough Mamie will be available not just in the city but in stores all over the country."

"Really? Well, that is impressive."

"Jennie is a very impressive woman," Aggie said. "And this cream of hers is really top-notch. In fact, Jennie probably knows more about dealing with conditions of the skin and scalp than anyone else in the city."

"Is that right? Well, that certainly is an endorsement coming from you, Aggie."

"I wouldn't say it if it wasn't true. And now with all the exciting things going on, Jennie has been thinking about opening a shop right here on South Parkway."

"Is that right?" Mrs. Nelson said. "Well, in that case you must meet some of the ladies from my club. As a matter of fact . . ." She reached into her purse and pulled out a small flyer. "It just so happens that we are cosponsoring the art exhibit this weekend. Perhaps you would like to attend?"

"She'd love to," Aggie said.

Jennie looked at him and then nodded. "I'd love to."

"Wonderful. And bring your daughter. I'm sure she'd enjoy it."

"I'll do that," Jennie said.

"Splendid. Tickets are ten dollars apiece," Mrs. Nelson said. "Aggie can give me your address and I'll have them delivered to your shop." She turned to Aggie. "You I will see next week."

"Can't wait," Aggie said. He waved as he watched her walk down the block.

He shrugged. "She's nice."

"Ten dollars? I don't have that kind of money to go to an art show, Aggie. Not yet anyhow."

"You are going to realize that sometimes you have to spend money if you want to make more. Anyhow I meant that, she really is one of the nice ones. You impress her, she's going to be telling all her friends how they have to make sure to go out and support your business. That's how she is, likes to feel like she's the one who discovered new talent. Besides, I bet it will be fun."

After that they went to the boutique and Aggie helped her pick out what he considered appropriate business attire. The dress he insisted was perfect for her may very well have been — but it also wasn't cheap. Aggie told her that, like the ticket for the art show, she should think of it as an investment. She was an actress, was she not? She knew very well that if she wanted people to take her seriously as a businesswoman she was going to have to make an effort to look the part.

Jennie paid for the dress. She realized as she did that she was spending money she didn't yet have. She tried to take comfort in the fact that Mr. Holder had told her she would receive half the money as soon as she signed her contract. Even if she didn't know what standard terms meant, she figured half of it should have been at least enough to afford a decent outfit.

It wasn't until she got back to her shop and saw Lala and Irene busy working inside that she remembered how upset she'd been when she'd left. She was calm now and felt bad about it.

"Hey, Irene. Hey, Lala," she said as she pushed through the door. "I'm sorry about this morning. Feel like I might have said some things I didn't mean."

"You told us you didn't want us working here anymore," Irene said.

"Did I? Well you know that's a lie. I'm not crazy, Irene. I know how much you do around here. Couldn't get along without you. And you, Lala . . . best believe I know how talented you are."

Lala nodded. "That right? Sure you're not embarrassed to have me working on your floor?"

"What? You mean on account of that sweet baby you've got coming? Pregnant or not you still get the job done. And really, that's all that matters to me." She frowned. "I didn't mean it," Jennie said. "I was upset is all. But it wasn't really you I was mad at. It was Tony."

"Tony?" Irene said. "What's he got to do with anything? I thought you got your divorce."

"I did. He managed to upset me while he was signing the papers."

"I don't know why you wasting time doing that anyhow," Lala said. "You and some Harperite man sound like a perfect couple to me, as much as you like to stand around and judge people."

"Girl, what do you know about being a Harperite?" said the woman sitting in Irene's chair. "Excuse me for getting into your arguments. But it bothers me when I hear people acting confused about Harper's message like that. Being a follower of Winston Harper isn't about judging other people. It's about self-respect."

Lala nodded. "I'm sorry, ma'am. I didn't realize you were one of Harper's people."

"Harper's people? Me?" The woman laughed. "I mean I was for a couple years. Long time ago, back when I was still married to my second husband. I guess some of it stuck."

"So you left the movement? Why?"

"Because I got Harper's message," she said. "Honestly? Things got real touchy with those people when it came to my divorce. My second husband hit me and when someone tried to tell me I needed to stand by him, find the strength to love him through his anger, I was out. I can't stick with nothing or nobody fool enough to ask me to stand around and let some man beat on me. And really, I didn't believe Harper

343

wanted me to. I feel like the Doctrine is what gave me the strength to leave my husband, even if it meant leaving Harper's Army too. Because it turned out that was what self-respect meant to me."

She stood up and walked with Jennie to the counter to pay her bill. "Harperites are just people. Some good, some bad, some stupid. But at least they're trying. And really, when you come right down to it, the Doctrine is just words. Can't nobody tell you what they mean. You've got to figure that out for yourself."

Then a bell rang. Jennie looked up from the register and, as she gave the former Harperite her change, saw Roderick walking through the front door with a smile on his face and an excited-looking woman in a tight dress clinging to his arm.

"Afternoon, Miss Jennie. Nice to see you again. Here with my sister. She was hoping to avail herself of some of your services."

"Which services?"

"All of them, honey," the woman said. "Hair, skin, makeup . . . He's paying, so I want the works."

"Well, that's not how things work around here. You got to make an appointment."

"Oh, Jennie, it's alright," Irene said. "I can do it."

The woman sat down in Irene's chair while Roderick looked around the shop and smiled.

"Nice place you got here. I mean, it's small, like Tony said. But nice. Just the three of you?"

"Why?"

"Just curious." He nodded toward the back. "What's behind that door?"

"What's behind that door is private," Jennie said. "And actually, I'm afraid I'm going to have to ask you to wait outside. Your sister should be done in a couple hours. You can come back to pick her up then. But we got a strict policy about men hanging around inside."

"Oh, you do, do you? Why? You got a problem with men, Jennie?"

"Honestly? Doesn't come up that often. On account of this is a ladies' beauty parlor."

Roderick nodded. "Yes, well, that's something I'd like to talk to you about. Been thinking you and me might be able to come to an agreement. I don't know if Tony told you, but I work for Dewey Jenkins. Our business, you might have noticed, is undergoing some structural changes at the moment. Looking to invest in a couple new locations."

"My shop is not for sale."

"Oh, I don't want to buy your shop. I want to rent out that back room, whatever space you got available behind that door. Temporary, just until all this trouble dies down. You can keep right on doing what you do out here while we set up in the back."

"What?" Jennie shook her head. "No. Absolutely not. I don't have any space for you. Not interested in nothing like that."

"You sure? Maybe you should talk to your husband about that. Because I'm pretty sure the man I work for has already paid in advance."

He turned to the woman he'd come in with. "I'll be back in two hours," he said and walked out the door.

"What's he talking about?" Irene asked.

"He's talking about numbers, honey," the woman said. "He wants to take bets out of your back room."

"Why would I let him do that?" Jennie asked.

The woman shrugged. "He works for Dewey. I imagine someone must have taken out a loan and not paid it back. That's usually how these things happen."

"I didn't take out a loan with Dewey."

"I imagine that's why he said you should talk to your husband."

346

Irene and Lala looked at Jennie. "You know anything about that?"

"No. I mean I saw Roderick with Tony yesterday when I went to get my divorce papers signed. But Tony didn't say anything about a loan."

She squinted at the woman.

"You're serious? He wants to work out of a beauty parlor?"

It was one thing to let someone come in to take bets from time to time. But using her beauty parlor as a base of operations?

The woman shrugged. "It's perfect, if you think about it. On account of no one would suspect it. Everybody getting real paranoid with all these shootings going on. All the old locations are already targets, so they trying to keep business going by finding new places to work until it gets sorted out."

"What, so my shop can be a target?"

"No, now, come on. Roderick's not like that. He's not trying to make anybody a target. He's not a gangster. Not like that anyhow. He's a businessman."

She smiled. "Anyhow, you might find it's not so bad having some men around with all this confusion going on. He's going to pay you rent, give you money on top of what your man already owes. Might be you'd find you like working for Roderick. I can tell you

347

from experience that it's not so bad. He likes keeping people who work for him happy. I mean, when he can."

Jennie nodded. "He really your brother?"

"Of course not. Don't be disgusting."

"But he told you to say all that?"

"He sure did. And now that I've said it, I want the works."

She leaned back in the chair and shut her eyes.

Jennie bit her lip.

"What's going on, Jennie?" Irene asked her. "Did Tony take out a loan from Dewey without telling you? Would he do something like that?"

Jennie didn't know how to answer. And so, for the second time in as many days, she found herself compelled to go see her husband.

When she got to his store, the sign the man had glued to the front window was still there but Tony had taken a smaller sign that read *"NEW"* and used it to cover up the man's *"UN."* Inside, the shop was empty except for Tony. He was reading a book as he sat behind the cash register. When he saw her walk through the door he smiled so brightly it startled her.

"Hello, Jennie. What a nice surprise. Does this mean you —"

"What's this I'm hearing about you taking out a loan from Dewey Jenkins?"

Tony stopped smiling. "Who told you that?"

"What difference does it make who told me? It's true, isn't it?"

"It's got nothing to do with you."

"No? Because your friend Roderick was just in my shop. He seems to think he's got some claim to it."

"Roderick came to your shop? Oh, now, that shouldn't have happened. Whatever he said, he didn't mean it. Just talking. He's not going to bother you. Trust me."

"Why should I trust you?"

"Well, for one thing we've been married for seven years. And I have never tried to take advantage of that situation and never would. If nothing else I would hope that by now you would at least consider me an honest man."

Jennie frowned. "I don't know you, Tony Marcus. I don't even know what you're talking about."

"I know you don't. That's my point."

She shook her head. "The whole reason I married you was to keep from dealing with people like Dewey Jenkins."

"I know that too."

"Then why would you?"

349

Tony shrugged. "It seemed necessary at the time."

"Necessary?"

Tony was quiet.

"Oh, so you expect me to trust you but you won't even tell me why?"

Tony looked at her. "Honestly? I used it to make a donation to Harper's legal defense fund."

"You're serious?"

She couldn't help it. She started to laugh.

"See? That's why I didn't tell you, because I knew you wouldn't understand. I was trying to send a message, wanted Harper to know that there are people out here who still believe in his work. You know it's easy to believe when everybody else does. But a true ally is someone that still believes when others turn away. I wanted him to know that no matter what happens, the movement would live on. That I intend to always live my life being the kind of man Harper taught me to be. But that's got nothing to do with you, Jennie. And that's why I was acting like that yesterday, about the two of us being married. I was trying to keep you out of it, to protect you."

"Protect me?"

It flashed through Jennie's mind, what Cutie Pie had said about Theodore doing things that were supposed to be nice but just wound up making her wonder if he was simpleminded.

"How much was it?"

"Never mind that."

"I asked you how much."

"It doesn't matter because Roderick is not going to bother you again." He looked at her. "Trust me, Jennie. I promise I'll take care of it."

Jennie walked back to her shop. She wondered if Aggie was right, if it was dangerous to walk around acting as if the world weren't real, as if the things that happened in it were someone else's delusion. If that part of Harper's philosophy hadn't worried her before she married Tony it was because, in truth, that was the part that had always made the most sense to her. Deep down, Jennie was a firm believer in the impossible. If she hadn't been she never would have made it to the city, to the life she was living now. She would still be in Alabama, possibly with Cutie Pie's father but more likely in jail or dead.

When she got back to her apartment, Cutie Pie was sitting on the couch, crying.

"What's wrong?"

"Promise you won't be mad."

"Why would I be mad?"

Cutie Pie shook her head. "I didn't tell you the truth last night. Theodore and I didn't just have an argument. We broke up."

"What? Why?"

Cutie Pie looked down at the floor. "He asked me to marry him."

"What?"

"He asked me to marry him," Cutie Pie said. "It was when we were coming home that night, after that engagement party I told you about. He started talking about how grand it would be to have a fine wedding like his friend was planning. I said I didn't think I was ready for all that. I said I wanted to graduate first, that I thought we were fine the way we were for now. But he took it as a rejection and said he didn't want to see me anymore."

"Really? He told you that?" Jennie was taken aback. "Because you told him you wanted to wait a few months?"

It was suspicious.

"There has to be more to it than that. Is there something you're not telling me?"

"No. There's not. I told you he was simpleminded sometimes. Always doing things that are supposed to make me happy and instead make me feel bad for not wanting them. Why is that?"

Jennie shook her head. The truth was she

had no idea. It did seem odd to be sitting there crying because some rich son of a doctor wanted to marry you. She stared at her child, trying to understand.

"Maybe you just don't love him."

"No. I don't and I'm sorry I don't, because I know I probably should. I know it's what you want."

"Me? No. You misunderstand. I just want you to be happy."

Jennie stared at her daughter. More than anything, she was just relieved that Cutie Pie hadn't told her she was pregnant.

"Don't cry, Cutie. It will be alright. Maybe Theodore is not the one for you," Jennie said. "I mean anybody trying to force a girl to marry them before she is ready is probably not someone you want to be with anyhow. If he tries to force you into something now, who knows what he might try to force you to do later, when you've already signed your name and don't have nothing to say about it."

The more she thought about that, the angrier she got.

"Stop crying, alright? Never mind Theodore. We don't need him. Plenty of boys out there. I mean look at you, about to get your degree from nursing school, about to have a fine job. That's why we're doing this, so you won't ever need a man to take care of you. Whatever happens, you'll be able to take care of yourself."

She smiled.

"Anyhow I like you standing up for yourself. Like you taking yourself seriously. You got to take yourself serious or else no one else will. Got to know your own worth. Took me too long to figure that out, but you already know it. Not gonna just settle for things because you know what you deserve. That's why you're going to have all kinds of things in life. Things I never could give you."

Cutie Pie wiped her eyes. "You gave me plenty, Mama."

"I did the best I could. But you? You're not going to have to do like I did. You've got that education, and that means you can make your own way, make your own choices."

She reached for her daughter's hand. "That's all I've ever wanted for you, Cutie. A choice."

11
THE KING AND I

The Starlight corporate headquarters was a ten-story stone building in the middle of a block of high rises on the northern side of Sutton Street, just a few blocks from Mr. Leclerc's tailor shop, identifiable by a logo hanging in burnished gold near the side of the front door. Aside from the logo it looked just like every other building on the block, but as soon as you passed through the door you realized they had their own thing going on. The front hall was a high-ceilinged rotunda flanked by eight-foot-tall bronze statues of the living logos that accompanied the copy for their most successful products over the years. Wally the Raccoon, Bennie the Baker, the Starlight twins with their big, beady eyes and toothy smiles — all brought together to stare down at visitors making their way to the lobby. As Jennie walked past them she found she couldn't help but think about Mamie taking her place among them one day. How dignified and regal she would look, eight feet tall and bronze.

She passed through another set of doors and entered the lobby. She walked across the thick red carpet, past a bank of low couches toward a large wooden desk where the receptionist sat.

"May I help you?"

"Jennie Williams. I have an appointment with Mr. Holder."

It felt good to say that, to know it was true.

The receptionist opened her agenda. "Oh. Oh, yes, here it is. We were told to expect you." She stood up. "Just one moment."

She disappeared through the door behind her desk.

Not having anything else to do, Jennie looked at all the framed photographs on the walls. Most of them contained images of white men either smiling and shaking hands or handing one another plaques of one sort or another. A few were framed articles taken from New York City papers, heralding the progress of Starlight Industries. They were full of headlines like *"Confident predictions"* and *"Increased market share all but assured"* followed by accounts of the various transactions that had mediated all the hand shaking. The most recent article was dated just a month before and was a triumphant account of the recent purchase of Better Butters Corporation. Jennie knew Better Butters, knew it so well in fact that it was hard to look at the name without thinking of their slogan.

Better Butters means it's never bitter.

It was a quality brand, but she had not approached them because they only marketed food.

"Yes, the latest headline."

She turned around and saw Mr. Holder push through the door, followed by the receptionist.

"Starlight has been on quite an acquisition frenzy lately. Gobbling up other companies left and right. We in product development have no actual say in this, of course. Just have to find a way to adjust." He smiled. "Hope you weren't waiting long, Miss Williams."

"Not at all," Jennie said and followed him inside.

They walked down a long hall lined on either side by small offices. Jennie noticed there weren't any other black people in there and assumed it was why more than a few people stopped what they were doing and stared as she passed. She didn't let that bother her. She'd worked too hard to get there and didn't care what anyone thought.

They might not know what she was doing there but she did. She was there because she'd been sent for; she was there because she'd earned the right.

When they reached the elevator Mr. Holder pressed a button. He turned to her and said, "Now, Jennie, when we get to the seventh floor I'm going to have to ask you to try to look past the current chaos."

"Chaos?"

"Yes, well, as I was saying before, Starlight has been on quite an acquisitions frenzy. And the truth is these expansions always necessitate a period of internal adjustment, a reconfiguration of the existing order. We are, at present, in the midst of such a period."

When the doors opened on the seventh floor she thought she understood his meaning. The place was indeed in apparent chaos, people moving frantically up and down the hall carrying large cardboard boxes and stacks of paper in and out of the offices that lined either side of it.

"What you see is largely a result of our most recent acquisition, Better Butters. We were approached with a private offering just a few months ago, a deal which, I imagine, must have appeared too tempting to pass over and yet, in my view, might have also been considered suspiciously cheap. We are now being told there is some question regarding the legality of the sale. It seems the heirs of the former owner were not at all in agreement about the asking price. Thus, due to a lack of diligence, Starlight finds itself, on top of all else, involved in a family dispute."

They walked past a man shoving papers into a shredder.

"An emergency board meeting has been called to discuss the matter. That's what all this is. Part of the scramble to make sure that everything is in order for their arrival."

He stopped in front of a set of double doors.

"You'll remember that, won't you, Jennie? What I just said? It is intended as a preface for our meeting, the circumstances of which, I assure you, are temporary."

"Yes, sir. I think I understand."

He nodded, then took a deep breath, gripped a handle, and pushed.

On the other side of the door was a conference room with a wooden table large enough to accommodate twenty people. To Jennie's surprise, a man was already seated at the head of it. He was wearing a dark suit and was scowling over a large stack of folders set out on the table in front of him.

"This is Mr. Dumont, who has come to us by way of just this acquisition we have been speaking of. He has asked to sit in on our meeting today," Mr. Holder said. "It seems Better Butters has taken a keen interest in our negotiations."

"Oh?" Jennie said. "Wouldn't have expected that."

The man looked up. "And why is that?"

"Because Better Butters manufactures food, of course," Jennie said. "My product is a healing salve."

Mr. Dumont looked at Jennie and frowned. "Perhaps I should clarify, Miss Williams. I have indeed arrived at Starlight by way of Better Butters. But I arrived at Better Butters by way of Pound for Pound. I assume you are familiar with that name?"

She was.

If you want the best value all around, look no farther than Pound for Pound.

They manufactured Rib King sauce.

She pulled back a chair and sat down at the table. "Mr. Pound, the founder of the company, retired seven years ago," Mr. Dumont said. "The company has been sold twice since then, first to Better Butters and then to Starlight. I was in charge of the sauce division, which meant, in truth, that I was in charge of the management of the company as a whole. For the value of Pound for Pound was, as you are probably aware, based almost entirely on the popularity of a single product."

He reached into his briefcase and, in an entirely unnecessary gesture, pulled out a mock-up of the Rib King label.

Jennie winced at the sight of it.

"It is my understanding that you know the Rib King personally. That in fact the two of you were employed in the same household when his original contract with Mr. Pound was signed. Is that not correct?"

Jennie said nothing. She looked at Mr. Holder, as at last she understood. The mention of chaos had not been in reference to whatever was going on in the hall, but rather to this man seated before her now.

"Miss Williams? Is that not correct? Are you not an associate of the man who posed for this image?"

"Posed for the image?"

Yes, she supposed he'd done that too. Murdered her employer, left her lying on the floor of a house he himself had set on fire. Then, without a word of explanation, left her to pick up the pieces of her life while he got fat and rich as the Rib King.

"That was ten years ago." Jennie shook her head and looked down at the table. "I have not seen the man since."

"Were you aware he intends to make an appearance this weekend?"

Jennie frowned. "I saw a flyer."

"And were you also aware that this appearance has been scheduled in flagrant violation of a cease and desist order?"

She looked up.

Mr. Dumont sighed. Instead of explaining he picked up one of the folders on the table in front of him and pushed it toward her with the flat palm of his hand.

"Miss Williams? When Mr. Sitwell signed his original contract, he was indeed given the rights to the title 'the Original Rib King' in perpetuity. However, it was also made clear that in making public appearances he would be serving as the embodiment of a trademarked icon. The Rib King represents the epitome of the reliable servant, the trustworthy black cook, the pinnacle of professionalism and decorum. Someone you trust to have your dinner prepared to the highest standard of quality and served on time. In other words, the validity of the contract is dependent on the maintenance of a certain standard of behavior. What amounts to an implied morality clause."

"Morality clause?" She opened the folder. Inside it was a series of newspaper clippings.

To her confusion and surprise, none of them had anything to do with the Barclay fire. Instead they were articles taken from outlets across the country, all outlining some tawdry incident of public indiscretion carried out by the Rib King over the course of the past five years. There were two citations for public urination in Kansas City. Disorderly conduct charges in Memphis, St. Louis, and Kalamazoo. An assault charge in Boston and an incident of public exposure in Pittsburgh. They were all fairly petty crimes and seemed to have been written up because they made an amusing headline, due to the fact that the Rib King was involved.

"Do you really think this is behavior befitting a beloved public icon?"

Jennie stared. The whole time she'd been sitting there she'd been waiting for him to say something about the fire. So it took a minute to process the fact that Mr. Dumont's agitation had nothing to do with that. It was something else, something that was happening now.

"It is the drinking, Miss Williams. That is the root of the problem. No one wants to picture the Rib King falling down drunk, frequenting gambling halls, or being swept up in raids in houses of fornication."

"Fornication?" Jennie blinked. "That's what you are upset about?"

It wasn't so much that she didn't understand what he said, because of course she could see how the type of behaviors he described were not befitting a public icon. It was just that they were all so petty in comparison to actual *murder,* which was what the Rib King was guilty of when he started his tour.

"Your associate's fondness for courting controversy has been allowed to go on for far too long. Perhaps it was tolerated under Mr. Pound, but the brand is now under new ownership. Your associate has been informed on several occasions that we no longer want him appearing as the Rib King. Yet he continues to tour, emboldened by his limited understanding of the term 'in perpetuity' and his awareness of certain irregularities with respect to the original patent on the product itself. He seems to be under the impression that he can disregard our wishes and continue to behave with impunity. I assure you that in this, he is mistaken. Such behavior will no longer be tolerated, and if your associate persists in coming here this weekend, we intend to come after him with the full force of the law."

"Why do you keep referring to him as my associate?" Jennie said. "I've already told you I haven't seen the man in ten years. I don't know anything about any clauses in the Rib King's contract. I was not present for his coronation. Anyhow, I didn't come here to discuss the Rib King. I came here to discuss Mamie's Brand Gold."

"That is precisely what we are doing," Mr. Dumont said. "Don't you realize that? Because you see, Miss Williams, I have had occasion to look at your proposal and was struck by its specificity and detail. It certainly did not escape my attention that the arrangement you appear to be angling for at Starlight is quite similar to the one signed by the Rib King."

"I don't know anything about that."

"No? Are we to assume that it is merely a coincidence? That two Negro inventors somehow miraculously emerged from the same household?"

"No, sir, not a coincidence." She straightened her back. "There was but one inventor to emerge from that household and it was me."

"You?"

"Mr. Sitwell didn't invent that sauce. Wasn't even a cook. He got that recipe from his mama, stole the seasoning from Mamie,

365

the woman who did cook for the Barclays. And yet somehow you have managed to make enormous quantities of money from its manufacture. Imagine what a company like Starlight could do with a real product, a product that is truly innovative and that has an actual unique value. Because that is what I have to offer, what I thought we were here to discuss."

"Be that as it may, Miss Williams, given my experience with your associate, I cannot, in good conscience, permit the board to go forward with any investment in your product without making certain they are aware of this unfortunate precedent. That given, I'm afraid it is highly unlikely that you will find the necessary support for Mamie's debut. Financing is subject to board approval, and given the circumstances, I'm afraid they will not want to take the risk."

"Risk? What risk? Because the Rib King is a drunk and a fornicator, I am a risk? How does that even make sense?"

"Perhaps it does not make sense. To you. And yet it is."

"But I don't even know the man. What is it you would have me do about the Rib King's behavior?"

"Can you make him disappear? Before

this goes to court?" Mr. Dumont asked. "Because I assure you the current situation will not be allowed to continue. But until it is resolved I'm afraid I simply cannot allow the board to permit this deal to go forward in good conscience."

He picked up his briefcase and left the room.

Mr. Holder looked at her. "I told you. Chaos."

He frowned. "I can't tell you how sorry I am about this. I realize this must be a great disappointment."

"I don't understand. So there is no deal for Mamie? Is that what you're saying?"

"No, that is not what I'm saying. As I told you before, I have every reason to believe it is only temporary. This situation with Better Butters . . . is not one that can sustain itself."

"Then what does it mean?"

"It means I have every intention of going forward with Mamie. But we shall have to wait until the current situation is reconciled."

"And until then? What am I to do?"

"Well, seeing as though Mr. Dumont was telling the truth, that you do in fact know this man . . . perhaps you should speak with him."

"Speak with him?"

"See if you can't get him to come to terms with Better Butters. Believe me, he will be forced to come to terms eventually. Mr. Dumont wasn't joking; the family he works for is quite litigious and has far too much invested in that product to allow the Rib King's behavior to continue unchecked. Perhaps you could try to speed things up by working through unofficial channels."

"Unofficial channels?"

"You could reach out to the Rib King directly while he's here in town. Do what you can to put our work at a safe remove from the onerous dynamic this acquisition has introduced. Convince him to adhere to the cease and desist order."

"And how do you propose I do that?"

"Well, Jennie, you clearly have a gift for marketing. You sold me on your idea. Perhaps you should think of it that way, as something you must endeavor to sell to him."

"That is your answer? That I try to sell the Rib King an order to cease and desist?"

"It is not my answer, no." He sighed. "But given the circumstances . . . all I can say is it would behoove you to try."

That was pretty much it. Mr. Holder stood up and they exited the conference room together. Then he turned left and Jennie turned right and walked back to the elevator alone.

She stepped back out onto the crowded street. It wasn't until she was on the sidewalk that she could actually feel it, the truth of what had just happened, and even then it didn't seem quite real. Because of something the Rib King had done, a product she had spent close to a decade working on would not be distributed by Starlight. She did not understand why she was repeatedly being made to pay for that man's crimes, or how it was possible she had been paying for so long.

She turned a corner and passed another ad for the cooking demonstration he was giving that weekend at the Fowler.

"Fuck you, Mr. Sitwell," Jennie said. She didn't even realize she'd said it out loud until she looked down and saw a little girl walk by, eyes staring wide at the outburst of profanity as she passed. She ripped the ad down, stuck it in her purse, and continued walking down the block, headed for the streetcar stop.

She climbed aboard a crowded car, and as she paid her fare, the implications of what Mr. Dumont said took firmer shape in her mind. No deal meant no Mamie on the shelves, no Mamie on the shelves meant no money. She had bills to pay and paychecks to sign; she had to come up with the money to cover Cutie Pie's tuition. In less than a week she had gone from thinking she was about to get everything she'd wanted to being faced with the possibility of losing everything she had. And all because of the Rib King, because the two of them were associated.

"Push back!"

She found a seat near the rear of the car. As she stared out the window, it occurred to her that this was hardly the first time she'd felt this way. How many times had she looked up to find that everything she thought she knew had changed? That one reality had been switched for another and all she could do was try to cope with it, find some way to keep moving, figure out some way to survive. If someone made a map of her life, all they'd see was a series of wild swerves out of which she had tried to forge something that resembled a path. Her mother leaving her, Cutie Pie being born, becoming the Williams Sisters, living life on a moving train. Then realizing Cutie was not a child anymore and settling down here, in the city. In some ways her whole life was just a struggle to stay upright, to maintain some sense of balance while the world pitched and rolled around her in ways she did not understand.

They reached her stop and she stepped off the train and found herself in the middle of a great throng of children marching two-by-two up the block. She grabbed one of them by the arm, made him stop and tell her what was going on.

"They got Bosswell."

"Who? The Good Time Gang?"

"No. The police. Set up some kind of ambush up near seventeenth. Shot him in his car last night."

"Last night? So what are you running now for?"

"We're going to the rally."

"What rally?"

"Harper's Army. They're protesting the violence. Want people to know they can't just shoot us in the middle of the street like that."

He took off running again.

Jennie shut her eyes and took a deep breath. Then she started walking again, headed toward Bosswell's Pool Hall.

When she got there, a dozen men in dark suits were standing just outside the door. One of them put his hand out to stop her when she tried to walk inside.

"Where do you think you're going?"

"I need to see Whitmore. Tell him it's Jennie Williams. He knows me. We used to work together."

The man squinted at her for a moment then disappeared inside.

A few minutes later, Mr. Whitmore stepped out.

"What the heck are you doing here, Jennie?"

"Hoping I could speak to you for a moment."

"Speak to me? Now?" Mr. Whitmore shook his head. "Not a good time."

"I wouldn't have come if it wasn't important. Won't take but a few minutes of your time."

Mr. Whitmore looked out on the street and then back at her. He nodded for her to follow him inside.

He led her down a dark hall, up a flight of stairs, and into an office on the second floor. He took a seat behind a large wooden desk and said, "What do you want, Jennie Williams?"

"Hoping you could help me with a problem I'm having. One of Dewey's employees, a man by the name of Roderick Peters, came by my beauty parlor yesterday afternoon and —"

"Let me stop you right there. I don't work with Roderick. He's one of Dewey's people. That's a different division. You got a problem with Roderick then you need to work it out with Dewey Jenkins."

"I don't know Dewey Jenkins. I know you."

There was a knock on the door. A man in a checkered tie walked in and whispered something in Whitmore's ear. Whitmore nodded and the man walked out again, shutting the door behind him.

"Jennie? Does it occur to you that I'm busy right now? Do you even know what is going on? We're not sitting in a kitchen anymore. There's a war going on. Police out there acting like they've lost their minds. They shot Bosswell and I'm in charge of security, which, for the time being, means I'm pretty much in charge of everything. I got an entire organization to think about. What makes you think I have time to talk about some beauty parlor?"

"That's my organization, Whitmore. My business. Might not seem like much to you but it's all I got."

Mr. Whitmore sighed.

"Alright, Jennie. It just so happens I do know what you are talking about. Your name did come up recently, on a list of locations we might consider investing in."

"My property is not for sale."

"Nobody said anything about buying something from you. I said investing. Dewey doesn't want to take your shop. He wants to share it with you for a little while. Things have gotten complicated lately and now that Bosswell is out of commission . . . Need some new locations to conduct business. It's just temporary. We got to be a little more mobile for now, switch things up a bit."

"It's a beauty parlor, Mr. Whitmore. I got ladies coming in and out of there all hours of the day. I can't have a bunch of men hanging out in there doing whatever it is they do. You'll ruin my business."

"I'm not the one doing it, Jennie. If I understand correctly, you did it to yourself. It's your man who took out the loan. Isn't that right?"

"That's what I'm trying to tell you. He's not my man. We had a business arrangement but it's finished now."

"If the two of you were married when he took out the loan then Dewey got a right to be paid however he sees fit. That's the law."

"The law? How are you going to sit there and talk to me about the law when everything you do is illegal?"

Mr. Whitmore frowned. "Oh, Jennie. You are confused, aren't you? I'm not talking about the Man's law. I'm talking about mine."

He shook his head. "You haven't changed, have you? I mean, look at you. Still fine. Still have terrible taste in men. Do you know there was a time when I thought you and me might have had something, some kind of connection? But you didn't pay me any attention back then, did you? So busy chasing after the Rib King." He smiled. "Looks like I got your attention now."

"What's that mean, Mr. Whitmore? You think I would have been better off with you?"

"Maybe. Probably not. All I know is I wouldn't have poisoned your soup."

Jennie nodded. "He's coming back, you know."

"Who?"

"The Rib King. Making an appearance this weekend."

"I don't have anything to do with that."

"No?" She looked at him. "You know what he's coming back here for?"

"I know it don't concern you."

"What's that mean?" She squinted. "You have talked to him, haven't you? What, you two still friends?"

"Friends? No. Not that."

"But you have talked to him. Now, how is that, Mr. Whitmore? Me you can't do anything for, but you're still in touch with him? Doesn't it make you angry? Thinking about what he did?"

"No, Jennie. Angry is not the word for what it makes me. Because I know it wasn't me he was trying to burn up in that fire, nor you either. We just happened to be standing a little too close to it is all. What it makes me is careful," Mr. Whitmore said. "You should be careful too."

He looked at her. "Listen, Jennie. I tell you what I'll do. I'll talk to Dewey. Do you this favor, for old time's sake. Make him give your husband an extension until the end of the month, tell Roderick not to bother you in the meantime. Would that help?"

"End of the month? It would. I mean if that's all you can do . . ."

There was another knock on the door. The man in the checkered tie rushed back in and started whispering again. Whitmore turned his head and stared at him for a moment, then nodded. As the man walked out, Whitmore opened the top drawer of his desk, pulled out a handful of bullets, and dumped them onto his desk.

"I should go."

"Yes, you should," Mr. Whitmore said. "Oh, and Jennie? In the meantime? Never mind about the Rib King. Hear me? Just forget about that. Looks to me like he's just coming in to put on a show for white folks, then leaving again. Got nothing to do with you. So just forget about it. Honestly? Seems to me you've got more important things to be worrying about now."

He reached into another drawer, pulled out a gun, and started loading the bullets into the chamber.

Jennie stood up. "I'll let you get back to your war."

She walked back outside.

So she had until the end of the month, a little more than a one-week reprieve, and that was the best she could do. It gave her a little time to think, but she didn't see how it would make much difference. All because she and the Rib King were associated. And the worst part about it was Whitmore was right. It was nobody's fault but hers. She'd done this to herself.

When she pushed through the door of her shop a voice called out, "There she is! Ms. Big-Time Corporate Executive!" and she looked up to see Irene, Lala, and Aggie standing in a row grinning from ear to ear.

Jennie nodded and set down her purse.

"What are you doing here, Aggie?"

"What do you mean? I came to ask about your meeting. How did it go?"

Jennie bit her lip. "It didn't."

"What?"

"There wasn't any contract. I got in there and all they wanted to talk about was the Rib King."

"The Rib King?"

"That's right. I was in a room with Mr. Holder and someone from the company that makes Rib King sauce. Apparently, the Rib King's behavior has become a problem for them. He's been drinking a lot, getting in fights, and peeing in the street."

She looked at Irene. "I told you I used to work with him. Somehow they knew it too. And because in their minds the two of us are associated, they consider it a risk to go forward with Mamie." She looked at Aggie. "I guess Mr. Holder wasn't interested in Mamie after all."

"No. That's not true," Aggie said. He looked confused. "I mean I know it's not. You saw how excited Mr. Holder was about Mamie."

"Maybe he was just acting excited."

"Why would he do that?"

"I don't know, Aggie. I don't know why other people do things. Maybe he was just playing with me. Men are like that sometimes."

Aggie frowned. "Men like Mr. Holder do not play, Jennie. That man doesn't have time for that. Why would he bother playing with you?"

"I'm just telling you what happened."

"And I'm telling you that if Mr. Holder wanted to talk about the Rib King he would have just come out and done that when you met him. Anyhow I've seen him since. He was going on and on about how excited he was to present your proposal to the board."

"Really?"

"Yes. Trust me, the man was serious. Something else must have happened."

He put his jacket back on. "I'm going to find out what."

He left.

Irene put a hand on her shoulder. "You alright?"

"No. Not really," Jennie said. "I'll be honest with you, it's pretty bad. I don't have a deal for Mamie and Roderick is breathing down our throats. And it's all my fault."

"Your fault? What are you talking about?"

"I'm talking about berries," Jennie said.

"Berries?"

"I never told you the truth about that Barclay fire. I was there that night. It's how I know the Rib King is the one who actually killed those people. It wasn't a white chef like everyone thinks. The Rib King killed him too; poisoned that man, same as he poisoned me."

"Poisoned you, Jennie? That's terrible. How come you never told us?"

"Because I never did anything about it. I knew I wasn't going to and I imagine a part of me was ashamed. So I didn't want to think about it. Because the truth is I don't just know what he did. I know how. Always have. You see, he showed me those berries, the ones he poisoned us with. Probably still out there, growing wild in what's left of the fields."

She looked at Lala and Irene. "And that's not all I know. You see it wasn't just us he poisoned that night. He killed a couple members of the Good Time Gang too. I read about it in the paper, when I was laid up in the hospital. Some strange deaths in the Magazine, the same night as the fire. Nobody bothered to look into it, I imagine, because they couldn't see how the two things were related. I could have explained it to them. But I didn't want to get involved."

"Are you telling me the Rib King was mixed up with the Good Time Gang too?"

"They weren't like they are now. This was ten years ago; union busters used to pay them to break up strikes, send them out to bust heads they wanted busted. That's how they got started. But it just so happens a couple of them came by the house the same day as the fire. I saw the Rib King talking to them. The kitchen boys told me there'd been some trouble the night before, that one of them had done something that got those men riled up and now they'd come to the house looking for some kind of payback. They told me the Rib King said for them not to worry, to just stay inside and let him take care of it. I reckon he did that because those men were dead by morning. Food poisoning. Same as me and the white chef, the Barclays, and their dinner guests. Same night, same poisons. Same man done it."

"And you never said nothing about any of this?" Irene asked. "Not even to us?"

"I was ashamed, Irene. I knew I should have done something, but the truth is I was scared. Scared that if I went to the police, tried to explain all that, it would just make me look suspicious. The way the police had it, the Rib King wasn't even in the house that night. According to the newspapers, he'd quit in protest when Mamie was replaced by the white chef they claimed had done the deed. But of course, he was there. It's just the only ones who could have confirmed it were the Barclays or the dinner guests or the white chef, all of whom were now dead."

"Except for you."

"That's right. Except for me. I didn't want to be associated with his crimes, and now I realize that somehow because of that, I have been ever since. Because it's meant I've been forced to feel like I was carrying around that man's secrets. Well, I'm not going to do it anymore. Those Starlight people want him to stop? Well, so do I."

"What's that mean?"

"It means I'm going to do like they want. Get him to retire. Tell him he's going to stop touring or else I'll make sure he winds up in jail. Might turn out it doesn't make any difference, that they never really were interested in Mamie at all. But at least I'll know I finally did what was right. Put an end to the Rib King once and for all."

Jennie looked up. "I just got to figure out how to get in touch with him."

"Well, shoot, Jennie. That's nothing," Irene said. "We're three smart women. We can figure that out."

They thought for a minute.

Then Lala said, "What about those ads? If he didn't put them up himself he must have paid someone to do it for him, right? Most likely they are in contact with him. I'd start there."

"That's a good idea," Jennie said.

"In the meantime, I'm going to make another batch of Mamie's Brand," Irene said. "We've had a few cancellations on account of those gangsters making people too scared to walk down the street. If you let me, I could start selling door-to-door, try to make up for some of the lost business. I mean if that's alright with you."

"It is, Irene. It's smart. It makes sense."

Irene nodded.

"See that?" Lala smiled. "We can work this out. Figure out a way to get through this."

She reached for Jennie's hand. "Just don't give up."

12
FOX TROT

It turned out Lala was right about the ads. It wasn't hard to figure out where they'd come from. There was only one black-owned printing press in the city that offered such services, operated by the same people that put out the community newspaper. The next morning, Jennie made her way over to their offices.

When she got to the building, Mary Jane and a few other Harperites were out front setting up a podium on the sidewalk.

"What's going on?"

"I'll tell you what's going on. Sabotage," Mary Jane said. "Newspaper published an editorial telling people not to participate in our march this weekend. They said that, given the recent violence, the march was 'ill-timed' and 'unwise.' I wrote an opinion piece of my own trying to explain that what was really ill-timed was the police thinking they can just come in here and shoot black people in the middle of the street. That what was unwise was not protesting injustice. Did they publish my opinion? Of course not."

She shook her head. "This newspaper, this so-called voice of the community has been trying to undermine Harper for years. But we're not going to stand for it anymore. We got a right to be heard too."

She went back to work setting up the podium.

Jennie didn't say anything. The whole time Mary Jane was talking all she could think about was the fact that she might lose her shop over a donation to Harper's legal defense fund. It made it hard to hear anything else.

She went inside and walked up to the information desk. When she inquired she found out that, yes, they had run off a 250-print order of the Rib King's ad. When she asked who had placed the order the man behind the counter looked through the records and came back with a name that was both familiar and one she had never heard before: Bart Ribkins.

Bart was one of the three kitchen boys Mr. Sitwell had taken with him when he fled town all those years ago, but Jennie hadn't known he was back in the city. As for the last name, she figured it was either a typo or a joke. Strangely, the man behind the counter hadn't even noticed the similarity between the name and the words in the ad until she pointed it out to him. When she asked if he could tell her how to get in touch with Bart he said he couldn't help with that; the order had been paid for in advance and with cash, so they hadn't bothered getting any other information from him. She wrote down her name and address on a piece of paper and, just in case Bart came back, asked the man to tell him she was looking for him. Then she thanked him and walked back outside.

On the sidewalk, Harper's people had finished setting up the podium. It was almost noon and a small crowd of people had gathered around to listen to Mary Jane read her letter out loud while they took their lunch breaks. When she was finished reading, another man on the podium took the bullhorn. He thanked her for sharing her thoughts, then started talking about the need for solidarity, how even those who disagreed with some of what Harper said should stand by him on principle. Because deep down, even if people didn't understand his strategy, they knew that Winston Harper had lived his life fighting for one thing and one thing only: the betterment of black people.

He said it was the real reason Harper had been sent to jail. Because he was a threat to the existing order.

"Is that right?" someone in the crowd shouted. "I thought it was fraud."

A few people laughed.

The man told them they needed to wake up. He asked if they really believed the United States government would have brought the full weight of the law down on Harper's head for the crime of defrauding other black people. He said that didn't sound like the United States to him; if cheating and exploiting black people was considered a serious offense in this country half the people in it would be sitting in jail. He told them to look around at all the other predatory members of society allowed to prey on the black community with more or less impunity. It was only when they presented a real challenge to the system that a person wound up incurring the government's wrath.

"What about Bosswell Banks?" another voice called out from the crowd. "Police went after him too. Shot him in the middle of the street like they were putting down a dog."

"Believe it or not, you're just proving my point," the man said. "Bosswell was involved in a turf war, was he not? A conflict with the Good Time Gang. And somehow that's when the police felt it necessary to intervene. Really, that shoot-out was just another example of white folks looking out for their own."

This provoked some ruminative mumbling from the crowd.

"Truth is, like it or not, we are all in this together," the man with the bullhorn said. "This world is not our delusion. But the only way we'll survive it is if we stick together. We've got to remember who we are, we've got to remember where. Bosswell and Harper, as different as they were, both ultimately found themselves subject to the same forces. I'm sorry for what happened to Bosswell, would loudly oppose the injustice that would cause any man to be treated that way. Even a lowlife like Bosswell Banks."

That was when the real heckling started. It was as if no one had heard anything else the man had tried to say before he called Bosswell a "lowlife"; now everybody was arguing among themselves about the virtues and vices that had ruled Bosswell's life. Jennie shook her head. She didn't understand how a speech about the need for solidarity could degenerate so quickly into a situation where everyone was just standing around arguing with everyone else.

Disgusted, she turned around and was just about to start walking back to her shop when she heard a popping sound, so close to her ear it made her flinch. Next thing she knew, everybody was running. While people pushed and shoved their way past her she watched a man stumble out of an alley, clutching his stomach with one hand and a pistol with the other. She recognized him by his checkered tie as the one from the pool hall, who'd been whispering in Mr. Whitmore's ear. He took two steps toward her, then dropped to his knees and fell out on the pavement.

When she got back to the shop, Irene, Lala, and Cutie Pie were waiting for her.

"How'd it go?" Lala asked her. "You find out anything?"

"You were right about those posters. I got a name, at least." She told them about Bart, Mac, and Frederick, the three boys Mr. Sitwell had taken with him when he fled the Barclay house. "Bart seems to be going by Ribkins. And from what I understand, Frederick calls himself Smith. I don't know where he got that from. Probably just made it up too."

"Wait a minute — Frederick Smith is the Rib King's son?" Lala asked. "I didn't know that."

"He's not the Rib King's son but the Rib King paid for his education. Frederick doesn't exactly advertise that."

"And the third one?" Cutie Pie asked. "Is he a Smith? Or a Ribkins?"

"I don't know."

"But you said his name was Mac, right?"

She handed her mother an envelope. Inside it were her invitations to the art exhibit.

"Came in the mail this morning. His name is on it."

Jennie looked at the list of artists who would be exhibiting at the art show. There it was: Mac Ribkins.

"Actually, if it's the same Mac Ribkins, then I've heard of him. He studied at the Art Institute. Now he's part of that arts collective, the Negro Art Brigade."

"Oh, I know NAB," Irene said. "They all live together near Barrington Square."

"That's a dirty part of town," Lala said.

Jennie looked at Cutie Pie. "How do you know so much about art?"

"I know about a lot of things, Mama."

"Why don't you take Cutie Pie down there this afternoon, see if you can't talk to him," Irene said. "Probably safer over there anyhow. Nothing to shoot at in that neighborhood but a bunch of anarchists and some broke artists."

All the members of the arts collective lived together in a three-story building at the western edge of downtown, a part of the city with a reputation for attracting a bohemian crowd. The neighborhood was pretty quiet that time of day, most folks apparently still sleeping off whatever mischief they'd gotten up to the night before. Jennie and Cutie Pie made their way through empty streets until they reached the NAB building and rang the bell. A window on the second floor creaked open.

"You here about the banner?" a voice called out.

"Banner? No. It's Jennie Williams. Looking for Mac Ribkins. He in there?"

"Miss Jennie?"

"That you, Mac?"

"Hold on a second."

A few minutes later the door opened and a young man wearing a paint-splattered T-shirt and dungarees appeared before them. He had big soulful eyes, warm brown skin, and he was missing part of his right ear.

"Why, Miss Jennie! Goodness it's been a long time."

"Oh, Mac! Is that really you?"

Jennie threw her arms around him, pulled him toward her, and gave him a tight squeeze. She took a step backward, looked at him, and smiled.

"Look at how big you are. And so handsome."

"Well, thank you, Miss Jennie. It's good to see you too."

Then he saw Cutie Pie. "And who is this?"

"This is my daughter, Cutie Pie," Jennie said.

"Daughter? Why, Miss Jennie. I didn't know you had a daughter."

"Well, I didn't bring her to work with me back then."

Mac put out his hand. "Pleasure to meet you, Cutie Pie."

They smiled at each other.

"What was that about a banner?" Jennie asked.

"Oh. Some of Winston Harper's people paid me to make something for them to carry at the march next weekend but it's taking longer to make it than I thought it would. I keep expecting them to come around asking for their money back."

"Well, we don't have anything to do with that."

"No?" He smiled. "In that case, come on in."

He ushered them into a large, dark room, empty save for a few cardboard boxes stacked on the floor, then up a metal staircase. When they reached the second floor, Mac led them down a long hallway, at the end of which was his studio. An apparent combination work and living space, there were several large paintings lined up against the walls, a bathtub in the middle of the room, and, in one corner, a single mattress sat on the floor. Aside from that the only furniture was two folding chairs.

"Welcome," Mac said.

Jennie looked around, surprised at how rough Mac was living. She'd always just assumed the three boys were well taken care of on account of all the sauce money the Rib King had made. Instead he appeared to be in a state of near destitution.

Cutie Pie didn't seem to notice. She walked around and stared at the paintings on the walls, almost as if she were in a trance.

"Did you do this?"

Mac smiled. "You like them? It's my

heroic series."

"Beautiful," Cutie Pie said.

Mac went and stood in front of a large painting of what looked like jagged slashes of bright black and blue suspended over a white banner.

"That's Toussaint L'Ouverture," Mac said. He nodded to the canvas next to it. "This one is Nat Turner. This one is Pancho Villa. . . . And that one —"

"Let me guess," Cutie Pie said. She stood in front of a painting of a glowing yellow circle against a dark blue background, wrapped around slashes of green. A tiny gold star had been painted in the upper left corner.

"Harriet Tubman?"

"That's right." Mac beamed from ear to ear.

Jennie looked at the gold star. It was just about the strangest painting she had ever seen.

"You do all these?" Jennie asked. Because even if she couldn't tell what they were pictures of, there certainly were a lot of them.

"That's right. They're part of an exhibit we're having this weekend."

"Oh, we know all about the art show. We're coming to it," Cutie Pie said. "Mama already bought the tickets."

"I'm glad to hear it. I'm still working on these. I'd love to hear what you think of them when they're finished."

"I guess people must think pretty highly of your work if they're paying ten dollars a ticket just to see it," Jennie said. She walked around the room.

"I suppose," Mac said. "Although of course that's not the point. It's about truth, about showing the world as I see it. The money is not important."

"So I see," Jennie said.

Mac smiled. "So what brings you around today, Miss Jennie? Not that it isn't wonderful to see you. Just been a while."

"Actually, I was hoping you could tell me how to get ahold of Bart."

"Get ahold of Bart? Now that is an interesting proposition. Mind if I ask why?"

"I need to talk to the Rib King."

Jennie reached into her purse and pulled out the flyer. "I understand Bart put these up for him. You know anything about this?"

"Me? Certainly not. I haven't spoken to the Rib King in almost two years."

"No?"

"I no longer have any contact with the man. Bart is in touch with him, but he doesn't really have a fixed address. Just kind of bounces around from place to place. A habit he probably picked up from our childhood."

Jennie frowned. "I take it the Rib King took you with him on tour?"

"Took us on tour, even had us performing with him for a while. For the first few years anyhow. After that I guess he realized that everything was just too complicated with us around. We were in the way. So he sent us to live with some of Mrs. Lawson's relatives for safekeeping."

Jennie blinked. She felt guilty hearing the details of Mac's childhood, as if he were telling her things she should have already known. She felt as if she should have kept closer contact with them, made sure they were okay.

"I'm sorry to hear this. Sorry you felt like you were in the way."

"Don't be. It was a complicated situation. I mean, he wasn't just touring. The real reason Mr. Pound hired him in the first place was so he could be a taste tester. Did you know that? He'd send him samples of popular products made by other manufacturers and have the Rib King give him a rundown of their ingredients so that he could market his own version. Corporate espionage is what it was. Mr. Pound made a lot of money that way, until the Rib King put a stop to it."

"How do you mean?"

"He started lying about ingredients in his reports. Let Pound put out products that contained substances that were harmless by themselves but made people sick if they were mixed together. Stomach cramps, vomiting, and nausea . . . Nothing fatal, but bad enough. Pound had about fifty products on the market by then, everything from flour and potato starch to cooking oil. And it was only the people using several Pound for Pound products in conjunction with each other who got sick. No one could figure out what was going on, but it spooked them." Mac shook his head. "It wound up destroying the company's brand. Which is why Mr. Pound had no choice but to sell the sauce to Better Butters."

"Interesting," Jennie said. She sat and thought about that for a moment, wondering if there was any way to use this new information to her advantage. "Can you prove any of that?"

"No, Jennie. And the only reason I'm telling you is so you will understand what I mean when I said getting away from him was probably for the best. I'm not even complaining, because I know he tried. For all his problems, he did try. And who am I to complain? Imagine there was a time when I actually thought we would somehow be a family. But I was a child then. I'm not one anymore. When I turned eighteen I told him to stop sending checks. I didn't want the Rib King's money, not when I knew very well where it had come from, what he had to do to get it. I didn't want to feel like I owed him my loyalty anymore. It's one of many things Bart and I do not agree on. The price of loyalty. And really, it's why Bart and I are not as close as we used to be."

"Shame," Jennie said. "You used to be like brothers."

"We still are, so far as that goes. Just not close. Point is, Bart may very well be running errands for him. But that's got nothing to do with me."

Jennie nodded. "So you really don't have any idea how to find Bart?"

Mac shrugged. "You could try the county jail."

"Jail?"

"I haven't spoken to him in almost a week. That's usually where he is when I don't hear from him in that long. Honestly I was thinking about checking there myself."

Jennie frowned. "Why would Bart be in jail?"

"You'd have to ask Mr. Whitmore about that."

"Whitmore?"

"That's right. Remember him? That's who Bart works for now. Has been, ever since he moved back here."

Jennie was quiet. So Mr. Whitmore had lied to her when he said he didn't know anything about the Rib King coming to town.

"You're telling me Mr. Whitmore is the one who paid Bart to hang up these advertisements?"

"I don't know. How am I supposed to know? All I said was that I know he's working for Whitmore. For about a year now. But I imagine hanging up ads isn't the reason he'd be in jail."

He shook his head. "He's crazy, you know."

"Who? Bart?"

"The Rib King. Well, Bart too, if I'm being honest. I don't know why you would want to talk to either of them, but I can tell you no good will come of it. Really, you should just stay away from them both."

"Unfortunately, my mother can't do that," Cutie Pie said. "Believe me, she wouldn't be trying to get ahold of him if it wasn't important. Is there really nothing you can think of that might help?"

Mac smiled. "If it's that important, you could try talking to Frederick."

"Frederick and the Rib King are still close?"

"No, Miss Jennie. Frederick hates the Rib King. But the weird thing is that, because of this, he tends to keep pretty close tabs on everything the Rib King does. It's like an obsession with him. I didn't understand it myself at first. But one day I realized Frederick's whole personality is based on trying to be the opposite of the man who raised us, trying to be everything the Rib King is not. I imagine he feels like if he doesn't keep track of what the Rib King is up to he might start to forget who he actually is."

"You make your brother sound very sad," Cutie Pie said.

"Well, he is sad. It's always sad when everything someone does is a reaction to shame," Mac said. "That's why I stopped taking the Rib King's money, why we don't speak anymore. Because I don't want to be like Bart or Frederick, don't want to be a reaction to someone else's madness. Bart idolizes the Rib King, and Frederick is so ashamed of him that the only way he knows himself is by what he does not want to be. But, see? I want to be free to define myself. As far as I'm concerned, that's the only thing really worth fighting for." He smiled. "That's why I love art."

"I love art too," Cutie Pie said.

Jennie rolled her eyes. She stood up.

"Thank you, Mac. But we should probably be going now. Come on, Cutie Pie. I'll try to talk to Frederick."

She looked around the room again. "You really make money doing this?"

"Sometimes. Not often, no. Right now though, I have an anonymous patron, he's the one who commissioned all these works."

"An anonymous patron?"

She remembered Lala complaining about the Rib King co-sponsoring the art show.

"Will the Rib King be at the art show?"

Mac frowned. "He might. He wrote me a couple weeks ago threatening to come. I told him I'd rather he didn't."

Jennie nodded. "Well, thank you for your time. Hope we didn't keep you from your work."

"Not at all. I'm glad you came by. If nothing else, you reminded me I need to finish that banner. I'm going to get it done in time for the rally. In fact, I plan on being out

401

there with them."

"I'm sure they'll appreciate the support."

"Least I can do given the circumstances." He kissed Cutie Pie on the cheek on her way out the door.

"Everybody knows Harper was framed," Mac said.

When they got back on the sidewalk, Jennie said, "Interesting."

"His art?"

"No. That stuff about an 'anonymous patron.' I'll bet you anything it's the Rib King."

"You think?"

"Of course. Now it makes sense. Why he's paying for that art show, why he's coming back. Who else would pay money for that stuff?"

"Mama! How can you say that? I think Mac's work is wonderful. If I had the money I would pay for it myself."

Jennie shook her head. "All those weird lines and crazy swirls? Couldn't make any sense of it. I've never seen such a thing before, calling itself art."

"Well, maybe that's why you don't like it, if all you're doing is looking for something you've seen before," Cutie Pie said. "Mac's paintings are unique, but that's why I like them."

"Is that why you were flirting with him like that?"

"I wasn't flirting with him, Mama."

"Oh, please. Who you think you talking to? You think I don't know flirting when I see it? Batting your eyes, telling him how 'amazing' he is." She squinted. "I hope breaking up with Theodore wasn't just an excuse to start fooling around with someone like Mac."

"What do you mean 'someone like Mac'?"

"An artist. If that's what you want to call him. What do you think you're going to do with him anyhow? That man can't do anything for you. He can't help you. He can barely help himself. No. You can't handle a man like that. Trust me, Cutie. I know his type."

Cutie Pie frowned. "Don't tell me what I can handle, Mama. And anyhow, I wasn't flirting with him. I just respect his art."

When they got back to the shop, Aggie was waiting.

"We talked again, when Mr. Holder came by to pick up his suit yesterday. This time I brought it up. His face got all red as soon as I mentioned your name and I could tell he was very upset. He said he thought the purchase of Better Butters was illegal, that the brothers who had sold it to Starlight were criminals who ought to be in jail as opposed to sitting in a boardroom. He said Starlight would regret their involvement and that he just hoped Mamie's Brand was not snatched up by a competitor before the matter was reconciled."

"That's what he said?"

"That's what he said." Aggie nodded. "See? I told you. The man wasn't playing. He was serious. All that stuff about you being an associate of the Rib King? He knows it was nonsense. Didn't affect his opinion of you or Mamie in the least. Matter of fact, he said he felt sorry for the Rib King. Like I said, he thinks the Farley brothers are criminals."

"The Farley brothers?"

"Jack and John Farley. They're the previous owners of Better Butters. It seems one sold the company to Starlight without getting proper approval from the other. Now they're suing each other over it. And whether or not the sale to Starlight is finalized, the Rib King is still their primary asset. Mr. Holder said those two are so crazy they would probably kill him before they'd let him do any more damage to their brand."

"Okay, Aggie. Thanks for letting me know."

"Sure thing." He smiled. "In the meantime I do have some good news. Remember Mrs. Nelson? From shopping the other day? She wants to come here with a couple of her friends on Saturday."

"Really?"

"That's right. It's a big deal. You impress them and you're all set." He looked around the shop. "Thing is, Jennie, and don't take this the wrong way, but they're going to need the whole place to themselves. Can't have any of your regular customers coming through, if you know what I mean." He frowned. "I'll just come out and tell you I'm talking about Maisy Day. Can you handle that?"

"If that's what it takes I'll do it. Can't be worrying about hurting nobody's feelings right now. I'm just trying to survive."

She thanked him for his help and walked Aggie to the door. Tony was waiting outside.

"What do you want?"

"What's this I hear about you going to see Mr. Whitmore, asking for an extension? Didn't I tell you to stay out of it? You don't want to get involved with all that."

"That's funny. Seeing as how you the one got me involved."

"You shouldn't be going over to that bar right now, Jennie. Those people are dangerous. Why can't you just let me handle it?"

"You want to handle something, Tony? Why don't you handle those Harperite friends of yours, out there shouting in the street? Because I happened to be at the newspaper this morning. I saw your allies — Mary Jane Whatever — screaming and hollering through a bullhorn about what a bad man Bosswell Banks was."

Tony shook his head. "That's not what they were doing there."

"Maybe that's not what they were supposed to be doing. But it is, in fact, what they were doing. Don't you realize you owe those people money?"

"I don't see how one thing has anything to do with the other."

"No? Just a delusion, is it? Is that what you think?"

"I can't keep people from saying something that's true, if that's what you mean. Everybody knows it's true so there shouldn't be any reason to get upset about it."

"I'm not talking about what should be, Tony. I'm talking about what is."

"All they're doing is telling the truth."

"Well, it was stupid," Jennie said. "Hear me? Sometimes telling the truth is stupid.

Don't you know that? Sometimes you just keep your mouth shut, nod your head, do what you got to do, and go on about your business. . . . Don't tell the truth unless you're ready to tell it. It's called being strategic."

"Is that right? Is that what it's called? Because what it is, is being a coward. You think people should only tell the truth when it's convenient? That otherwise they should just go along to get along? A real man, a true man, stands up not because it's convenient, but because it's the right thing to do."

"Yeah? And what does a real woman do? While you all are just standing around?"

Tony shook his head.

"That's what I thought," Jennie said. She turned around to walk back inside.

"Where are you going?"

"Don't worry about me, Tony. I'm just doing like a real woman. And actually handling the situation."

13
A ROMANTIC QUEST

Of the three boys who'd once worked with Jennie in the Barclays' kitchen, Frederick was the one who had done the most with what he'd been given. With the help of the Rib King he'd gone to college, then medical school, and then set up his own practice in DC. Jennie knew all this because of an article she'd read on the society page of the community newspaper, the subject of which had been Frederick's engagement to the daughter of Dr. Langston Livingston, a prominent local political figure and civil rights advocate of national renown. That article was the first Jennie knew that Frederick had moved back to the city, and when she read it she was stunned. The Livingstons were one of the most influential black families in the city and now Frederick was about to become one of them. This would have been an impressive feat for any man, but when Jennie considered who he'd been when she'd met him, it was downright astonishing.

According to the article, Dr. Livingston had put his future son-in-law in charge of the planning and development of a new medical training facility for black doctors, the first of its kind in the country. Private funding for the facility had already been secured, and until it opened, Frederick was working out of Dr. Livingston's office, a handsome brick building on a tree-lined corner of South Parkway.

That was where Jennie went to see him the next morning. She pushed through the door and smiled at the woman sitting behind the front desk.

"May I help you?"

"I'm here to see Frederick Smith."

"Dr. Smith is in a meeting right now. Is he expecting you?"

"Should be. His brother Mac told him I was coming."

"I'm sure he'll be out shortly then."

Jennie took a seat in front of the receptionist's desk as she went to tell Frederick Jennie was there. When she knocked on his office door a voice said, "What is it?" She pushed it open and Jennie heard men laughing from inside. Then a voice said, "What? Who? Oh, you're kidding. . . . No, wait. It's fine." It was quiet for a moment, and then there was more laughter as the receptionist walked out and shut the door behind her.

"He'll be right with you," she said and sat back down at her desk.

A few minutes later the door opened again and four men in business suits filed out. As they walked toward the door the man bringing up the rear turned and smiled. Jennie saw the three faint lines of a butcher's fork on his left cheek and knew it was Frederick.

He walked the other three men to the door, shook each of their hands, and then came back.

"Jennie Williams. Is that really you? My goodness it's been a long time."

Jennie stood up to shake his hand. "Oh, Frederick! It's so good to see you. I hope you know how proud of you I am. I mean, look at you. You've done so well and now to see you're about to marry such a lovely girl."

"Thank you, Jennie. I appreciate that." He kissed her on the cheek. "And I must say, you look wonderful. It's like you haven't aged a day."

"I have though," Jennie said. "If you can't see it, I sure can feel it."

He led her into his office and gestured for her to have a seat in front of his desk.

"And how have you been since last I saw you?"

"I own my own hair salon now. On Thirty-Seventh Street, just off the main strip."

Frederick frowned. "Been a bit of trouble in that area lately, hasn't there? Criminals and gangs . . . You alright? Keeping safe? Is that what you came to see me about?"

"Me? No, it's not that. Didn't Mac tell you? I was hoping you might be able to tell me how to get in touch with the Rib King."

Frederick stiffened at the sound of the Rib King's name.

"Yes, well, that situation is . . . complicated." He glanced toward his open office door.

"When I talked to Mac yesterday he seemed to think you might know how to track him down."

"Did Mac say that? Because he knows very well that the Rib King and I . . . do not engage socially anymore."

He stood up and closed his office door.

"Can I be honest with you, Jennie? My relationship with my benefactor is not good. I prefer not to even talk about him here. All that Rib King business has not been easy for me. I don't mean to sound ungrateful because I do appreciate some of what the man did for me as a child. But the fact is

411

that, as I've gotten older, the more accomplished I've become, the more my relationship with him has become an obstacle to my career."

"I can see how it might," Jennie said.

"Yes. You've seen the ads. Everyone has. It's humiliating, being associated with some minstrel act I never wanted anything to do with. Did Mac tell you we used to perform with him? It was back in the beginning, when Mr. Pound was still trying to establish the brand."

"Yes, he told me. It's terrible and I'm sorry for it," Jennie said.

"Yes, well, it was a long time ago. But when people find out . . . it's almost as if they were there in the audience. Sometimes it feels like it's all they see when they look at me. You have no idea what it's like having to live in the shadow of that ad campaign. But I can tell you that it has meant I have always had to work that much harder to prove I belong. And it just won't end. I've tried everything to make him stop."

Jennie nodded. "Then perhaps you'll take some comfort in knowing that's actually why I'm here."

She told him what had happened. About Mamie's Brand Gold and her deal with Starlight; how her association with the Rib

412

King had proven the greatest obstacle to finalizing it. She told him how the people at Starlight had suggested she try to talk to him in the hopes that she could convince him to retire. She told him that she had resolved to do it, that there were certain details about the Barclay fire that Frederick might not be aware of but that she was certain the Rib King would not want made public.

When she was finished talking, he nodded.

"So you are here as a representative of Starlight Industries?"

"What? Me? No, of course not. I'm here as a representative of myself. But, yes, they were the ones who told me about his current state. Or, rather, Better Butters did. . . . The point is that he is damaging the brand."

"And what exactly did they tell you, Jennie? About the Rib King's current state?"

Jennie shrugged. "They didn't tell me so much as show me. They had a whole folder full of newspaper clippings. I could see for myself just from reading the headlines that he's been making a fool of himself all over the country."

"Which section of the paper?"

"Excuse me?"

"The clippings. Which section of the paper

were these headlines taken from? I'm trying to figure out what exactly you've been told."

"I don't know. I wasn't paying attention to that."

Frederick reached into his desk drawer. He pulled out a larger folder, very similar to the one Mr. Dumont had shown her during her meeting at Starlight, and set it on his desk. It too was full of newspaper clippings.

"You know, Jennie, I've always said it is very important for our people to read the entire paper. Not just the funnies . . ."

Jennie looked through the folder. The articles it contained were taken from the same newspapers Mr. Dumont had shown her during their meeting. But they weren't the same articles. None of the headlines made any mention of the Rib King and they'd all been cut out of a different section altogether.

They were obituary columns.

"I don't understand," Jennie said.

"That's because you're still only reading headlines. If you look more closely, you will see that they are all dated within a week of one of the Rib King's appearances. You will also see that they all make mention of an incident of accidental poisoning that took place while he was in town."

She closed the folder. "My goodness,

Frederick. You really do hate the man, don't you? Just like Mac said. Please tell me you don't think the Rib King has something to do with all these people being poisoned. Just because you don't like him it doesn't mean that every time someone is poisoned it's his fault. That's crazy thinking. Paranoid. It doesn't help you, me, or anyone else."

"Yes, well, actually it was not the poison that first drew my suspicion. It was the shared place of origin. I realized it was part of a pattern that in truth started with the Barclay fire."

"The Barclay fire? How?"

"The dinner guests that night. Do you remember where they were from?"

Jennie had to think for a moment, but then realized she did remember. Florida.

"Look at the articles. If you read them you will find that all these poison victims have some connection not just to Florida, but to Seminole County. The same county that is the Rib King's true place of origin."

She looked back at the articles and saw that it was true. Every one of those obituaries made some mention of the victim's connection to Seminole County.

"Do you remember back at the Barclay house, the day I was imprisoned at that fair? When we were down in the cellar I told you about it, how the Rib King warned me about what had happened to his friend, Wash Talbot. I couldn't see it at the time, but now I realize he never really recovered from whatever happened down there. I think when he saw those two cousins sitting in Mr. Barclay's parlor, he must have recognized them. And something just snapped."

"Snapped?" She had to think about that. All this time she'd assumed the Rib King's intended victims were the Barclays. Now she was being presented with an alternative version of events, one in which the Barclays were only minor characters.

"And after? You think he just kept going? Tracking people down, getting revenge for murders that took place in his hometown years ago?"

"Basically. Yes. I mean, it's probably not what he'd say. I lived with that man for three years. There's always a reason for the things he does, some extenuating circumstance he will claim forced his hand. But that is the real reason the Rib King will not stop touring. It's got nothing to do with sauce. It's a revenge tour."

Jennie looked back at the articles.

"Still don't believe me? Too cryptic? Perhaps you're thinking how could anyone have noticed such a thing unless they were looking for it? And yet I tell you I was not looking for it. I started collecting those newspapers when we were sent to live with Mrs. Lawson's relatives, out of pride and affection for the man I once considered the closest thing to a father I would ever have. Because he was on the road so often it was my way of feeling close to him, by keeping track of all the places he was going while on tour. I forgot about them when I went to college, and so it wasn't until I graduated medical school that I happened to go through that box and actually read them. Without even wanting to I began to see it: a pattern."

She shook her head. If what Frederick was saying were true it meant that over the past decade the Rib King had killed at least twenty men.

"I don't know what to say, Frederick. I mean it's crazy. . . . But then again it's crazy to think that an entire town was burned to the ground over a stolen mule."

Frederick frowned. "Please don't repeat that ridiculous lie. I can't tell you how much I despise that story, that absurd fiction. What happened to the Rib King had nothing to do with a mule."

"It didn't?" Jennie was confused.

"Of course not. It was about money. The

land the Rib King's people had built their settlement on. Oil deposits had been discovered nearby and a group of developers wanted to drill beneath it. And the fact is those people had no legal claim to it. They were squatters. They were told to leave and, when they refused, were forced out. Why do you think so many families like the Farleys are so wealthy now? It wasn't because of a mule. It was business."

Jennie felt sick. "That hardly makes it any less cruel, Frederick."

"No. But it doesn't make it any crueler either." Frederick sighed. "How I hate the way people lie to themselves, come up with fanciful stories and ways to romanticize the surface of things. When all along the real truth is right there, staring them in the face. That's how you wind up with the type of psychosis the Rib King suffers from. The man actually believes he's on some sort of romantic quest, avenging the great wrong done to his people many years ago. He doesn't even realize that not only is he fighting the wrong war, he's not even on the right battlefield."

Jennie didn't know what to say. The whole thing was crazy. And yet . . . as many times as she'd told herself the Rib King had been out to get the Barclays it had never really

418

made sense to her either. She looked at Frederick.

"If you believe this then why haven't you done anything? Why haven't you gone to the police?"

"Perhaps I will. It's certainly what I threatened to do. But of course, the situation is complicated. After all, he is the man who raised me."

"Loyalty then? After everything you've said you still —"

"No. Not loyalty. It's the fact that we are associated. If my association with the man causes me this much trouble now, can you imagine what it would be like if people knew the Rib King is actually psychotic?"

She frowned. "An honest man does not tell the truth simply when it is convenient. He tells the truth because it's the right thing to do. If you believe the Rib King is out there killing people then you have to do something to stop him. At the very least you should tell the people at Starlight."

Frederick gave her a pitying look. "Oh, Jennie. You really are confused, aren't you? I already have."

"What?"

"A long time ago, I'm afraid. Long before they called you in for that meeting and showed you what sounds to be a very carefully curated sample of the Rib King's clippings from his tour." He shrugged. "I was trying to be strategic. Make the best of a truly horrible situation. I was hoping I could convince someone to donate money for my future father-in-law's medical training facility."

"The training facility? What does that have to do with this?"

"The Farley brothers. That is the name of the family that is currently in a legal dispute with Starlight over the sale of Better Butters. They're from Seminole too. The family was already quite prominent locally when the Rib King lived there. Their father was one of the men who instigated that attack, but like many of the others who were directly involved, he is now deceased. When I figured out my benefactor was targeting heirs, I tried to warn them. One brother threatened me with legal action if I ever spoke publicly about how the family's wealth had been acquired. Then he purchased Better Butters, no doubt thinking that by becoming the Rib King's corporate sponsor he could exert control over the man. But the other brother, John, agreed to my terms at once. He confessed that in truth both he and his brother, Jack, already knew about the murderous rampage that took place in the village and that it had always troubled him that his family's fortune had been derived from so much suffering. Given the circumstances, John felt that endowing a black medical college, a place of healing, was not only appropriate but the least he could do."

"So that's where the money for the medical facility is coming from? John Farley?"

"Can you imagine? An honorable man attempting to pay for the misdeeds of his ancestors in the most honorable way possible. With money. And that, unfortunately, was how we found out about the exorbitant amount his brother, Jack, paid to acquire ownership of Better Butters from Mr. Pound. The sale was completely unauthorized and left John, the good brother, without the liquidity required to honor his commitment to us. That is why, upon acquiring a court decree that declared Jack's purchase illegal, John initiated its immediate sale to Starlight, even though it meant even further financial loss to his family. In part I suppose he did it to teach Jack, the bad brother, a lesson. But also, and more importantly, it allowed John to honor his commitment to us."

Jennie stared at him. "What are you talking about, Frederick? What does any of that have to do with what's going on?"

"What do you mean?"

"The Rib King. He's still out there, isn't he? Still poisoning people? Killing them, if what you say is true?"

Frederick shrugged. "I'm not sure what more I can do about that. I have told people who are better equipped to deal with the situation, people who have far greater resources than I. And it appears that they are taking steps to deal with it. Including, it would seem, contacting you."

He frowned. "You had no idea, did you? I'm sorry, but it's probably the real reason they took an interest in your beauty cream."

"It's a healing salve," Jennie said.

Frederick nodded. "Well, I am sorry. Sorry they didn't tell you the truth, although, as you can see, they had more than enough reason not to. And this salve of yours, I'm sure it is a fine product. It's just that there are forces at play here much larger in scope. I hope you did not take offense."

"Naw," Jennie said. "Take a whole lot to offend me, if that's what you were trying to do."

"I wasn't, Jennie."

She nodded, then put her hat back on. "Anyhow I got other stuff on my mind."

By the time she walked out of there she did not doubt Frederick was telling the truth. It made her sick inside to realize that the only explanation for what the Rib King had done that made sense was the one that confirmed he was insane. That seemed clear enough now and perhaps should have the whole time.

It was also clear that Mr. Holder had lied to her. He must have known what was going on at Starlight and yet he pretended it had nothing to do with his interest in her. Just like Whitmore had known, then saw fit not to tell her. It seemed as if every time she turned around there was some man trying to make a fool of her, a fact that had the effect of producing an intense rage. And this rage in turn seemed to produce a certain clarity of thought. Because all at once she realized she knew exactly what she needed to do.

She caught the streetcar and rode up to Starlight's corporate offices. She walked straight through the lobby and stood in front of the receptionist's desk.

"I need to speak with Mr. Holder."

"Do you have an appointment?"

"You just go on back there and tell him it's Jennie Williams. Tell him it's about the

Rib King. Trust me, he's going to want to talk to me."

She wasn't kept waiting long. The door opened and, instead of Mr. Holder, Mr. Dumont walked out to greet her.

"We weren't expecting you back so soon," Mr. Dumont said. "Does this mean you have actually managed to solve the problem?"

"Depends on which problem you are referring to," she said. "You all seem to have a lot of problems. No, I'm here to negotiate terms."

"Terms? What do you mean?"

"You want me to get rid of the Rib King, don't you? Get him to sign that cease and desist order? Convince him to stop touring? All of that requires effort on my part. This effort is called work. And when I work I expect to be paid."

"Paid?"

"That's right. Cash."

"I don't understand," Mr. Dumont said. "I thought we explained to you that your deal with Mr. Holder will not go forward until the Rib King has been dealt with. You want to see Mamie on those store shelves, don't you?"

"Keep Mamie out of this. We're talking about the Rib King now. Mamie has nothing to do with the Rib King. And you and I both know it."

Mr. Dumont nodded. "Miss Williams? I hope you realize that we don't actually need you to solve the problem. There are other ways we could have dealt with it."

"And yet you haven't. And we both know why. You want to keep selling that sauce, am I right? I don't see how that would be possible if the general public were to find out what the Rib King's been up to while on tour. And I am not talking about peeing in the street."

Mr. Dumont frowned. "What I meant was that reaching out to you was in fact the humane choice."

"Well, sometimes the humane choice is also the smart one, I guess. Sometimes it charges a fee."

She picked up a pen and a piece of paper from the receptionist's desk and wrote down a number. She handed it to him.

He looked at the number and then back at her.

"I'll need to get authorization for this."

"You do that. Go and get authorized. I'll wait right here."

He went back inside. A few minutes later he came back with an envelope.

"Take it. But understand, it is not a gift.

425

Not a handout." Jennie put the envelope in her purse.

"I'm serious, Miss Williams. I do not want to see that man again. If you do not stop him you will never have a deal with Starlight. In fact, I will personally make sure that your product will never be on any store shelf anywhere in this country."

She started to leave but he stopped her.

"Also, when you speak to him, be sure to let him know that as soon as I saw those ads he had posted about his upcoming appearance I informed the chief of police of the threat to public safety he might pose. As a result, both Farley brothers have retained the services of additional security, off-duty officers handpicked by the chief. These men will be armed, Miss Williams. Do you understand? I gave you that money because you're right, sometimes the humane choice is the smart one. But it's not the only choice. Your associate would do well to remember that."

Jennie turned around and walked back outside.

She went to Bosswell's Pool Hall. She waited until the man at the door waved her inside then walked up to Mr. Whitmore's office and placed the envelope on his desk.

"What's this?"

"The money Tony Marcus borrowed from Dewey."

He looked inside the envelope. "Where'd you get this?"

"A representative of Better Butters Corporation gave it to me. I take it you're familiar with the brand? They want me to get the Rib King to retire before the Farley brothers show up for some board meeting because, apparently, that's why he's coming. To try to kill them. But you already know that, don't you? Just like you know exactly what the Rib King has been doing on tour. Because you've been helping him do it."

"Me? Helping the Rib King? I don't think so."

"No? Mac told me Bart works for you. And I know Bart is the one who put those ads up all over town. You're going to tell me you didn't know anything about that, that you just happen to have his son on your payroll?"

She shook her head. "Just so you know, as a result of Bart's enthusiastic distribution of those advertisements, they've hired additional security. Mr. Dumont told the chief of police about possible threats to public safety. You should tell your friend the Rib King that those Farley brothers will be surrounded by a security detail composed of off-duty police the whole time they are here. And those officers will be armed, Mr. Whitmore."

"Is that right?" He smiled. "Good."

"Good?"

"Listen, Jennie. I didn't lie. I don't have anything to do with what the Rib King is planning. But that doesn't mean I don't have the basic intelligence to realize it presents an opportunity. One I intend to take advantage of."

"An opportunity?"

"That's right. You see I couldn't care less about the Farley brothers. That's the Rib King's madness, not mine. But those off-duty officers they're bringing in to do security? I know them. Some of them were involved in that ambush of Bosswell and there's got to be an accounting for that."

Jennie squinted. "What are you talking about?"

"Just what I said. I know those men. I've known them for a very long time. Some of them used to be a part of a gang that ran me off a good job when I first arrived to town. It's how I wound up working for Barclay. I've been tracking their movements ever since, trying to figure out just how they operate. They called themselves the Good

Time Gang."

"The Good Time Gang?" She frowned. It occurred to her that that was how the violence started, with Bosswell encroaching on their territory.

"You had something to do with starting that turf war, didn't you?"

He shrugged. "That was business. Sometimes business makes people do things they might not otherwise do. Sometimes it just so happens I don't mind."

"So you're hoping the Rib King will miss, is that it?"

Mr. Whitmore laughed. "Oh, no. The Rib King doesn't miss. He's been doing what he does for ten years without being caught. What he will do is create confusion. That's what I intend to take advantage of. You see, Bart's going to be there too and he is a very good shot. While everybody's worrying about those two brothers, he's going to be aiming at the real targets. The security detail."

"That's why you had Bart put up all those flyers? So they would hire extra security?"

"I'm just trying to be strategic," Mr. Whitmore said. "You think I like what's been going on lately? All the shootings and chaos? It's a waste. Waste of time, waste of talent, waste of money. What purpose does it serve? And the only reason it's happening is because people don't know who is in charge. Seeing Bosswell gunned down like that has produced a powerful confusion in a lot of folks' minds and now they're acting out. It's childish, but it's not going to stop until someone calms them down. So that's what I'm going to do. Something that will shut them all up, make them understand who is really in charge. Then we can stop all this nonsense and get back to the real business of making money."

He smiled. "So you see? I didn't lie. I don't have anything to do with what the Rib King is planning and none of it actually concerns you."

Jennie stood up. "All y'all make me sick."

When she got back to the shop she told Irene and Lala that she'd paid Tony's debt and that Roderick wouldn't be bothering them anymore. When they asked her how she'd gotten the money she told them about her visit with Frederick.

"Well, look at that," Irene said. "I guess race hate really is killing white folks too."

"I don't understand." Lala shook her head. "How can they know all that and just keep going on selling that man's sauce? Haven't they got any shame?"

"Something is wrong with them, that's for sure," Irene said. "You got a salve for that, Jennie? Something to soothe that over?"

Jennie shook her head. "The one I feel sorry for is Bart, being manipulated by both the Rib King and Mr. Whitmore like that. It's not right."

"You tell Tony you paid off his debt?" Lala asked.

"For what? He'll figure it out. I'm tired of talking to that man."

Irene nodded. "Well, the important thing is . . . now that you know who these people are, what they are capable of, you've got to stay away from them."

"Don't worry about me."

"I mean it, Jennie. These are some shady folks you are dealing with. I don't just mean Whitmore and the Rib King. From what Aggie said, these Farley brothers sound like bad news too."

"I hear you, Irene. And believe me, I'm done," Jennie said. "I don't want to have anything to do with any of those people anymore."

The following night was the art show. After the stress and chaos of the past week, Jennie wasn't in the mood to go and would have stayed home if she hadn't already paid for the tickets. But Cutie Pie was excited.

"Come on, Mama, it will be fun."

While they got dressed Cutie Pie tried to remind her of all she had to celebrate. She'd solved the problem with Roderick. Irene was doing so well selling Mamie's Brand door-to-door that she'd hired two other women to help. Jennie should have been feeling good, but she wasn't. Because those victories had come with the knowledge that the Rib King had been out there killing people the entire time he was on tour. And somehow just knowing had the effect of making Jennie wonder if she wasn't also, in some way, responsible.

They got dressed up and walked to the art show. It was being held at the Cornelius Street YMCA and by the time they arrived there a large crowd was already outside. A lot of them were people she had never met before but recognized from the community newspaper's society page. Together they stepped into a large hall.

"Oh, my goodness," Cutie Pie said as she gazed around the room. "Isn't it beautiful?"

Jennie nodded. The exhibition featured work by some of the most well-known black artists in the country. There were sculptures, photographs of moving street scenes, meticulously crafted portraits, and still lifes. And then there were Mac's giant canvases full of wild splashes of color.

"I love it," Cutie Pie said and stared rapturously at the one he'd titled *Nat Turner.*

Jennie nodded and said nothing. His work certainly stood out, although in Jennie's mind it was not in a good way.

They walked around the main hall, admiring all the work on display when a cheery voice called out, "Hello, Jennie Williams!"

She turned around and saw Mrs. Nelson making her way through the crowd, arms outstretched and a bright smile on her face. She gave Jennie a quick embrace then kissed the air near Jennie's cheeks.

"I thought I . . . recognized . . . you. So glad you could make it. Isn't it wonderful?"

"Yes. It is," Jennie said.

Mrs. Nelson looked around the room and smiled at both the art and all the people who'd come out to see it. "This is what it is all about after all," she said. "All the beauty our people have created in this world. All the beauty we are capable of, given half the chance. That is what inspires me." She smiled at Jennie. "I'm so happy you could be a part of it."

She reached for Jennie's hand. "Come

now. There are some people I'd like you to meet."

She led Jennie across the room to a group of well-dressed women standing near the buffet table. They smiled and shook Jennie's hand as she was introduced to each of them in turn. It felt good to be so warmly welcomed by these women, women who, when they looked at her, she could sense all understood the hard work that had gone into crafting not only her product but herself — the woman who had created that product. When she stood among them, she felt recognized.

After about a half hour, a high-pitched ting rang out. A man was standing near a set of double doors at the back of the gallery, tapping a pen against the side of a wineglass. Dr. Livingston's presentation on the future of black art and culture was about to begin in the room behind him.

Jennie thanked the women and went back to find Cutie Pie. She found her standing just a few feet from where Jennie had left her, only now she was talking to Mac, who was holding one of his wild paintings.

Jennie frowned as she watched her child smile and blush. She didn't understand how her daughter could be standing in a room surrounded by eligible bachelors and not even notice because she was so busy wasting time talking to Mac.

Mac smiled. "Evening, Miss Jennie. So glad you could make it."

Then he took a deep breath, opened his mouth, and began reciting a speech Jennie could tell by looking at him was something he'd already practiced in front of the mirror several times.

"Miss Jennie Williams. I cannot tell you what a pleasure it has been to reconnect with you again after all these years. And also what a pleasure it is to become acquainted with your lovely daughter, Cutie Pie. You have always held such a special place in my heart and I will never forget the kindness you showed me as a child. As a token of my affection . . ."

He picked up the painting and held it in front of him. "I would like you to have this."

Jennie stared at a glowing orb and a small gold star.

Cutie Pie gasped. "Oh, my goodness, Mac. That is so thoughtful of you. So amazingly generous and thoughtful. Isn't it generous and thoughtful, Mama?"

Jennie looked at her daughter.

"No." She shook her head. "I can't accept that. I don't have money to buy something like that from you."

"Oh, no," Mac said. He lowered the painting and smiled. "It's a gift. I wouldn't accept your money anyhow, Miss Jennie."

Jennie nodded. She looked at her daughter, who seemed giddy with excitement, and then looked back at Mac. Her left eye began to twitch.

"Won't accept my money? Is that what you just said? Why not? Don't you need money? Isn't that the point of all this? You trying to sell your art, make enough money to pay your rent, and not be dependent on some anonymous patron we both know is really the Rib King?"

"Mama!"

"It's the truth. Just the other day you were going on and on about how you want to be your own man. How do you expect to ever do that if you just stand around giving all you've got to sell away for free? Here you are in a room full of people who got enough money to pay ten dollars to come to some art show and you're wasting time talking to me? You ought to be out there hustling, trying to sell something to someone who can actually afford it."

"Mama!"

"It's the truth, Cutie Pie, and you might as well hear it, because really I'm talking to you too. You children are going to have to grow up sometime." She looked at Mac. "What if you decide you wanted to get married someday, Mac?"

"Married?"

"That's right. I don't know if you've given much thought to such matters, but what if you were to meet a nice girl and decide you want to have a family? How do you think you could afford to ever take care of a wife if you don't have sense enough to take advantage of an opportunity like this?"

Mac stared.

"I understand." He nodded. "You make some good points, Miss Jennie. Imagine I'd do well to listen to you."

He looked at Cutie Pie and frowned. "But I'd still like you to have the painting."

He handed it to Cutie Pie and then, without another word, turned and left.

Cutie Pie watched him go.

"You alright?" Jennie asked. Cutie Pie's lip was quivering.

"I'm sorry about that, Cutie. But it needed to be said. Because it's the truth. Everything I just told that boy is true, and by the way you've been standing around grinning at him I know it's long past time you heard it too. You break up with a man like Theodore just to take up with someone like Mac? And expect me to not have an opinion about it?"

"You told me you understood about Theodore."

"I was trying to be nice. I'm always trying to be nice to you, Cutie. Because I love you. But I'm also your mother. And sometimes a mother's love isn't about just standing around, watching you make mistakes I know you'll regret. Sometimes loving you means telling you when I think you're doing wrong."

"Well, I think you're doing wrong, Mama. How about that? All Mac did was try to give you a gift. You didn't have to humiliate him for it."

"It was a gift he couldn't afford to give."

"And yet he did anyway," Cutie Pie said. She picked up the painting and carried it down the hall.

"Wait a minute —"

Jennie started to go after her when she felt a hand tap her shoulder.

"Why hello, Miss Jennie."

She turned around and saw Frederick standing behind her, dressed in a fine white suit.

"What a surprise seeing you here. I hadn't realized you were a patron of the arts."

"My daughter likes it."

"Daughter? I didn't know you had a daughter. Is she here?"

"She's here somewhere. . . ."

But by then Cutie Pie had disappeared into the crowd.

"And the matter we discussed yesterday?" Frederick asked. "How is that coming along? Any progress?"

"No." Jennie frowned. She'd lost all enthusiasm for any kind of confrontation with the Rib King. After what Frederick told her, she no longer knew what she would say to the Rib King if she did see him. How could she threaten a man with exposure when everyone around him already knew the truth?

Frederick gave her a serious look.

"I'm glad I ran into you. Ever since you left my office I've been concerned that I hadn't done a good job explaining things."

"You were pretty clear."

"I don't mean about what the Rib King has done. I mean what I haven't done," Frederick said. "You have to understand, Jennie. I know how terrible it is. But I also know how much harm to our people, to the cause of civil rights, my benefactor has already caused just by way of the image he promotes trying to sell that sauce. Can you imagine what would happen if the general public were to find out what he has really been up to? The panic it would cause? 'This is what freedom has wrought,' they will say. 'You cannot trust them in your home.' One black man running amok like that could lead to violence on a national scale. That's the real reason I didn't go to the police. Because we are all associated with the Rib King, whether we like it or not."

Jennie had to think about that. It was an aspect of his crimes she had not yet considered: the fact that they were all associated. Not just her.

She nodded. "I understand."

"Good. Because it's important that we are all on the same page. All working together to solve this problem. And now that I know we are . . . there is someone I'd like you to meet."

He looked up and nodded across the hall toward a tall, handsome woman in a blue satin gown standing near the double doors to the lecture hall. The woman had pale skin, long black hair, and the most piercing hazel eyes Jennie had ever seen.

"My future mother-in-law," Frederick said.

Mrs. Livingston walked toward them, a small rhinestone-studded clutch purse in one hand, a flute of champagne in the other. She seemed to glide across the room, moving swiftly through the crowd, before coming to stand beside Jennie and Frederick.

"I'll let the two of you talk," Frederick said, and left the two of them alone.

"So you are Jennie Williams?" Mrs. Livingston asked. "The one Starlight has assigned the task of putting the Rib King out to pasture?"

She sipped her champagne.

"I understand that the two of you are old friends," she said.

"Who? Me and Frederick?"

"The Rib King."

"No, ma'am. Not at all." Jennie shook her head. "As a matter of fact —"

"Do not dissemble. Is that what you are trying to do? I'm not judging you for it. I just want an explanation," Mrs. Livingston said.

"An explanation?"

"Why is he doing this? Is it some sort of political agenda? Make the white man pay for his crimes? Does he not realize that the entire country has profited off the suffering of our people? Does he intend to take them all out?"

The woman had the most riveting gaze of anyone Jennie had ever met. Jennie found herself twisting her head nervously, trying to find a distraction from it. "You are asking me?"

"It would appear so."

Jennie watched two waiters loading empty champagne flutes onto a tray on the other side of the room. She shook her head.

"I could not presume to know that man's intentions. But from what I gather it is not political at all. On the contrary, it seems to be very personal for him."

"In that case, you should understand that it is personal for me as well. You see, unlike my future son-in-law, I do not believe for an instant that Jack Farley's purchase of Pound for Pound was an irrational response to the potential threat posed by the Rib King."

"You don't?"

"Not for an instant. That might have been part of the reason, but it was not the main one. The main reason, I am quite convinced, was spite."

"Spite?"

"Yes." Mrs. Livingston took a final sip of champagne. "Deliberate, vindictive spite. Race hate, in other words. An insidious, psychotic delusion entirely underresearched by the psychiatric community. And because it is a psychosis, I do not believe it can be resolved simply through the Rib King's retirement."

"I'm afraid I don't know anything about

442

the Farley brothers."

"It's not complicated. There are two of them. A Jack and a John. Jack Farley purchased Better Butters at a great financial loss to himself for the simple reason that he hates black people. Whereas John Farley has the most well-developed understanding of the tragedy of his social status of any white man I have ever known. And despite what your friend the Rib King might think, he is operating out of the most noble impulse that one could ever expect of a man of his social standing: shame. He has dedicated his adult life to making reparations and since coming into his inheritance has donated a fortune to the cause of Negro improvement. Unlike his brother. Who will of course insist on far more security during their impending visit due to paranoia and fear. Making John Farley, the good Farley, the easier target for the Rib King's wrath. Now do you understand?"

"No," Jennie said.

Mrs. Livingston frowned. "I'm trying to explain to you that Jack Farley is a bad man, a very bad man. The world would be better off without him. It is therefore critical that the Rib King and those of his ilk, do not, in seeking out a suitable target for their bloodlust, mistake the Johns of this world for the Jacks."

Jennie shook her head. "I still don't understand. What does any of this have to do with me?"

Mrs. Livingston sighed. "My concern is that no harm befalls the wrong Farley who, in a larger sense, is the right Farley. If your friend is intent on killing someone, he needs to make sure he knows what he is aiming at."

Jennie blinked. A chill ran up her spine.

"Ma'am? Why are you telling me this?"

"Because I want you to tell the Rib King, of course. You tell him that if he hurts the wrong Farley, shoots a John when he could have just as easily shot a Jack, then he will have to deal with me."

Then she turned and walked away.

Jennie looked down and realized she was holding an empty champagne flute. Sometime during their talk, Mrs. Livingston had handed it to her to dispose of, without Jennie even being aware of it.

She watched Mrs. Livingston enter the lecture hall. She felt light-headed and wasn't certain if it was the intensity of Mrs. Livingston's presence or her actual words that had left her so disoriented. Those words had been strange and terrifying and Jennie could scarcely believe they'd been said. Because it sounded like Mrs. Livingston wasn't interested in stopping the Rib King so much as making sure he shot the right Farley. And for some reason, she'd felt it necessary to tell Jennie that, hoping she would pass that message along. Which, if true, was insane. Just as it was insane to think Jennie would have anything to do with it.

The doors to the lecture hall closed and Jennie looked around the gallery, empty now, save for a few waiters walking around the sides of the room, stacking empty glasses onto trays. She handed one of them Mrs. Livingston's empty champagne flute and walked outside.

She needed some fresh air and stood on the sidewalk, shut her eyes, tried to regain control of her breathing. She wondered what kind of woman Mrs. Livingston had mistaken her for. Because if one thing was clear it was that Mrs. Livingston had mistaken Jennie for someone she was not — the kind of woman who would involve herself in someone else's murder, for any reason.

That was not Jennie Williams at all.

"You alright, Miss Jennie?"

A young man was watching her while he stood on the corner smoking a cigarette. He flicked the cigarette into the street then walked toward her, limping as he did.

"That you, Bart?"

"Yes, ma'am." He smiled. "Long time no see."

"What are you doing here, Bart?" She squinted. "You're not here to start any trouble are you?"

"Trouble? Me? No ma'am. Came to see my brother's show."

"That right?"

"It is," Bart said. "Making all those pictures? Spending all his time trying to find some beauty in this world? I'm proud of him."

He smiled. "He told me you've been looking for the Rib King. Still want to get in touch with him?"

"No. Not now. Please." She'd had enough for one night. She didn't want to think about the Rib King anymore.

"Suit yourself," Bart said. "But if you change your mind, he's staying at the Fowler. They got a couple rooms in the back for performers coming through town, keep them separate from the white folks. He takes his morning meals in the main dining hall, after they've finished with the breakfast service. That's always a good time to catch him."

Jennie frowned. "You know what hurts me the most about all of this? Seeing you mixed up in it. I know it's been a long time, but I remember you. Such a mischievous child, such a wonderful imagination. I don't think I ever told you back then, but out of the three of you boys? You always were my favorite, Bart."

Bart blushed and looked down at the ground. "That's real nice, Miss Jennie."

"Nice? I'm not trying to be nice. Because that boy I remember? As naughty as he sometimes was? Deep down I always knew he could tell the difference between right and wrong. I realize that you've probably been through a lot since then. But I believe deep down you still know. That's why I'm trying to understand it, how you wound up involved in something like this. You got your whole life ahead of you and there's so many things you could be doing. If you go through with this thing Whitmore has convinced you to do, you're not going to have a future."

Bart shook his head. "You misunderstand the situation, ma'am. Whitmore didn't convince me to do nothing. I volunteered."

"What? Why? Why would you want to do that?"

Bart frowned. "I don't have any toes, Miss Jennie. Someone cut them off when I was

447

seven, to keep me from running. And I might not agree with everything the Rib King and Whitmore do. But that don't mean I don't understand why they're mad."

He walked away from her, still shaking his head.

Jennie watched him disappear around the corner then stayed outside for a few minutes, trying to muster the strength to go back inside. By the time she did, the talk was over and the guests were on their way out. She found Cutie Pie sitting in a corner of the gallery, once again talking to Mac. This time when he saw her heading toward them, he turned and walked away.

Cutie Pie stood up. "Let's go."

"I'm sorry, Cutie Pie. Maybe I overreacted. Or it came out wrong anyhow."

"Don't lie. I know you meant it. Because that's what you believe."

"It is what I believe," Jennie said. "But honestly? It's not all I believe."

"And what about what I believe? Do you ever stop to think about that? Just because you don't think love means anything doesn't mean I think that too."

"Don't think love means anything? How can you say that? You know I love you. I've spent my whole life trying to take care of you for no other reason but love. But see, you don't understand what that means because I never let you. All your life I just did what I had to, trying to take care of you. Trying to keep the bad off of you. To keep it to myself, just smile, and keep going."

"Yeah? Well you didn't do a very good job then."

"What?"

"Of keeping it to yourself. I know exactly what you've been through, Mama. Because I went through it too. I was right there with you the whole time. Know what that taught me? That there are some bad people in this world, but there are good people too. You are a good person, I know that. I know how fortunate I am to have you for a mother. I know all you've done for me. But maybe Mac is a good person too. Maybe being good doesn't have anything to do with how much money you make or how suitable other people might think you are."

"Is that what it sounded like I was saying?" Jennie asked. "That's not what I meant. That's not what I meant at all."

Cutie Pie picked up the painting and walked back outside. The two of them walked home together, and when they got there, Cutie Pie unwrapped the painting and hung it up on the wall over the couch.

Then she went to bed.

Jennie sat in the living room and stared at it. She wound up staring at it for a long time, every now and then tilting her head from side to side as she considered it from different angles.

After a while, a strange thing happened. She realized she could see it. Maybe not Harriet Tubman, maybe not what Mac was trying to do. But what he'd actually done. It was beautiful.

14
THE RIB KING

When Jennie woke up the next morning she
still felt so exhausted that she had a hard
time dragging herself out of bed. She knew
she needed to get up and get ready, that
Mrs. Nelson and her friends were scheduled
to come to the shop that day but it was also
the day of the Rib King's cooking demonstration, and every time she thought
about that she felt sick inside. Sick, because
she knew what he was planning and sick
from knowing how many people were waiting for him to do it. The Rib King was
murderous and crazy, but everyone around
him was so devious and calculating that
they'd managed to do something she would
have never thought possible just a few days
before.

They'd made her feel sorry for the man.

She walked to the bathroom, turned on
the shower. She got dressed, plucked her
eyebrows, and curled her lashes. She ap-

plied rouge to her cheeks. She looked at her face in the mirror.

She wondered why it seemed like every time she solved one problem another seemed to appear in its place.

She shut off the light, locked the door behind her, and walked downstairs to her shop.

The first thing she noticed was the bouquet of roses sitting in a vase next to the register. The floors had been cleaned, walls scrubbed, windows washed. Someone had even polished the metal fixtures.

"Surprise," Lala said.

"You did all this?"

"Me and Irene. Last night, while you were at your fancy party. How was it? Did you have fun?"

"It was alright," Jennie said. She smiled. "But this is beautiful."

"Well of course we wanted everything to look right," Irene said. "Probably not be as fancy as what these ladies are used to. We intend to make sure they know that we can shine too."

At eleven a.m. the ladies arrived. There were eight of them in total, including Mrs. Nelson. They pushed through the door looking regal and imposing in their long dresses and large hats. Irene and Lala greeted them at the door with bright smiles and complimentary refreshments. They took the ladies to their chairs two at a time while Jennie gave those waiting for their turn a demonstration of how to use the various products she had created for sale in the shop.

Everything seemed to be going well when, at a little after one p.m., she looked up and saw Tony standing outside.

She excused herself and walked to the door.

"Not a good time, Tony Marcus —"

"Why didn't you tell me you paid that debt?"

"Because I didn't feel like telling you." She glanced over her shoulder and smiled, then looked back at him. "Just assumed you were smart enough to figure it out on your own."

Tony nodded. "I told you I'd take care of it."

He reached into his jacket pocket and pulled out an envelope.

"What's that?"

"It's your money. From Roderick."

Jennie took the envelope. Inside was a roll of money tied up with a rubber band and a handwritten letter that went on for seven pages.

"I don't understand."

"It's an apology, Jennie. For bothering you the other day. He's real sorry about that."

"That's what he told you?"

"He's been coming to meetings for a couple months now. I knew he wasn't happy. Thing is, he'd been working for Dewey for so long he didn't really see any way out of it. That's part of why he's been acting so crazy lately."

She looked down at his letter.

"What are you saying, Tony? You converted him? To Harper's Army?"

"I just helped him find a door. He's the one who found the strength to walk through it."

Jennie stared at Tony, mystified. Somehow a man she'd given up on just a few days before had converted Roderick to a movement that a lot of people said didn't even exist anymore now that their leader was in jail.

"So all that talk about standing by someone when everyone else has given up on them. You weren't talking about Harper, were you? You were talking about Roderick?"

"I was talking about all of us," Tony said.

Jennie glanced back at the ladies. "I can't really talk right now. But I've got to admit.

You surprised me, Tony. I'm impressed."

"Thank you, Jennie Williams. I do try. And speaking of trying . . ."

"Yes?"

"Now that we're not married anymore there is something else I'd like to ask you. Something I've been wanting to ask you for a very long time now."

"And what is that?"

He took a deep breath. "Would you like to have dinner sometime?"

She stared at him. "You're serious?"

"I am."

"But I'm not a Harperite."

"Well, from what I'm told, neither am I at the moment. It seems you weren't the only one who disapproved of my efforts with Roderick."

Again, Jennie was speechless. "I don't know what to say."

"Then say yes."

"I mean, I'm flattered and all, but . . ." She squinted. "How long have you wanted to ask me that?"

"Honestly? Since the day I met you."

Jennie nodded. "Alright, Tony Marcus. Dinner it is."

He tipped his hat. She watched him walk back down the crowded sidewalk, merging with the great throng of people moving up and down the block. Then she went back inside.

The ladies looked beautiful. Every single one of them had a new hairstyle and perfect makeup. Lala and Irene were now handing out gift baskets while the ladies put on their jackets and started walking toward the door.

Before they left, Mrs. Nelson came and shook Jennie's hand. "Thank you, Jennie. This was wonderful. You have developed a unique and valuable product. I think you have all the skills you need to be a success."

"Thank you, Mrs. Nelson. Hopefully we will be seeing each other again very soon."

Mrs. Nelson nodded and looked around the shop.

"A word of advice? If you really are planning on opening a shop in our neighborhood, I hope you will remember how important it is to know your market."

"What do you mean?"

"Well, for one thing, you have what appears to be a pregnant teenager doing people's hair."

Jennie looked at Lala, smiling and chatting on the other side of the room, a five-months-pregnant belly sticking out in front of her.

"She's older than she looks," Jennie said.

"Is she married? I noticed there is no ring

on her finger. Believe me, it is the sort of detail other women will notice too. Perhaps that is a temporary issue. But the other one? The one with the disfigurement?"

Jennie looked at Irene. She was standing near the door, passing out samples of Mamie's Brand, her always immaculate hair and makeup framing the long, thin scar that ran down her left cheek.

"A bit controversial for a beauty salon, don't you think?" Mrs. Nelson said. She frowned. "Forgive me for being so blunt. I only say these things because I care. I know how much Aggie admires you, and now that I have seen your work I understand why. I think you could do well in our community. But you have to understand, we live in a world where appearances matter. We know how closely we are watched, how cruelly we are often judged. We didn't make this world, but in order to survive it we have come to understand the need to be strategic. I know it sounds harsh, but it is a truth which, I'm afraid, would reveal itself in sales."

Mrs. Nelson kissed her cheeks then walked out the door.

"I think that went well," Lala said.

Jennie looked at her two assistants. "You both did great. I could not have been prouder."

She reached for her jacket.

"Where are you going?"

"I've got to go run an errand."

"Now?"

"Looks like it. Can you two handle things here while I'm gone?" Jennie smiled. "But see, I don't even need to ask that question, do I? Already know you can. Because you always have."

She picked up her purse and walked out the door.

She caught the streetcar and rode it to the Fowler Hotel.

When she got there she found out that Lala had been telling the truth: they didn't let black people in through the front door. One of the doormen stopped her at the entry, asked her what her business was, and tried to shoo her down the steps while the white patrons in the lobby stared. There was no official policy about that and technically it wasn't even legal. But like a lot of places in the city, they had ways of keeping people out, letting people know they weren't welcome. Black people could get jobs holding open that front door, but walking through that door was an entirely different matter.

Fortunately it was not the only door.

She walked around to the side of the building until she reached a steeply descending flight of stairs that led to the basement and the employee entrance. It wasn't locked, and when she stepped inside, a tired-looking woman was seated behind a metal desk with a large clipboard to take down names and clock the time of entry for everyone who passed through it.

"Who are you?" the woman asked her.

"Jennie Williams. Hairdresser." She reached in her purse and handed the woman one of her business cards. "I received a call about an emergency on the seventeenth floor. I was asked to be discreet."

"Seventeenth floor? Those are the Hardings' suites."

"Yes, Mrs. Harding is the one who requested me."

The woman squinted. "Mrs. Harding? Of New Hampshire?"

"Well, technically I believe Mr. Harding is the one from New Hampshire. It appears Mrs. Harding is from New Orleans."

The woman's eyes opened wide.

"You understand my meaning? She asked me to be discreet."

"So Mrs. Harding is from New Orleans?" The woman shook her head. "You know something? I'm not even surprised. As soon as I saw that woman I had a feeling, something not quite white about that woman."

"It seems she is having some sort of hair emergency, which she does not even want her husband to know about. But I cannot assess the situation until I have actually seen it."

The woman nodded and stood up from her chair.

"I understand. You just wait here for a moment. I'll get someone to escort you to the seventeenth floor."

She hurried down the hall.

"I hope I can trust you to be discreet," Jennie called after her. She watched the woman disappear through a metal door. She waited a few moments, then went in after her.

She pushed through the metal door and up a short flight of stairs and found herself standing in a low-ceilinged, ill-lit corridor littered with boxes of cleaning supplies. It was the service hall that lined the back of the lobby.

"Who are you?" an angry voice called out.

She stopped walking. When she turned around, a reedy-eyed white man in an ill-fitting blue uniform was glaring at her from the open doorway of a small office.

Jennie bowed her head quickly and curtseyed. "Apologies, sir. Must have got turned around. I'm new here. Chambermaid. Supposed to work the evening shift and came in early so as I could orient myself."

"New girl, huh?" The man looked her up and down. "Well you can't just be wandering around back here, don't you know that? Who is your supervisor?"

"Supervisor?"

He shook his head at her ignorance. "The one that hired you, girl."

"I don't rightly remember her name, sir." Jennie started looking in her purse. "I mean I wrote it down, I got it in here somewhere. . . . I was just so excited to be working in this fine hotel. Ain't got no hotels like this where I come from. And all these fancy people in it . . . got me so nervous and happy I figure I just forgot everything else. 'Cept the time and place. And I didn't want to be late. . . . I'm sorry, sir. I didn't mean to disturb you."

The man sighed. "What time you say your shift start — two?"

"That's right."

"You working with Hattie then. You need to just turn around, walk back down that hall, look to your left, and count out three doors. You can count to three, can't you?"

"Yes, sir."

He looked her up and down. "Go on and get yourself straightened out then come

461

back to see me. Got a couple other things need explaining if you want to keep this job."

"Yes, sir. Thank you, sir."

The man shut the door.

Jennie frowned. Instead of turning left she turned right and pushed through a swinging door.

A short flight of stairs led her out into the lobby. She kept her head down and walked quickly toward the dining room. She pushed open the door and found him, sitting by himself, reading the newspaper while he ate his breakfast from behind a screen that had been placed around his table.

The screen was one of several ingenious ways places like the Fowler thought to deal with the problem posed by black people wanting to eat in the dining hall. It was usually placed around a table where black patrons sat, to keep them out of view of other patrons. But the Rib King was alone in that room.

While she stood there, pondering the necessity of the screen in an empty dining hall, the Rib King looked up. He stared at her for a moment, then continued eating.

"Hello, Jennie," he said. "Been a while."

"That it has," Jennie said, still standing by the door. How strange it was to be standing so close to him again after all that time. How different he looked from the man who had spent the past decade grinning at her from the label on the front of a can. He'd gained weight and his hair had gone gray over the years since she last saw him in person. But Jennie still recognized him. Not as the Rib King, but Mr. Sitwell.

"My boys tell me that you are doing well. I'm glad of that."

"Are you?" Jennie said. She walked across the hall and went to join him behind the screen. "I imagine it must come as a surprise, considering the state I was in when last you saw me."

She nodded to the screen. "What is all this?"

"Protocol." He shrugged. "I know it is considered an insult by some but I actually prefer it. Becomes a makeshift backstage for when I am not performing and sometimes I just want to eat in peace without worrying about conforming to others' expectations. Perhaps some things are better left unseen. Just as perhaps some things are better left unsaid."

"Some things," Jennie said. "Not all. And not always."

The Rib King frowned.

"I hope you know I never meant for that

463

to happen, Jennie," he said. "The Barclay fire. I never meant to hurt you. I only meant for you to sleep for a while."

"While you killed the Barclays' dinner guests?"

"Yes. It had to be done. I know it sounds terrible and I don't expect you to understand. It didn't occur to me that that white cook would insist you clean the upper chambers. If not for him, you would have simply had a good night's sleep and by the time you woke up it would all be over. If not for him, the Barclays would have received the same dessert as you."

Jennie nodded. "So you did not mean to kill the Barclays then?"

"Kill the Barclays? No, of course not. Why would I do that?"

"I have no idea. I don't know why you would do any of it."

"The Barclays were to receive the same dessert I'd prepared for you, Jennie. But the cook forced my hand. He's the one who insisted I serve them the dessert I'd prepared for the guests. By then it was too late to change course."

"And so they are all dead."

"Yes. They are," the Rib King said.

"And what of the fire? Did he force you to start that too?"

"That was an accident. You see I'd never actually used that poison before. I knew what it did, but I forgot about the spasms it caused while doing it. It was horrifying, watching them thrash around in that dining room. One of the four of them knocked over the candle on the table and the next thing I knew, fire."

He shook his head. "It really was terrible, Jennie. And it seemed to happen so fast. I didn't know what to do, didn't know what I was doing at all really. But it is an image that has haunted me ever since."

He frowned. "Is that why you wanted to see me, Jennie? What you wanted to talk about? You want an explanation? An apology? After all this time?"

"No." She shook her head. "I'm here because I want you to stop. You see, for ten years now I have been carrying the pain and horror of what happened that night. And somehow it is only lately that I have realized how deeply I have let it affect how I see the world, how I see myself, my ability to love. And I'm tired of that. It's got to end. And it occurs to me the only way that will truly happen is if I stop trying to ignore what you are doing, stop pretending that we are not associated, and the things that happen to you have nothing to do with me. Which means I had to at least try to keep you from walking into this trap."

"Trap?"

"Your anger, Sitwell. Do you not yet realize it is a trap? Everyone knows what you are here to do. Everyone is just waiting for you to do it, so that they can commit crimes of their own. You are ill, Mr. Sitwell. You have suffered a great loss and never fully recovered. Vengeance will never solve it and perhaps the reason you have not realized that is because you are surrounded by people who prey upon your delusions. And it appears have been preying on those delusions for a very long time."

"Yes, Jennie. You are not telling me anything I don't already know. The thing is I don't care. All they care about is selling sauce, about making money. And in exchange they leave me alone. Everybody wins."

"Wins? How can you say that? When your image alone has hurt so many? And when you are exposed, when the truth comes out, others will bear the burden of that as well."

The Rib King frowned. "I can't help that, Jennie. I'm sorry for it but I can't worry about those people. I've got to think of my own. Or do you not realize I am the last of my kind?"

466

"There was a time when I thought I was your kind, Sitwell. That you were my people. I know Mamie felt the same."

"You and Mamie never even knew my name."

"Then tell it to me," Jennie said. "That's all you had to do."

Jennie shook her head. "I'll bet you haven't even looked for survivors."

"What?"

"Survivors. Have you even looked for them? Or have you been so busy killing people you didn't have time to get around to that?"

"There were no survivors."

"How do you know? Perhaps you are not the only one. If you got out, there is a chance others did as well. Perhaps there are other people out there hiding, as you were when we met. Waiting for somebody to call them by their name."

The Rib King stared at her for a moment, as if considering it. Then a bell rang. He turned and looked toward the door.

"That's my cue." He wiped his mouth and stood up from the table. "It means my audience is about to arrive. It also means that you should leave."

He pushed back the screen and reached for her hand.

"Please don't do this," Jennie said as he led her across the dining hall. "There is still a way out, you just have to have the strength to find it. It's not too late to stop."

"It is for me."

He led her through a swinging door and into the kitchen. "Listen to me carefully. I'd rather not have you get hurt again when there is no cause. So I need you to do exactly as I say."

He nodded toward the rear of the kitchen. "Back there is the service entry. I want you to walk downstairs to the basement. Then go straight back; on your right you will see a small narrow door near the main service entry. This door will lead you even further underground and allow you to pass safely beneath the streets. It was sealed up for years, but you'll see I have opened it in preparation for today's performance. You see, many of these old buildings downtown are linked by way of underground passageways. Did you know that?"

Jennie shook her head.

"You don't have to do this. What about forgiveness? The possibility of redemption?"

"Redemption?" The Rib King gave her a pitying look.

"Ask my mother about that," he said, and pushed back through the door.

Jennie stood alone in the kitchen. On the other side she could hear his audience filling up the room, the sound of chairs being pulled back from tables, a spoon tapping against the side of a glass. For a moment everything was quiet. And then the sound of applause.

She looked at the kitchen. What more could she do? She didn't even know what he was planning, only that it was something homicidal and insane. And perhaps she would be implicated in it, simply by being here. . . .

She realized he was right, that she needed to leave quickly. She turned around and saw another door. But when she pushed it open, instead of an exit she found a supply closet. A middle-aged white man in a rumpled gray suit was tied up and stretched out along the floor inside it, a gag placed inside his mouth.

Jennie gasped, then bent down to remove the gag from his mouth.

"Please," he said. "Whatever my brother is paying you . . . I will double it, I swear."

"Mr. Farley?"

"Yes, that's right. John Farley. If it's money you want, I can —"

"No, no. It's alright. I don't want your money." She reached around and began trying to remove the knots on the rope that held his arms bound behind him.

"My brother did this. . . . His goons . . . He is insane."

Outside the door there was a sound like breaking glass, followed by a woman's scream.

"We've got to get you out of here," Jennie said. Then the swinging door fell open and the Rib King rushed back inside.

"What are you still doing here, Jennie?" There was another scream in the dining hall.

"Did you bring this man here?"

"No. He was a gift, from his brother. Two of his security people brought him to me this morning. I didn't know what to do with him, so I stashed him in here. It seems he is being offered up as a sacrifice."

He shook his head. "Never mind him," the Rib King said. He glanced behind him toward the swinging door. "You're the one I'm worried about. You really must go."

Jennie shook her head. "No. I'm not going to just leave and let you hurt this man."

In the dining hall they heard another scream.

"What on earth have you done?" Jennie said.

"It seems some of the guests have taken ill." He smiled. "Dreadful chaos at the moment. Police will no doubt be here soon."

He frowned. "I really should get you somewhere safe."

"I'm not leaving without him."

"Very well. We'll bring him with us. It's what I was planning anyhow."

The Rib King replaced the gag in Mr. Farley's mouth and pulled him to his feet. He pulled the man by the rope and led them through another door that opened onto a stairwell. They walked down the stairs and to the basement then along a dark corridor until they reached a steel door half-hidden beneath a stack of boxes, which the Rib King pushed aside. The Rib King opened it and they found themselves walking through a long tunnel that ran underneath the city street.

They walked for a long time, then climbed up another flight of stairs, pushed through another door, and found themselves standing in a back alley between two tall buildings. In the distance, Jennie could hear the chanting of what she knew was Harper's march. The Rib King led her through a back door of another building and onto a service elevator. They got off on the tenth floor, and it wasn't until she looked out the window that Jennie realized they were now directly across the street from Starlight's corporate office.

"What are you up to?" she asked him.

The Rib King continued walking down the hall, then stopped and knocked on yet another door.

He got no answer.

"Who is in there? Is it Bart?"

The Rib King raised a finger to his lips in a gesture for her to be quiet. He leaned his ear against the door and knocked again.

Again, there was no answer.

He reached into his pocket and pulled out a gun.

Jennie gasped. "What is this? Who is in that room?"

The Rib King shook his head. "Trust me," he said. "Wait."

He put his hand around the doorknob and pushed it open.

He'd only opened it partway when a shot rang out. The Rib King crumpled to the floor, the weight of his body forcing the door open the rest of the way. Inside, Mrs. Livingston was sitting in a chair by an open window, two men in dark suits beside her, a pistol in each of their hands.

Neither one of them was Bart.

"He was warned," Mrs. Livingston said.

Later, Jennie found out from Bart that the Rib King's plan was to shoot Jack Farley from the window and then stage the scene so it looked like John Farley had shot his brother and then shot himself. But it turned out Mrs. Livingston had spies everywhere; she'd known about the Rib King and Mr. Whitmore's plans, had found out about the Rib King's escape route, and had been lying in wait. Jennie was certain if John Farley hadn't been there to witness it, she would have killed the Rib King, instead of having him shot in the leg. As it was, she had simply done a good deed, acted as necessary to save the good Farley's life.

It turned out that was the only shot fired that day. Mr. Whitmore had positioned Bart on the roof of the same building, but when it came time to do what he'd been tasked with doing, Bart hadn't actually gone through with it. "Started thinking about some of that stuff you told me; I kept hearing your voice in my head," Bart told her. "I was sitting there, trying to aim, but it was like you were right there standing next to me, telling me how people were taking advantage of me, how I knew I was wrong on account of deep down I was a good boy."

"That was your conscience, Bart," Jennie told him. "That wasn't my voice. That was your own voice talking to you. Because you are a good man. And deep down you do know you were doing wrong."

"No, I'm pretty sure it was you," Bart said. "Produced a powerful confusion in me for a couple minutes and the next thing I knew I'd missed my chance. Honestly? As soon as I realized I felt bad about it. Because I had a clear shot. I might not never have one like that again. Plus, now I got to find a new job. Mr. Whitmore says he's done with me."

Mr. Whitmore, in truth, was furious. "You think you've done something good, Jennie? By messing up my plan? Because you haven't. All you've done is prolong the inevitable."

He was convinced that as a result of her fixation on saving Mr. Farley's life, all she'd done was ensure that the street fighting would continue. It meant the loss of more black lives, more black talent.

"That's why this shit never ends," he told Jennie. "You are very confused."

Jennie didn't have anything to do with that. Not anymore and she was glad of it. Instead of moving to South Parkway, she used the money she'd gotten from Mr. Dumont to do some renovations to the shop. Irene was put in charge of the day-to-day operations of Mamie's Brand and, under her supervision, established a network of

474

saleswomen that eventually stretched across the country, all trained to sell and promote the healing powers of Mamie's Brand Gold. She didn't get everything she wanted, didn't get to see Mamie on those store shelves, but she found a way to get her healing salve to a great many women, all of whom were grateful for it. And when, a few years later, Starlight introduced its own version of her healing salve, everyone who'd had the opportunity to sample both would confirm that Starlight's was, in truth, the inferior product.

ACKNOWLEDGMENTS

I would like to acknowledge my editor, Patrik Henry Bass, and my agent, Ayesha Pande, for their advocacy and support of this work. Fellowships from Writers in the Woods, MacDowell, Sewanee Writers' Conference, Vermont Studio Center, and Art Omi facilitated its completion. I would also like to recognize Marta Savigliano and Christopher Waterman for their guidance during the writing of my dissertation about travel to the Chicago World's Fair of 1893, the research for which ultimately formed the contextual grounding for this novel.

I am grateful to Jami Attenberg, Daryl Chou, Eve Ewing, Maria Hinds, Randall Kenan, Jesse Lee Kercheval, Sarah Lazar, Zachary Lazar, Bernice McFadden, and Marc Perry for their insights during the writing of this book. More broadly, I offer my gratitude to the Black Lives Matter movement, the emergence of which was, among other things, an important reminder of how deeply the answers we come up with are shaped by the questions we are asked.

Thank you to my mother Jacqueline Hubbard, my uncles Charles, James and Peter, my aunts Jackie and Sandee, my father Grigsby, my sister Sage and my brother Haven for being family. Thank you to Allison Warner and Loren Hamilton for being family too.

I am as always indebted to Barbara Christian and Toni Morrison, whose examples remain an abiding source of inspiration and strength. And thank you to Christopher Dunn, Isa Yasmin Gonzalez, Joaquin Hubbard Dunn, and Zé Hubbard Dunn for your love, patience, and solidarity.

ABOUT THE AUTHOR

Ladee Hubbard, who studied under Toni Morrison at Princeton University, is the author of the 2017 debut novel *The Talented Ribkins,* which was an Indie Next pick and won the Hurston/Wright Legacy Award for Debut Novel, a Rona Jaffe Foundation Writers' Award, the Ernest J. Gaines Award for Literary Excellence, and the William Faulkner-William Wisdom Creative Writing Competition. Hubbard is a 2019 MacDowell Colony fellow. Born in Massachusetts and raised in the US Virgin Islands and Florida, she currently lives in New Orleans with her husband and three children.

PORTLAND PUBLIC LIBRARY SYSTEM
5 MONUMENT SQUARE
PORTLAND, ME 04101